mostly loathing you

*If you related a little too much to Monica in
Season 7 Episode 13 of Friends, this one is for you.*

PLAYLIST

You're On Your Own, Kid by Taylor Swift
You're So Vain by Carly Simon
Idfc by Blackbear
Let's go to Hell by Tai Verdes
Don't Blame Me by Taylor Swift
Tear You Apart by She Wants Revenge
Cruel to Be Kind by Letters To Cleo
Mirrorball by Taylor Swift
Question...? By Taylor Swift
Damned If I Do Ya by All Time Low
Not Like I'm In Love With You by Lauren Weintraub
Jealous by Nick Jonas
The Archer by Taylor Swift
Car's Outside by James Arthur
False God by Taylor Swift
I Hate You, I Love You by Gnash ft. Olivia O'brien
Peace by Taylor Swift
Matilda by Harry Styles
Dammit *Cover* by Alexandra Kay
Your Biggest Fan by Jonas Brothers & China Ann McClain

ONE

LIAM

"You used to be way nicer to me!" Hannah's shrew voice travels through the air, pulling an unwilling eye roll from me.

Much to my dismay, there is no avoiding our joint family trip—you would think in the twenty-seven years we've been coming here together, I would give up on that pipe dream.

"That was your first mistake," I say with a chuckle, bumping my arm into Jackson's.

Jackson and his sister Hannah are the children of my parents' absolute best friends, George and Linda, so naturally we grew up together. While Jackson and I have always shared a friendship as a result, his sister Hannah has been the bane of my existence for years. There is something about her that just makes me want to scream, and not in the fun way.

"Yeah, yeah," Jackson laughs in response, letting my words roll off his back per usual.

Jackson started at Baker & Park, my father's law firm, a little under a year ago, so we've spent more time together recently, and thus have gotten much closer than we once were.

Unfortunately, that has been met with more than one visit from his devil spawn of a sister.

Gen, Jackson's girlfriend, is standing next to him, equally lacking interest in engaging my disdain for Hannah. That's fine—I'll hate her enough for all three of us.

I venture outside to help my dad tend to the grill before heading back in with a plate stacked with sirloin steaks. Each one is cooked to a perfect medium rare, while the outside still manages to have a delicious-looking sear.

"Well—your inability to admit you want to sleep with Liam is nasty." Gen's voice carries out of the kitchen as a roll flies past my face in the entryway. I stifle the gag this pulls not because the thought of sleeping with Hannah grosses me out at face value, but because, once I consider her personality, I'm steadily returned to Ew-ville.

"Don't speak those disgusting thoughts of yours into existence. I would rather take a hot poker to the eye."

Okay, Hannah, that was a bit dramatic.

"That can be arranged..." I say, grabbing Hannah's dinner roll on its way to her mouth and stuffing it in my own. This elicits the reaction I am looking for, as Hannah huffs. However, I don't appreciate the searing pain that throbs from my foot as the heel of her sandal digs into my bare flesh. I do my best to bite back the remark that bubbles up; giving her attention only makes it worse. Typically I'd chase it, but I don't want her to break skin.

We make our way out to the back patio, each with a dish in hand. In the middle of the table is a big bowl of lemons surrounded by an array of greenery. Chargers are placed in each place setting, where crisp white plates lay on top. Why my mother insists on decorating for what are essentially just family meals, I will never know.

After a while, we settle into a rhythm as the fairy lights draped over the table start to blur into tiny little sunbursts: the effect of the fifth margarita I've guzzled. I reach for the pitcher anyway, pouring myself another glass goblet of George's famous cocktail.

"Sure you need another?" Hannah asks. If I didn't know her, I would think it concern.

"It helps drown out your squeaky voice, so yes...because I can still hear you."

This barely earns me a shrug, which I don't appreciate. Her reaction is what it's all about. She pushes shoulder-length blonde tendrils behind her ear, barely looking at me.

My eyes roll so aggressively and dramatically that I think they might strain.

This also doesn't earn me a response. What gives?

It's then that I realize everyone has their eyes fixed on the beach, so naturally, I stand to look.

Jackson is out there, down on one knee, a ring box in his hand. A gasp falls from my lips before I can stop it, and all eyes —including Jackson's and Gen's—turn to my own. I pretend to zip my mouth shut and toss the key, mouthing "sorry" toward the happy couple.

He's seriously proposing? I mean, I know he's been in love with Gen since we were kids, but one vacation and ten months of dating hardly justifies a marriage. It all just seems a little fast, but if you ask Jackson, he'd say it's been a lifetime. The two dated when we were teenagers, but it ended badly. That was, until about a year ago when they somehow ended up on the same vacation together, and, well...the rest is history. I can, however, admit I'm just being a bit too cynical for those around me. Hannah's elbow finds my ribs, signaling for me to shut up, and to my surprise—I listen.

Hannah's hair catches in the wind and a piece sticks to her lip gloss, leaving me fighting the urge to remove it. She's fixated on what's unfolding in front of us, but all I want to do is remove that damn piece of hair. The gleam of her gloss catches the light, pulling attention to her pillowy lips, but it exaggerates the clump attached to it like a vise. It shouldn't be there; it's disgusting.

Finally, she reaches up and grabs it.

"Congratulations!" Voices ring out in unison as Gen and Jackson make their way back to the yard, hand in hand, Gen's left hand sparkling in the moonlight.

Linda pulls her into a hug, mumbling something about the daughter she always wanted. This shouldn't bother me, but as my eyes dart to Hannah, who barely reacts, I'm reminded that it isn't new.

We all make our way back into the yard, crowded around the table once more, this time talking about Gen and Jackson. The group drones on about the wedding, when it might be, who might be invited, and who will be in the bridal party.

"Hannah will be in Atlanta, so that will make things easier for you, Gen!" Linda says with a gleam, pulling an awkward shift from Gen. Hannah and Gen had a falling-out years ago, and while they're okay now, they're not where they once were. Linda can't seem to take that hint, but it's not my business to insert my opinion on the matter.

"Atlanta?" The question gets asked, and a few seconds go by before I realize it's my own voice. I'd asked the question.

"What? Your ego too big to not suffocate me by being in the same city as you?"

"More like the stench of you might evacuate the metropolitan area..."

This gets the reaction I've been chasing all night, pulling a scream from Hannah's lungs as she jumps from the table. Her face is about as red as a cherry Popsicle and I grin in response.

"You're a dick!" Hannah stomps into the house, dramatic as ever.

I don't really care if she's in Atlanta, as long as she stays the hell away from me.

TWO

THREE WEEKS LATER

HANNAH

As much as I love my brother and Gen—and I do, I love them tremendously—I am so happy to no longer be staying with them. If I have to wear earplugs to bed one more time, I might actually self-destruct. Genuinely, I think the sound of my brother having sex is seared into my brain, and it's a trauma I cannot undo.

I've avoided eye contact for a week and a half.

Not to mention being around two people so disgustingly in love when you're terminally single is just plain sad.

My older brother and my best friend since kindergarten reignited their relationship last year after mutual friends set them up on a trip to Saint-Tropez. At first I was thrown by it, but honestly, seeing them together feels right. When they broke up in high school, I didn't handle it well, so having Gen back in my life has been a welcome change.

I just wish we weren't still tiptoeing around the past because neither of us wants to bring it up and talk about it.

"Are you planning on helping?" Jackson huffs, dropping a brown box marked *Kitchen* onto the low-pile carpet. He pushes his dark brown hair back, the combination of the sweltering Atlanta heat and the walking up and down two flights of stairs causing sweat to soak his skin.

"But you do it so well..." I pout.

"Hannah—"

"Fine." I put my can of Diet Coke on the credenza, following Jackson out of the apartment I will be inhabiting for the next year.

Thankfully, when I'd decided to move to Atlanta, Wes, Jackson's best friend, said his sister's roommate was moving out and that she needed a new one. At first I was nervous, but once I learned that it was because she was moving in with her boyfriend and not because Sage was a raging psycho, I agreed.

Sage Buckley meets us right outside the building, her beautiful, highlighted curls pushed into a ponytail on top of her head. Her golden-brown skin looks almost ethereal peppered with a dusting of sweat. Her hands are on her hips as she sucks in air, evaluating the U-Haul still half-full of my belongings.

"How do you have so much shit?" she laughs, nodding her head toward the heap.

"It's not shit, it's *memories*."

Truth be told, I didn't need to bring every memento from every production I'd ever been in when I moved to New York. I considered them reminders of why I worked so hard, and when I opted to move to Atlanta, I couldn't find it in me to part ways with them.

Especially my wig from *Little Shop of Horrors*. The very wig that fell off my head as they fed me to the man-eating plant, Audrey II. I was cast as Audrey Fulquard, the female lead in the production. Even though I'm naturally blonde, I refused to cut it, so I opted to wear a platinum blonde bob wig. While the show was one of the most fun I'd ever done, I can still feel my cheeks flush in embarrassment when I remember the crowd laughing as the wig hit the wood of the community theater stage despite it being the saddest scene in the show.

I've been in over thirty productions since middle school between school and community shows, yet despite my love of the arts, I've yet to be cast in a professional production.

Getting your union card in New York is harder than I expected. I considered going to Chicago, but ultimately I felt like I was going to run into the same problem.

Homesick.

Atlanta isn't Live Oak, *thank God*, but Jackson lives here and it's one of the most up-and-coming theater districts in the nation.

Heaving the box up to cradle it in my arms, I move back toward the building, hoping we'll finish sooner rather than later. Gen, Sage, and Jackson each grab a box as well, following me in a much-less-fun version of Follow the Leader.

Sweat pools at my brow as I make my seventh non-stop trip from the truck to my new apartment. As Jackson drops the last box onto the living room floor, I throw myself onto the couch, my eyelids fluttering shut as my head meets the headrest.

"Beer?" Sage's voice travels from the kitchen.

"Sure!" Jackson and I yell in unison.

Sage comes out to meet us, four cans of Sweetwater 420 between her fingers in a claw-like grip. I grab the ice-cold relief from her, pop the tab, and take a huge gulp within seconds.

I'm not typically a huge beer person, but the arctic salvation leaves me worshipping the fresh, hopsy flavor on my tongue.

Each of us swallows it down—even Gen, who I have never

seen drink beer. Then again, I haven't drunk around her much in the past decade.

"Hey babe." A tall, blond guy appears in the open doorway, pressing his lips to Sage's cheek.

I don't miss how she pulls away from his affection.

"What are you doing here?" Sage asks.

"I am heading to the gym...I figured I'd stop by and see my girl."

Despite my efforts to not be obvious, I feel my eyes bug out of my head at his words. I didn't realize Sage had a boyfriend.

"Not your girl...but you can stay," she sighs, grabbing a box off the floor and handing it to him. "Put this away."

He doesn't even question her and I am reminded that I really don't know much about this girl. I've met her a few times, mostly at events thrown by Wes and Savannah, but as for her personal life, I know next to nothing.

"Boyfriend?" I ask, hushed in tone.

"Oh God no," Sage laughs. "I worked with him at the golf course last summer. He's fun—but no."

Her shrug keeps my questions at bay. I look to Jackson, who doesn't seem remotely fazed by this.

Okay then.

A crash sounds from the kitchen, causing me and Sage to jump slightly.

"Sorry—" The random blond guy's voice rings through the air with the sound of glass being swept up. He emerges from the kitchen with half of my teapot in one hand, the other half in shambles in the blue dustpan in his other hand.

"No..." I whine, grabbing Mrs. Pots—or what's left of her—from his grasp.

The teapot is one of the few things my parents have gifted me that made me feel like they knew me. It was for my thirteenth birthday and I've treasured it since that day, bringing it to every new apartment.

"We'll replace it." Jackson's voice cuts through my panic as I struggle to keep tears at bay.

Objectively, I realize it's just a teapot, but it's more than that and he should know that.

"Jackson..."

"I know, bug...but we'll replace it."

I nod, unsure of what to say other than that you can't unbreak porcelain.

The half still intact lands in the empty trash bin, the sound of it cracking again causing me to jerk in response.

Don't cry, don't cry, don't cry.

By a stroke of a miracle, I don't.

Remind me to pat myself on the back.

Gen, Jackson, and Sage's not-boyfriend finally leave. A chime cuts through the apartment before a whirl of caramel curls darts past me to open the front door. Sage grabs the box from the delivery driver, filling the space with a delicious fog of pepperoni and pineapple. I'm relieved that it took barely half an hour to get our order—leaving New York made me nervous.

"Thanks for buying the pizza," I say, grabbing a piece and plopping it onto a paper plate at the kitchen counter.

"Of course—I mean, after all...you're unemployed."

The joke has been following me all day. First, Jackson said it, and it led to everyone following suit. I start at Baker & Park on Monday, so this "unemployed" joke only really works for the thirteen days I've spent between my waitressing job in New York and here, but Jackson couldn't resist.

"Barely."

"Still counts!" She chuckles, stuffing half a piece of pizza into her mouth after she folds it in half.

Before we know it, the box is nearly empty and we're both a human embodiment of Violet in *Willy Wonka and the Chocolate Factory*, busting at the seams.

"So, what's the deal with the blond guy?" I ask, approaching the topic I've been feeling her actively avoiding all day.

"*As I said*—just some guy."

Normally, I'd read into it. I mean, most people who say it's nothing when referring to a romantic entanglement are typically downplaying, but something about Sage's demeanor has me thinking it really is to be taken at face value.

"Fuck buddy?"

"Basically, yeah. I don't know. I get bored." She shrugs, pulling her fourth beer to her lips. "What about you? Anyone special in your life?"

I should have seen the question being returned, but it still stings on impact.

"No," I say as Sage looks at me as if the answer isn't good enough. "I was seeing this girl in New York, but she was kind of a commitment-phobe...like someone I know."

"I'm not a commitment-phobe...people just suck."

"Fair point."

"So, this girl...any actual feelings?"

"Ish—I don't know...it's hard to date in the theater scene in New York; everyone knows everyone and, frankly, it started to feel like my hometown after a while. But she was fun."

Downplaying things with Esme stings, but I can't find it in me to think about it right now. Telling a practical stranger that your ex-girlfriend didn't think you were exclusive and subsequently slept with over half of the acting community while you were the picture of commitment is embarrassing.

Sage nods, and I can't tell if it's because she's deep in thought or is just absorbing what I said.

"What do you do?" I ask.

"A little of this, a little of that—a career isn't really a goal of mine." Sage shrugs as she stands up to grab another beer from the fridge. "Want one?"

"I'm good, thanks." My mind travels back to the guy from earlier. "At least you're getting laid. I'm pretty much terminally single."

"Terminal means it will kill you..."

"It might."

"Okay, Miss Drama Queen."

"It's what I do, Sage. It's what I do."

She laughs, tossing a throw pillow in my direction as she finds her way back to the couch, popcorn and beer in hand.

I can't say I'm disappointed as we settle into a rapport together. Moving in with a near-stranger is stressful, but I'm sure Sage and I will undoubtedly make good friends.

A yawn pulls from my throat as the day catches up with me. I look down at my iPhone to find that it is almost midnight, and I have to be up early. Sage, however, is bopping around, filled with energy as if it is midafternoon.

"How are you not tired?"

She responds with a shrug as she pulls the throw pillow into her lap, lifting the remote to turn on the TV.

Dozing off, I jerk awake thinking that no time has passed, and Sage is still next to me. I peek down at my phone and see that it's now nearing 2:00 AM.

Jeez.

"I'm going to bed."

Once again, Sage nods, not pulling her attention from the episode of *Hell's Kitchen* that has her enraptured. Popcorn litters her blanket, but she barely seems to notice as her eyes are glued to the screen. Walking past her, I grab the now-empty bowl of popcorn and put it in the sink. I make my way back to my new bedroom, only to be reminded that I didn't put the sheets on my bed earlier in the day, when I insisted I would remember.

Apparently...not.

Typically, I would take the time to do it, but as my head hits my pillow, I pull a throw blanket off the stack of clothing and laundry Gen had unpacked earlier and nod off, naked mattress and all.

THREE

LIAM

"How is it that we continue to have this conversation?" Jackson says, squeezing the bridge of his nose between his fingers.

"Because I am forced to see you continuously bring that MacBook in every day."

"It's my computer..."

"It's just further evidence that the masses will always choose an inferior product if it looks cool." I laugh, tossing a ball in Jackson's direction.

He is unfortunately becoming much more attuned to knowing when I'm about to throw something, as he catches it with ease, stopping it inches from his face. Setting the ball down on his desk, Jackson continues typing away on his god-awful MacBook, refusing to engage the topic any further.

"So, marriage, huh?" I say, leaning back in my desk chair, playing with a fidget toy in my hand.

"Yes, marriage. Was there a question in there?" Jackson looks up from his computer, his brows raising in the process.

"The question is...you're getting married, huh?"

"You were there..." Jackson doesn't seem to be as amused as me as I've been distracting him for most of the morning.

"Yeah, I know..." I contemplate my words for a moment, "but marriage?"

"Yes, marriage," Jackson scoffs.

"Hey man, I didn't mean that in a shitty way. I like Gen, but aren't we a little young to be getting married?"

"You are too young...at least...*intellectually*. I, however, happen to like the idea of declaring in front of our friends and family how much I love Gen."

"Fair, fair."

Marriage is a concept I've just never understood. I realize the fault in that logic as I've never been in a long-term committed relationship, so I realize that I might just not get it... but what's the point?

Knock.

Our heads jerk toward the door as it slowly opens, revealing my dad standing in the doorway, his coffee in hand.

"Hello, boys," he says with a grin, closing our office door behind him.

People say I look like my dad thirty years ago, and while the years between us make it harder to draw the comparison, I definitely see the similarities. He's Korean and I am therefore half Korean—obviously, that's kind of genetic—but I like to think I inherited his hair. Well into his fifties and the man still has a full head of hair; fingers crossed I age the same way.

"Hey, Dad, what's up?"

"Good morning to you too, Liam."

The room grows silent as my dad clears his throat, Jackson and I waiting for whatever reason fueled his coming into our office for the first time in a month.

"As you know, I've been wanting to up your workloads.

Especially you, Liam," he says as his eyes meet mine, an understanding between us. "I'm not getting any younger and I need to start grooming you for the future."

Ah, this again.

It's not that I don't want to take over Baker & Park; I do—it's always been my goal. However, in recent years it has become so much more in the forefront of my dad's mind, and he doesn't let it go. I'm twenty-nine, and I want to feel young for a little bit longer. Then again, I look over at Jackson, who is ready to do just about anything to establish his career at Baker & Park, and I find myself wondering if I'm the best fit to take over when my dad retires.

"That being said, I am looking to get you guys an assistant to help with your load in taking on more work."

Typically, associates at the firm don't have assistants, so that seems weird, but given everything, I guess it makes sense. The shine of the glossy windowpane bounces off my desk, casting my dad in an aggressive stream of direct sunlight, reminding me that it's nearing the end of the workday.

"Sounds great," I respond, noticing that Jackson has said little and just nods.

"I'm glad you think so, Liam. Hannah will be starting Monday."

Hannah.

"Hannah?" I ask, knowing exactly what is coming but still tensing as I wait for confirmation.

"Hannah Thatcher-Miles," he says, straightening his tie.

My eyes dart to Jackson, whose eyes are fixed on the floor at my dad's feet. This has got to be a joke. Hannah is an actress, for crying out loud—what the hell does she know about being a law assistant? Even more so, what kind of a sick joke is he playing thinking Hannah and I would work well together?

"This is a joke, right?"

"Liam." My dad's stern tone chills me to the bone, causing me to slump into my seat. He's never been a fan of the back-and-forth between Hannah and me, so I can't imagine he'll be accepting it at Baker & Park. My eyes dart to Jackson, whose eyes are now on me.

"Did you know about this?"

He nods in my direction but looks away as he does.

It's not a secret that Hannah and I don't get along. We have been at each other's throats for pretty much our entire lives. This is something my dad is very aware of, so the idea of hiring Hannah to be my assistant feels like either a manipulation tactic or just a dick move. Either way, I'm not about to call him out on it.

"Monday," I reiterate.

"Monday," my dad responds. Straightening his suit jacket once more, he walks toward the door and clicks it behind him without so much as a goodbye.

The room grows quiet, a stark contrast to the constant conversation that normally fills our office.

"Seriously, man?" I ask, but Jackson doesn't look up from his computer.

"She's a tiny blonde, she can't even do a push-up...I don't know why you're so scared of her..."

"I'm not afraid of her!" I react before I realize it, eliciting a grin from Jackson.

"Awfully defensive." Jackson *tsks*, still not looking up from his computer, judgment filling the air.

Here we go again.

"No," I snip, standing from my desk to grab a bottle of water from our mini fridge on the far wall by Jackson.

CHAPTER THREE

"I'm just saying, you're awfully defensive when it comes to her."

"Stop," I say. Jackson has gotten it into his head that there is something between Hannah and me, which is just offensive. I would rather stab myself in the jugular than touch that demonic little blonde. However, Jackson sticks to his theories. I'm not sure if he genuinely believes it or just enjoys fucking with me.

"So...this medical malpractice suit..."

Jackson is back to work without pause as he perks up at my question. "What about it?"

"It landed on my desk this morning; is there any way you can take it on? I know your client roster is pretty full, but my dad just added me to the Tollies case and it's taking more time than I anticipated."

The Martin Tollies case has been ongoing for months and it's finally going to trial, so I'm not entirely surprised they needed more help on the case.

"Yeah, man, no problem..."

I don't say it, but my mind is far from law.

FOUR

HANNAH

I really shouldn't be this nervous.

It's just a job, one that involves me working with people I've known my entire life, yet as I stand in front of Baker & Park, my anxiety is at an all-time high. Flattening my pencil skirt against my thighs, I let out a heavy breath, forcing myself to push through the front door.

The moment I enter the foyer, an intense desire to quote *The Wizard of Oz* comes to mind.

We are certainly not in Kansas anymore.

I've never been to Kansas.

"Hey, bug!" Jackson's arm slings over my shoulder, pulling me into a side hug.

The relief I feel knowing that Jackson will be by my side through this is comforting, but at the end of the day, this is a means to an end and everyone, including Stephen, knows it. Honestly, I don't even think there was an actual job available— he just made it happen.

I adore Stephen, but sometimes I wish I could just do something on my own without requiring intervention.

Jackson has always been on this path. He knew from a young age he wanted to be a lawyer, which I always assumed was because he adored Stephen so much. However, it's just not for me. I cringe at the thought of working at a law firm in general. I'm meant to be acting, but damn, getting your union card is a bitch.

"Hey, Jackson!" I force a pep in my voice, hugging him back.

"Are you excited?"

"That's one word for it," I laugh as Jackson presses his name badge to the turnstile at the front of the building, allowing us into the overly shiny entryway.

Baker & Park is in one of the largest towers in downtown Atlanta. There are upwards of fifty companies functioning within these walls, Baker & Park Law being only one of many.

The coffee cart in the corner smells like heaven, but I've already had two cups of coffee and I don't need another dose of caffeine or my anxiety surrounding starting a new job could very well venture into heart palpitations territory.

"Hello, Hannah!" Stephen's familiar voice travels from behind Jackson and me as he walks toward us from the coffee cart, a large coffee in his hand.

"Hey, Mr. Park!" I force a grin from ear to ear, attempting to hide my nervousness.

"What is with the two of you? Jackson did the same thing when he started. It's Stephen. Hannah, I was at the hospital when you were born—calm down."

With that, my nerves are surprisingly quelled. I was anxious that the dynamic with him would be different in a professional environment, but I'm happy to see he's still the same Stephen Park I've known my entire life.

Stephen and his wife, Caroline, have been best friends

with my parents since long before Jackson or I were born. I adore them; they've always treated me as family, sometimes more so than my own parents did.

"Of course. I'm sorry, Stephen," I say, leaning into his outstretched arms for a hug.

Stephen embraces me and holds me there for a moment. He whispers in my ear so quietly that I'm pretty sure I'm the only one who can hear, "You're going to do amazing, Hannah."

How he manages to sooth me so much better than my own parents is jarring.

"Thank you," I whisper back, squeezing him tightly before pulling away.

"So..." Stephen turns to Jackson, "I'm assuming you will be showing her your office?"

His office?

I hadn't really thought about who I would be assisting during my time at Baker & Park, but I didn't think it would be Jackson. This should be comforting, and it is for a moment... until I remember who he shares an office with.

No.

"Yes, sir. Maintenance brought her desk up Friday afternoon and set it up in the outer office. We're heading up there right now."

"Excellent—" Stephen's attention veers to someone behind me and Jackson. "I'm glad I caught you two, but I am actually meeting a client. Hannah, have a good first day."

I offer a smile and a nod, and Stephen is gone in an instant.

We make our way up the escalator before we are ushered into an elevator. This place really is a maze.

"Your office?" I whisper to Jackson.

He pins me with a glare. "Hannah, don't. I can't deal with both of you about it."

I stifle the urge to roll my eyes in response. Liam has no reason to complain; I am a fucking delight. Much to my surprise, I manage to keep that thought to myself.

Jackson pulls out his scan card, pressing it to the office door, where I find an empty desk void of charm. I assume it's mine, and set my purse in the seat before he directs me toward another door directly to the left of my desk.

His office...or...*their* office, I guess.

The moment the door beeps, Jackson pushes it open to reveal a room, much like the rest of the building, glistening from floor to ceiling. Except for their respective desks.

I've been here a few times before, so I knew what to expect, but it's still so weird to know I work here now.

In the room, my eyes meet Liam's and my stomach lurches. He glares at me, his piercing, borderline insidious brown eyes fixed on my eyes. Normally I would meet his presence with unwelcome disgust, so why am I fixated on his strong jawline like it has appeal? His perfectly styled, thick, dark hair should make me want to dishevel it to cause him anger, so why am I thinking about what it would feel like to touch it? This is *Liam*, Hannah, get it together!

The combination of excess caffeine and anxiety over the day has me reacting in weird ways, that's for sure.

"Park," I quip before turning away from him, instantly allowing my previous diversion from sanity to wash down my spine.

"Satan spawn."

"Guys," Jackson interjects, rubbing his eyes in irritation, "we have to work together. This may be okay when we're on family holidays, but it can't be like this at work."

I know he's right, but damn does it make me feel like a reprimanded child to be reminded of the fact. I look over at

Liam, who doesn't seem even remotely concerned with what Jackson said.

"Work would imply she's going to do anything." Liam's eyes shift to mine, a look of disdain that I know all too well aimed back at me. "You may have convinced my dad that you're going to work while here, but you and I both know you're not going to do shit. Act like you're not a princess all you want, but you forget I know you—"

"Liam." Jackson's voice travels out of my periphery, quelling the building rage in my stomach.

"Jackson."

"Guys." Normally I would find amusement in them butting heads, but this seems like a lot.

"Look—" Liam sighs, getting up from his seat, buttoning his suit jacket as he stands. I struggle not to notice the way the fabric of his sleeves hugs his arms as he stretches. "Jackson, I realize she's your sister, but if she's going to fuck around and be hanging around in our office without a purpose, then it's going to be a problem."

"She won't." Jackson grits his teeth as he forces the words out.

I can't quite figure out why what Liam is saying hurts so much. He's said far worse than this to me over the years, but something about him attacking my work ethic stings. Working hard has never been an issue for me. I work to hide the sting in my chest and eyes as I look away from him and Jackson, allowing them to hash their shit out without my input.

"Good." Liam turns to sit down, unbuttoning his suit jacket in the process. He pulls it from his frame, draping it over the back of his chair before rolling the sleeves of his shirt to his elbows. The muscular strain of his forearms pulls my attention before I jerk my gaze away in an attempt at being discreet.

Beautiful fucking asshole.

Look, it's not that he's unattractive—objectively, at least—but his personality is easily one of the most unappealing things about the man.

"I'm going to, um..." I say as I point toward the door to the outer office before darting out the door, Jackson on my tail.

"Are you okay?"

Nodding, I turn on the monitor fixed to my new desk before pulling out my favorite office supplies from my bag. Jackson is still lurking and I try my best to avoid looking at him. He can read me like an open book and I don't want to admit Liam got to me.

"Okay, well...text me if you need anything..."

I nod again as he walks away. The moment he's gone, I allow the tears welling in my eyes to drop before wiping them away rapidly in hopes of it going unnoticed. Just as I level myself out, I look up to find a petite brunette standing in front of my desk. Her long, brown, highlighted locks are draped over one shoulder and if I wasn't in such a sour mood, I would almost consider flirting with her.

"Is Liam in?"

And suddenly, the thought of flirting with this nitwit dies. I nod, fighting the curiosity about whether it's of a work or personal nature, but given how she asked...I'm assuming the latter.

"Yeah, uh...go right in."

FIVE

LIAM

"What are you doing tonight?" Veronica asks as she rests her ass against the wooden edge of my desk, a seductive grin plastered across her lips.

She's worked at Baker & Park for a little over a year, but it's only been the last few months that she's even remotely frequented this side of the office. Popping in every so often, Veronica is a sight for sore eyes on a bad day.

"I'm getting a couple beers with the guys." I grin, attempting to match her enthusiastic inflection. "Why? What are *you* doing tonight?"

"Apparently...getting some beers with the guys."

Jackson clears his throat, pulling my attention to him.

My eyes drift to him as he shakes his head frantically at me. It's not that Jackson doesn't like Veronica—at least not enough to have voiced it—but this isn't my first rodeo. She does this at least once a week and sometimes tags along, but she can be...a lot when she drinks.

"I'm sorry, Veronica, guys' night. Rain check?" I smile up

at her only to find a disappointed pout on her lips. Not this again.

"Promise?"

"Would I ever lie to you?" Truth be told, there is no precedent to say I wouldn't, but I'm not about to mention that.

"Okay." Veronica reaches forward, squeezing my hand as she stands up. Her expression sours as her gaze drifts toward Jackson.

All right, so that dislike is mutual, apparently.

As the door clicks closed, Jackson lets out a breath that in my opinion is far more dramatic than the situation calls for.

"Penny for your thoughts, Jax?"

He glares at me, but I pretend not to notice it. "You're toying with her."

The judgment I'm met with leaves me irritated. He knows I'm not that kind of guy—I intentionally work not to be.

"Oh, fuck off," I say, rolling my eyes in irritation.

"She likes you, man. Speaking from experience, being toyed with is not fun. Stop."

Veronica is attractive; hot, even. She's the full package, but I try my best not to shit where I eat. At least that's what I tell myself.

"Whatever, man..." I toss a stress ball at his head, but he dodges it with ease, the ball barely skating over his dark brown hair, so lightly it doesn't even displace it. He really is getting too used to this. I need to up my game. "So, we still hitting Harry's after work?"

Harry's is a small hole-in-the-wall bar around the corner from our office. It has become a sort of go-to place for us over the last year. It doesn't exactly provide much by way of ambiance, but it gives us the laid-back environment we all want after a long day at work.

"Yeah, Wes is meeting us a bit later after his shift is up, but Gabe said he'll be there."

I nod in response.

The rest of the day drags, a fresh client file landing on my desk as the clock displays 5:00 PM.

That is a problem for tomorrow.

I pack up my things in record time, but Jackson is still typing away on his computer.

"C'mon, let's go."

"I'm almost done," Jackson says, not even looking up from his task.

Making my way into the outer office to start shutting off lights, I notice Hannah still typing away as well. Since our earlier interaction, her hair has shifted into a haphazard mess of a bun atop her head, her glasses fixed to the bridge of her nose.

I didn't know she wore glasses—weird.

"Wrap it up, princess."

She responds with a nod, and much like my interaction with Jackson moments ago, she keeps typing.

Does no one listen to me?

Unlike Jackson, I don't totally care how late she stays as long as she shuts off the light and closes the outer office door before she leaves. Jackson, however, I care about, since the rest of his evening is integral to my own plans.

"Jax, c'mon." The moment the words leave my mouth, he is shutting his MacBook.

As we make our way out of the office, Hannah is still working and, from the looks of it, has no plans of stopping any time soon.

Whatever.

"Don't stay too late, bug, okay?" Jackson says to her,

messing with the bun on top of her head in a noogie-type motion.

"I'm almost done." She doesn't look up at him, so something tells me her words are just to make him feel better.

"Okay...well, we're heading to Harry's."

"Dude, let's go..." Irritation bleeds into my voice as I say it, but I can't will myself to care if I'm appearing crass. I want a beer.

"Yeah, yeah."

By a pure stroke of luck, we arrive at Harry's just as Gabe sits down at the bar, the pretty redheaded bartender waiting to take his order.

"Hey, man!" I smack him on the back as I sit, causing him to jump a bit. "You okay?"

"Yeah, uh, I'm good. Long day."

I've known Gabe long enough to not pry when he's like this. It honestly could be anything and it's not like he's prepared to tell me anyway.

The bartender—Brittany, apparently, according to her name tag—takes our order and before I know it returns with three draft lagers in hand.

"Thanks."

Gabe's phone dings on the bartop, causing my eyes to instinctively travel to the light.

KARA

you can't be serious. you are LUCKY to have me, and if you think there's another woman on this earth who would actually fucking date you, then you've got another thing coming.

Woah, what the fuck?

"Gabe?" I say, concern seeping into my voice, but he

doesn't respond. He simply looks down and flips his phone over, the screen now facing the wood.

Despite my efforts, his eyes travel pretty much anywhere but mine.

"You excited for the wedding?" Gabe shifts in his seat to face Jackson, ignoring me entirely.

Should've seen that coming.

It's not uncommon for Kara and Gabe to fight, but sometimes I wonder how bad it is when people aren't around. However, I try not to pry.

"Very. Well, I'm excited to be married to Gen...and also to be done having Savannah blowing my phone up about stuff I don't understand...did you know that off-white and cream aren't the same thing?"

"Yes," Gabe and I respond in unison, eliciting a groan from Jackson.

"I get your point. But...just trust that it's a lot." Jackson clears his throat. "What about you, Gabe? You and Kara have been together a while."

I tense.

Despite years of pushing him to break up with Kara, Gabe still insists on staying with her. Do I think eventually they'll get married? Maybe, but I sure as hell hope not.

"Not for a while, man," Gabe says with a chuckle, pulling his beer to his mouth.

Both sets of eyes divert to me and I freeze, nearly choking on the sip of beer already in my mouth.

"Ha, fuck no. What about never? I'm not the settling-down type. Dad wants me to step into a more prominent role at Baker & Park...I'm going to focus on that."

This seems to quell them, and they shift toward their own conversation while I sit still, marinating on the thought.

It's not that I don't want to settle down, it's just that I can't think of a single woman in my life that I would want to settle down with. I never really have. In my twenty-nine years, I've never had a serious relationship and I don't plan to start now—it's just drama.

A hand clasps down on my shoulder, pulling my attention. Wes appears out of what feels like nowhere and takes the seat on my other side.

"Hey, man!" I return the gesture.

We exchange pleasantries amongst the group before Jackson clears his throat, causing all of us to look in his direction.

"The, uh...the girls are heading down..."

Letting out an exacerbated groan, I realize I am the only one reacting in an irritated manner.

"When?" Wes asks the question I'm resisting the urge to ask myself.

"Uh...now." The moment the words leave Jackson's mouth, an arm wraps around my middle, squeezing me from behind. I turn my upper body to find a familiar grin staring back at me: Sage.

Sage and I have gotten close over the past six months. When we first met, I'll admit I was distracted by how beautiful she was. Between the tight ringlets and light brown skin—which, frankly, was tantalizingly peppered with sweat on the golf course the day I met her—I wouldn't be human if I didn't notice.

Luckily for both of us, we fell into a much different rhythm after that, and I am proud to call her a friend. At first Wes didn't love the prospect of his sister hanging out with us, but after a while I think he realized it was the path of least resistance. There is rarely a scenario in which Sage doesn't get what she wants, so...it's typically best for him to just steer clear of trying to prevent it.

"Hey!" My tone shifts as I reach around to hug her back. My stomach instantly sours as my eyes meet the jade ones of the blonde standing behind Sage.

Hannah.

She's still in her clothes from work, but her hair is now down in a cascade of waves. If I hadn't seen her earlier, I would have never known her hair was up before.

Intentionally, I don't acknowledge her.

Is it a dick move? Probably. However, just because we're in the same group of friends now and she lives in Atlanta and managed to convince my dad to give her a job...that doesn't make us friends.

"Hi, baby!" Savannah squeals as she wraps her arms around Wes's neck.

Waving to the bartender, I ask for a shot of Patrón. She reappears instantly and as the fiery liquid coats my throat, I find myself relaxing despite the hostile company.

I will never grow used to Hannah being here; I wish I didn't have to.

Believe it or not, it hasn't always been this way between Hannah and me. When we were kids, some would have even called us friends. We bickered...but were friends. Something changed along the way. I try to prevent the tequila from coming back up as I recall that at one point I actually had a crush on her.

I am well aware of how disgusting that is. Lucky for me it was short-lived.

Hannah squeezes in beside me at the bar in an attempt to get the bartender's attention. As she orders a shot, I order one as well and, although we're not taking the shot *together*, we do take our shots at the same time.

Despite the burn, I fixate on the way her throat moves as she swallows it.

The tension in her throat stretches down the expanse of skin of her decolletage. She was wearing a blazer earlier, but the dress she had underneath goes from office to night out so seamlessly that I'm convinced there's no way it is work-appropriate. But somehow, it was.

"Hey, Liam!" Gabe yells from the pool table, thankfully pulling my attention away from Hannah.

Clearing my throat, I push my shot glass to the back lip of the bar, signaling to the bartender that I'll have another.

"One sec," I respond, grabbing my newly provided shot and guzzling it down before heading over to join Gabe. "What's up?"

The look I'm met with causes my stomach to sour.

"No." I attempt to shut him down instantly.

"I'm just sa—"

"No," I reiterate.

"No, what?" Jackson appears out of nowhere at the absolute worst possible time.

"Gabe just being a dipshit," I say with a grin.

"Yeah, just, ya know...drunk and stupid." Gabe forces a laugh as he scratches the back of his neck.

Thank God.

SIX

HANNAH

If you had asked me a year ago what I'd be doing right now, sitting in a meeting at Baker & Park taking notes for Jackson and Liam, I would've said you were delusional. I never wanted to do this.

My agreeing to take a job at Stephen's law firm was far from a rash decision; it was suggested by my parents for years. They have never agreed with my decision to pursue acting and when I opted to move to Atlanta, I am pretty sure they were convinced they had won.

Won they have not.

That being said, money is a necessary evil in life and when I moved to New York, it was made clear that as long as I was pursuing that path, I would have no financial help from my parents.

So here I am, sitting in Conference Room B taking notes I am almost positive neither Jackson nor Liam will be looking at. It's just the three of us, so I'm not even sure why we booked a conference room.

"What do you mean his alibi fell through?" Liam sighs, rubbing his hand over his face in exhaustion.

We've been in this meeting for over an hour rehashing the Martin Tollies case. Liam was assigned to take lead on the case and it's been made pretty clear through our meetings that he's intent on leaving no stone unturned.

"His neighbor that he said would vouch that he was at his apartment that night couldn't corroborate," Jackson responds, and I instantly write it down.

Liam's forehead meets the tabletop in frustration. He groans, lifting his head to look at Jackson again. "Okay, well... we need to figure out another way to corroborate his alibi. I'll call his landlord and see if there's any sort of security that can confirm. Jot that down, Hannah."

As I'm already halfway through writing it down, this earns him an involuntary eye roll.

"Did you have something to say?" As Liam leans back in his chair, his hands crossed over his chest, I feel my stomach churn.

He's taunting me, I can feel it.

Yet I don't walk away.

In any other environment, I would snap back at him. I would tell him to eat a bag of dicks. But I need this job and I have absolutely no faith that he wouldn't throw me under the bus the first chance he gets.

"No." I speak quietly, the sting of my nails biting into the palm of my hand.

I can't let him rile me up.

"That's what I thought." Liam's eyes divert to Jackson's, but I don't miss the smirk he wears. "I think we've got everything we can at this point."

With little pleasantries, we wrap up the meeting.

My phone pings as I'm standing to gather my things. Despite this, I don't check it in an attempt to get out of the room as soon as possible. I jump up in an effort to get to my desk without another snide remark from Liam.

As I make my way down the hallway back to my desk, the sound of Liam's overpriced loafers catches up, on my tail despite my efforts.

"Hannah!" he yells from behind me, causing me to stop in place.

"What's up?" I resist the urge to bite his head off, and as people pass us, I am reminded of just how inappropriate that would be.

"I need you to go through the notes sent over from Tollies's old representation and compile it for review. It needs to be more digestible for my 9:00 AM tomorrow, so I need it by end of day."

"But it's almost 5:00 PM. That's going to take me hours." *Don't snap, don't snap, don't snap.*

"Then get to it, princess." With that, he walks away without another word.

It's not that sifting through notes is a skilled or difficult task, it's just tedious and can't really be expedited...a fact with which Liam is very well acquainted.

I've been biting my tongue since starting because I want to remain professional, but the more I'm around Liam, the more I find my resolve deteriorating by the minute.

He's such an asshole!

Plopping into my chair, I reach for my phone, pulling up the email that came through, hopeful.

My stomach sours in an instant as I realize it's yet another junk email and not the director of the show I auditioned for informing me I've been cast.

In the four weeks I've been in Atlanta, I've gone to three auditions; this is now the third audition they have passed me over for. The stats really aren't looking great for me.

I reach up to rub my eyes, remembering just how long of a night I have ahead of me.

"Hannah." Liam's voice carries out to my desk, causing my stomach to sour.

Leave me alone, *fuck.*

"Yes, Liam?" I allow my annoyance to seep into my words, the veil I've been fighting to keep in place slipping.

"*Hannah.*" His voice drops to a growl, a reprimanding tone. It causes the hair on my arms to stand, a shiver running down my spine.

Fine.

It's no secret that I've always had a flair for the dramatics, yet even I am surprised when I barge into Liam and Jackson's office without a shred of decorum.

"What could you possibly want, Park?" Crossing my arms over my chest, I feel the blood rush to my face as I barely keep my rage at bay.

If we're being honest, I'm surprised I've made it this long.

He feigns surprise as I glare down at him, his fingertips tapping against his chin in a thinking pose. "I don't know, Hannah...for you to do your *job?*"

Jackson clears his throat, pulling my attention away from Liam's irritatingly smug face. As my eyes meet his, he is shaking his head, presumably telling me to stand down. Normally, I wouldn't entertain the idea, but this isn't summer at the beach house or winter in Vail. He's my boss...and the reminder leaves a sour taste on my tongue.

Gritting my teeth, I turn back to Liam. "I'm sorry. What do you need?"

His grin of triumph has me fighting every instinct in my body to flip the contents of his desk onto the ground.

"I want you to work on compiling those notes in here. Jackson is heading out—you can work at his desk." Liam waves his hand in Jackson's direction as he looks back down at the document in front of him.

Dude, *why?*

I clear my throat, turning to Jackson in a silent plea. He just shrugs.

Always Mr. Helpful.

"Of course." I grit my teeth, my jaw locking in place. Why Liam insists on micromanaging me, I will never know. I am not incompetent like he paints me to be. I'm capable of going through notes on my fucking own, thanks.

I make my way out to my desk to grab my laptop. The heated flush in my cheeks creeps down my neck, leaving me feeling like this office is scorching.

"Hannah." Jackson's calm voice does little to quell my anxiety.

"What's up?" I try to sound unaffected.

Turning to make my way back into their office, my eyes meet Jackson's, an expression of sympathy painted across his face.

"Don't let him get to you."

"Easier said than done." I swallow, feeling my heart rate finally starting to settle. "He just—he does it on purpose. He's trying to get under my skin."

"Probably," Jackson sighs, "but knowing that, don't let him win, okay?"

"Why aren't you sticking around tonight? I mean, why is Liam and not you?"

"It's his client, but also...I have plans with Gen. We're tasting wedding cake."

Of course, *Gen*.

It's not to say I don't like Gen. I adore her; we've been friends forever. However, it stings every time I'm reminded that Jackson knows her far better than I do anymore.

When we were little, Gen and I were inseparable. She was at our house every day for years and, while I'm not naive enough to say it was 100% about me, I miss it.

Also, my parents doting on her constantly is enraging.

"Well, have fun with your precious Genevieve. If there's blood on your envelope opener tomorrow, mind your business."

I walk away before he can reprimand me.

While Jackson's desk chair is far more comfortable than my own, I must admit the view leaves something to be desired. The incessant clicking of Liam's pen has my irritation growing higher, the semblance of calm I'm attempting to hold onto dying with every passing second.

"Why do you insist on being a dick?" The words tumble out before I can shove them back in.

Liam's brows shoot up to his hairline, his expression hardening for a split moment. He moves his jaw from side to side, almost as if I've hit him and he's calculating his retort.

"Trust me, princess, you haven't seen me be a dick. I will ride you so hard that you fall asleep standing up, so don't test me." He just looks down at his paper and continues the incessant clicking as if he didn't just say that.

I'm slack-jawed at his words.

"Stop staring, Hannah." He doesn't look up from the

document in front of him. The annoyed tone in his voice leaves me wanting to chuck Jackson's stapler at his head.

"Stop clicking your pen, *Liam*."

He pauses his clicking as he looks up at me before looking back down at the task in front of him.

Click.

SEVEN

LIAM

I swear this case is going to be the death of me. It feels like with every victory comes three more setbacks.

When my dad said he wanted me to start taking on more responsibility at the firm, I knew it would mean taking on bigger and more powerful clients, but all I can seem to think about with this case is how royally screwed I am if I mess up.

Do I need to stay with Hannah while she goes through these notes? Probably not, but I refuse to allow something to get missed, because at the end of the day it falls on my head, not hers.

That's not even to say that I think Hannah will mess it up; she's moderately competent. She graduated from the University of Tennessee with honors. Acting major or not, that is still a massive undertaking.

"Why do you want to work here anyway? It's not exactly Broadway." I toss one of my squishy stress balls up in the air. I've been wondering since she started at Baker & Park, and while I didn't anticipate myself actually asking, now I'm curious. "You're not qualified," I say, a coldness in my voice that the topic doesn't warrant.

Hannah's jaw tenses, a telltale giveaway that I'm getting under her skin. It's also something I've been seeing a lot over the past week.

"If you must know…" she labors the words out as she grits her teeth, "it was your dad's idea. It's not long-term, but it's necessary."

"What? Can't find work?" I chuckle, intending it as a joke to poke at her, but the expression glaring at me isn't just that of disdain, but pain. I struck a chord.

She says nothing in response, much to my dismay. The game only works when she responds.

Whatever.

The wall clock ticks as we approach 7:00 PM, my stomach reminding me that I've once again worked through dinner.

Hannah brushes a piece of her golden-blonde hair behind her ear and I watch the way her hand traces down her neck as she gazes at her laptop. The expanse of skin that trails from her ear to her collarbone is far more distracting than it should be. She holds her hand there, causing my eyes to linger.

I clear my throat, pulling Hannah's attention from the task at hand.

Shit.

"How are you doing over there?" I ask, not really concerned about it, but flustered when she catches me ogling.

Well, not *ogling*.

Observing.

Hannah's brows shoot up at my question, causing my stomach to squeeze like a vise.

"Oh—um," she clears her throat, clearly unsure about my

sudden onset of brain malfunction, "I'm actually having trouble finding the document they're referring to."

Wait, what?!

No, this can't be happening. This is supposed to just be last-minute note compiling to prepare for my meeting with the client tomorrow. We can't be missing documents.

This could lose me the client. They're already feeling skittish after firing their old representation.

I jump out of my chair, causing it to spin behind me, and dart over to look at what has Hannah perplexed.

"Show me."

Hannah tenses at my sudden intrusion, but quickly relaxes. "The document, uh—it says it's the Wellington statement, but I can't find it on the flash drive you gave me."

Fuuuuuuuuck.

"Shit, uh—" I scratch the nape of my neck. "Pull up the flash drive, please."

Her expression shifts to something of confusion at my use of pleasantries.

Jesus Christ, Hannah, I'm not a Neanderthal. I understand basic human decency.

She does as I ask, pulling up the contents of the drive. She's right—there isn't anything labeled "Wellington." Sweat begins to pepper the back of my neck as I flush. This can't be happening.

"Open the file marked 'Irrelevant Evidence,' please."

Hannah does as I request, opening the folder that houses an absolute headache of chaotic folders and files, none of which have consistent names to even point us in the right direction.

See, this is why we are so meticulous in our naming conventions here at Baker & Park.

"There," I say, leaning forward to look closer at her screen as I point to a file named "Well-Depo."

Once again, she does as I ask and, to my relief, it's the statement we were looking for.

"Oh, thank God," Hannah whispers to herself in relief.

It is then that I realize how close I am; so much so that I smell the faint mixture of citrus and ylang-ylang mingled with peppermint.

It's nice.

"Yeah...thank God," I sigh, noticing the skin on her neck pebble as I say it. Why that is, I can't be sure, but it's odd.

My hand grips the back of her chair, my body still leaning over hers. The realization hits me that this is the closest we've been in years, and that revelation should horrify me. The air around us seems to thicken, yet I don't move...I feel paralyzed. I notice the way Hannah's breathing becomes more labored, the rise and fall of her chest causing my eyes to wander... clinging to areas I shouldn't peruse.

The scan card lock beeps on the office door, causing me to jerk away from Hannah as if I was doing something lewd, not helping her with a work task.

Jesus, what the hell is wrong with me?

"Liam." My dad's deep voice carries, pulling my eyes to his.

I button my suit jacket, making my way back to my desk in an attempt to find a level of familiarity.

"Hi, Stephen." Hannah's voice is peppier than it ever is when directed at me, the false kindness causing me to resist the urge to gag in response. If it were anyone but my dad, I would, but that sounds like a one-way ticket to being reprimanded and potentially a mandatory seminar on proper workplace etiquette. He's typically a relaxed guy in most respects, even with employees, but he has a serious stance on anything that could be construed as hateful or rude amongst staff.

"Hannah." He grins at her before his eyes dart back to my own. "Why is she still here?"

This earns an eye roll from me, one that I hope he doesn't notice. "She's helping me compile notes for the Tollies case."

To be frank, I probably could have handled it myself, but what is the value in having an assistant if they aren't going to make your life easier?

"Are you almost wrapped up?" he asks, a gentleness in his voice toward Hannah.

"I think so—"

"Head home, Hannah."

Wait, what?

I understand it is his company, but telling Hannah to leave when I've clearly given her a task is undermining, and I don't like it. Though I've never really cared about that, now it has me fuming.

"We're working on something," I say, trying to keep my irritation at bay.

"If you had checked your calendar, you would know that her parents are in town. I'm due to dinner in a half-hour with them, with *her* in attendance."

Why he thinks I should have a handle on his social calendar, I will never know, even if he insists on adding them to my own.

"I didn't reali—"

"It would do you well to attend, Liam. George and Linda would appreciate seeing you." He turns from me, aiming a more docile expression toward her. "Head out, Hannah. Go home, freshen up, and we'll see you at Andre's at 7:30."

Once again, my dad undermines my authority in my own office. I can't say I'm shocked.

To my surprise, Hannah's eyes meet mine, an expression of conflict on her face. I nod in her direction, causing her to close her laptop and pull it to her chest as she jumps from her seat. Hannah places the flash drive she'd been working on on the corner of my desk and I snatch it up instantly.

She makes her way out to her desk, the door clicking shut behind her.

"Are you out of your mind, Liam?" His stern tone causes a shiver to run down my spine.

"Dad, she's my assistant. If you didn't want her to work, I don't know why you got her the job in the first place."

I try my best to keep my annoyance at bay, pressing the drive into the USB port of my computer, pulling up an array of documents meticulously organized. It's so orderly that I would think I'd done it myself.

"I got her this job as a favor to her father. Yes, I want her to work, but during her *working* hours. Your personal vendetta against the girl needs to be left at the door."

"I didn't—"

"You did, and I expect it not to happen again. If you need her to stay late, it needs to be approved. Until then, she leaves by 5:30."

That is hardly standard practice at this firm, but I'm not going to bring that up right now.

Gulping, I nod, my eyes not meeting his.

"Dinner with George and Linda, be there."

As quickly as he enters, my dad is gone again, leaving a sour feeling in my stomach at his words. I'm meticulous about being professional in the office with our employees, so for him to insinuate that I would weaponize Hannah's job against her doesn't sit well with me.

Did I, though?

My eyes return to the screen in front of me, all the documents I need for tomorrow's meeting laid out in order of necessity, as easy to navigate as if I had handled it myself.

I reach up to rub my eyes in exhaustion before flipping my laptop shut, stuffing it into the padded compartment of my bag. As I exit my office, I see Hannah is already gone, except I notice the case files printed and stacked on the edge of her desk. She took the time to print these for me before she headed out? I don't like the feeling this causes in my stomach.

The papers crinkle slightly as I snatch them up, heading back into my office to set them down so I have them for tomorrow.

As I leave the Newmont tower in which Baker & Park is situated, I question what direction to go. Should I go to our joint family dinner, or go home?

My stomach growls, a not-so-subtle reminder that I really should just attend.

I make my way down to Andre's, a bistro only a block from the office. The memory of their chicken melt has my mouth watering, but as I approach the restaurant, I stop in my tracks as I catch a glimpse of Hannah across the table from my parents, a laugh being pulled from her far more effortlessly than I am used to. It's nice, but I don't have the time to unpack that thought.

My hand reaches for the doorknob, but I pause. I should go home.

I don't want to be around her any more than I have to.

The grin plastered across her face as she presses the glass of red wine to her lips causes me to step backward, making my way back to the parking garage. I pull out my phone as I walk away.

LIAM

Can't make it to dinner, something came up. I'll see you in the morning.

Knowing him as well as I do, I don't expect a text back from my dad. My stomach growls as I reach my car, pocketing my cell phone.

Bojangles it is.

EIGHT

HANNAH

My head hits my pillow. The wine haze from the restaurant has the ceiling spinning in a counterclockwise motion. It's not even to say that I got drunk at dinner—I only had three glasses of wine—but unfortunately for me, I've always been the world's biggest lightweight.

Once again, I spent the evening being bombarded by my mother, so the fact that I only had three glasses is a miracle in and of itself. Dinner with the Parks always seems to spiral into her hurling not-so-subtle jabs at my accomplishments as a way for her to praise Jackson and Liam. Now, with this wedding on the horizon, it's just another opportunity for her to reduce me to being a lesser option to Jackson and now...Gen.

I reach over to plug my phone in, a text from Jackson popping up on the screen.

JACKSON

did you get home okay?

HANNAH

yeah, just got home.

> are you okay? i know mom was a lot
> tonight…

I'm honestly a little surprised he even noticed since it didn't revolve around him or Gen. I tamper down that thought and try to be thankful that he cares.

> yeah, im fine. thank you though.

> however, im heading to bed. ill see you in
> the morning.

> sounds good. love you, bug.

> love you too.

To say today was weird is an understatement. Even if you remove my mother and her insistence on being a bitch at dinner from the equation, my mind still keeps wandering to earlier in the day. I can't find the words to unpack all of it. The memory of Liam's breath skating over my neck as he leaned over me still sends shivers down my spine. I don't want to think about why my body reacted the way it did. The warmth between my legs from earlier creeps back with full force, causing my mind to wander to places it shouldn't.

Damn it, Hannah. Get it together.

The spinning from the alcohol starts to subside, giving me a sense of calm rather than distress. Drifting off into oblivion, a comforting warmth spreads as sleep overtakes me.

"Trust me, princess." Liam's voice, commanding, a near growl, travels up my neck. The familiar feeling of my skin prickling crawls up my spine, bathing me in the memory. "You haven't seen me be a dick. I will ride you so hard that you fall asleep standing up, so don't test me."

Unlike the actual moment my thoughts recall, this time Liam's hand trails up the back of my neck, yanking the hair at the nape and eliciting a gasp from my lungs. My skin erupts in goosebumps, a warmth spreading at the simple aggressive action.

I'm pinned against his desk, my hands braced onto his tabletop calendar, the paper crinkling under the pressure as my hands form into fists. He yanks my head back, causing it to lean against his shoulder, his breath dancing along the shell of my ear as he whispers.

"Be a good girl and don't make a sound. We wouldn't want anyone to hear you."

His free hand begins to snake down my back achingly slowly until his hand crawls around, lifting the hem of my skirt before his hand dips below my panties, inches from oblivion.

"Fuuuu—"

In my hazy half-asleep state, the lines between reality and dream begin to blur. The moment Liam's fingertips reach my wet heat, I slip my hand below the waist of my pajama shorts, finding myself exactly as expected.

Dripping.

My middle finger finds my clit and I gasp, the pressure pulling a moan from my lips.

"Hannah," Liam reprimands, causing me to bite my bottom lip, "I said be quiet. I need you to fucking listen."

The phantom sting at the base of my scalp sends a delicious bolt of electricity down to my pussy. I circle my bundle of nerves more rapidly, biting my lip to remain quiet with so much effort I'm convinced I can taste blood. In my fantasy, it's his hand bringing me pleasure.

In that moment, the fantasy changes.

He's here.

Liam is in my room with me, but he doesn't touch me. He simply watches and I revel in it.

"If you insist on doing it yourself, let me see." His voice carries as I let out a moan, the raspy baritone pulling me back. "I said be quiet, Hannah. Don't make me tell you again."

I comply, pulling my pillow to my chest, resting it just over my mouth as a buffer to my mewls.

A finger dips inside me, leaving me aching, wishing for more...wishing for him. I fuck myself with my hand, muffling my moans in the pillow pressed to my lips.

The pressure building inside me causes my strokes to become more frantic, a constant shift between caressing my clit in circular motions and pressing inside. I tense, biting back a scream behind the cotton.

"That's it, Hannah. Come for me." Liam's voice swarms my brain, pushing me over the edge. Ecstasy overtakes me, pushing me past the point of no return. My orgasm hits me, the pulsing sensation consuming me.

Fuck.

The buzzing feeling overtakes my entire body, carrying the pleasure through every expanse of skin.

Coming down from my orgasm, I attempt to quell my racing heart, but it's no use. The warm, all-encompassing state of satiation unfortunately doesn't stick around.

The reality of what I just did hits me, along with a healthy dose of shame. I can't think about him like that, and the reminder of how utterly intolerable his personality is causes my stomach to churn. The memory of his smug expression when he reprimanded me earlier in the day is enough to throw me into a shame spiral.

I'm no novice to the concept of post-orgasm clarity, but if it isn't a bitch anyway.

Yet, the memory of him leaning over me with his mouth mere inches from my ear, invading my space, has me questioning my sanity and if I have managed to go crazy in the week and a half I've been working with him.

That is the most logical conclusion: insanity.

The clock on my nightstand reads 4:00 AM and I groan, rolling over onto my side. I have to be up for work in two hours and, despite my exhaustion and what should be satiation, I'm wired. I squeeze my pillow to my chest and shift back onto my back, staring up at the ceiling, begging for some relief from my mental agony. I lift it to my face and do the only thing I can—I scream.

NINE

LIAM

"How did it go?" My father appears in the doorway of Conference Room B, his hands in his pockets as he leans against the frame.

I gather the papers from the conference table, compiling them into a stack and stuffing them in my padfolio.

"It went well. They appear to have faith in their new representation. Can't wish for much more at this point."

He nods in response, but judging by the expression painting his brow, I have a nagging feeling he's holding something back. As I turn toward him, he pushes off the frame, a piercing look on his brow.

"I can hear you thinking, Dad."

"Do you have any reservations about your preparedness?"

His thinly veiled implication stings. "Do you think I should?"

Dad shakes his head as he clears his throat. "Of course not. I just wanted to be sure. This is your first big client. I know Jackson has been working on it with you, maybe he could—"

"It is my client, Dad. I have a handle on it."

He nods. "Good. I am working to lay the groundwork with the board in grooming you."

This isn't the first time my taking over Baker & Park one day has come up recently. My dad isn't getting any younger, so it's not really a surprise, but it's always felt like this far-off concept. I thought I had at least another five years before this conversation would be had.

I've been a lawyer for two years and I've yet to have the opportunity to do anything fulfilling. Baker & Park seldom takes on much outside of corporate law and criminal law when it comes to defending our corporate clients. I had high hopes in taking on the Tollies case, but the further I dive into it, the more I come to realize it's just another favor to one of our many corporate clients. A romantic partner of yet another CEO thinking their money can get them out of trouble.

Fortunately for my record, that is appearing to be true, and what once threatened to be a months-long trial appears likely to be settled before ever seeing a courtroom.

While I was pushed into pursuing law, my intentions were entirely altruistic. I don't know if I had a skewed view of what Baker & Park does or thought I'd eventually find a way off the track that was set for me as a child, but the closer I get to the day of taking over my dad's position, the more I want to just get in a car and drive.

"Sounds great, Dad," I sigh, rubbing my brow. "I'm starving, though, so I'm going to head back to my office then go grab some lunch."

He nods in my direction before disappearing down the hallway.

My stomach growls as I make my way back into my and Jackson's shared space.

"Andre's?" I ask as I drop my meeting notes on my desk.

Jackson appears to consider my suggestion before nodding in response, grabbing his suit jacket off the back of his desk chair.

Hannah appears in the doorway—I swear she has a sixth sense for when I'm in a shit mood.

"Lunch?" Her peppy tone has me resisting the urge to retort.

"Yeah, we're grabbing Andre's," Jackson responds.

"Can I come? I'm starving!"

"Nope." I button my suit jacket closed, not even bothering to look up at her.

"Why not?" A slight whine warps her voice.

"Because you weren't invited," I say, looking up at her, "and I personally would like to enjoy my small window of Hannah-less time. You're always around, and it's getting fucking irritating."

"You're not exactly preferred company either, Park." Her peppy tone from before is nowhere to be found. "In fact, I'm not even sure why Jackson is friends with you. It made sense when we were kids, but why would someone *choose* to be around you?"

"Guys," Jackson chimes in. "This isn't some family function. This is work—act like it. We get it, you hate each other. In any other situation, I would let you duke it out, but I'm starving and kinda don't care to deal with it today."

What crawled up his ass?

My gaze travels back to Hannah, and a wounded expression meets mine. Oh, *come on.* As quickly as it's there, it's gone again, but it's a manipulation tactic I'm well acquainted with, and it won't work. I'm not going to give her the attention she clearly wants, nor do I care to indulge her theatrics.

"Besides, Hannah, it'll give you a chance to do a single one of the tasks that I asked you to do this morning." My attention shifts back to Jackson. "Let's go."

We make it down to the street entrance of the Newmont building before Jackson says anything.

"You didn't have to be a dick, you know. She's been having a hard enough time adjusting to Atlanta. You doing shit like that doesn't exactly help."

"She's a big girl, she's fine."

"It doesn't mean you have to make it harder for sport."

For some reason that stings a bit, but I try not to read into it too much.

I look down at my phone, altering my Andre's order on their app, hoping that they catch the change before we get there.

The crisp air today is unseasonably chilly for October in Atlanta, but as someone who prefers cooler weather, I welcome the reprieve from the constant ninety-degree days we've had for the past week and a half. For once, I don't feel the urge to strip off my suit jacket the second I step outside.

The moment we enter the familiar restaurant, I'm hit with the scent of roast chicken, one of Andre's signature dishes that you had better believe I ordered for my lunch.

"Pickup for Thatcher-Miles, please," Jackson tells the bartender. He is met with a nod as the man disappears behind the exposed separation between the bar and the pass into the kitchen. He reappears with a brown paper box, handing it to Jackson and accepting his card.

I do the same, except I am handed two boxes, my total being close to double Jackson's. He pins me with a confused look before thanking the bartender.

"What? I'm hungry. I didn't eat breakfast."

This earns me a nod of understanding as we make our way out into the cool air, the walk back to our office a welcome break from the hectic days I've been having at the firm.

The moment I reach my desk, I open the box of food from Andre's, the smell of roast chicken and potatoes causing my mouth to water. Fishing around in my desk drawer, I struggle in my attempt to find a fork from a previous takeout order as I forgot to grab one from the restaurant.

Of course, there isn't one.

I jump out of my seat and go to fish around in the drawers in the kitchen on our floor, my stomach growling, borderline eating itself in the process.

Letting out a cheer of triumph, I discover a wrapped-up set of cutlery from a catering order a few weeks ago stuffed in the back of the drawer that is typically reserved for rejected and unneeded sauce packets. Despite the busted McDonalds honey mustard cup that apparently spilled and now coats half the set, I grab it anyway, tossing the plastic in the trash can.

The thought of my roast chicken has my mouth watering in anticipation, the lack of breakfast this morning attacking me with full force. In a near run, I power-walk back to our office to find a confused Hannah staring down at a brown takeout box on her desk identical to the one calling my name.

"Where did this come from?"

I shrug in response, attempting to get back into the office without conversation. "I don't know, Jackson must have grabbed you lunch since you wouldn't stop bitching about it."

She appears to accept this answer without so much as a snarky response, opening the box to find her favorite chicken penne inside. She doesn't get it very often despite Andre's being my parents' go-to when George and Linda are in town.

However, I've seen the way she reacts when she gets it against her mom's insistence that she get a salad.

"Thank God." She moans as she takes in the scent. I refuse to acknowledge what that sound does to me as I dart past her into my office, clicking the door behind me.

It's not that deep—it's just a fucking lunch.

TEN

HANNAH

No matter how many of these family meals I've been forced to endure in my life, it will never become enjoyable. It's formulaic at this point. We sit down, we exchange pleasantries, then at some point during the meal, after my parents are done fawning over Jackson—and now Gen—my mother, without skipping a beat, shifts to criticizing my life choices. Whether she focuses on my career, what I'm eating, or my hair, she always has something to nitpick. I can't even really blame my dad because I'd be hard-pressed to believe he even notices she does it.

While New York sucked in a lot of ways, something I loved was that I didn't have to be around my parents unless I came to visit, because God knows they never came to visit me. When my mom was being a bitch, I could just hang up the phone—it's not like she was about to show up at my apartment in Brooklyn. I can't even say with certainty that she knew my address, and I lived there for five years.

New York City is crowded, infested with rats, and essentially a lottery when it comes to launching an acting career, but distance was the one thing it always managed to give me. It's not a coincidence that I chose to attend the University of Tennessee before moving to New York...a university precisely 520.5 miles away from the hellhole that is Live Oak, Georgia. Too bad living in Atlanta, they have no qualms with traveling the five hours to visit. I'm not deluded enough to think that has anything to do with me, though.

The menu in my hand is nothing more than a formality. Andre's has become something of a go-to for these meals, but the brunch menu at the very least offers more variety.

I opt for the eggs Benedict as my mother orders a fruit parfait, a scolding, judgmental expression searing into my periphery as I read it off the menu.

For someone who detests being around me so much, she really knows how to pick apart my choices, down to the side of hash browns I order.

"Gen!" My mother perks up, shifting in her seat to face my childhood best friend. "Have you gone wedding dress shopping at all yet?"

Like clockwork.

"Not yet. Savannah's been traveling a lot so I've been holding off until I have someone to go with me," Gen responds, taking a sip of her water in the process. This reminds me just how dry my mouth is at the topic at hand. My mom has been obsessing over Jackson and Gen's upcoming nuptials.

Genevieve soon-to-be-Thatcher-Miles, the daughter she never had.

"Hannah could go with you!" My mom's offer causes my glass to pause halfway to my mouth, a stinging sensation sent straight to my heart.

It's not that I don't like Gen. I love her; she's family at this point. However, despite being friendly again and happily hanging out socially, we haven't had a single real conversation since last summer, when I gave her some tough love about her situation with my brother Jackson.

The two of them have been completely in love with one another since we were kids, so when they found themselves back in each other's lives, Gen managed to do what she does best...she ran. I, however, was not about to allow her to do that to my brother yet again, so I showed up at her apartment to talk her into accepting her feelings for him.

I still don't know how much of an impact that had—maybe she would've come to that conclusion eventually on her own.

"I'd love that!" Gen's peppy tone shakes me out of my frozen state at my mother's statement.

My stomach sours, but I don't have it in me to tell her no. I want to find a way to be close again, I just don't know how.

"We'll figure out a time." I force a smile, gulping my water down.

Thankfully, the conversation drifts quickly as the server returns with our dishes, setting the most mouthwatering eggs Benedict in front of me. The Hollandaise sauce cascades over the side of the muffin, encouraging me to reach for my fork without hesitation.

"Hannah, *manners*," my mother scolds, causing me to drop my fork to my plate.

The server makes her way around the table, placing everyone's dish in front of them. I wait until someone else reaches for their fork before I dig back in, not wanting to attract the wrath of Linda Thatcher-Miles.

"So, Liam, Stephen tells me you've taken on your first big client," my dad says, turning his attention to Liam seated next to me.

Their closeness has always been weird to me. How my dad

manages to have so much interest in the life of his best friend's son but can't even muster the words to know a single thing about my life confounds me. As his only daughter, you would think it would be different.

"That's correct," Liam responds, reaching up to wipe his mouth before continuing, "It's been going well. I'm confident we'll get the outcome we're hoping for."

Despite their close relationship, I notice the way Liam doesn't divulge any details, keeping his professional demeanor intact while discussing client information.

"How are you liking it at the firm, Hannah?" Stephen's kind eyes meet my own, shifting the topic toward me, much to my dismay.

"It's nice!" I don't provide much more detail outside of that. I could tell him how insufferable it has been working so closely with Liam. However, given past experiences, I can't imagine that complaint would go over well in the current company.

My parents, mostly.

"How is she doing?" My mom looks at Jackson and Liam, her eyes rapidly shifting between the two.

I'm prepared to be ripped to shreds by Liam. It's no secret that he doesn't exactly have the best opinion of me.

Jackson goes to speak, but hesitates for too long. I know any opinion he could share would be diluted the moment it left his mouth anyway. Every defense he's ever had for me has been met with questioning.

"She's been great. Very organized." Liam's response is concise, professional. He cuts into his eggs, clearly declaring that to be the extent of it.

I gape for a moment, shocked that he didn't take the opportunity to knock me down a peg. The moment I realize my mouth is hanging open, I snap it shut in an effort to avoid further ridicule from my mother.

"You really should check with HR about opportunities to segway this assistant position into an administrative career."

Suddenly, I know why she's randomly developed interest in how I'm doing at work.

We've had this conversation many times over, yet every time it hurts.

"I don't want an administrative career," I mumble.

"Mom." Jackson attempts to divert her attention without success.

"Want or not, you need to get realistic. Acting was cute for a while, but you're twenty-seven. It's time to start thinking about your future."

"I am thinking about my future."

"Clearly you're not. You continue to chase these fantasies of acting professionally, but it's not going to happen. Community theater is fine, but you need to find a long-term job with a 401K."

"I have an audition this week that I'm perfect for, I have a good fee—"

"You always have a good feeling. It's time to be responsible."

I struggle to keep the tears from spilling free. Based on experience, I can confidently say nothing positive would come from crying in front of my mother. The pressure behind my eyes and nose increases, leaving me staring up at the ceiling in an attempt to keep the tears at bay.

"Linda, that's enough."

At first I think it's my dad, but it's not until I see the look of confusion on my mother's face that I realize it is Liam who spoke up.

His eyes are pinned on her, his jaw locked so tightly I fear he may explode. I'd expect that response from Jackson, even my dad on occasion when he's aware enough of what is going on, but never Liam. I would even expect it from Gen before I'd expect it from him.

Unfortunately, this progression of events urges the tears on even more, so much so that I'm sure they're going to fall any second.

"Excuse me, I have to use the restroom."

I don't wait for a response from anyone before I dart toward the single-stall restroom, locking it behind me. The frosted glass of the door is cold against my skin.

Why I let her get to me so much, I'll never know.

The tears begin to stream down my face. An unfortunate side effect of bottling so much up around my parents is that when I do cry, it's nearly impossible to stop.

What feels like forever passes, yet the tears continue to pepper my cheeks, streaming down to land against my collarbones.

Knock, knock.

"Just a minute." I wipe the moisture from my face, looking over at the mirror in an attempt to make myself more presentable. There is no hiding how red and splotchy my face is, the watery rim around my eyes still stinging.

Taking a deep breath, I open the door, expecting to find an impatient woman waiting for the only women's restroom in the restaurant, or maybe Jackson or Gen.

I'm shocked to find Liam standing on the other side of the door, leaning against the wall in the hallway.

"What do you want?" I snip.

"Don't make me regret being nice, Hannah." He exhales, examining my clearly swollen eyes. "You look rough."

"Thanks, asshole. If I wanted to be told how terrible I look, I would go find my mother."

His jaw tenses again, much like when we were at the table. "Fair." He clears his throat as he steps away from the wall, invading my space. "Are you okay?"

I nod. "Why do you care?"

"I don't," he says with a sigh, "but you look like you could use a hug."

Much to my surprise, I do want a hug, desperately. I step toward him, aching for the human contact. My hands meet his sides as he pushes my forehead backward with the heel of his palm.

"I'd be happy to go find Jackson." He grins, the obvious joke rolling off his tongue. Except, it doesn't sting like normal. There is a humor in his demeanor that I don't typically see.

Rolling my eyes, I pinch his side, pulling a laugh from him and from my own lips as well.

"We cashed out." His laugh drops, a serious expression painting his face again. "Honestly, I wouldn't be surprised if your parents already headed out."

I know I shouldn't find that comforting, but I do. "Are Gen and Jackson still here?"

"Yeah, they're waiting at the table. I told them I was going to the bathroom, so don't tell them I checked on you...wouldn't want it to ruin my street cred."

"What street cred?" I laugh, met with a terribly stifled grin. "Not like they'd believe it anyway."

"You wound me." He mockingly drives a fake knife through his heart, causing me to smack his arm. "But fair. Seriously though, Hannah. Don't let her get to you."

I nod as he steps away, making his way back over to the table.

What *Twilight Zone* alternate universe I just stepped into, I can't be sure.

"Hey, bug." Jackson steps toward me as we approach the table, handing me my purse. "Are you okay?"

"Yeah, I'm fine." I force a smile up at my brother, hoping to ease the sad expression looking back at me.

I feel bad for how brunch went, but then I remember that I was goaded into my reaction. My mother pushes me on purpose, and while I know that objectively, I also know that what she says has merit.

Am I making a mistake in not finding an alternative career path with acting not working out? I can't accept that yet. I've worked far too hard for far too long to accept that it's not meant to happen.

"Let's get going." Jackson forces a smile, the four of us making our way out of the restaurant.

As we walk down the sidewalk, I feel a hand entwine with my own and squeeze. Instinctively I think to jerk away, then I realize it's Gen.

And weirdly, it's more comforting than anything else.

ELEVEN

LIAM

"You're late," Sage sighs as she opens the door to her apartment, her exacerbation at my tardiness clear.

"I'm like five minutes late…" I can't resist rolling my eyes at her dramatics as I close the door behind me.

Sage walks over to the kitchen, grabs two beers, and hands one to me.

Over the summer, Sage and I developed a habit of watching Braves games from the balcony of her apartment. The apartment that I'm almost positive she—or Hannah, now—doesn't pay full rent for has an unobstructed view of Truist Park, home of the Atlanta Braves. While I have never been a massive baseball fan, I'll admit there is a certain level of community surrounding our local team, leaving me catching far more games than I would have prior to meeting Sage.

The regular season is over, so unfortunately we won't be viewing the game from above, but with the Braves playing the World Series, Sage has moved her flatscreen TV out onto their covered balcony for a "similar experience."

"We could have just watched the game inside, you know."

"And miss this ambiance?" Sage waves her arms around to the sunny but blistering hot October day right as a bird drops a massive dump on the railing only inches outside of the overhang. "Not a chance in hell."

She lifts her feet to rest them on the patio coffee table, popping the top of the Sweetwater 420 in her hand before she takes a massive gulp.

"Who are they playing?"

"Phillies." She barely looks up from the TV screen.

My attention diverts to the game on the screen, right at the exact moment a Philadelphia player hits a home run, giving them an early lead in the second half of the first inning. Sage groans, then takes a large gulp of her beer.

"Heads up, Hannah is supposed to be home soon, so don't be a dick."

"Who, me?" I feign offense at her words.

Truth be told, my mind hasn't diverted from Hannah and the brunch yesterday much, if at all.

"Yes, you." Sage glares at me before shifting her attention back to the game.

I've witnessed Linda go after Hannah on more occasions than I would like to admit, and I've always felt it wasn't my place to say anything. Hell, even yesterday I cringe at the memory of inserting myself into their family issues.

Yet, I can't say I wouldn't do it again.

I can still imagine the look on Linda's face when I said something, and my stomach knots at the memory. Despite this, my mind wanders to how Hannah looked when her mom was berating her, and suddenly I find myself filled with the same level of irritation toward her mother as yesterday.

It's just unnecessary.

My family isn't perfect, but I could never imagine either

of my parents talking to me the way Hannah's mom talks to her. I can't wrap my head around it. I can't even fathom my dad not stepping in to defend me if my mom ever reacted the way Linda did and always does when it comes to Hannah.

The frost of my full beer bites into my hand, causing me to shift it to my other. I pull it to my lips and down a large gulp.

"Penny for your thoughts?" Sage's eyes shift to mine for a split second before she returns to watching the game, but her focus is still on me, expecting a response.

"About what?"

Her eyes move back to mine, a look of *Really, Liam?* painted across her brow.

The TV roars to life, pulling our attention back to the game as a blur of white jersey with "Braves" plastered across the front slides into home, earning our team just shy of a grand slam, with three players running home as the ball sails over the far outfield wall.

"Fuck yeah!" Sage yells, her previous prying mentality lost in the excitement of the game.

My dynamic with Hannah has always been a point of amusement for Sage. When it was decided that Hannah would be moving in with her, I dealt with weeks of questioning from her about my disdain for her impending roommate. Unfortunately, it has only gotten worse as they've become friends and Sage insists on picking apart every interaction between the two of us.

As if Hannah's ears are ringing, a key turns in the apartment door, the sound of the door swinging open traveling out the open balcony door.

"Sage?" Hannah yells, a distance in her voice as she sets her keys down on the entry table.

"Balcony!" Sage responds, her eyes not moving from the lively screen in front of her.

"Why is the TV on the balcon—" Hannah's voice skips as her eyes meet my own, her amused expression shifting from jubilant to sour in a matter of seconds. "Park," she quips before shifting her attention back to the screen in question.

"Hannah."

"Braves are in the World Series," Sage says, her attention not breaking from the screen.

"Ah." Hannah fakes interest, standing awkwardly in the doorway. "Well, as fun as *this* is," she waves her hand at the display in front of her, "I'm hopping in the shower."

"Have fun!" Sage yells as Hannah disappears into the apartment, her attention still focused entirely on the game.

My eyes linger on the door for a moment before shifting back to the game. Much to my dismay, Sage is staring at me when I look back toward the TV.

A few moments pass before the lingering silence outside of the speakers gets to me.

"What is it?"

"Are you into Hannah?"

I nearly choke on my beer at her words. "Jesus Christ, Sage. No."

Her expression lets me know that she more than likely doesn't believe me. I'll be the first to admit things have been weird with Hannah recently, but I'd hardly call that interest.

I can feel Sage's invasive gaze on me as I chug the rest of my beer, grasping onto any opportunity to get away from her scrutiny.

"I'm grabbing another beer. Do you want anything?"

As if this pulls her out of her thoughts, Sage's eyes drift

back to the television, and she gulps down the remaining beer in her can before she hands it to me.

I'll take that as a yes.

The moment I step back into the apartment, I hear music emanating from the bathroom at the end of the hall. The clear tune of the *Hamilton* soundtrack carries through the space, causing me to unintentionally start humming along to "Wait for It."

"*Hamilton* fan?" Hannah's voice startles me as I step into the kitchen, a smirk painted across her lips. She's standing on the tile, the water from her hair dripping down her decolletage before soaking into the towel wrapped around her body. My eyes can't help but fixate on the way her breasts are barely contained under the terrycloth.

"Jesus, Hannah!" I yelp, my hand covering my heart.

"Oh, don't be dramatic."

"Me, dramatic?" I scoff. "What are you doing anyway?"

She reaches for the kitchen table, grabbing a bottle of shampoo from inside a Publix bag. "I forgot my new bottle." Yanking the bottle off the table, she goes to turn around.

"Are you okay? After yesterday, I mean." I'm talking before I can stop myself.

She slowly turns on her heels, shifting her attention back toward me with a puzzled expression on her face. "Why do you care?" The aggression in her tone doesn't go unnoticed. "I'm just a spoiled princess with no work ethic, right? I would think you'd agree that I need to change course for my career."

To my surprise, this stings.

I've expressed that exact sentiment on numerous occasions, so why does it suddenly bother me that she thinks that is what I think?

"For what it's worth, I don't think that."

A sardonic laugh leaves her lips as she sets the bottle down and crosses her arms over her chest, unintentionally pushing her breasts up in the process, allowing the towel a slight gape at the top.

"Well, you've told me enough times—excuse me for believing you."

She starts to walk away, but I reach my hand out to grab hers. Hannah pauses and doesn't look at me, but also doesn't pull away.

"I don't think that," I say quietly, repeating myself in a near-whisper.

A moment of silence passes, her eyes pinned on the wall to her side, anything to avoid looking back at me.

"Hannah, I—"

"Well," she says, yanking her hand from my grasp, refusing to look at me, "it's semantics, because believe it or not, Park, I couldn't care less what you think of me."

With that, she saunters away, her shampoo bottle still balancing on the edge of the kitchen table.

A few moments pass.

I don't know why I do what I do next, but my feet are moving of their own volition before I get the chance to stop myself, her shampoo in hand.

Steam flows from below the bathroom door and through the small crack left in the door, allowing light to seep into the otherwise dark hallway.

Despite my brain telling me to walk away, screaming at me that this is a bad idea and to go back outside and finish watching the game with Sage, I stay.

Hannah drops her towel and my eyes rake over the soft, tanned expanse of her skin. My mouth grows dry, but I can't look away. I've never noticed the clear dip of her waist, her hips sloping downward to quite possibly the most perfectly apple-shaped ass I've ever seen. Her tan lines from the waning summer take me back to a distant time when the thought of me touching her didn't cause her skin to crawl.

She climbs into the shower, the frosted glass only traveling up to around her belly button, leaving me with a view of her from the waist up. I'm unsure why I'm still standing in the doorway, peeking through the small crack in the door without concern of being caught.

Is that a tattoo?

"Shit." Hannah exhales, looking around the shower to realize she left the new bottle of shampoo in the kitchen. She reaches up to shut off the water, grabbing her towel from the hook just outside the shower.

I back away, darting down the hallway to the kitchen as quietly as I can before I set the unopened bottle on the kitchen table.

In an attempt to get back out to the balcony before Hannah comes out here looking for her shampoo, I reach into the fridge haphazardly, grabbing two fresh beers from the top shelf, not worrying to check the label.

Thankfully, I make it outside just as I hear Hannah venture back into the kitchen. I hold the extra can out to Sage and am met by a puzzled expression looking up at me.

"Liam."

"What?"

"That's a Sprite."

It's then I realize I am holding two bright green soda cans in lieu of the beer I'd gone in for.

"Oh, I, uh, figured we could switch it up."

"Very funny, go get me a beer." She laughs, her eyes drifting back to the television, the score now 2-3 Braves. It's the bottom of the fourth inning, making me realize just how much of the game I've missed already. The hot day has grown cooler as the sun sinks below the skyline.

A mosquito bites my arm, causing me to slap it, squashing it against my tanned skin. Brushing it away, I turn on my heels, relieved to find a Hannah-less kitchen upon my return.

I let out a sigh, pulling two fresh cans of what I am 100% sure is beer from the fridge, stepping in a small puddle of water in front of the table.

Fucking Hannah.

TWELVE

HANNAH

Today has proven to be one of the longest days of my life.

Jackson took a day of PTO to go tour wedding venues or test caterers with Gen...I think. To be completely honest, I'm not really sure what they're doing—all I know is he's not here. Subsequently, I've been forced to spend the last five hours with Liam.

"Do you still need that phone call transcript for the Tollies case?" I ask as I stand in the doorway of Liam's office.

Liam's eyes rise to meet mine, an exasperated expression painting his face. "Hannah, this is the fifth time you've come in here to ask me a question in the last hour. You could just Teams me, but if you insist on coming in here, just work in here. Jackson's desk is empty."

He looks back down at the document in front of him, rubbing his brow in what appears to be exhaustion. He's been rather tight-lipped all day, only talking to me when absolutely necessary. If it were any other person, I would be sitting here questioning what I did and why they didn't want to talk to me. However, I know Liam well enough to know that he pretty much never wants to talk to me. So questioning that isn't even worth the brain cells I use thinking about it.

I turn on my heels as I make my way back to my desk to grab my laptop. When I return to his office, Liam is just as entranced with his task as before, except this time I notice he's loosened his tie. The once perfectly tied skinny tie is now lying with extra slack, a lasso draped around his neck loosely. His hair is mildly disheveled, but not enough to cause concern. Just the result of him running his fingers through it one too many times.

"So, do you need it?" I ask.

"Need what?" He doesn't look up at me right away, but when I don't respond immediately, he pins me with a glare.

"The Tollies transcript," I reiterate, my brows raising in irritation.

His gaze lingers for a moment before he clears his throat, looking back down at the document in front of him. "No, that case has come to an agreement, so it won't be going to trial anymore."

My face flushes as a noticeable warmth spreads to my ears. "Why didn't you tell me that? I spent over an hour dictating that recording!"

The timid expression he was sporting before is nowhere to be found as his eyes meet mine again, a cold determination in his gaze. "Well, as an assistant at Baker & Park, you don't exactly need to be in the know about our cases." His attention shifts back to the document as if he isn't actively choosing his words to hurt me. "You are a worker bee; worker bees do as they're told. Anything outside of that is vastly above your pay grade, princess."

I'm fuming, but I've done this song and dance long enough

to know that he is more than likely looking for a reaction—a reaction that I won't be giving him.

"Of course, my mistake...Mr. Park." My attempt at professionalism feels slimy as it rolls off my tongue. I'm sure we're both aware of just how disingenuous it is. The anger bubbling up in my stomach grows tempered as embarrassment sets in, wanting with every fiber of my being to be able to erase my words from the air. His face drops, but he bounces back quickly.

"Mr. Park?" Liam quirks a brow as an amused smirk paints his lips, his eyes meeting my own with a surprisingly light expression. "Are we finally shifting into professional decorum, Miss Thatcher-Miles? I thought we abandoned that around the seven-hundredth time you called me a dick at work."

His words sound aggrieved, but the expression on his face is nothing short of...playful? It nearly gives me whiplash how quickly he can shift his demeanor. However, I don't miss the way his joking tone causes my stomach to twist.

"Don't be cute with me, Park," I say as I roll my eyes, biting back the grin that tries to crawl up to the surface.

He nibbles at the end of his pen, his gaze still fixed on me. "You think I'm cute, huh?"

I glare at him, finding a not-so-subtle cocky grin pointed across the room at me. "About as cute as an oozing sore on my ass."

"You wound me."

"No, I don't."

Liam shrugs, biting back a grin. His attention again returns to his work.

We go on like this for a while, silence falling over the room, but, unlike other times this has happened, it's comfortable.

The shift in the air is noticeable, but I worry if I acknowledge it I will ruin it and the pleasantries will die on contact.

"You did a good job on these," Liam says, his voice cutting through the stark soundlessness of the office. I try not to share my surprise, but as my brows raise, he chuckles. "Don't look so shocked."

"On what?" I try to focus my attention on the task to which he's referring and not the way the compliment makes my stomach flutter.

"The case files for the Reinman case are far more organized than I ever would have been able to do."

I shrug my shoulders before I drop them, trying not to look him in the eye amidst his praise, knowing that the surprise plastered on my expression is unavoidable.

"Thanks," I whisper.

Liam looks up at me before standing from his seat, moving over to my side of the room and resting against the edge of the desk.

"Hannah." His playful tone is gone, a serious air about him setting in, but he's not angry.

"Yes?" I don't look up from my computer.

"Hannah, look at me." The commanding tone he uses shouldn't do something to me, but it does. To my surprise, I listen without a fight.

"What?" The moment our eyes meet, my stomach flutters, an unwelcome swarm of butterflies descending.

"When people compliment you...believe them."

My eyes stay pinned on his. I'm unsure what to say.

It's not that I can't take a compliment, but when they come from him, I find myself questioning how genuine they are. Their sheer rarity and his otherwise detest of my presence doesn't exactly lend itself to hearing a compliment and not instantly questioning his motive.

When he's like this, I'm reminded of the boy I used to know, the boy who held my heart in the palm of his hand and chose to tear it to shreds anyway. I'm reminded of who I thought he was all those years ago... I just need to remind myself that he hasn't changed; he's never been that boy.

"Be careful, Liam," I say, my words a hoarse whisper. "Keep saying stuff like that and people might start to think you actually care about me."

He shifts from his serious demeanor back to playful, the stark change causing my head to spin.

"No one would ever believe that." He scoffs as he adjusts the cuffs of his shirt and stands, but he doesn't move away from my side of the room. "But seriously, Hannah, you shouldn't let people talk down to you...even me. I know I seldom get away with that without you biting back, but I wish you'd find that with other people."

I know he's referring to my mom in the way he says it, which shifts the butterflies in my stomach to a churning sensation.

"I bite back because I hate you," I grit out, the animosity not finding my eyes.

"You really are a good actor. Sometimes I even think you hate me...but we both know that's not true." He smirks again with a wink, this time turning away to walk to his desk.

My mouth drops open as I stare at him walking away.

"You'll catch flies with your mouth hanging open like that." He doesn't even turn around as he speaks.

How the hell does he do that?

Despite my shock, it has the desired effect, and I snap my mouth shut to stop my gawking.

"Go ahead and head out."

"But you said you needed me to stay late with you."

"Yeah, but there's no point in us both being stuck here late. You got me your notes and that's all I needed from you, so go home."

I remain in place despite his words.

"Hannah, go home." The commanding tone from before returns, igniting the same reaction.

Butterflies...that need to be squashed.

As I stare at him, our eyes linger far longer than feels appropriate. Yet neither of us is willing to break contact.

I clear my throat, peeling my eyes away from his with the nagging desire to rid myself of the flutter that's taken up residence in my stomach.

"Gladly—to get away from you." My scorching tone appears to throw him off, the playful Liam from before nowhere in sight.

"Exactly." He sits back down at his desk, the cold demeanor I've grown accustomed to back in place as if it never slipped.

THIRTEEN

HANNAH

Oddly enough, this is the first time I've been fully alone with Gen since I moved out of their house. Not for a lack of her trying, mind you, but I've been struggling to find a new normal between us after everything that has happened.

When we were kids, Gen's crush on Jackson was harmless, or so I thought. When they broke up, it was more than their romantic entanglement that fell apart. Gen and I stopped hanging out that day and, up until they returned into each other's lives, it stayed that way.

While we talked about it briefly the day I went to her house to try to get her to give him a chance, we haven't discussed it since then.

I miss her, but I don't know how to say that. It's starting to feel like I've ruminated on it for too long and now it would be weird to say something.

"Are you two ready to order?"

I don't realize the server is standing over us until she speaks. I've barely looked at the menu of the pho restaurant that Gen suggested. Frantically I start scanning the menu, trying to figure out what to get.

"Can we get a few to look over the menu?" Gen politely responds to our server, making me realize how rude I had been.

"Of course, I'll be back in a few minutes." The server disappears almost as quickly as she appeared, leaving Gen and me to bask in the silence.

I bite the inside of my cheek as I investigate my options on the menu, ultimately settling on the beef pho. Unfortunately for me, I no longer have a valid reason to stare at my menu like it's going to sprout two heads.

"Han?"

"Hm?" I respond, barely looking up from my menu despite having made my selection.

"I'm sorry." Her voice is reserved, almost nervous.

"For what?"

"Everything—" As the word drifts off her tongue, my eyes are pulled to hers, an expression of anguish mirrored back at me.

"Gen, it's fine. Seriously. Bygones and all that." I wave my hand in an attempt to let it go, but she continues.

"No, it's not. I wasn't a good friend in how I handled things with Jackson. I knew you were upset, and I didn't try to push. I know it was a long time ago, but I really want to be able to get closer to where we were...I miss you."

I spent years wanting an apology from her and yet, now that I have it, I realize that I have already forgiven her. How things transpired hurts to think about, but I know she was being driven by her love for my brother—how could I fault her for that? Is holding onto past pain worth keeping her at arm's length?

"I miss you too...and I didn't handle any of that great, either. We were kids."

"Are we okay?" Gen's voice carries through the air, her glassy expression causing a pang in my stomach.

"Yeah..." I sigh, but she doesn't appear to believe me. "We will be."

This seems to appease her as a grin spreads across her lips, the previously anxious pinch in her brow nowhere to be found.

"How is it going at Baker & Park?" Gen asks.

"It's going fine." I try not to be snippy, but I've had a week straight out of the Twilight Zone and thinking about that place is about the last thing I want to be doing. "Honestly, it should be the tenth circle of hell being near Liam for eight hours a day."

Gen chuckles, causing me to shoot her a glare.

"What's so funny?"

"Nothing, that is just nearly verbatim the way your brother describes working with the two of you at each other's throats."

Somehow, my glare intensifies, but this doesn't deter her.

"I'm just saying, you and Liam fighting is hardly a new thing, so why does it suddenly bother you?"

While I know she's right, that isn't what has my head spinning, but I don't want to tell her that.

Something has shifted in Liam and the fact that I can't pinpoint what, exactly, is driving me mad. He'll go from normal to nice within a matter of minutes and it's giving me whiplash.

I mean, that whole thing with my mom—what the hell was that?

Don't even get me started on that comment from yesterday. Something has changed and I'm not sure I'm welcoming it. Then again, I don't miss the way my stomach flutters when I think about him these days. I don't know if it's some weird form of Stockholm syndrome or what, but I need to squash it sooner rather than later.

Occasionally nice or not, he's still an ass.

"Whatever, he's not important enough to even warrant this conversation," I say as I pick at my cuticles. "How's wedding stuff going?"

Gen takes the change in conversation in stride, shifting the topic away from Liam and me and toward linen colors and their top three choices for first dance songs. I ask about trivial wedding aspects: church or beach, big or small, whether she's found a dress.

"Unfortunately, no." Gen sighs. "I've looked online, but I haven't had the chance to look at options. Since we're not having a long engagement, it's proven difficult to find stuff off the rack that works and I like."

"Well, it doesn't hurt to try things on."

Our server approaches, and this time I actually know what I want.

"Beef pho, please." I smile politely up at her as she takes my menu.

"I'll have the same," Gen says with a grin, allowing the server to walk away from our table before continuing, "I was actually hoping we could go dress shopping after we get back from Vail next week."

I pause, expecting myself to feel a certain way about the idea of going wedding dress shopping with Gen. There is so much history between us, a lot of which involves my brother, but I realize for the first time in all of this that the anger and resentment over the years has faded so much that I don't feel anything about it except joy.

Joy for two of the most important people in my life finding happiness in one another.

Even without a single prospect in my life, a pang invades my chest at the thought. While I am so beyond happy for Jackson and Gen, the jealousy that took up residence in me a long time ago has yet to subside.

"Sounds great." I smile as the server sets our food down in front of us. She silently grabs our glasses and is gone again within seconds.

"Good. Actually...I've been meaning to talk to you about something..."

My stomach sours at her words as I anticipate a painful blow.

"Okay..."

"I was wondering...if you'd be willing to be one of my bridesmaids?"

Well, that wasn't what I was expecting to come out of her mouth. However, it's in this moment I realize I didn't even consider I wouldn't be a bridesmaid. I just assumed, given everything, that I would be, even if only for the simple fact that I'm Jackson's sister, although I'd much prefer it not just be about that.

"Are you sure?" I ask, earning a confused look from Gen.

"Of course, Hannah." She reaches across the table, grasping my hand in hers. "You have been one of my best friends for pretty much my entire life. I couldn't imagine this day without you by my side. Jackson or no Jackson."

A warmth blooms in my chest at her words of reassurance. "I'd be happy to be in the wedding, Viv."

The childhood nickname feels weird rolling off my tongue. Over the past year, I've grown accustomed to calling her "Gen," short for Genevieve, whereas my brother goes back and forth. This glint of familiarity draws a smile from her, so infectious that it spreads to my lips.

"I'm glad." She squeezes my hand before pulling her hand back right as the server reappears with our refills.

The rest of our lunch goes by quickly, and while I'm not typically a huge soup person, the pho hits the spot, especially given the cooler-than-normal fall we're having.

"Hey!" Sage's voice rings through the air as we make our way out of the restaurant, the air hitting my face in a gust as it nearly takes the door with it.

"Hey, what's up?" I respond as she approaches Gen and me, Savannah at her side.

"We were just doing some shopping!" Savannah's peppy voice cuts through the wind that the buildings downtown exacerbate.

I've known Savannah for years, given her relationship with Jackson's best friend Wes. She's always been someone I liked, but I've spent the last year unpacking the fact that she's essentially Gen's number one now.

Well...other than Jackson.

Savannah and Gen have developed a bond that she and I just don't have anymore. I used to be able to know exactly what Gen was thinking. Her favorite foods, her hobbies. While I have learned so much over the year we've been back in each other's lives, it still stings every time I am reminded just how much I missed.

All because I couldn't handle her relationship with Jackson.

Not anymore—I've grown. At least that's what I tell myself.

"Do you guys want to hit Harry's?" Sage brushes a curl gone awry from her face just as the wind pushes another one across her nose.

We all nod in unison as we follow Sage, her walking backward toward the all-too-familiar dive bar.

Harry's has become somewhat of a stomping ground for our group of friends. Only a short walk from Gen and Jackson's place as well as Baker & Park, it's the most logical place to grab a drink after a long day at work.

If only the one thing I left work wanting to forget didn't end up there alongside me much of the time.

We sit down at the bar, thankful to see that it is pretty much a ghost town. It's not particularly surprising given that it's 3:00 PM; most of the Saturday foot traffic probably won't make their way in until dinner time. The neon beer sign behind the bar flickers as it basks us in hues of yellow and red, the bar far darker than you would expect in midafternoon.

Sage swivels back and forth in her chair as she waits, becoming increasingly irritated as the bartender still takes close to fifteen minutes to bring us our drinks despite us being the only people in the bar.

"So, Hannah," Savannah turns in her seat, narrowing her attention on me, "how's Baker & Park?"

I've known Savannah long enough to know that she seldom asks a question for the sake of pleasantries—there is always a reason. If only I knew what it was with this one.

"It's fine," I say as I pull the straw of my tall Titos and cranberry to my lips.

"How is it working with Liam?" Her enthused tone coats the question, which I'm sure she knows won't garner a positive reaction.

"About as enjoyable as getting a colonoscopy."

"Have you ever actually *had* a colonoscopy?" Gen asks.

"Accept the analogy, Gen."

"I don't know, Hannah, he's kinda hot…" Savannah trails off, her eyes meeting Sage's glare. "It's an observation. Trust, Wes is the best f—"

"Okay, that's enough." Sage cuts her off, pulling a laugh from my lungs. A disgusted expression paints her face. Once the trauma of Savannah's comment wears off, Sage's focus shifts back to me, a perplexed expression on her face.

I try to ignore it, but it's almost as if her gaze follows mine, refusing to pull away. The intensity of her attention only grows as I try to avoid her. She gets to the point of physically moving her body so as to not allow me to escape her advances, her butt hanging halfway off the chair.

"What, Sage?" Irritation seeps into my words.

"Nothing."

"*Sage…*"

"It's interesting is all."

"What's interesting?" I sigh, taking a large gulp of my drink.

"You and Liam."

Here we fucking go again.

"Don't start, Sage."

"Mhmm," Sage hums as she rolls her eyes, clearly not saying something that's on her mind. I, however, have been through this song and dance enough times with my brother to know when not to take the bait.

An all-too-familiar tune comes blasting through the speakers and I know before I turn around that the guys are here. The unfortunate sound of Toto's "Africa" is a dead giveaway. Don't get me wrong, I like the song, but after the thirtieth time of them playing it every time we're here, it loses its novelty. A hand slaps down on my shoulder, causing my chair to turn around and face the phantom.

"Hey, bug." Jackson grins from ear to ear, pulling a smile from me.

As quickly as it hits my lips, the smile is gone as my gaze finds a much darker pair of eyes behind my brother staring back at me, the unwavering contact causing my skin to chill.

Liam Park.

FOURTEEN

LIAM

We've made a habit of going golfing most weekends that we're all available. This weekend, Wes was surprisingly not working, so we had...let's just say...a few drinks on the course. By the time Wes got a text message from his wife, Savannah, saying to meet them at Harry's, I was already past tipsy.

If that wasn't the case, I would have probably made up an excuse and headed back to my apartment.

I know what awaits me at the bar.

Yet, I feel a certain sense of excitement in it.

Hannah is beyond irritating, but I've started to find enjoyment in my time around her, even if I refuse to admit that to anyone out loud.

The hurricane hitting Florida has caused the wind this afternoon to kick it up more than a few notches. As a result, by the time we were halfway through the course, it was nearly impossible to shoot straight. Thus, we all had historically terrible games and were also all moderately inebriated by the time we walked into Harry's, which to my surprise was pretty empty except for the girls. People start to filter in behind us, but it mostly appears to be college students.

My eyes lock on the all-too-familiar beautiful blonde in front of me. The sunshine in her hair doesn't reflect in the icy gaze staring back at me, the startling green that typically borders on blue now a near-emerald as she glares up at me, making it very clear that she is extremely displeased with my presence. I can't be sure whether the change in color is because of me or because of the terrible lighting in the bar despite it being midafternoon.

"Hannah," I say, nodding toward her.

I've been working constantly recently and, as a result, I've spent significantly more time with Hannah than I have in probably the last ten years of my life. I've always enjoyed the games we play and baiting a reaction from her. Recently, however, I've managed to develop a conscience about it. I used to revel in the way her cheeks would flush when she would throw what I could only describe as a temper tantrum at the things I said. Now, the second I see that pink hue, I feel my stomach plummet to the floor.

"Park," she quips, my neutral, almost cheery disposition foiled with her clear distaste for my presence.

Whatever.

"Actually, it's Liam." I grin at her, not being rewarded with even a sliver of amusement.

"Drunk already?" She snickers. "Some say being wasted at 3:30 PM is a cry for help."

"I'm not that drunk, princess."

"Whatever."

Some douche in a Ralph Lauren polo approaches Hannah, his lips skating over her ear as he says something to her. I can smell the half-bottle of Axe body spray that he pretty much bathed in. The laugh that his words pulls from her causes my stomach to churn. I get little time to react as she walks away with him without so much as a goodbye to me in the process.

My eyes are locked on her as she approaches the group of college guys at the back of the bar.

"Still don't want her, huh?" Sage's amused but borderline condescending words cause me to pin her with a glare as she hands me a tall draft beer, two shots of clear liquor in her other hand.

"Trust me, I have absolutely no interest in Hannah Thatcher-Miles." I taste the lie as it glides off my tongue, but I attempt to wash it away with a gulp.

"Uh-huh," Sage says with a laugh before handing me a shot of tequila.

It burns as I swallow it down, but the lie I just spewed still coats my tongue.

As the day moves into evening, more people fill Harry's. By the time it's 7:00 PM, the bar is standing room only for most people and another bartender has come in to accommodate.

I can't say that the service is much better with the additional assistance, as it appears the bartender from earlier just took it as an opportunity to take a step back and let the petite redhead run around like a chicken with her head cut off.

"Two shots of Jose Silver, please," I say with a smile, eliciting one from her in return. I can't be sure if it's just her being pleasant for her job or genuine interest. My game has felt so off lately.

"Coming right up."

As she walks away, I can't resist my attention shifting toward the corner at the back of the bar where Hannah is now sitting in the lap of some douchy frat guy.

It's not that I have an issue with frat guys. It was never my thing in college, but Wes, Jackson, and Gabe were all in fraternities and they're my best friends.

But something about *this* guy bothers me.

His cocky demeanor doesn't sit well with me, and the way his hand rakes over the hem at the back of Hannah's shirt causes my hands to ball into fists.

"Who is that?" I nod my head in the direction of Captain Douche, pulling Savannah's attention.

Her expression perks up almost instantly—Savannah has never been known for not getting involved in other people's business.

"No idea. He's cute, though," she says with a grin. I watch the amusement drain from her eyes, replaced by an expression of concern. "Why? Is there something wrong with him? Should I go get Hannah?"

Would I like her to? Yeah, I'd fucking like that a lot. Should she, though? Probably not. I'd never live that one down.

"No, I don't know the guy. I was just curious."

This appears to satisfy her, but I know better than to accept Savannah being satisfied by anything that could instead be molded by her.

The bartender reappears with my two shots of tequila, both garnished with a lime wedge.

My original intention was to bring the other to Gabe, but as I make my way to the back of the bar, I am standing in front of Hannah before I realize what I'm doing.

"Take a shot with me," I demand, causing her brows to shoot up to her hairline.

"Why would I do that?"

"Humor me." My dry tone is clear as I refuse to break our

eye contact. This lingers for a few moments before Hannah reaches out and grabs the shot glass from me. However, she doesn't do what I ask.

"Okay." Her head turns to Dr. Douchenozel with a sly grin painted across her lips. "Body shot?"

I watch hesitation coat his expression. "I would, but...I don't do tequila. I'll end up throwing up on you."

Grow up.

But also, the disgusting image this paints is not even close to gross enough to quell the sense of relief I feel at his refusal.

Hannah pouts for a moment before turning back toward me, prepared to hand the shot back.

"Why don't you take the body shot off of her, Liam?" I know the voice from behind me as it crawls up my neck, causing me to turn on my heels.

Sage.

"You see...I would, but..." I clear my throat, trying to think of a reason not to. "We have two shots. We're trying to figure out what to do with hers."

"I'll take the extra shot if Hannah doesn't want to return the favor." The implication in Sage's words causes my skin to heat. "Off you, of course."

The gasp this pulls from Hannah is nothing short of vindicating. Her flustered expression is all too familiar, but it's been years since I noticed the current look in her eyes.

Jealousy.

"Don't be ridiculous," Hannah grits out, only to be returned with an expression of defiance on Sage's face.

"Fine." Sage appears to concede for a split second. "I'll just take the other shot...but Liam still has to take his off you."

The red painting Hannah's face causes my blood to heat, a hopefulness strumming through my veins that she's caving.

"Okay." She nearly gasps as she says it.

My brows lift before my attention shifts to the clearly uncomfortable guy she's currently sitting on top of.

Yeah, I don't really care.

As much as I'd been hoping for this outcome since the topic came up, the realization of the implications sinks in, causing me to get frazzled. I sure as hell don't want Jackson seeing me taking a body shot off of his fucking sister, no matter how long we've known each other.

"Patio," I demand, walking away from her, not waiting for a response.

FIFTEEN

HANNAH

I stare up at Sage with my mouth agape at what just transpired. He can't be serious...can he?

The hand that has been wrapped around my waist since Liam walked over is now slack, a tenseness in his expression that I can't quite place.

"Are you okay?"

"Why wouldn't I be?" Noah says just before he gulps down the second half of the beer in his hand. "I need another drink." He taps my leg, instructing me to stand up so he can make his way back over to the bar.

As soon as he's out of earshot, I notice Sage's eyes still on me.

"What?" I can't resist the snippiness that settles in.

"Are you going to head out to the back patio?"

"Of course not!" I huff, adjusting in my seat to divert my eyes from hers.

In true Sage fashion, she doesn't allow this as she sits down in the seat in front of me. "Go."

"I said I'm not doing it."

The glare pinning me in place heats my skin. My hand balls into a fist as I turn my attention to the patio door, an overwhelming sense of cognitive dissonance settling as I remind myself this is a bad idea, but also feeling myself being pulled toward the door to find Liam outside.

"I'm not here to judge, or even tell anyone, but you and I both know you want to go out there...so just do it."

I've been biting my inner cheek so hard it's starting to feel raw; I need to make a decision. I either fall victim to the same reality of allowing him to touch me that fucked me over nine years ago, or I resist exactly what I want to do.

My desire to do it wins as I stand and move toward the door, Sage's voice fading into my periphery.

"Don't forget the lime!"

Fuck off, Sage.

Wind hits my skin the moment I step out onto the completely enclosed patio.

"Took you a while." Liam grins, the shot of tequila sitting on the glass tabletop in front of him, the lime taunting me with what comes next.

"Didn't want to come." I refuse eye contact.

"But you did anyway." He continues to grin, standing up from his seat, shot in hand as he approaches me. His eyes don't break from my own as he encroaches on my space. I back away from him instinctively until my back is flush against the concrete wall of the bar and he's mere inches from my face.

"Have you done one of these before?"

I nod, swallowing the lump in my throat. Liam's eyes linger on the way my neck moves before darting back up to my face.

"Once back in college."

"Good." His voice grows husky, but I wonder if I'm reading too much into it.

"Good," I whisper.

Liam lifts the shot, urging me to grab it from him. I do as he requests with little resistance, pushing the cold shot glass into my cleavage until it's secured between my breasts. His eyes follow my movements. While normally I'd reprimand him for looking at me there, my skin heats on contact as I bathe in his focus.

"Now what?" My voice comes out breathier than I intend, eliciting a borderline cocky grin from him. I want to smack it off his face and taste it in equal measure.

"Salt."

This returns me to reality, but no matter how many times I urge myself to put on the brakes, I can't figure out a way to verbalize it.

"Okay."

Liam leans forward, his lips centimeters from my ear. At first I think he is going to say something, but the moment he extends his tongue and swipes it across the flesh below my ear, I gasp. He reaches over to the table and pulls the salt shaker from the center basket, sprinkling it over my now-damp skin.

The lump in my throat makes it nearly impossible to say anything, so I stand there entranced by him. I plead with the universe that he can't tell I'm essentially a ball of putty in his hands.

"Lime," he commands as he holds the lime wedge against my bottom lip, forcing me to yield to his demand. I allow the piece of fruit to rest between my lips, all of it so completely at odds with our normal interactions.

"If I'd known this would make you so agreeable, I would've tried it ages ago."

My jaw drops, allowing the wedge to drop from my lips.

He's prepared for this and catches it in his hand without a second of hesitation.

"Hannah, it's called a joke. Now open."

I don't know what this foreign hold is that he has over me, but I part my lips without so much as a second of resistance despite being irritated seconds ago.

"Good girl." This sends tingles down my spine, but I refuse to unpack that right now. "Are you ready?"

All I can manage to do in my current predicament is nod.

He steps into me, invading my space with his body pressed against my own. My mouth waters at his proximity. The moment I swallow, I feel his tongue dart out against the salted expanse on my neck, licking upward at a languid pace. He lingers there for longer than makes sense, but the longer he does it, the more out of touch with reality I become.

Liam's face dips downward, his stubble from the weekend scratching against my breast as he wraps his mouth around the glass. His lips graze my flesh, heat shooting straight to my core, and I have to bite back the whimper that attempts to crawl up my throat.

He tilts his head back to allow the fiery liquid to hit the back of his throat, causing quite possibly the most vulgar and entrancing view as he swallows, his Adam's apple bobbing in the process. Once he sets the shot glass down on the table next to us, he's ascending toward the lime—the lime that's in my mouth.

Suddenly, it's as if we're in slow motion. As he approaches me, I can count every second, every freckle, every look as he encroaches on my space.

His lips graze mine as he grasps the lime between his lips, his tongue gliding over my bottom lip.

It's intoxicating.

CHAPTER FIFTEEN

He sucks the lime while it's still between my lips. At some point I drop the lime, but his lips remain a whisper from my own. Our staggered breaths create a medley between us.

I suddenly find myself internally pleading for him to step closer; to allow himself a moment of weakness; to allow his mouth to linger, sans lime this time.

"Liam," I whisper, but it comes out as a breathy moan.

This sets something off inside him and he steps forward, pressing his entire body against mine. His hands find my hips as he pins me in place, not giving me a moment of reprieve before his lips crash into my own, the fiery taste of liquor mixing with the taste of peppermint on his tongue as he pries my lips open.

It's not tepid; it's a full-on blaze consuming me in one fell swoop.

As if of their own volition, my hands creep upward, wrapping around the back of his neck to pull him closer to me, as if that's even possible.

We linger like this for a while—how long, I can't be entirely sure.

He's intoxicating in the way that speeding down an abandoned country road brings a rush. It's invigorating because it could very well kill you in the process. Safety seldom makes you feel alive.

I'd be content going out that way, I think.

"Hannah," he whispers, pulling from my grasp, his lips still against mine.

"Hm?"

"Why do you hate me so much?"

Like a bucket of cold water, this brings me back to reality.

"You know why." I glare up at him as he puts distance

between us, probably to prevent me from rearing back and kneeing him in the crotch for touching me.

"I really don't."

I feel paralyzed at his reveal, unsure how to proceed. Yeah, he's an ass—he's always been an ass—but the current iteration had a moment as its catalyst, the moment that caused my heart to sour toward him...nine years ago.

"You not remembering is honestly probably worse." I harden immediately, pushing his chest away from me. To my surprise, I find an expression of anguish and hurt staring back at me.

I will not fall for his shit again.

"Hannah."

"Let it go, Park."

The door to the inside of the bar crashes behind me, hitting me with warm air—exactly what I need to pull me back off the ledge of quite possibly the second-worst decision of my life.

Liam Park...again.

SIXTEEN

HANNAH

I didn't exactly plan on getting drunk and being home in my bed by 9:00 PM yesterday when Jackson and I agreed to go for a run today. What was supposed to be a quick drink after lunch turned into a sloppy day of drinking. Normally I would consider that a great use of time, but the memory of my actions yesterday is seared into my mind like a bad tattoo.

Why the hell did I let that happen?

I skate my fingers over my bottom lip, still remembering the way Liam's felt and tasted. The tender burn from his scruff left my skin raw, the memory sending shivers down my spine.

The sun barely crests over the horizon as Jackson comes into view, jogging in my direction. Oak trees umbrella over the park, creating a calm, sated environment to bask in.

"What about me says 7:00 AM run, Jackson?" I huff, extending my hand to give him the bottle of water he asked me to bring from my apartment.

"I've grown to like it."

"*I* don't like it, though," I say with a grimace, the memory of tequila and hard cider threatening to come back up with vengeance.

"Are you sure you can run? You look—"

"I'm aware I look like shit."

"I wasn't going to say *like shit*. Unwell, maybe." He opens his bottle of water and takes a gulp, the alcohol he drank yesterday not even a whisper of a memory. "Drink too much yesterday?"

"You could say that." I don't care to talk about this at all. If we start talking about yesterday, I'll eventually have to come face to face with my actions, and there is nothing I'd like less than to relive that. "I'm good to run. Let's just go."

Jackson jogs in place, warming his muscles against the early morning chill in the air. I turn on my workout playlist and tuck my phone into the pocket of my leggings. We begin to make our way through the park, the sun warming the air at a startlingly quick pace as it creeps over the horizon.

I've never been a fitness enthusiast. I seldom choose to run for fun—I don't know how Savannah and Wes participate in so many marathons—but being in shape is a necessary evil when performing. You would be surprised just how much havoc being on stage can have on your body, especially if it's a musical. The combination of breath control and multiple dance numbers often leads to a very exhausted Hannah.

Running helps, even if I hate it.

The *Heathers: The Musical* soundtrack rings through my AirPods, my steps falling in time with "Candy Store" as I hum to myself.

We approach the fountain at the center of the park, circling it to make our way in a different direction; unfortunately this causes us to run directly toward the sun.

My eyes water as I squint, but I don't complain. It should

get better as the sun moves, which it appears to be doing rather rapidly. We thankfully turn onto a trail, shading us back under the canopy of oak that shelters most of the park.

It reminds me of home more than I would like to admit. I avoid going back to Live Oak most of the time, but there are a few things I miss about it.

My parents? No.

High school? No.

The perfectly manicured oak trees in our neighborhood? Possibly.

We run for about forty-five minutes before we're back where we started, a few feet from the parking lot where only our two cars reside.

Jackson gulps down half his bottle of water and I do the same, the sweat pebbling on my brow cooling me from the now-balmy Georgia morning.

"You happy we have a short week?"

What a loaded question. Am I happy to be away from Baker & Park for a few days? Yes, but unfortunately the single reason I want to avoid work will be with me, so is it really a break?

"Meh, pretty indifferent."

"Don't act so enthused to celebrate my pending nuptials," Jackson says with a dry tone before cracking a grin. "I get it, but I promise you'll have fun. You like skiing."

He's right, I do, but something about the company has me ready to upchuck the very alcohol that has made this morning run brutal. I'm not ready to unpack what happened between Liam and me with Jackson. Not that I think he'd care—I just don't think I'd hear the end of it.

"You're right. I'm just...on edge. I have an audition later this afternoon."

"I'm sure you'll do great." Jackson tries to give me a reassuring smile, but it seems more like a grimace. I've been auditioning without luck for way longer than I would like, and I can feel the people around me growing tired of me bringing it up.

"Thanks." I clear my throat. "I'm going to head home and get ready."

"You're gonna kill it." He smiles, a bit more genuinely this time. "Come here."

Despite the disgusted expression I offer him, Jackson pulls me into a hug, his sweaty shirt sticking to my own.

"Ew."

"Just let it happen."

Like I have a choice—he has me in a vise grip. Lucky for me, it's over quickly.

"I'll call you after."

I walk back to my car, hopeful, but I can't shake the sour feeling in the pit of my stomach.

I tap my foot, my nervous tic overly obvious to the room around me as I hum my audition piece under my breath.

While I was relieved to have had an extra few days to prepare after auditions were pushed back due to a scheduling conflict, it's also given me a couple more days to internally freak out about it. I've prepared three different songs for this audition, none of which I'm 100% confident about. While one of them shows my range better, I also have one in mind that I've performed hundreds of times and would nail easily, though it doesn't have the same key changes and higher-register parts.

"Nervous?" A beautiful brunette sits down next to me, clearly dressed for the same audition. I hate knowing that we're more than likely going for the same role, but I don't have it in me to wish her ill will or to hope that she flops.

Okay, maybe a little bit, but definitely not out loud.

"A little, you?"

"Petrified." She laughs, turning her upper body toward me, and extends her hand. "I'm Luna."

"Hannah." I smile, shaking her hand politely. To my surprise, her kindness calms me a bit, but not enough to take down my guard.

"Who are you auditioning for?"

"Annabeth, you?"

She cringes for a moment before painting on a smile. "Annabeth."

Of course she is.

"Well, I wish you luck." The lie tastes bitter as it rolls off my tongue. "Are you from Atlanta?"

"Originally, no. I'm from Illinois, but I've been here the past few years."

"Makes sense. What brought you to Atlanta?" My incessant need to fill silence leaves me asking questions to which I don't totally need the answers.

"Girlfriend—" She pauses. "Well...ex-girlfriend now, I guess."

"I'm sorry to hear that." I genuinely mean it.

"I'm not, she was terrible. I broke up with her." She laughs, adjusting the sheet music in her hands.

"Oh," I laugh. "Well, good riddance then."

"Amen to that."

We make small talk and I actually think I may be finding a friend in Luna. It can be hard making industry friends because so often they consider you competition. I can't say I don't fall into that trap more often than not.

As we exchange numbers, what appears to be an assistant appears in the doorway.

"Luna Aguilar?"

"That's me!" Luna perks up before turning to me. "Seriously, good luck."

Suddenly I feel like a dick for hoping she flubs her audition.

Looking around, I fixate on all the other women in the room who are more than likely also going for the role of Annabeth. While it only takes one "yes" to get your big break, it's starting to feel like it's never going to happen for me.

I've gone to sixty-eight auditions this year, received nine callbacks, but ultimately haven't booked anything. I was offered a job swinging for a small regional theater's production of *Mrs. Doubtfire*, but it didn't even pay enough to cover my phone bill during the run and I can't afford to not work at Baker & Park if that's the case.

"Hannah Thatcher-Miles?"

"That's me!" I try to hide the shakiness in my voice, but it's obvious.

I follow the assistant into a room, where I see three individuals behind a table and find myself alone on stage with nothing but an accompanist. Sheet music in hand, I provide him a copy before shifting to center stage. I feel like I'm staring the judges down as I await that first note from the piano.

The piano part to "I Don't Know How to Love Him" from *Jesus Christ Superstar* begins to play, a brief prelude before I need to sing.

The first verse allows me to settle into my falsetto, but not so much that I'm straining myself to reach into my upper register. I wipe the sweat from my palms as I attempt to quell my anxiety.

As I drop into my chest voice, I feel much more confident, but I struggle a bit shifting back into my falsetto. Luckily, I am allowed a few seconds of reprieve as I prepare for the moment in the song that has me nervous. It's not to say that it's a super high note—as a mezzo-soprano, I actually have a decent range, able to reach a high C despite being most comfortable in the middle of my range. However, it always results in me messing up when rehearsing.

My eyes fix on the judges in front of me as I lift my soft palate in an attempt to round out the note. I have a tendency to go nasal if I'm not careful.

That's when my greatest fear comes to fruition.

My voice cracks as I hit my note, startling me so much that I squeak in the process. I watch the joy leave the judges' eyes at the exact moment I realize I just bombed this audition and the chances of me getting any part, let alone *the* part, is slim. Despite this, I finish the song in an attempt to remain professional.

The last notes of the piano fade as I stand there, essentially a deer in the headlights as I await a response.

"Thank you, Hannah. We'll be in touch."

With that, I know with certainty I bombed it.

I power-walk to the lobby, darting directly past Luna chatting with another person.

"How did it g—"

"Good. I gotta go, Luna. Text me, okay?" I all but sprint to my car, not waiting for a response from Luna.

Slamming the door behind me, I instantly call Jackson. My brother has always been the person who could give me perspective after a bad audition or a shitty day.

"Hey, bug, what's up?" He sounds distracted.

"I completely bombed it, Jackson." My voice cracks, but I am doing nearly everything in my power to prevent myself from breaking into a full-out sob.

"I'm sure you didn't bomb it," Jackson says before whispering something to someone with him as he tries to muffle a chuckle. "Babe, I promise, I'll be out there in a sec."

"I fucked up my vocal audition, colossally."

"Uh-huh." He's clearly further from the phone than before as I hear rustling, but no actual response to my words.

"I don't know what happened, my voice just—"

"I hate to cut you off, Han, but I really need to go."

My stomach sours, but I try not to reveal my disappointment. "Okay."

"I love you."

"I love you too."

The line goes dead and I drop my phone in the passenger seat, at a complete loss. I don't know who else I could call without feeling like I was annoying them.

So I sit in my car...and cry.

SEVENTEEN

LIAM

It's been years since I've been to Vail.

We used to come every Christmas, but in recent years we have all been busier and fitting in the summer trip is enough of a struggle to get everyone together at the beach house. Although we're still a few weeks early for the holiday crowd, it feels just like it did when I was a kid.

Something about the crisp winter air makes me feel alive, unlike the muggy southern heat of Atlanta. Even now, in the second week of November, we left a temperature of around seventy. It should start to dip a bit soon, thank God.

The group arrived at the house early this morning and were out on the slopes within an hour, our bags a heap on the floor in the entryway.

I trip as I walk in the door, yelping on instinct. "Shit!" I throw my shoe off and grab my sock-clad foot to apply pressure to my toes. "Who the hell left their bag right in front of the door?"

A mixture of *"Not me,"* *"I don't know,"* and *"Not I"* fills the rooms, which only irritates me further. Everyone filters in out of the cold with Hannah at the back of the pack.

"Or you could watch where you're going," she says as she rights the suitcase that caused me to trip.

Of course it was Hannah's.

I wouldn't say things have been weird since the bar the other day—things have been nonexistent. Even at work, she would only communicate with me via Teams or email, or when feeling exceptionally petty she'd send messages via Jackson, who mentioned he felt like something was off, but lucky for me didn't question the why of it all. Fortunately, my tumultuous past with Hannah is actually working to my benefit.

"Or maybe you could be courteous to others rather than being rude for no reason."

I expect a snippy remark, but all I get is a shrug as she walks away, closing her bedroom door behind her.

With everyone here, unfortunately most of us don't get our own room. Gen and Jackson took one of the guest rooms, Gabe is on the pull-out couch in the office—because, surprise surprise, him and Kara broke up again—Sage and Hannah are in one of the guest rooms, Savannah and Wes are in my parents' room, and I'm in my room.

I could have offered Gabe to stay in my room, but why would I do that when there is a perfectly good pull-out in my dad's office?

Also, I like my privacy.

The plan for the evening has been to head over to one of the villages and hit the bar for a while, but the last thing I want right now is to leave the house again. My body is sore as it is, but now that my foot is throbbing thanks to Hannah's stupidity in leaving her suitcase in the doorway, I feel like a mess.

"Why don't we just have a party?" I ask Jackson as I shuck off my outer layers and reach for a mug from the cabinet.

Jackson turns to Gen, who shrugs in response, appearing indifferent to the matter.

This trip is to celebrate with friends before the big day. With their wedding the second week in December and only a few weeks to go, it was important to the two of them for us to get out of Atlanta as a group.

"Sounds good to me—anything not to have to layer up again." Savannah's voice carries from behind me, essentially securing Gen's vote.

"I'm down for a party," Gen finally responds, looking up at Jackson.

We've had parties at my parents' house in Vail before, but not since we were old enough to drink...or at least old enough to drink legally. Such an occasion was always contingent on bribing some idiot at the resort to buy a bunch of teenagers alcohol.

Lucky for us, now we're all full-grown adults and can order alcohol for delivery and not have to go back out into the cold.

I send out a text blast to the locals and seasonal guests I know are in the area right now, then head to my room to get cleaned up for the night.

Hopping in the shower, the hot water sears into my flesh, prickling my chilled skin. It takes a minute or two, but I finally find a comfortable temperature. I towel off before walking into my bedroom, thankful that I was able to keep hold of my room and, with it, my private bathroom.

As I knew we would be out on the slopes for most of our time here, I packed simple clothes—we're only here for one night as it is. No rest for the wicked, or whatever they say. It's mostly because Wes has to get back to the hospital.

I pull on my dark wash jeans before pairing them with a heather gray Henley, thankful to be dressed. Though it has modern amenities, the house is older and doesn't have the best insulation, so, despite the heat being on, there is still a bite in the air.

When I finally venture out into the house, people are starting to trickle in, and I calculate that I know at least 90% of the guests.

"Hey man, it's been a while!" I plaster on a grin before smacking a guy I know on the back, not allowing myself to be distracted when I'm on a mission.

Hannah.

My eyes find her in what I would call an unseasonably short yellow dress. It hugs her perfectly, and if we weren't in a room now nearly filled with twenty-somethings, most of whom are single, I'd enjoy the vision.

"Little cold to be dressing like that, no?" I reach past her, grabbing a red cup from the stack and pouring myself a serving from the keg. You really can order anything for delivery these days. When she doesn't answer me, I look up to find her eyes fixed on me. "Cat got your tongue?"

As if something shakes her out of her trance, her expression shifts from perplexed to irritated. "Just trying to figure out what made you think you could talk to me."

There is the Hannah I know.

"Noted." I lift my beer in a toast before walking away from her, but I can't manage to pry my eyes away entirely.

Cold or not, that yellow dress is doing things to me. I've always noticed the way her body looks, but it's as if the other day flipped a switch in me, making it impossible to ignore. The cotton fabric hugs her ass perfectly, stretching to barely cover it. If she bent over, I wouldn't be shocked if I got a full view of what's underneath.

I adjust my pants at the thought of what that could be.

"You're staring at her." Sage once again appears out of nowhere, earning herself a glare. "Hey there, killer, I just call 'em like I see 'em."

"I was not staring at her." I drink the rest of my beer right as Gabe appears, giving me the opportunity to push the plastic cup into his palm to avoid going back over to Hannah, who is still leaning against the keg on the other side of the room.

"Okay, so I guess I'm getting you a beer." If Gabe is irritated, he doesn't show it.

He's been in a foul mood the past few days because of Kara. I was hoping that this trip would pull him out of it, but I'm starting to think it might just make it worse. Yeah, they fight all the time, but every time they fight and break up, he's sure it's for good.

However, it never is.

"Pong?" Sage asks as Gabe reappears with my beer in his hand. I nod toward her and we head over to the table.

Thankfully, my night begins to ramp up. Sage and I win not one round of beer pong, but two. Gabe played against us with this local named Justin for the first game, but ended up bowing out for the second. Justin seems to want to keep going as we approach our third round, but the girl he was partnered with didn't want to play anymore.

Hannah appears, much to my dismay, to ask Sage something, which unfortunately sparks an idea for Sage.

"Do you want to play beer pong with us? Justin needs a partner."

Hannah's eyes divert to mine for a split second before she smiles in Sage's direction. "Sure!"

My attempts to avoid her tonight are officially foiled. The bright side, at the very least, is that she's on the other side of the table.

"Have you ever even played beer pong?" I scoff.

"Once or twice."

I regret asking almost immediately.

"Left corner cup." Hannah lifts her arm to toss the ping pong ball, her dress riding up her leg in the process. She appears to be wearing some sort of boy shorts or Spanx underneath, but it doesn't stop my imagination from going haywire.

With a plop, the ball lands clean in the left corner cup, allowing her a second turn. I toss the ball back across the table as she calls out again.

"Back right." Once again, the water splashes as she makes a clean shot.

"Once or twice?" My brows draw upward as she looks up at me.

"Once or twice...or I was the Tau Kappa Iota beer pong champ for Greek Week three years running."

"Once or twice, my ass," I chuckle, fishing the ball out of the cup before setting myself up to take my shot.

"Don't I get another shot?" Hannah pouts, exaggerating her voice to sound almost childlike in her plea.

"House rules, princess." I wink, earning a huff in response.

Despite my attempts to get her to lose, the game ends in record time with Hannah sinking multiple shots every time the ball is in her hand.

"Okay, this isn't fun anymore." Sage laughs despite her words before grabbing her cup off the edge of the table and walking away, effectively ending our game.

Hannah walks by my side of the table. I expect her to just

walk away, but she pauses before she looks up at me. "You know, you have the confidence of a much taller man. You should work on that."

My mouth falls open, completely flabbergasted, so much so that I can't think of a single thing to say. She disappears into the crowd before I get the chance to get a word in edgewise.

At this point, the party is in full swing and, thankfully, I lose Hannah in the shuffle. However, I want to shake myself for allowing my eyes to still scan the crowd, trying to find her. The moment I spot her, my stomach sinks.

If I had a nickel for every time I scanned a room and found Hannah sitting on a guy's lap recently, I'd have two nickels. That's not a lot, but it's enraging that it has now happened twice.

Hannah is sitting on Justin's lap, whispering something in his ear that causes him to laugh.

Oh, give me a break, she isn't that funny.

My stomach drops at the sight as I pull my beer to my lips, gulping down the remaining liquid in an effort to quell my irritation.

After what happened no more than five days ago, she's all over some guy she doesn't even know. It's taking everything in me to not say anything right now, but my patience is wearing thin.

I latch onto Sage's arm as she walks by, halting her advance in Gabe's direction.

Their dynamic is weird—has been since we met Sage, really—but I would argue that neither of them is in the right place to be talking to one another, not with both of them drunk.

"Kiss me," I plead, but it comes out more of a demand.

Sage laughs, which I try not to take personally. "I would rather gnaw off my own arm, thanks."

Okay, *that* I take personally.

"Try not to sound so disgusted," I say with a gasp. "I am a catch."

"No one is saying you're not. You're just...not my type." She places her hand on my arm before yanking it away and taking a sip of her beer. "Besides, I would prefer not to get stabbed in my sleep by my roommate."

It's now that I notice Hannah, who's stopped interacting with Justin despite sitting on his lap, her eyes locked on me and Sage, her expression murderous.

Interesting.

EIGHTEEN

HANNAH

I've always liked the cold.

When I was a kid, I always loved coming to Vail, but I really began to fall in love with colder weather when I moved away to college. It's not to say Tennessee is the tundra, but it's colder than Georgia.

The day out on the slopes was exactly what I needed to shake myself out of this funk I've been in. I'm not typically one to marinate on a bad audition, but given everything else this week, it hit me harder than it typically would.

I was tipsy earlier, but now, hours later, the house dark and empty of guests, I feel myself sober as a judge. Thirsty as hell, but sober nonetheless.

Pulling my wool socks on to combat the cold tile floors, I don't worry about putting much else on besides my sleep shirt. It's almost 4:00 AM and I'm not getting dressed to grab a glass of water from the kitchen. The floor creaks beneath my feet, reminding me just how old this house is despite its updated amenities.

The kitchen light causes me to squint as my eyes adjust. I

make my way all the way into the kitchen before I realize I'm not alone, although the light being on already really should have been my first clue that someone was up.

My eyes lock on the expanse of muscular back of the man currently facing away from me, inspecting the contents of the fridge.

Liam.

I gulp, my eyes fixed on the way his muscles contract as he reaches inside the fridge, pulling out all the fixings for a sandwich.

We stopped at the grocery store on our way into town in the hopes that it would keep us sated when going out for food wasn't an option. I don't think anyone expected the appetites of the three men currently on this trip. I thought it was a dramatic amount of food for a two-day, one-night trip, but apparently not.

I shake myself out of my trance, pulling my attention back to why I'm in here—water.

"I need a glass," I say, my voice groggy as I reach past him at the counter where he is now assembling his sandwich. He jumps slightly at the sound of my voice before I come into vision, but I don't miss the way his eyes linger on the hem of my shirt riding up my thighs.

"The polite thing to do would be to ask me to move." His voice is raspier than normal, the mixture of sleep and something foreign filling the air.

"Why would I be polite?" I grab a glass from the cabinet and head over to the fridge to fill it to the brim from the water dispenser in the freezer door.

"Good point. You've hardly been polite all night, so I can't imagine why you'd start now."

Okay, he's mad. If only I had insight into why.

"Excuse me?"

"You heard me." His gruff tone, which I'd previously interpreted as tiredness, is now clear: irritation.

"What could I have possibly done today to have your panties lodged so far up your ass?"

He scoffs, ignoring my question as he cuts his sandwich into two triangles before lifting one of the halves to his mouth. I swat it from his hand, the plate clanking against the counter as it lands.

"Don't be a bitch."

Oh, fuck no.

"Well, don't be an asshole and I won't be a bitch. Seriously, what is your fucking problem?"

I know in almost an instant that I have made a massive mistake. He abandons his plate as he turns toward me. With every step he takes in my direction, I back up until my back is pressed against the counter.

"You're my problem." His jaw is locked as he grits his teeth, the annoyance verging on full-blown rage as he speaks. "You and this constant bullshit. One, it's rude, but it's also disrespectful as fuck and I'm over it."

"What did I do to disrespect you?" The confused expression plaguing my face only appears to anger him more.

"Justin."

Who the hell is Justin?

My thoughts must paint my face because his expression contorts even more into disgust.

"You don't even know his name? Damn, Hannah, you had his dick lodged against your ass for half the night. I didn't take you for the type."

"Don't talk to me like that."

"Like what?"

"Like you get to judge me. Slut shaming is unbecoming of you."

This seems to return his decorum to him.

"I—that's not what I meant."

"It's what you said." I gulp as I realize just how close to me he is, his body only inches from my own. My attempts to hide what it does to me don't go unnoticed as I watch his eyes linger on my chest, ruminating on the way my nipples are hard and visible through my sheer white sleep shirt.

"I'm sorry. I—it was just rude," he says with a gulp.

"Why do you consider it rude? It had nothing to do with you," I say breathily.

"You can't honestly be that clueless, Hannah."

I think on it for a moment before it hits me—he's clearly upset about the other day.

"Liam..."

He steps away from me as I speak, raking his fingers through his sleep-tousled hair.

"Liam, we were drunk when that happened."

"You think I don't know that?" The methodical combing of his fingers through his hair ventures on pulling as his frustration appears to grow. "You think I don't know that is just about the last thing I should want?"

Blood rushes straight to my face as realization dawns on me. I've been beating myself up over the sudden resurgence of attraction to him. We've spent so much time at one another's throats that it didn't even feel like a possibility he might be dealing with the same anguish I've been enduring.

Suddenly I am aware of every movement he makes as he paces back and forth across the kitchen, his bare feet padding on the floor as his sweatpants barely graze the tops of his feet. He's wearing nothing but a pair of dark blue joggers and it's not until this moment I realize just how little is left to the imagination.

"Wh—" I clear my throat, trying to think of the right words. "What do you want?"

My words settle in the air, staling as he doesn't respond for more time than I am comfortable with.

"Hannah."

"What?" My voice is barely audible.

"You should go to bed." He says it like a suggestion but it reads like a command. I hate the way my body reacts to that. His deep brown eyes are locked on mine and they manage to feel darker, like a scathing abyss threatening to drag me down to the depths of hell.

"No," I mouth, but no sound leaves me.

His gaze drifts to my mouth, lingering on the way my lips move, his jaw locking.

"I said go to bed." Liam steps toward me, his words less demanding and more suggesting than before. Hell, maybe it's a taunt—I can't be sure.

"And I said *no*." I try to muster up the confidence to not stand down to him, but as he encroaches on my space, the air I'm searching for to bring me solace lodges in my throat.

My back presses firmly against the counter once more, but this time Liam doesn't appear to be stopping his advance. He rests his hands on the counter on either side of me, bringing his body flush with my own. The sensation of my sensitized nipples grazing his exposed chest sends shivers down my spine.

Unfortunately, he notices.

"Something bugging you, princess?"

I swallow before attempting to compose myself. "Yeah,

you're near me. That tends to cause involuntary negative reactions."

"Is that so?" he whispers in a taunting tone. "What sort of involuntary reactions?"

"The negative kind. I just said that."

"More specific." He steps closer still, bringing his mouth just shy of my lips, so close that our breaths intertwine. Liam's hand leaves the counter before snaking down my side to find the hem of my sleep shirt. He doesn't lift it, but simply rubs the hem between his fingers.

"Irritation." I try to stand firm in my words, but my body betrays me as I press further into him.

"Doesn't seem like irritation to me," he says with a smirk, allowing his fingertips to dance along the hem of my shirt before resting on my inner thigh. "Care to test that theory? Because I would venture to bet that it's something else."

Liam squeezes my inner thigh, reminding me just how close to my core he is.

"Liam." I mean it to be a plea—to reason with him that this is a bad idea—but it comes out reminiscent of a moan.

"Do you want me to stop?"

I can't tell if he means it genuinely or if he's taunting me for amusement. Either way, it sets me ablaze.

"No, I don't want you to sto—"

A loud yelp escapes me as he lifts me without warning, my bare ass now against the cold marble countertop as my shirt bunches to my hips. He steps between my legs as he pulls me toward him, his mouth lingering against my own, yet still not kissing me.

"Last chance to back down, Hannah. Because I'm telling you right now, I have no intentions of stopping this time."

NINETEEN

LIAM

"For the love of God, do you ever stop talking?" Hannah asks in a breathy tone, causing me to fixate on her mouth more than before. I reach one hand upward to entangle my fingers in the hair at the back of her head, yanking it hard in response to her insult.

Hannah moans, and this is the only indicator I need to advance as I press my lips to hers, the taste of spearmint sweet on my tongue. I squeeze her inner thigh, allowing my nails to scrape down the tender flesh as I pull her legs further apart and move in closer. My hard length presses against her heat, which pulls a soft whimper from her lips.

That is quite possibly the best sound I've ever heard.

Allowing my fingertips to dance along her thighs, I'm enamored by how soft her skin is. Her tanned skin is cold to the touch, at complete odds with the energy in the room. Despite the chilly atmosphere, I am on fire.

Snow begins to fall at a rapid pace outside the window above the sink, encasing us in what feels like a secluded cocoon despite the nagging reminder that at any moment one of our friends, including Hannah's brother, could walk in on us.

I hate the way that eggs me on further.

Hannah's legs wrap around my hips, pulling me closer. Her oversized T-shirt bunches around her waist, giving me full view of the cotton cherry-printed boy short panties hiding beneath.

I've spent the better part of the last month aching to touch her, fighting my instincts to reach out and seize her, consequences be damned. What happened the other day was a breaking point for me, finally giving in to what haunted my thoughts ever since she showed up in Atlanta.

However, the ache I've been fighting pales in comparison to feeling her skin against my fingertips.

"Liam," she moans against my lips, pulling my erection flush against her cotton-clad pussy, eliciting a groan of my own.

Okay, I like that a lot. I've heard her say my name a million different ways over the last twenty-seven years. Well, twenty-four years; Hannah was a late bloomer when it came to talking. She has said my name with indignation, irritation, amusement, anger. She has called me every name in the book, though seldom the good ones, but nothing causes me to react quite like the sound of her moaning my name.

It's like a jolt straight to my cock, which I know with certainty she can feel with absolutely no plausible deniability.

Trailing my mouth down her neck, I catalog the way she trembles at my touch, especially when I graze my tongue against that sensitive area below her ear that pulled a similar reaction from her only days ago.

"Fuck," she moans again, this time far louder than before. I reach up, pressing my hand to her mouth to quell the sound.

"Shhh, we wouldn't want someone to hear you." I'm

convinced she can hear the grin seeping into my words.

I'm still in awe that this is even happening, but as she reaches forward to palm my cock through my sweats, any reservations I had become a moot point.

"Fuuuu—" I groan at the touch, pulling my hand away from her mouth in the process.

Since Hannah started working at Baker & Park, I haven't had sex with anyone. It's not even to say that she was the reason—she's *not* the reason. I just haven't wanted to. It could be that I've been so irritated by the time I'm heading home that the thought of seeking a woman out was more effort than I was willing to put in. I've unwillingly become far too acquainted with my right hand, so much so that I've felt like a teenager all over again.

Maybe that's why the slightest touch from an attractive woman has me so reactive.

It has nothing to do with it being Hannah.

"Shhh, Park. Wouldn't want anyone to hear you," Hannah says, biting back a laugh.

"Touché."

She grips my length through the fabric, causing my eyes to roll back as an intoxicating feeling shoots up my spine.

I need to regain control of this situation, because I can feel myself dissolving into putty in her hand.

Wrapping my hand around her wrist, I set her palm flush against the countertop.

"Keep this here," I demand.

Her brows raise for a split second and I await a retort. It's not in her nature to be easily subdued.

"Yes...sir." Despite the sarcasm dripping from her words, I can't ignore the way her response shoots straight to my dick.

I step back into her, pressing a kiss to her lips, far more

gentle than the situation calls for.

"Good girl."

She melts into my touch with ease, apparently shelving her indignation for a later date.

As I thread my fingers through the sides of her panties, her breath hitches, giving me the confidence that, regardless of my anxiety, this is what she wants.

"Lift your ass," I demand.

She complies with ease, lifting her rear off the counter to allow me the chance to pull the scrap of fabric from her. I drop the panties to the ground with no hesitation.

My eyes meet Hannah's, seeking any indication that she's having reservations. Everything up until this point could be backtracked, but moving forward is embarking on a situation we might not bounce back from.

As if she can read my mind, Hannah leans forward, her lips crashing into mine with far more urgency than before. Something inside me snaps and I yank her ass to the edge of the counter, bunching her shirt up, exposing her to me entirely.

I pull away before leaning down to kneel in front of the counter, wrapping my arms under her thighs. The sight of her glistening with anticipation causes me to groan, my mouth watering at the thought of tasting her.

"You don't look half bad on your knees for me, Park."

"Trust me, princess," I grin as I bite her inner thigh, gentle but hard enough to potentially leave a mark, "I will always be willing to worship you the way you should be worshipped."

While I intend it to be sexual, the implications of my words cause Hannah's eyes to widen. I don't give her the time to retort as I lick her pussy languidly from bottom to top, flicking my tongue across her clit.

A gasp escapes her—a gasp so intoxicating I'm convinced I'd be satisfied leaving this world with that being the last thing I hear. Her thighs tighten around my cheeks, filling me with resolve. I repeat my action, eliciting a moan from her, louder than before. The more I feel Hannah's thighs tighten against my cheeks, the more I inch forward, chasing her release like it's my last meal. Every inch she gives me, every sound she makes, cements in me the need to have her.

"Liam, I—"

I suck her clit between my lips, and her head falls back at the sensation. Her legs tremble slightly, which only encourages me more. The sweet tang of her on my tongue is all-consuming.

"Yes?" I whisper, only pulling away from her heat for the second it requires me to speak. Her eyes lock onto mine as I lick her intently, a man on a mission.

"I'm going to, I'm going to—" Her head falls back again, but this time it's a clear indicator that she's close to climax.

As I press my middle finger inside her, she lets out yet another intense moan. I make no effort to quiet her. The gusts of wind outside fill the kitchen with noise, muting the pants and moans rolling off her tongue.

I add a second finger, curling them upward as I tease her bundle of nerves with the tip of my tongue. She squeezes tightly around my digits, indicating that she's getting close. The moment I look up at her, I find her staring down at me, an expression of pure lust painting her face. Refusing to break eye contact, I fuck her methodically with my fingers, not relenting my assault of her clit as I do so.

"Oh my gah—" She breaks our eye contact as her head falls back, a medley of expletives and moans consuming the room. Despite this, I don't stop. We could wake the entire mountain and I would still stop at nothing to ride out her orgasm for her.

Her pussy pulses around my fingers as they pump in and out of her, the sweltering heat of her core encouraging me. The tension that consumes her body seems to calm. I pull my fingers from inside her as I pepper kisses along her inner thigh before standing up, adjusting my dick in my pants in the process.

I expect her to need a moment, or even potentially to tell me this was a mistake in her post-orgasm clarity, but she doesn't. Hannah curls her fingers over the waistband of my sweats, pulling me toward her. Her lips melt against mine, undoubtedly tasting herself on my tongue.

"Fuck me," she mumbles as she reaches her hand inside my pants to palm my cock, slowly stroking it from root to tip.

Fireworks erupt behind my eyelids as I tilt my head back in euphoria at the new contact. What I would give to bury myself to the hilt inside her wet heat right now—but we're in the kitchen and it would be presumptuous, even for me, to bring a condom to the kitchen to make a sandwich for myself in the middle of the night.

"Come to my room." I struggle to get the words out, my mind a foggy mess as she continues to tug on my dick.

"No, here." She sucks my bottom lip into her mouth before biting it hard enough to nearly draw blood, then releases it with a pop.

"I don't have a condom in here."

"I have an IUD." She says it so matter-of-factly, like she's been thinking about it this entire time. The mere thought of sliding into her bare sends shivers down my spine, and maybe a few hours ago when I was tipsy I could have justified it, but I can't.

No, I don't think she has an STD. Do I believe that blindly? No, but I also spend an exorbitant amount of time with her roommate, enough to know that they both went for their regular checkup recently. Sage waved a clear bill of health in my face, literally...it was kind of weird, but that's Sage.

"Give me two seconds," I say, pressing my lips to hers before pulling away. "I have one in my bag, it'll take me two seconds."

She doesn't say anything, so if my insistence on using a condom bothers her, she doesn't let it show. Honestly, if she did, I can't say for sure if I wouldn't cave.

I run to my room and sift through my backpack to find the single condom I brought along, thankful I'd had the delusional idea that I might actually get laid on this trip.

Well, technically I was right, even if it is Hannah.

I would not have put money on that, though.

As I reenter the kitchen, I notice she's still sitting on the counter, and she's eating my fucking sandwich.

"Seriously?" I laugh, pulling the triangle from her hand and placing it on the plate, setting it on the other counter.

"What? Orgasms can knock it out of ya, and you were taking forever, so."

I yank her forward and bite her bottom lip, causing her to yelp before she melts into me, matching my frantic, borderline aggressive kiss.

As I pepper kisses down her neck, she yanks my pants down before wrapping her hand around my length, causing me to groan. I step back from her touch to pull the condom from my pocket, ripping it open and sheathing myself with one swift motion.

"Get inside me, Park," she demands playfully.

"Don't tell me what to do, Hannah." I yank her to the very edge of the countertop, so far that her ass is nearly hanging off.

Lining myself with her entrance, I look up at her, wanting one final go-ahead, because I'll be damned if, come tomorrow, she acts like the she-devil I know well.

"Lacking follow-through?" she taunts, giving me exactly the stamp of approval I need, and I slide into her. She's so wet that I manage to be buried to the hilt within a few strokes.

"Fuck, Hannah," I gasp, trying to remain composed as I bury my face in her neck, biting her flesh in an attempt to muzzle my noise.

My lack of recent action immediately bites me in the ass as I stand still in an attempt to gain composure. She doesn't push me, which is a surprise, and about a minute passes before I start to move again, thrusting in and out of her in slow strokes.

This almost makes it worse.

With every thrust, I feel her tighten around me, causing me to nearly see stars. This is quite possibly the best feeling I've ever experienced, but I'd be hard-pressed to tell Hannah that.

"Fuck me, Liam." She says it like a demand, but it comes off like a plea, one which I don't have it in me not to fulfill.

I pull out, then thrust into her, burying myself deep inside before pulling back and burying myself again and again. With every thrust she gasps, a clear attempt to quell her moans as she holds her own hand over her mouth.

I reach up and yank her hand away as I bury my face in her neck, the hypocrisy of my action not lost on me.

"Liam," she moans, egging me on as I sink into her at a quickening pace. She wraps her legs around my hips, pulling me deeper with every thrust. My thumb dances over her clit, circling to match my thrusts, but she quickly swats my hand away. The bite of her nails against my back only pushes me further into oblivion, the delicious mixture of pain and pleasure sending me into a haze.

I continue to pound into her, my advances becoming more and more frantic with every push inside. She grows louder with every stroke, forcing me to cover her mouth with my hand.

Our pants mix with the billowing winds against the exterior wall and window as I attempt to keep my orgasm at bay. My efforts are futile, though. Within a few moments I tremble and gasp harshly as I surrender, letting out a long, shuddering breath. I gasp against her neck, struggling to catch my breath. By some instinct, I lean over and press my lips to hers, far gentler than I had before. To my surprise, she welcomes it, reaching her hand up to rest against my cheek for a split moment before she yanks it away.

I pull out of her, then toss the condom in the trash can, but I attempt to hide it below beer cans and the pizza box from earlier. Handing Hannah her underwear, I feel the energy shift. She goes from pliable to combative as she yanks them from my hand and jumps to her feet, stepping away from me as I struggle to stifle the desire to ask her to stay in my room.

She'd say no anyway, so there is no use wasting my breath.

I walk over to the opposing counter to grab her glass, filling it with fresh water and ice before handing it to her. She looks alert, like she expects me to throw it at her, or poison it.

"It's just a glass of water," I reassure her, but my voice betrays my annoyance.

She yanks it from my hand as she swivels on her heels, walking back toward her room without as much as a thank-you.

And with that, she's back. It was nice while it lasted.

TWENTY

LIAM

The smell of bacon wafts into the air as I attempt to cling to the last bit of sleep I can get. Despite falling asleep around 5:00 AM, I haven't allowed myself to let go of the pipe dream that is getting a lick of rest. This is a vacation, so I shouldn't be forced or coerced out of bed.

Knock, knock.

I groan as I roll over onto my stomach and bury my face in my pillow, hopeful that whoever is knocking will get the hint and leave me be. Instead of a second round of knocks like I expect, the door creaks open, revealing my best friend with two mugs of coffee in hand. I squint up at him over my shoulder, causing him to chuckle.

"Rough night?" Gabe laughs.

Talk about understatement of the year.

"Nah man, just couldn't sleep." I reach out and grab the coffee from his outstretched hand, pulling it to my lips.

"The claw marks on your back would beg to differ."

I nearly choke on my coffee before setting it on the bedside table.

"And that," I say with a laugh.

"Did you end up hooking up with that Melanie girl last night?"

Who the hell is Melanie?

"Yeah, uh. She came back over."

This seems to curb his interest as he sits on the edge of the bed, the smell of roasted coffee beans waking me up even though I've had only a few sips.

"Did someone make breakfast?"

"Yeah, Wes did, but everyone just headed down to hit the slopes before we leave tonight."

This shouldn't relieve me like it does. I don't regret last night, not in the slightest, but I've known Hannah long enough to know she's going to backtrack colossally. This isn't my first rodeo with Hannah Thatcher-Miles.

"Why didn't you go?" I ask as I take a sip of my coffee.

"Kara wants me to call her at noon."

Ugh.

Just like this isn't my first time experiencing Hannah's hot and cold reactions, it's also not my first time dealing with an infamous Gabe and Kara break-up.

I try to be supportive—he's my best friend, after all. However, Kara is awful. She's terrible to him, and she's also not particularly kind to his friends. To my understanding, he's only brought her around his family a few times, even though they've been together for three years.

"What does she want?" My attempt to hide my disdain is met with a glare.

"She wants to talk about what happened."

"So, she wants to con you into thinking she's changed and you'll inevitably take her back?"

Gabe isn't an angry guy. He actually may be the most

even-keeled person I know, but Kara brings out a side of him that scares me. Not that he gets angry, actually quite the opposite. She treats him like a doormat, even if he would never admit that.

"She's trying." He sighs. "That's all I can ask for."

"No, you can *ask* for her to respect you."

"She does respect me." The lie of the century rolls off his tongue so well I genuinely wonder if he believes it.

"Are you going to meet up with everyone after your call?" I ask, trying to steer the conversation away from Kara as it never goes the way I intend it to. It always results in me sounding like a dick. I'm pretty sure Kara hates me, but I don't care.

"I don't know, haven't decided. Probably depends on how this call goes." Which is code for *if we don't get back together, I may throw myself off the ski lift.* "What about you? You plan on getting some time in on the slopes before we head back home?"

"Nah." I don't elaborate as I stand up and adjust my sweatpants around my waist so that they sit straight.

In the kitchen, I find a plate piled high with crispy bacon and a pan of scrambled eggs. They must have just left, because the food is still a little warm. I fix myself a plate and dig in, desperate to wash the taste of last night off my tongue. Brushing my teeth didn't do it, so maybe this will.

Our flight is scheduled to leave at 6:00 PM, giving me just enough time to go back to bed until everyone returns from skiing. I wake up to pounding on my bedroom door, this time far less pleasant than Gabe's gentle knocks in the morning.

"What?!" I yell, making my irritation evident as I bury my face in my pillow.

The incessant pounding on the door doesn't stop and I'm forced to stand up and stomp over to open it. I repeat myself as I swing the door open. "What?"

An irritated Sage is standing on the other side. Typically, she's the picture of carefree, but something seems to have crawled up her ass and died today.

"We leave in an hour." She's short with me, which is unusual.

My irritation melts away, replaced with concern. "Are you okay?"

Sage pauses before shaking her head as if to convince herself. "Yeah, I'm fine. But you need to get moving." I don't expect her to be forthcoming—she seldom is—but it's obvious something is bugging her.

Is everyone completely discombobulated today?

"Ma'am, yes ma'am." I mockingly salute her, causing her to finally smile.

"Don't call me that," she says with a laugh before pushing me into my room. "Now get packed."

I finish packing my belongings, but given the one night we've spent here, it doesn't take me long.

We pile into the SUV we rented to get around town and back to the airport. Unfortunately for me, since I'm the last to head out to the car, I get no choice in where to sit. As some sort of sick joke from the universe, the only free seat is next to Hannah.

I crawl into the car and squeeze in next to her. My arm brushes against hers, and Hannah tenses at the contact.

This is about to be the longest thirty minutes of my life.

"Did everyone have fun?!" Gen's excited voice is like daggers on a chalkboard as I attempt to keep my distance from Hannah, even though we're stuck directly next to each other.

"Yeah, it was great!" Savannah matches Gen's tone, which thankfully pulls Gen's attention in her direction.

Hannah is still tense as I try to scoot away from her, but I realize quickly there isn't anywhere for me to go. The floral scent of her perfume is far more prevalent than I remember it being last night, but it hits me just the same. It's new to me, but for some reason it just screams Hannah, making it familiar.

There is a mark on Hannah's neck that she appears to be trying to hide as she pulls her hoodie up over her head. I know I bit her there last night, but I didn't realize quite how easily she would bruise. I hate the way the memory bathes me in heat, especially as Hannah glares at me as if she can read my thoughts.

"Stop looking at me."

"I'm not looking at you," I scoff.

"Are so."

"What, are we twelve?"

A pregnant silence falls over the vehicle as we drive over gravel, the sound of the crunching snow a soundtrack to my misery.

My arm grazes Hannah's once more, causing her to pinch my exposed skin, and not in a playful way. I bump my arm against her in an attempt to tell her to stop, but this only causes her to pinch me harder.

"Dude, stop!" I try not to yell, but it causes everyone in the car to turn around and look at us nonetheless.

"Move," she demands.

"In case you didn't notice—and I get it, it's hard to catch the obvious with such a smooth brain—there aren't any empty seats to move to."

"Then switch with Sage," she grits out through her teeth as she glares at me.

"No," I nearly whisper, shifting from irritation to amusement at angering her. It's a pastime that I know far too well. If she's going to be like that, I'll happily serve it back to her.

"Guys." Jackson turns around in his seat, pinning us both with a glare.

I raise my hands in a sign of surrender, but not to Hannah.

Gen turns around next to Jackson, her eyes fixing on Hannah for a long moment, clearly staring at my handiwork on her neck. Hannah lifts the collar of her sweatshirt in an attempt to hide it, but it's too late.

However, Gen doesn't say anything, especially not to Jackson. She just wears a faint grin.

As the airport comes into view, I feel a sense of relief wash over me, because I know that my seat on the plane isn't next to Hannah. We pull up to the curb, the snow crunching below the tires and subsequently beneath my boots as I step out, slamming the door behind me in the process.

Hannah swings the door back open, her face flushed with rage.

"Asshole!" Her voice cracks, causing me to smile.

TWENTY-ONE
NINE YEARS AGO

HANNAH

I was hoping that as an adult—a whole-ass bona fide high school graduate—I would have even the slightest input on the family trip to the Parks' beach house. I should be back home, spending my last summer with friends before leaving for college in a month and a half, but I'm not. I'm stuck sitting here in a folding pool chair listening to Jackson and Liam go back and forth on who to invite to the party they insist on throwing tonight.

Jackson has been drinking a lot. I want to think it's just normal college guy stuff, but I'm growing worried that it may run deeper than that.

He's been off all year, and I wish I didn't know the probable reason behind it.

I scroll through my Instagram feed, seeing all my friends from back home having the time of their lives at Eric Cline's pre-college rager since his parents have never cared about us drinking there. However, I'm stuck in Florida for two weeks because my parents can't entertain the thought of skipping one summer.

Switching to the search bar, I fight and ultimately lose to the urge to look up Viv's Instagram in hopes of seeing what she's been up to. We haven't spoken in eight months and it's killing me. Despite this, I can't get myself to reach out. She completely wrecked Jackson, but I'd be lying if I said her breaking his heart was why I told her I didn't want to be friends anymore.

She chose him, even if she swore that wasn't what she did. Genevieve knew that her and Jackson breaking up was always going to be a possibility and that our friendship would hang in the balance. Yet, she did it anyway, showing me that she was willing to choose Jackson over me.

Everyone chooses Jackson over me, and I don't need that in a best friend.

My impulse wins as I scroll through Viv's feed, not seeing many pictures at all except for one from freshman orientation. Mine is in a few weeks and I can't wait to get away from my parents, nor can I wait for school to begin in the fall. My mom isn't exactly thrilled that I'm choosing to go to school for a Bachelor of Arts in Theatre.

She's never gotten it...or me.

I enlarge the image to find Viv grinning ear to ear and plastered to the side of a petite redhead, the photo captioned with the words *"Found my roomie!"*

It shouldn't hurt to see her moving on and finding new friends, but it does.

Liam runs around the pool, his legs barely kicking up a splash of water, so fast it seems as if he's ice skating. His dark brown hair is damp, sticking to his forehead in wet strands. He cannonballs into the pool without warning, causing water to splash high, getting me wet in the process. Luckily, I have an

OtterBox on my phone or I would be punching him for his stupidity. I settle for yelling instead.

"What the hell is wrong with you?!"

He looks over to me with a smirk on his face and doesn't respond. Typical Liam.

As he pulls himself up from the cool water of the pool, I admire the way the droplets cling to his skin, slowly sliding down and collecting in the crevices of his toned muscles. Something changed in Liam over the last year. He left for college the same scrawny nerd I've known for my entire life and came back...not that.

I scrunch my nose up at the fact that I allowed myself to even think something like that.

Liam walks directly over to me. I expect him to say something shitty or tell me to stop being such a girl about it and that I shouldn't be sitting next to the pool if I don't want to get wet, but he takes it one step further. He doesn't say a word as he hangs his head over me and shakes it aggressively from side to side so that the water soaking his hair flies haphazardly all over me and my phone.

"Asshole!" I scream, causing Jackson to turn his head, but the moment he sees it is a reaction to Liam, he turns back to his phone.

This bro loyalty thing is getting old.

I jump up from my chair to go inside, walking past Jackson en route. "Try being a good brother for once!"

This pries his attention from his phone for a moment. "Oh please, I'm a great brother. But I've lived enough years on this earth to not get involved in—" he points to me and Liam, "that."

Liam and Jackson's friendship has always perplexed me.

How my brother could be friends with someone so annoying and so unlike him is beyond me.

I yank the sliding screen door to the side, dripping water as I walk into the kitchen. It could be worse; I could have been thrown into the pool, but the water on me boils my blood just the same. Hurriedly, I run up the stairs and change, thankful that my hair was already up in a bun, so the damage to it is minimal.

People should be arriving soon, much to my dismay. Our parents are gone for one night and having a party with such little time to clean up feels risky. However, Jackson and Liam seem confident that it will work out. Worst case scenario, I pretend I went to bed, took a large dose of melatonin, and slept through the entire fiasco.

Not that they'd believe that.

The banister creaks under my hand as I carefully walk down the staircase after getting ready. My loose bun is now in a more polished topknot. I opted to trade my denim shorts and tank top for something a bit more party-ready: my brand-new yellow dress. It is tighter than the clothes I typically wear, but is part of my "New Town, New Hannah" wardrobe for the fall. Despite the clothing change, the scent of chlorine lives rent-free on me, more than likely until I take a shower.

As soon as I get down to the main floor, I hear the music playing from the backyard. The scent of chlorine heightens as I step out onto the concrete pad around the pool, where the chairs are now pushed to one side to allow room for people to move and mingle. My eyes dart around to see a variety of faces I know, and some that I don't.

A head of dark brown curls steps into view. I would simply ignore the person impacting my view of the party, but as she turns around, my breath catches in my throat.

I don't know her, but I want to desperately.

Her sea-foam-green eyes meet my own with a grin, pulling a matching smile from my lips. Most of the girls Liam and Jackson invited are regulars in the area; some of them live here. However, this girl I can honestly say I've never seen before.

"Hi," she says with a grin, not being immediately forthcoming with her identity.

"Hi." I smile back, attempting to hide how nervous interacting with her makes me.

"I'm Olivia."

"Hannah." My stomach does an array of flips and twirls, an entire flight of butterflies taking up residence in my abdomen. She's gorgeous, but I can't figure out why I'm reacting the way I am.

I mean, I know, but I'm not ready to unpack that quite yet.

We chat for a while, but none of the conversation ventures past face value. She's new to the area, her family having just moved here from Wyoming. She recently graduated high school, like me, but doesn't plan to go to college.

I considered doing the same; I could just move to New York City without pursuing a degree first, but my mother might actually send me for slaughter if I even entertain that idea.

As the night progresses, I find myself pacing the pool. The nervous energy from before is only exacerbated by the alcohol now running through my veins.

Jackson, the sad puppy that he is, hasn't left his spot by the pool, his eyes fixed on the way the water dances and ripples as people jump and move around.

I feel for him, but not enough to allow my night to be dragged down.

Pulling the screen door open, I venture into the

kitchen to get ice from the fridge. The guys got a keg, but I'm not a big beer drinker. Maybe that will change when I go to college, but right now I'll stick to Mountain Dew and UV Blue. The bottle glugs as I pour it, the heavy stream of the blue liquid filling up a solid three-quarters of the Solo cup in front of me. As I add the Mountain Dew, the blue shade shifts to a pretty electric green.

I lift the drink to my lips as I shift on my feet to lean against the counter. The house is full of people now, various partygoers covering just about every sitting surface available. The always-present smell of the chlorine is now mixed with the yeasty smell of cheap beer.

The moment my eyes land on Liam, my stomach sours. Not in the typical way, when his presence leaves me wanting to gouge my eyes out because he's being annoying, but in a foreign, unfamiliar way.

Olivia, the girl I was talking to earlier, is now sitting in his lap. The irritation that flows through my veins isn't about her, though, and that startles me. The way she touches him, her hand pressed firmly to his taut T-shirt, has my blood boiling, and I find myself ready to lunge across the living room couch to get to them. I taste blood as I bite down on my bottom lip far more aggressively than normal.

I don't like this. I don't like this at all.

So why am I walking across the room?

The moment my feet skid to a stop in front of the recliner they're parked in, I realize I don't have the slightest idea of what to say. What the hell does someone say when they suddenly find themselves jealous over the single person in this world that they'd love to watch rot?

"Liam, I need to talk to you."

This pulls his attention from Olivia for a split second before he leans back into her touch, ignoring me.

"Liam..." The pleading tone that slips from my lips seems to wake him up and he turns to me, a concerned expression on his face. He taps Olivia's leg to instruct her to move, and she does without hesitation.

She'll make someone very happy one day, I'm sure of it, but I'll be damned if it's Liam.

He follows me to the laundry room and I click the door behind us, trying to find a shred of privacy. What will we talk about? Hell if I know, but he's the hell away from her.

"What's up?" The concerned tone in his voice makes me feel almost guilty—almost.

"Um—" I gnaw at the inside of my cheek, struggling for a reason to justify pulling him away from the party. "Oh, I, uh," I say as I clear my throat, "I can't find the laundry detergent. Someone spilled beer on my dress and I need to change."

That's not *not* true. I look down at a small brown spot staining my yellow dress on my hip from some idiot who tripped on his way into the house.

Liam pins me with a puzzled expression and I find myself trying to figure out a way to backtrack.

"You pulled me away from the party...from a hot girl sitting on my lap...for laundry detergent?"

"Yes!" I yelp, my nervous energy seeping into my words. "It's an expensive dress."

He squints at me, confusion plaguing his expression. "What is wrong with you?"

"Nothing's wrong with me! Can't a girl care about her appearance? I know caring about that is foreign to you."

"There she is," he says with a grin. "For a second there, I was thinking this was a ploy to get me away from Olivia."

A scream crawls up my throat at his statement, but I swallow it down, not wanting him to know what I'm thinking.

"Where is the laundry detergent, Park?" I sigh, forcing my anxious energy to present as irritation.

He pauses, looking at me, perplexed, before pointing to the top shelf where the pods are clear as day. Okay, I should have found a better excuse.

"Silly me. Silly little bird brain, thanks." I go to push him toward the door, but he latches onto my wrist.

"What is up with you?" He sounds almost concerned again, but I can't escape the way the heat of his palm sears into my wrist.

"Nothing," I say as I yank my hand away before reaching for the hem of my dress.

I pull the dress over my head, toss it into the top-loading washer, throw a laundry pod into the drum, and slam the lid. Heat crawls up my neck as Liam clears his throat, reminding me that I am now standing in front of him in a lace bralette and a thong.

Why the fuck did I just do that?

The thought dies on my tongue as I turn around to find his eyes on me, the irritation from before nowhere to be found. His expression is something I've never seen from him. Well, something I've never seen directed at me, anyway.

"Hannah, you're naked." He says it but doesn't seem bothered by it, only confused.

"No, I'm not." I clear my throat. "I'm clearly wearing a bra and underwear, it's nothing worse than a bikini."

"True. But *you* don't wear a thong bikini...ever."

"So?" I pin him with a glare, irritation crawling up my spine at his picking me apart. "You basically see me like a sister, so it really shouldn't matter to you. It's not like I'm walking around outside like this."

I reach to grab a T-shirt from a hanger above the washer, but Liam's hand wraps around my wrist again.

"I don't," he whispers.

"You don't what?" A lump lodges in my throat, but I don't yank my hand away.

"I don't see you as a sister...not even close."

The revelation causes my eyes to dart to his, and a heady expression paints his face. I may not have ever seen it directed toward me, but I know that look. Lust.

Realizing this warms my skin, at the very least because I know that this new attraction isn't one-sided, even if I would love nothing more than to steep myself in a bucket of cold water.

"What do you see me like?" The question comes out nearly as a whisper; I'm not even sure he hears me.

"Don't play dumb, Hannah."

"I'm not playing."

A smirk washes over his lips, causing me to smack his shoulder with a grin. "Shut up."

I expect this to lessen the tension in the room, but it does the opposite. The air is so thick it's unavoidable. The hand wrapped around my wrist loosens. I think he's about to retreat, but the moment I feel his hand skate upward to cup the back of my neck, my stomach lurches.

I'm in complete disbelief and entirely consumed by him in the same thought, the cognitive dissonance causing my head to spin.

Liam leans in, his lips a whisper from my own. He pauses, I think to see if I'm going to pull away from his touch. I know I should; my brain is screaming at me to back away.

I close the distance, my lips melting against his. It's gentle at first, but quickly becomes frenzied. Every shred of reservation I had before is replaced with an undeniably clear emotion.

Desire.

TWENTY-TWO
PRESENT DAY

HANNAH

"I'll have the chicken penne, please," I say with a grin up at the familiar waitress at Andre's as I hand her the menu. Not that I need the menu—we come here far too often.

The rest of the table places their order and hands her their menus one by one. As soon as she is out of earshot, the table erupts into chatter, all surrounding Gen and Jackson's wedding.

Sage and I are both bridesmaids, while Savannah is Gen's Maid of Honor...or is it Matron? I'm not super sure, I just know it's not me. I find that both heart-wrenching and a relief all at the same time.

I wish Gen and I were as close as we once were, but I'm thankful for the growth we've made. It was bumpy at first, but since I've been living in Atlanta full-time we've gotten a lot closer again. At the very least, Gen is about to be my sister-in-law, and you can't trump family.

"Have you thought about silhouettes?" Savannah asks with a grin, resting her chin on her hands, her fingers intertwined.

"Not really." Gen takes a sip of her water. "I know I don't

want it to be too boobie, but other than that I'm open to most anything."

"Why not? You've got a great rack. I'm sure Jax would approve." Savannah chuckles at her own joke as I do everything in my power to keep myself from gagging. I'm not sure I will ever grow used to how flagrantly she talks about my brother, although I know that I wouldn't bat an eye if Gen was marrying someone that wasn't my flesh and blood.

The clattering of cutlery fills the air as people hustle to find a seat, pouring in from the street like ants. Bright light floods through the windows, revealing twinkling lights strung between the ceiling beams. Andre's succulent roast chicken is Tuesday's specialty and you can smell it all the way from the doorway. It draws a full house even on a weekday at noon.

We all took the day off work after getting back from Vail a few days ago because Savannah was fortunate enough to get Gen an appointment at one of the more exclusive bridal boutiques in Atlanta. Anya Baron's Bridal Atelier caters exclusively to women from wealthy families, and only a small number are allowed entry into their showroom each month. Getting an appointment requires going through several layers of bureaucracy and is usually as hard as winning the lottery.

In this case, Savannah Newmont is one of those women.

"Can we not talk about my brother's sexual interests?" I make a disgusted expression before I crack, a laugh falling out of my mouth.

"It's never ending, she does it about my brother all the time." Sage matches my grossed-out expression, which causes Savannah to roll her eyes.

"Well, I'm married to your brother. Are you aware of what married people do, Sage?" Savannah lifts her brows with a mocking smirk.

Sage responds by miming a gagging motion, pointing into her mouth.

Our food arrives in surprisingly quick time despite the restaurant being extremely busy. I will never grow tired of their chicken penne. Their cheese sauce gives the pasta a rich creaminess, and the tomato adds an earthy sweetness that just makes me swoon with delight. I nearly moan as the taste invades my senses. It's literally the best thing I have ever tasted, no matter how common a dish it might be.

Andre is a man after my own heart.

We settle into a rhythm as we discuss details necessary as the time grows closer to Gen's appointment, which is luckily right around the corner from the restaurant.

"Did everyone have fun in Vail?" Gen asks it as if she is asking about the weather, because I guess to her it's not quite as weighted of a question.

"Yeah," I say quickly as I shovel a bite of pasta in my mouth, hoping this conversation falls off fast. I don't want to relive Vail; I don't want to think about it. Actually, I would prefer if I could just go back in time and rewrite my choices on the trip. However, the hickey the size of a quarter on my neck is an unfortunate reminder that it wasn't just a really detailed dream.

"Hannah sure did," Sage says with a laugh, knocking her leg against mine under the table. I kick her back in response, causing her to yelp. "What? You did!"

I don't want to talk about this, and the moment all three of their eyes are on me, I find myself wanting to crawl into a hole.

"Justin?" Gen grins, reminding me she already noticed my indiscretion and apparently thinks it was Justin. I can work with that.

The door swings open and nearly slams against the side of

the old building. The wind is finally starting to dial down compared to last week, but it's still pretty intense. The gust chills my skin, but not nearly as much as the man the wind dragged in with it.

Liam stands at the bar with a credit card in hand, clearly picking up his lunch.

I must have been a mass murderer in a past life—that's the only explanation for my luck today.

"Park!" Sage yells, but while I call him by his last name in a negative context, somehow it comes out endearing when she says it.

I need to come up with something different to call him... "ass-wipe" has a nice ring to it.

As Liam approaches, brown paper takeout bag in hand, Savannah picks the worst possible moment to continue the conversation that Sage so kindly started.

"So, who's Justin?" Savannah asks while shoveling a forkful of salad into her mouth.

"The bestower of that hickey on Hannah's neck." Sage laughs to herself before turning to Liam, whose eyes are now on me.

His attention lingers, almost inspecting—or realizing for the first time that he branded me.

"Justin, huh?" he says with a smirk.

I lift the collar of my shirt to attempt to cover the hickey that I clearly didn't do a good enough job of covering with concealer this morning.

I'm so happy that he finds amusement in my utter humiliation.

"Yeah, Justin. The super-hot guy I was hanging out with the other night." I pin him with a glare, but it doesn't dissolve his amusement; it appears to only egg him on further.

"Well, seeing as I didn't hear anything out of the ordinary, I'd assume he wasn't all that great at the end of the day."

"Actually—" Sage talks with her mouth full, and I know the moment she starts that she's about to make me want to kill her. "From what I was hearing that night, he was great. She was like...so loud."

Oh my God, oh my God, oh my God.

Liam purses his lips as he bites back a cocky grin.

"Honestly, I wouldn't be surprised if it was the best sex she's ever had. Girl was loud."

Jesus Christ, Sage, SHUT THE FUCK UP!!

Blood rushes to my face and I attempt to hide it, but the red flush overtakes me anyway. It's unavoidable at this point, so I pin her with a glare. "Can you not?"

"Best sex of her life, huh?" The cocky grin Liam was attempting to quell before is on full display, but it's a common enough expression for him that I can't imagine anyone notices the connotation but me. Liam rocks back and forth on his feet, his perfectly polished brown dress shoes glistening from the overhead lighting.

"Meh—kinda sucked." I take a sip of my water before cutting into the chicken in my pasta, refusing to look up at him. I look at Savannah instead. "You know those guys who think they're great, but really they just thrust blindly, so hard that you're loud? They think it's because you're enjoying it, but really it's because your head keeps being slammed into the headboard. Or backsplash, depending where you're doing it."

The smile on Liam's face drops as I look up at him, his cocky grin now plastered on my face.

"No...I can't think of a single instance of that ever happening to me," Savannah says with a puzzled expression.

"Lucky girl—it's terrible."

This seems to pull Liam out of his game as I watch him clear his throat. "Well, as fun as analyzing Hannah's sex life has been—seriously, riveting—" he says, his sarcasm dripping off every word, "I need to head back to the office."

"Shame." I mockingly pout at him, earning me a glare.

"Bye, Liam!" the other three women at the table say in unison as he walks away, but I don't join the pleasantries.

"Do you think it would be possible for you two to coexist at this wedding without being on top of each other like that? You're walking with him, for crying out loud." As the words leave Gen's mouth, I struggle not to laugh at her inopportune choice of words.

"I can promise you, going forward that won't be the case."

"Good," Gen says as she digs back into her roast chicken, but I don't miss the way Sage's eyes are pinned on me.

I refuse to look at her.

TWENTY-THREE

LIAM

Despite the fact that we've been tiptoeing around one another all week, I find myself working with Hannah with no buffer come Friday afternoon. Jackson has a lunch meeting followed by a different meeting across town at his client's office. He's not coming back before the weekend, meaning for the next six hours I'm stuck having to interact with Hannah directly.

Okay, to be fair, I don't have an issue with it—she, however, does.

Hannah has barely come into my office, but her presence is everywhere in this damn space. Starting with that stupid Duke Blue Devils bobblehead she gave Jackson that is taunting me from across the room. I pull out my phone, the inevitability of the situation spurring me on.

LIAM

come here

I set my phone down on my desk face-up, though I expect her to just walk in. I've stopped locking my office door when it's just me and Hannah because usually she's in and out constantly.

HANNAH

why?

I rub my brow, her refusal to be cooperative seeping through the shred of professionalism I have left.

because i told you to.

and im your boss

Three dots appear, indicating she's typing, each dot an exclamation point of rage and fury, coming in quick succession before disappearing and leaving me to wonder if she is done or just taking a breath to continue. My office door creaks open slowly. I'm actually a bit surprised by her obedience, but when I see a petite brunette in the doorway, I realize that's not the case.

"Hey, Veronica," I say with a smile as I lean back in my chair to give her my complete attention. "What can I do for ya?"

"Nothing, I just thought I'd stop by to say hello." She grins from ear to ear as she leans against the edge of my desk, pulling her highlighted waves over one shoulder in the process. Veronica's perfume is subtle and sweet, and appears to be freshly sprayed.

I'm somewhat surprised that Veronica hasn't been by at all this week until now. She used to stop by at least once or twice every week, but I haven't seen her as much lately.

"Well, that is always welcome." I grin up at her, earning me an even bigger smile than before.

The door to my office swings open with a thud, far more

aggressively than when Veronica entered. I know without having to look up that Hannah has entered the room and is more than likely pinning me with a glare.

"What did you want?" She barely makes it in the door before her hand is on her hip, an irritated expression painted on her lips.

Her irritatingly pillowy lips.

I would make a smart-ass remark, but given that we're not alone, that doesn't exactly feel professional. Now that I think of it, neither is the fact that Hannah has yet to acknowledge Veronica, who is sitting on the edge of my desk, only about a foot from her. She doesn't just fail to acknowledge her; it almost seems like she's intentionally refusing to offer pleasantries.

"Hannah, have you met Veronica? She works down in Accounting." I force a neutral smile in her direction, but it doesn't reach my eyes.

"Yep." She turns her head toward Veronica and gives her a curt nod before turning back to me. "Now, what did you want?"

It's a struggle not to snap at her when she's like this, especially toward someone she barely even knows.

Unless...no. There is no way she's jealous.

"Did you pick up that thumb drive from my dad like I asked you to?"

"I don't know, are you blind?"

Okay, so we're not even attempting to pretend to get along in front of other employees.

"It's sitting right in front of your keyboard."

"Ah, well...thanks," I grit out, clearly caught.

I expect her to gloat at her triumph in catching me in my false pretenses, but she just glares at me.

"I'm gonna go," Veronica says as she looks back and forth between me and Hannah. I don't even blame her, as the air in this room is so thick with animosity that I would like to escape it, too.

"Okay." I sit upright as I sort through the papers on my desk, handing her the one with the Baker & Park letterhead that she's been asking for. "Here are the expenses you were asking about."

"I'll get this logged and bring it back to you for your records." She awkwardly backs away, exiting without a single word to Hannah.

"Seriously, Hannah?" I exhale as I try to keep my cool. Her clear tantrum has me on edge.

"What?" she sighs.

"You can't treat people here like that." I rub my eyes as I set my elbows on my desk, the exhaustion of an earlier day than normal wearing on me.

I expect an apology, or at the very least a "fuck off," but Hannah just turns on her heels and heads toward the door. She's not one for backing down from a fight with me, so I take the win when I can get it.

That is...until she locks the door and turns to face me.

I'm prepared for a screaming match—it wouldn't be the first time we've had to duke it out in private. Standing, I prepare for battle. I can't give her even the slightest leg up on me; she'd exploit it without fail. I start to roll my sleeves up, the warmth thrumming through my veins causing me to grow flushed.

I don't miss the way her gaze lingers as I do it.

"I'm ready. What's your problem? Or are you finally ready to talk about what happened?"

The pin I just pulled from the grenade that is Hannah

Thatcher-Miles has me on guard, ready to bite back at whatever insults she's about to hurl at me.

Hannah walks toward me slower than I am comfortable with. She seems calm...too calm. Angry Hannah I know; calm Hannah scares me.

It's not until she's standing in front of me that I get my bearings, preparing for my rebuttal to whatever she's about to say. Her floral perfume consumes me, discombobulating me in the process.

However, her words don't come.

Hannah lifts onto her toes and presses her lips to mine. The taste of Starburst candy invades my senses, the slightly sour yet sweet flavor consuming me as I relish in the taste on her lips. She pulls away for a split second. Her sudden shift in attitude has my head spinning, but her treatment of Veronica has me equally confused.

"Han—" The last shred of reservation I have is eviscerated the second her tongue skates over my bottom lip, and all I want is to feel it tangled with my own.

A groan escapes me as she bites my bottom lip. It's not sweet or tentative—she intends it to hurt—but it only urges me on.

My hand snakes upward as I drag it over the gold buttons that span the back of her black dress, grasping a fistful of hair at the nape of her neck. Hannah gasps at the sudden pain, but as her eyes meet mine, I know with certainty that it was the right move.

"You won't treat Veronica like that again," I reprimand her.

Hannah isn't a compliant person; she isn't malleable—at least not for me. However, I'll be damned if this isn't something she listens about. It makes me look bad if I allow her to get special treatment and disrespect our employees. It's a Human Resources complaint waiting to happen.

"Yes, sir." The breathy sound mixed with her words shoots a sensation straight to my cock.

I don't know where this version of Hannah came from, but I refuse to not engage it.

"On your knees."

I anticipate a shitty remark, a retort, a "go to hell." What I don't expect is for her to do exactly as I say without so much as a huff of defiance.

The moment her knees hit the carpet in front of my chair, I look down and find a doe-eyed expression looking back up at me. She's breathtaking like this. There is just something so enrapturing about someone who is typically so formidable giving up control willingly.

I allow my thumb to trace over Hannah's bottom lip, causing her breath to hitch. Cradling the back of her neck in my palm, I use my other hand to unbuckle my belt with a clank. The cognac leather sits slack on my hips as Hannah reaches upward, her eyes not leaving mine. I can't tell if she is looking for a word of encouragement to keep going, but I provide it anyway.

"Unzip my slacks."

Without hesitation, Hannah releases the button and unzips my pants with one quick motion. Now that my slacks are undone, my erection is glaringly obvious. Lucky for me, there is nothing about this situation that calls for subtlety.

"Get my cock out," I say, my voice ragged as I attempt to hold tightly to what little control I have. It may look like I'm in control, but I've never felt more exposed to Hannah than I do right now.

She tries to hide her gasp at my crude words, but I hear it

with clarity. As her hands wrap around the waistband of my boxer briefs, I hold my breath, the anticipation causing my heart to pound so loudly I worry she might hear it.

I can't let her know how much she affects me, though I suppose she'll know soon enough.

Hannah wraps her hand around my still-restrained cock, and her firm grip pulls a strangled groan from me.

The ticking of the analog clock on the wall is the only sound I hear as she pulls me free, my sensitive, hard length now standing at attention only inches from the Eden of Hannah's mouth.

She gulps, leaning forward, and presses the tip to her lips before extending her tongue to taste the drop of pre-cum that's begun to pool there.

It's like a jolt of electricity as my head lolls back, the muffled moan that I try to bite back slipping through my lips. This appears to only urge her further as she takes my length into her mouth, easing herself down until it hits the back of her throat. The moment Hannah wraps her hand around the three inches that don't fit in her mouth, my composure breaks.

"Fuck, Hannah." The moan that leaves my lips is anything but reserved; there's no questioning how incredible this feels. I unintentionally jerk forward, pushing my cock against the back of her throat. Hannah gags slightly but doesn't allow it to deter her as she holds me deep within the warm, wet euphoria of her mouth.

Knock, knock.

We both freeze, turning to stare at the door in silence. I'm thankful that Hannah had the forethought to lock the door and the only way to get in would be with a scan card. I press my pointer finger to my lips to encourage her to be quiet and, to my surprise, she listens...until the doorknob begins to turn.

"Fuck," Hannah mumbles as she backs under my desk, not having the time to compose herself or give even the slightest bit of deniability to what we were doing.

I sit down at my desk as I tuck my dick back inside my underwear, hopeful that whoever it is doesn't have a need to walk around my desk for any reason.

Veronica's head pokes through the now-cracked door and she makes eye contact with me. "Oh shit, I'm sorry. Karen gave me her swipe to drop this on your desk, I figured you ran out for lunch since the door was locked."

"I—it's okay." I struggle to get the words out as I feel Hannah's fingers curl around my waistband below the table, causing my cock to jerk.

"Is Hannah okay? She seemed off today," Veronica asks at the exact moment Hannah pulls my dick free.

A gasp lodges in my throat. Thankfully, Veronica doesn't seem to notice.

"Oh yeah, she's, um...she's fine."

Hannah seizes this moment to take me into her mouth in one swift motion, the sensation of my head hitting the back of her throat with little prelude nearly making me buckle over.

"She...um, she's stressed I think."

I'm not normally this short with Veronica, but I am unsure if I have the capability to carry a conversation right now without making it glaringly obvious what Hannah is doing. I reach under the desk with the intention to yank her backward to encourage her to stop, but I find myself nudging her further down with my hand flush against the back of her head, her blonde strands entangling with my fingers. The gagging sound that carries from below the mahogany wood is faint, but enough to make me cough in an attempt to disguise it.

"Oh, that's unfortunate. Well, hopefully she feels better

soon." Veronica begins to rock on her feet, obviously trying to find an out from our conversation.

"She'll be fine," I quip, much shorter and quicker than I intend. "Thanks for dropping this off," I say with a forced smile, grabbing the piece of paper from her hand, "but I have to jump on a call."

"Understood. Sorry about that." She smiles as she moves toward the door. I attempt to extend some sort of pleasantries about hoping she has a good rest of her day, but Hannah chooses this exact moment to circle her tongue over my sensitized tip. I grip the edge of my desk so hard that my knuckles go white.

"Be sure to close the door," I grit out, focusing my attention on the paper in front of me without the slightest concern for its contents. As Hannah speeds up her advances, the tingling sensation at the base of my spine grows in intensity. I'm on the precipice of coming, but I'll be damned if I have to hide that too.

The moment the door clicks shut, I reach back under my desk and nudge Hannah's head back down, lifting my hips to deepen the thrusts as I dance with her gag reflex. To my pleased surprise, she takes every inch of my cock into her mouth with enthusiasm.

My orgasm assaults my senses, pulling a groan from me that is far too loud for discretion. With every jerk of my cock, Hannah keeps me seated entirely in her mouth. The sensation of her swallowing around me causes my eyes to roll back at quite possibly the single most intoxicating feeling I've ever experienced.

Panting, I jerk backward, the wheels of my chair gliding effortlessly over the hardwood floor.

"Hannah," I reprimand. "That was risky."

She crawls out from under my desk, wiping the rogue lipstick from the corner of her mouth with a smile. Her hair is disheveled, and she attempts to flatten it with no luck. "Are you saying you didn't like it?"

"That's not what I said." I tuck myself back into my underwear before refastening my pants and belt.

"Okay then." She grins as she steps into me and presses her lips to mine. It's tepid and gentle, a far cry from moments ago.

"Come over tonight," I say before I even realize it comes out.

This isn't what we are—we don't hang out. We don't just spend time at my apartment of our own free will.

Then again, we also don't fool around at Baker & Park, so I suppose it's a day of new things.

Hannah looks taken aback by my request, but she doesn't reject the idea immediately, just stares at me with a confused expression. "Liam, I—"

"Please, Hannah. Come over tonight." The earnestness in my voice seems to break through her hard exterior as she nods up at me with a weary expression.

"Okay." It's barely a whisper, but I'll take what I can get.

TWENTY-FOUR

HANNAH

My day passes at snail speed.

I don't know what came over me when I saw Veronica trying to flirt with Liam, but it awakened something in me that I neither recognize nor trust. Why I would be jealous over someone flirting with—of all people—Liam, I don't know. However, the events my jealousy set in motion were nothing short of intoxicating.

The taste of his orgasm still lingers on my tongue far into the afternoon, so when Veronica walks by my desk as I'm packing up to leave, I actually manage to feel a level of guilt with which I'm not comfortable.

"Hey," I say as she passes me, stopping her in her tracks.

"Oh, uh..." Veronica stops, but it's clear as day that she doesn't want to. "What's up?"

"I was rude earlier, I'm really sorry about that." Liam got inside my head about the way I conduct myself at work, even if I know for certain Veronica's intentions with him are far from platonic or altruistic.

This seems to relieve her and she exhales before saying, "It's fine, Hannah. Seriously. We all have bad days."

God, I hate that she's so likable. She's supposed to be a bitch, she's supposed to be annoying, anything to justify the anger that bubbles up inside of me whenever she's around.

"Thank you for understanding." I force a smile as I look across my desk at her. It's not Veronica's fault that she clearly likes Liam. Is her infatuation a clear sign of a deteriorated mental capacity? Sure, but it's not a moral shortcoming.

She gives me a nod as she walks away, allowing me to finish stuffing my water bottle into my tote bag alongside my laptop.

***

The anxiety that crawls up my spine as I stand in front of Apartment 42 of the Westmoor downtown is nothing compared to the panic that sets in as Liam opens the door. I've never been to his apartment in the city, so the idea of losing what little control I have in this situation causes bile to crawl up my throat.

Liam waves me into his space without a word and even I'm shocked that I don't fight him on it. I'm here, after all, so any plausible deniability has long since gone out the window. I enjoy having sex with him—that doesn't mean I have to trust him.

Expansive dark hardwood floors meet me at the entryway and travel back to cover the entire apartment. The open concept of the space is awe-inducing, rivaled only by the view of the Atlanta skyline visible through the floor-to-ceiling windows that span the entire right wall of the living room.

The musky scent of a mahogany teakwood candle is only

masked slightly by the smell coming from his kitchen, the combination of food and masculine cologne oddly pleasant as it grounds me.

"What are you making?" I ask as I walk across the threshold into the kitchen, which is only separated by a large marble island from the rest of the living area. Dark wood cabinets span all the way up to the ceiling. I can only hope I don't need something from the top shelf while I'm here, because I would undoubtedly need Liam's assistance.

"Chicken parm." Liam tosses a kitchen towel over his shoulder before opening the oven, and the delectable aroma of the dish he's cooking completely overtakes the smell of the candle.

"That smells incredible." I nearly moan as I take a deep breath, causing Liam's gaze to linger a few seconds longer. Chicken parmesan has always been my favorite meal, a fact which I doubt Liam would pay enough attention to know.

"Thanks," he says as he pins me with a puzzled expression, as if my giving him a compliment is such a bizarre concept. He acts like I'm this evil person. Just because we don't get along doesn't mean I can't extend a simple compliment.

Gripping my phone in my hand, I stand awkwardly as I watch him pull the cast iron skillet from the oven, the delectable scent even stronger than before. It's not until now that I realize he doesn't have a dining room table. The open-concept floor plan doesn't lend itself to a huge table, but where the assumed dining area resides there is a desk with three monitors topping it, along with an assortment of Mountain Dew cans stacked up rather than in the trash.

"Ever heard of throwing stuff away?" I laugh as I approach the desk to get a better look at the computer tower. It has sides of mesh through which a bright blue light seeps. I would like to pretend I don't know what the setup is for, but having grown up spending multiple vacations every single year for the past twenty-seven years with Liam, I know it's for gaming.

"Yeah," he says with a chuckle as he begins to scoop portions of chicken on top of beds of what looks to be buttered spaghetti noodles on two plates, "it's been a hectic week. I need to clean up."

I realize most of his apartment is pristine, cleaner than any space I've ever lived in...except for his desk. Almost as if he compartmentalizes his mess, managing to be both a clean freak and a slob all in the same apartment.

"Apparently." I chuckle as I lean against the island and watch him continue to plate our dinners.

He pulls two forks and two knives out of a drawer in front of him before walking to the living room with plates in hand. I stay behind in an act of defiance.

He comes back from the couch with a puzzled but amused expression. "Plan on joining me for dinner, or...?"

"Well, seeing as you didn't tell me that we were going to the living room..."

"And here I thought you had at least a base level amount of brain cells. Stupid me for assuming you could deduce that on your own."

"Funny."

"Red or white?" He doesn't look away from me as he shuffles around in a drawer before pulling out a corkscrew.

"What?"

"Wine." He raises his brows. "Red or white?"

"Oh, uh...red." I don't know why such a simple question has me discombobulated. It's not that it's a hard question, but the longer I spend in this apartment, the less I feel like I have a footing on solid ground.

He reaches into a rack on the counter and pulls out a bottle of Pinot noir with an intricate script on it, but I can't make out what it says. He reaches into the same rack, where there are multiple types of wine glasses, and selects the ones reserved for red wine.

Liam has to be the only single twenty-nine-year-old man I know who has an assortment of wine glasses and doesn't just drink boxed wine out of a dinner glass.

He passes by me with the bottle and glasses in hand before turning around. "Do I need to give you a play-by-play on how to walk to the living room?"

"Do I need to give you a play-by-play..." I mock him as I follow anyway, my hunger winning over the desire to irritate him.

I plop down on the plush navy sofa and sink a few inches, the lush fabric bringing me a sense of relaxation that I desperately need after the day I've had. The day that I have no intention of bringing up with Liam, given that I would probably have to answer questions about why I acted the way I did.

Liam hands me a plate and silverware before sitting down directly next to me, his side flush with my own. I struggle to formulate a shitty remark at his proximity, but as he hands me a glass of wine, it dies on my tongue.

"Do you want to pick something to watch?" He asks it so nonchalantly I almost answer without quip, but I stop myself. I just stare at him, a puzzled look on my face.

He looks at me with an equally confused expression. "What?"

"You're being weirdly nice..."

"Believe it or not, princess, I am a nice guy."

I scoff, earning me a scowl, but he doesn't retort. The

nickname that he started using when we were kids as a way to taunt me whenever I was demanding—*his words, not mine*—rolls off his tongue, but it doesn't irritate me like it normally does.

"Fine. Remote, please."

He hands it to me instantly and I begin downloading the Disney+ app, but he doesn't question me until I start typing in my selection.

"What are we watching?"

"You'll see," I say with a laugh as I continue to type.

J...O...N...A...S.

"Please tell me we aren't watching that stupid show. It's terrible!" Liam laughs but doesn't attempt to take the remote.

"Of course we are! It's a television masterpiece."

"It's a children's show with terrible acting."

"It's nostalgic," I say with a pout, eliciting an eye roll.

"Fine."

Liam sits back without creating distance between us. He starts eating without any additional qualms about my choice in show, even if he doesn't pay attention.

After a while, our plates on the coffee table are empty except for sauce residue, and he suddenly very much isn't annoyed by my choice of television show as we switch to *Jonas L.A.*, the second season of the franchise.

"Okay, but why isn't he into her? It's so obvious!" Liam asks as he pours himself another glass of wine, unable to pry his eyes from the television.

"Oh, he is, just later in the season."

He acts over-dramatically offended. "Woah, spoiler much?"

"Shut up, it's not like you actually care," I choke out

through a laugh as I polish off my second glass of wine, leaning into him.

Another episode goes by along with the bottle of wine before he bursts out laughing. "Hannah, this is awful."

"Yeah yeah, I'm sure you're the pinnacle of cinematic taste." My sarcasm doesn't reach him—or if it does, he ignores it.

"Actually, yes. I like to think I have exceptional taste in movies."

"Like what, *John Wick?*" I mock, flailing my arms around for emphasis. I'm fully aware that's his favorite movie franchise.

I yelp as he pins me to the couch, his body flush against me. The laugh that escapes me is nothing short of a maniacal cackle, causing Liam to dig his fingers into my ribs as he knows how much I detest tickling.

"Stop, stop!" I laugh as I attempt to pry his hands from my sides, but he doesn't let go. He does, however, grab me tightly, the tickles quickly a memory. As my laughter dies on my tongue, his eyes meet mine, shifting from amusement to need in a matter of seconds.

Every other time anything has happened between us, it has been intense, like we were letting the pressure out of a valve in the hope that it would prevent the air from entirely combusting. That intense, all-consuming mixture of anger and desire is intoxicating, but nothing when compared to the look he's giving me right now...like he could eat me alive.

The realization—without anger, without the heat of the moment—that I still want him to close the distance and kiss me has me ready to crawl in on myself.

I can't want this; I can't want him.

As soon as Liam's lips meet mine, tender and investigating,

I'm reduced to a puddle on the floor. I can't want this, I can't want him, I can't *like* him.

The realization is worse than any hurtful thing he could ever say to me, because I know the ending is ten times worse.

"Stay the night," Liam whispers, his lips lingering against mine.

I try to search for a reason to say no. I have to be up early, I have an appointment in the morning, I forgot my phone charger, Sage and I have plans—*something*...but nothing believable comes to mind.

As a gulp rolls down my throat, his eyes meet mine.

I nod as I whisper, "Okay."

TWENTY-FIVE

LIAM

Sunshine drifts through my bedroom window so tepidly that I'm sure it has to be insanely early in the morning. I would typically get up and head to the gym for a quick morning workout before starting my day, but as I remember Hannah is in my bed, I instantly melt into her.

The sweet floral scent of her perfume lingers on my sheets from her night of tossing and turning, but there is nothing quite as intoxicating as the feeling of her hair draped over my shirtless chest, her face only inches from my heart.

I press my lips to her forehead, a gentle gesture that I can only reserve for when she's asleep or not paying attention, without her psychoanalyzing it. However, the simple action bathes me in a calming sensation that I don't recognize, so maybe she's right to question it.

Slipping out of my crumpled navy sheets, I tiptoe out to the kitchen so as not to wake her from her slumber. Pots and pans line the counter as I maneuver the context of my cabinets to get to the griddle sitting at the back of the space. As I finally reach it, I pull it onto the counter and begin mixing boxed pancake mix. While homemade pancakes are irrefutably better, I can't will myself to make them at 7:00 AM on a Saturday morning.

Pancake batter hits the electric griddle with a sizzle as Hannah comes into view, her bright blonde hair disheveled as she rubs the sleep from her eyes.

"Good morning," Hannah yawns out as she approaches the counter.

"Morning." I smile up at her before returning to my task of removing golden-brown pancakes from the heat and piling them onto a ceramic plate. The single most convenient thing about pancake mix is that, despite it being the easiest thing under the sun to make, it still comes out looking impressive. I'm the master of adding water to powder and mixing.

"You made me breakfast..." The puzzled expression on Hannah's face has me questioning if this was too intimate of a decision.

I just thought that typically people get up in the morning and eat breakfast and it would be rude not to make something for her. Now, as my eyes meet hers, I realize that it tends to be a statement to make an overnight guest breakfast in the morning. While my intentions started out purely logical, the implications of it don't exactly deter me.

It's not an automatic death sentence to actually enjoy the company of the person you're sleeping with. I like Hannah. I'm not sure exactly how long that's been the case, but it's not the most foreign feeling to me. She, however, treats the idea as if it is my personal goal to ruin her life in the process.

With that thought, I choose my words carefully so as to not scare her off.

"It's just pancake mix, Hannah, relax. It's not a marriage proposal." I slide the plate across the island.

This seems to quell her anxiety. She moves to sit on a stool, her shoulders finally deflating as she reaches for the maple syrup, glugging it onto the short stack with little concern for the sugar coma it is sure to induce.

"Would you like some pancakes with your syrup?" I laugh as I sit down next to her and grab the bottle from her, drizzling a normal amount of syrup onto my pancakes.

"Oh, shut up, I'm not the first person to like maple syrup." She nudges her arm into mine as she lifts her fork to her mouth.

"Maybe not, but you are the first person I've met that I worry might actually willingly inject maple syrup into their veins."

Hannah nearly chokes on her bite as a chuckle breaks free, which plasters a grin to my lips. She recovers quickly. "Idiot," she says, but the insult doesn't meet her eyes as she grins.

Maple syrup lingers on her lips, and without a second thought I lean over, brushing my lips over hers. The sugary, rich, caramelly flavor lingers as my tongue ghosts over her bottom lip, causing her to melt into my touch.

Ding-dong.

The ring of my apartment doorbell startles us from our embrace. Hannah's surprised expression meets mine, but I'm just as confused.

"Who's at your door?"

"Do I look like I can see through walls?" I snip as I jump from my seat.

"Well, what do we do?" She's frazzled and it would honestly be cute if I wasn't concerned with who might be at my door.

"Uh..." I look around the room, the open floor plan of my

apartment now an inconvenience. "Go hang out in my bedroom for a while, I'll get this handled."

I lean in and tenderly kiss her; it's so instinctual it nearly tosses me off my axis. The nonchalant nature of it is terrifying, but I don't have the time to unpack that.

My hand swats her ass as she runs to my bedroom, my T-shirt from last night hanging loose on her small frame. The moment I open the door, I see quite possibly the worst person who could possibly show up while Hannah is in my apartment.

"Hey, Jackson, what's up?" I say as I wave him into my space despite wishing I could justifiably do anything but. He's drenched in sweat, his T-shirt and sweatpants clinging to his frame. "Did you...run here?" I can't hide the amusement that seeps into my words.

"What?" He looks confused until he looks down at his body. "Oh, hah. No, well...technically yes, but not *to* here. I was on my morning run."

"Something about physical fitness just made you think of me?" I slap him on the shoulder with a shit-eating grin. "I mean, I get it. I have a great body, so I don't blame you, but I don't see you like that, buddy."

"Fuck off," Jackson laughs as he swats my hand from his shoulder. "No, I wanted to talk to you about wedding stuff before I forget again."

"What about the wedding?" Though this will clearly be a loaded conversation, I want nothing more than for him to leave.

"Viv is worried about you and Hannah walking together. She seems to think something bad is going to happen if we don't change the lineup."

My tumultuous history with Hannah has become something of legend in our friend group, but most of it they've never seen. It's more implication based on our bickering, but no one, not even Jackson, knows the full extent of my history with her.

"Trust me, Jackson, we'll be fine. We're adults—I think we can play nice so as not to ruin our best friends' wedding." Not to mention, he's her brother, and it kind of bugs me that he assumes she wouldn't put our issues aside for the sake of him and Gen. "She loves you and Gen. Both together and as people. She'd never do something to ruin your wedding."

His confused expression makes me realize my misstep faster than my brain can register it. "I wouldn't let her, is what I mean. You have my word: I won't give her a single reason to have an outburst at your wedding."

I suddenly find myself pleading that my walls are thicker than I think, because I can't imagine Hannah would love to hear about her brother's lack of faith in her. We have our issues, I'll be the first to admit that, but I've never agreed with the way her family treats her and how little they think of her. It's not right, but it's not my place to say something, so I keep quiet most of the time.

"Thanks, man," Jackson says as he takes in my apartment, the normally pristine space a litter of discarded clothing, my coffee table still topped with two wine glasses, and my kitchen island clearly displaying two half-eaten plates of pancakes. "Uh...get laid last night?"

"Yeah, uh." I scratch the back of my neck, trying to think of a reason to get him to leave. The only solution I can come up with is the truth. "She's actually in my room right now, so if you could..." I wave toward the door.

"Oh, shit, yeah. Sorry about that. I should have called." He turns back toward the front door before turning around with a grin. "Have fun!"

As the door clicks shut behind him, I resist the urge to break out into laughter at the utter insanity of the situation. It's not uncommon for the guys to discuss my single life, as the rest of them are in long-term relationships, but even I know that if Jackson knew it was Hannah, he would probably gag at the realization.

"He's gone," I yell to Hannah a few seconds before I hear my bedroom door creak open. "It was your brother."

"What did he want?" she asks, but she doesn't seem to care.

I'm sure at this point she knows what was said, but to my shock she doesn't say anything about it. The painful reminder that she's used to it makes me want to pull her into my arms, but then I remember I've never been much better than her family.

Who does she have, then? It sure as hell has never been me.

"Just wanted to stop by on his run. Although, once he took in the state of my apartment, he deduced pretty quickly that someone was here."

"Did you tell him it was me?" Her eyes go wide as she asks.

"What? No, of course not! I just said there was a girl in my room and that he should go."

She nods, gnawing on her bottom lip. What she's thinking, I can't be sure. Her thoughtful expression morphs as a smile spreads quickly across her lips before she breaks out into laughter.

"Fucking Jackson." She shakes her head as she continues to laugh, sitting down at the island as if nothing happened.

"Yeah, fucking Jackson." I smile at her, my anxiety from before melting the moment her eyes meet mine.

Despite my insistence that she stay a bit longer, Hannah is insistent that she has to get back to her apartment.

"I have an audition coming up and I really need to rehearse," Hannah says as she frantically moves through my apartment, looking for her keys. Although they are sitting clear as day in the bowl on the entry table, I don't say anything. Her inability to find them is buying me precious time to convince her to stay.

"You could rehearse here!" I blurt out without realizing how frantic I sound, causing Hannah's eyes to lock on me with a perplexed expression.

I'm also confused.

"I don't have my sheet music, or my monologue...nor do I have my laptop with the accompaniment for the song."

"Do you have the sheet music and monologue in digital form, by any chance?" Why I won't let this go, I'm not sure; I just pray she doesn't register my desperation despite it being glaringly obvious.

"I guess I have them on the cloud, but that doesn't solve the track being on my laptop. It's fine, Liam, it's not a big deal. I'll just head home."

"I have a keyboard! I could play it," I blurt out.

Hannah looks up at me with her brows scrunched together. I can see her mind working a mile a minute behind her eyes. "You...play piano? How did I not know that?"

"And guitar."

Her wide, piercing green eyes stare up at me, the confusion enmeshed with what appears to be interest as she steps toward me. "Here I thought I knew everything about you."

"Happy to still be able to keep you on your toes." I grin down at her before pressing my lips to her forehead. I'd done it earlier this morning, but she was in a sleepy daze. This time, I don't miss the way she tenses at my tender touch.

"Okay...I'll stay." She doesn't say anything about the forehead kiss, which I'm thankful for.

I pull my silver keyboard from where it's lived for the past six months, untouched, at the back of my living room closet. I haven't had a lick of inspiration, so I've spent most of my time gaming or taking work home with me.

As I set the instrument onto its fold-out stand, Hannah steps up next to me, admiring the keyboard silently.

"Did you print the sheet music?" I ask as I turn the instrument on. It emits a faint electrical hum as it powers up.

"Yeah," Hannah says, reaching over to my printer and pulling off two matching sets of sheet music with "I Don't Know How to Love Him" scrawled across the top in big block letters.

"Jesus Christ Superstar?"

"How could you possibly know that?" She chuckles as she yanks the sheet music from my hands, revealing the smaller font below the song title indicating the show it's from. "Oh."

This appears to appease her as she hands me back the papers. I prop them against the music stand attached to the back of my keyboard and await her cue to start playing.

Hannah nods in my direction and my fingers begin to tickle the plastic ivory-colored keys, my hands gliding over the black and ivory with as much finesse as one would expect after six months of not playing at all.

The moment Hannah starts to sing, the hair on my arms stands to attention, her voice slipping up my neck in a way that sends shivers down my spine. I've heard her sing before, but never like this—never with her actually trying. I wouldn't consider singing along to Lady Gaga in the car to be trying, nor do I remember much from her forcing performances on us when she was little. This is different.

This is incredible.

I find myself wondering if her mom is aware of how talented her daughter is, or if she refuses to have faith in her abilities despite them being irrefutable.

As she embarks on what I assume to be the hard part of the song, she navigates it with grace. Hannah reaches for the highest note in the song, her finger pointing upward as she urges herself forward. She doesn't appear strained, so the moment the song comes to an end and Hannah tosses her sheet music in frustration, I find myself puzzled.

"What's wrong?"

"I messed up," she huffs, picking the papers back up off the couch and inspecting them for damage.

"I thought it sounded great," I say as I reach for her hand now holding the papers. "Hannah, you're insanely talented."

She allows my hand to linger for a moment before her eyes meet mine, a level of vulnerability in her gaze that I haven't seen in a long time.

"I'm serious, Hannah, you're amazing."

"Not amazing enough to book a job," Hannah says. She pulls her hand from mine, but she doesn't walk away.

"It'll happen, it just hasn't been the right job."

The room grows quiet—too quiet. Yet, it's not uncomfortable; it's a content kind of silence.

"Thank you." Hannah's faint voice lingers in the air, the whisper barely leaving her lips.

I wrap her up in my embrace and instinctively take note of her rhythmic breathing as she rests against me. I am sure of one thing.

I'm completely fucked.

TWENTY-SIX

LIAM

The moment my ass meets the leather seats in the back of our Uber to head to the next bar, I realize for the first time since we embarked on this bizarre bachelor party evening that I might actually be drunk.

Jackson asked not to go to a strip club, and while I get it, also...what the hell, man? Not everyone here is about to get married. Even married guys like strip clubs—you don't have to touch in order to watch.

Whatever. I lost that fight to Wes and Jackson pretty quickly.

As we pull up in front of Enigma, I can't resist letting out a groan.

The entrance to Enigma resembles an old vintage movie theater, which I think it actually might be. A glowing marquee comes into view, reading something about their nightly drink specials, but as we enter the club, it shifts from bright city lights to complete darkness. Strobe lights of varying speeds give us a faint view of the rest of the crowd.

A U-shaped bar sits in the middle of the room and flows back into the dance floor, which is flush with the edge of a stage. The DJ is set up center stage toward the front with a few girls lined up down the stairs to stage left, waiting to put in their requested song for the night.

Bumping music matches up perfectly with the light intervals, making it nearly impossible to ascertain faces amongst the crowd. However, I spot the unmistakable head of shoulder-length bright blonde hair facing away from me and know instantly who she is.

"Wes...what did you do?" I don't dare pry my eyes from Hannah for fear that she might disappear into the crowd.

"What do you mean?" he says as he grabs his double shot off the edge of the bar, placing a twenty-dollar bill in its place.

"Are the girls here?"

"Shouldn't be, why?" Wes scans the room, but the lights make it nearly impossible to make out faces.

We stop questioning it the moment our eyes land on Jackson, who is now pressed flush against his soon-to-be-wife near the far wall.

"Jackson..." Wes and I say in unison as we realize exactly what he did.

Gen's bachelorette and Jackson's bachelor party were scheduled for the same night on purpose, but we were intentional in trying to choose places that wouldn't cause us to cross paths. When Jackson mentioned that he wanted to go to Enigma, I found it random, but not so much that it caused concern.

Now I realize it wasn't random at all.

Wes is still silently scanning the room and I notice when his eyes land on the radiant redhead only feet away from Gen.

"Go find your wife," I say with a laugh, waving him in her direction, "I'll go do...something."

He doesn't question me as he steps into the darkness, barreling directly toward Savannah with a grin plastered across his lips.

My eyes lock on Hannah once again, but this time she's staring back at me. As much as I want to approach her, claim her mouth for the entire world to see, my feet are cemented in place. I wish I could tell what she is thinking right now, but something about the way she turns away from me to move fluidly against a petite girl with purple hair causes my stomach to bottom out.

I've never considered myself a jealous man. Typically, I'm pretty even-keeled and neutral, even if someone I'm seeing flirts with someone else. However, the moment Hannah's lips graze the shell of the girl's ear before pressing to the flesh of her neck, I see red.

Darting across the room, I latch my fingers around Hannah's wrist without warning, pulling her away from the embrace of the girl. Within seconds I have her pinned with her face against a wall, desire and anger creating a toxic combination.

"What the hell do you think you're doing?" I grit out as my lips ghost over the shell of her ear, causing a shiver to run down her spine.

"Dancing," she responds breathlessly.

"I don't appreciate being lied to." My jaw nearly hurts with how hard I clench it as I force out the words. I yank her head back by a fistful of her hair, her face now a whisper from my own.

At first, she winces, but then she quickly melts into my touch. "It's not like it matters. Not like we're together."

Her breathy response shoots straight to my cock but is quickly tampered by her words.

"We may not have a label for it, princess. But I need to make one thing clear—you're *mine*." A whimper leaves her lips as I tighten my hold. "I may not own your heart, but you so much as let another person touch you like that again and you'll see for the first time just how mean I can actually be."

I expect her to push me off of her, to yank herself out of my hold, yet when the moment allows her to escape my grasp, she only pushes back into me further. A groan rolls off my tongue as I press into her more, and her breath hitches at my obvious hardness.

"What's going on over here?" Wes's confused but clearly amused voice travels from behind us, causing me to yank away from Hannah in an instant.

"Nothing." I try to catch my breath without being explicitly obvious.

Wes isn't known to be an idiot, and I'm sure he has a good idea of what was just happening, but I'm thankful he isn't much for gossip.

"Liam was just being an asshole, per usual." Hannah pins me with a glare that at first I think is an act, but as her gaze remains hard as stone and Wes's eyes divert to look at me, I know I must have misstepped in some way.

"For a second I thought you two were..."

"Not a chance in hell, man." I force a laugh, but Hannah's glare only intensifies. The anger in her expression is only matched by the obvious hurt in her eyes. I want to reassure her that I only said it because I don't want it to get ruined, but when I go to close the distance between us the moment Wes walks away, Hannah slips out of my grasp.

CHAPTER TWENTY-SIX

"Hannah, I—" I circle her wrist only for her to yank it away instantly.

"Don't start." She doesn't sound angry, she sounds defeated...and that's honestly worse.

TWENTY-SEVEN

HANNAH

The anxiety stirring in my stomach doesn't abate as the small alert sound from the Outlook app on my phone dings out. I know exactly what it holds, and it could either be the best thing to happen to me or just another rejection masked as a cast list to add to my list of failures. I can feel the excitement mounting with each second.

When I didn't receive a phone call last week, I knew it was probably indicative of a rejection, but I've been holding out until the cast list goes up.

I open the email to find the cast list entirely void of my name. While I want to say I'm surprised, I'm not in the slightest. There have been auditions where I thought I did amazing and got rejected—those hurt like a bitch—but I knew I tanked this one, so the rejection is just a reminder of my colossal mistake. However, it doesn't make it hurt any less.

Blood whooshes in my ears as I attempt to quell my unrest. Despite my disappointment, I scan the cast list for familiar names.

Luna Alvarez is Havannah Rose
Esme Eaton is Annabeth Cash
Aaron Hessville is Richard Callahan
Penelope Edmonds is Rosalyn Worthington

My stomach sinks as my eyes lock onto Esme's name. I didn't even know she auditioned for this production, so it's a discomforting combination of disappointment and irritation that someone who hurt me so much is still managing to win over me. My lip quirks upward as I notice that while Luna didn't book Annabeth like she'd originally been hoping for, she did book the other main lead, Havannah.

HANNAH

congrats on getting havannah! you're gonna kill it

LUNA

thanks hannah! heading up to nyc this week to start rehearsals before the tour starts in a few months, fingers crossed it goes well

it will

thank you

Switching back to scroll through my emails, I come across one I know all too well: the newsletter of upcoming auditions that I qualify for. Most of these are in New York City, and while I know that moving back would make more sense, a cold shiver passes over me at the thought. New York was such a lonely experience for starting my life both as an adult and in the industry.

I exit out of my email and switch instantly to my text

thread with Liam, one of which I realize that, outside of work-related texts, we haven't used in years.

HANNAH

come over tonight

LIAM

do I look like your own personal fuck toy?

ask nicely

fuck off

come over tonight...please

was already planning on it princess. see you at 6

My doorbell rings at 6:00 PM sharp. Despite expecting Liam, the sudden noise still causes me to jump. Sage has been working late at her new bartending job the past few nights, so I've grown accustomed to stark silence in the evening. The aroma of pasta sauce and cheese carries from the kitchen into the entryway along with me.

The moment I open the door, Liam walks inside with a backpack slung over his shoulder. As he enters my space, I step into him without a second thought, my face pressing against his T-shirt-clad chest. He wraps his arms around my shoulders as he presses his lips to my forehead.

"You're awfully sweet today...should I be scared?" He laughs as he pulls back slightly to look down at me.

My emotional exhaustion melts the moment his eyes meet mine. I push his chest in a joking manner as I step out of his grasp.

"Actually, yes. You should be scared," I say as we step into the kitchen, where the smell of lasagna is far more pungent.

"You...cooked?" The shocked look on his face is almost enough to invoke my anger, but even I know that cooking isn't exactly my forte.

"Don't jump off the balcony quite yet—it's a frozen lasagna."

The relief that I see physically wash over Liam makes me laugh, but I try to curb it because the last thing I need is him thinking he's funny.

"So..." he says as he steps toward the stove, where the lasagna sits fresh out of the oven, the smell of the bubbling cheese wafting into the space. "What is the occasion?"

"What do you mean?"

"You've never invited me over."

"Not true, you've been over here dozens of times." I wave my hand in dismissal.

"Yeah...with Sage. *You* have never requested I be here..."

"*Oh,*" I mouth with little bravado.

The weight of my asking him to come over hasn't hit me until now, but as he steps into me again, I feel it melt down my back.

"It's not a bad thing that you want me here, Hannah." Liam pushes my hair behind my ear as his eyes meet mine. "What's going on?"

"Shit day." I'm typically rather forthcoming, but something feels uncomfortably intimate about the way he's looking at me right now.

I'm thankful he doesn't pry or try to push me to open up; he just steps toward the cabinet that houses the dinnerware and pulls out two dishes. I would question why he knows his way around here so well, but then I remember his friendship with Sage.

I don't know why I've never really felt jealous of them.

They're together a lot, but I know it's not an issue. Whether it's due to Sage's insistence in shutting him down in those early months of knowing each other or her not-so-thinly veiled crush on his best friend Gabe, I've never questioned if she's something to worry about.

Not to say I should be worried about him being interested in another woman. He's a free man, after all.

"What's going on in that head of yours?" he asks as he turns back to me, his eyes pinning me with a knowing look.

I hate that he can do that. His ability to read me like an open book terrifies me, but it also hurts when I remember that there have been so many times he's intentionally disregarded my feelings.

"Nothing," I say, forcing a grin, but it dies the moment I look up at him. "I was rejected for a show I really wanted earlier. Just put me in a funk."

This seems to quell his interest as his shoulders deflate. "You'll book something soon."

I don't miss the warmth that blooms in my stomach as he reassures me; it has way more weight coming from him than when Jackson says it.

"Thank you," I mumble.

"You're welcome. Now, no more of this." He points to my frown before placing a tentative kiss on my lips. "Let's eat."

The lasagna is passable, but nothing to write home about. There is no unique flavor or pizzazz, just a basic frozen lasagna. Liam seems to enjoy it though, as he has already eaten two pieces. He wipes his mouth with a paper towel and cleans away the rest of the sauce, causing my gaze to linger a moment too long.

"Eyes up here, princess." He winks as the realization dawns on me that I have been staring.

"Shut up," I scoff before taking the last bite of my food.

The moment the plates land in the sink, Liam is on me like a fly on honey, his lips grazing the shell of my ear as I attempt to wash the dishes.

"Liam," I sigh. I intend it to be a reprimand, but it comes out more akin to an invitation.

"Yes?" he murmurs, the rough rasp of his voice vibrating off of my pebbled skin. As his tongue circles that sensitive place below my ear, I feel myself lean back into him. His breath tickles me and he doesn't yield as he stands firmly, allowing my weight against him.

Butterflies swarm my stomach. Their fluttering wings and rapid motions churn my insides like a living, breathing entity. As his tongue grazes my wet, sensitive skin, I let out a soft moan. The sponge squelches in my hand as I squeeze it tight, the residual moisture and soap slipping between my fingers and dripping back into the sink.

"But..." I gasp, my voice barely audible, "I bought pie."

Liam pauses before reaching onto the counter to grab a paper towel and pat my hands dry. "Okay, pie." His words linger in the air far longer than they justify.

As I pull the packaged chocolate pie from the fridge, Liam grabs it from me and sets it on the counter. "Whipped cream?"

"Wha—" The innocent question dies on my tongue as he swipes the edge of the pie with his finger and brings it to his lips. He licks the rich mousse off his finger at a snail's pace, the languid movement shooting a bolt of electricity straight to my core.

My fingers trace the back of the refrigerator, grazing a box of baking soda before they close around the cold metal cylinder. I pull the carton away from the door and peer inside at what looks like a brand-new can of whipped cream. God bless Sage and her weirdly specific shopping choices; I need to remember to replace it tomorrow.

"Whipped cream," I say with a grin, and my breath catches in my throat as his eyes meet mine.

Liam's hand wraps around my own as he pulls the bottle from my grasp and snaps the cap off. He squirts some of the frothy milk-based foam into his mouth before he invades my space once more.

"Open," he demands.

I open my mouth as wide as I can, prompting him to press the cold metal dispenser tip to my tongue. My mouth is instantly flooded with a cold, sweet coating, so delicious that it's only matched by his advance. Liam's lips melt into mine before he pries my mouth open with his tongue. Our tongues intertwine as the sugary-sweet flavor consumes my senses.

As quickly as his mouth is on me, it's gone again. He steps back only inches before he lifts the bottle to my collarbone and sprays a dollop of whipped cream along my skin. The memory of a few weeks ago consumes me, the intense wave of desire from that day only a fraction of the need I feel now.

Liam swirls his tongue against my heated skin, lapping up any remnant of the sweetness.

The oversized flannel I'm wearing appears to be of inconvenience to him and he attempts to release the buttons without setting down the whipped cream.

"Unbutton your shirt," he demands, nodding downward.

I want to protest, if only on principle, but any will I have not to give into him dies before it leaves my lips.

With every button I spring free, I watch his eyes grow headier. If he's impatient, he doesn't show it as he intently watches me pull each button through its respective hole. As my unfastening ventures past my sternum, it becomes abundantly clear that I am not wearing a bra below my shirt. I intentionally allow the shirt to rest over each breast, leaving only a sliver of skin visible once I'm done fulfilling his request.

My breath catches in my throat as he steps toward me, so close that I have to tilt my head upward. I think he might kiss me, but instead he dips down to kneel in front of me, his eyes not leaving my own, his face level with my chest as it heaves in anticipation.

I expect him to reach for the waistband of my leggings, but I gasp when the cold air hits my nipples as my shirt flutters to the floor.

"Much better," he whispers as he grins up at me. He presses the cold nozzle of the whipped cream can to my flesh once more, this time against my left nipple. The frigid metal causes my sensitive nipple to pucker before it's covered in the creamy froth, managing to make it colder than before.

Liam remedies any discomfort within seconds as his mouth closes around my tender flesh, biting down on the stiff peak as he laps at the sugary substance. A gasp falls from my mouth at the sensation, which only encourages him further. He releases my nipple with a pop before he shifts to my right breast and sprays whipped cream against my flesh like before. This time, when Liam's mouth latches onto my nipple, the gasp that leaves my lips earns me a groan from the intoxicating man kneeling in front of me.

The moment he releases my nipple, he gazes up at me, setting the cylinder on the tiled floor.

What on God's green earth is he doing?

The question never graces my lips as he curls his fingers around the waistband of my leggings and tugs them down to the floor in a swift motion. Liam taps my thigh, urging me to lift my legs one by one. I do as he instructs me to, allowing the ball of cotton to land next to my foot.

Whipped cream coats my inner thigh within seconds before Liam's tongue is lapping at my skin once more, the scruff of his jawline tickling the sensitive flesh only centimeters from where I want him.

His tongue lingers against the seam of my panties, but he doesn't nudge them to the side. He sits back on his heels.

"We should eat the pie before it gets too warm."

My breathy suggestion is futile—Liam shakes his head.

"Unless you want me to lick chocolate mousse off your pussy, then fuck the damn pie. I'm quite famished, but I couldn't care less about pie." He grins as he yanks me forward.

"How could you still be hungry? We just had dinner." I grin down at him, and he rolls his eyes in response. He chuckles before yanking my panties so hard that it pulls a yelp from my lungs.

The sound of lace ripping fills the room and, while I should care about the wasted underwear, I don't. The pale pink scrap of fabric falls to the ground as Liam leans in further, his hot breath ghosting over my wet slit. The mixture of sensations causes a chill to roll down my spine, but nothing prepares me for the jolt of pleasure that washes over me the moment his tongue traces me from bottom to top, followed by him swirling his tongue over my clit so meticulously that I think I might faint.

"Liam," I gasp, combing my fingers through his hair. Despite our current predicament, it still sits perfectly coiffed. That needs to be remedied immediately, so I grasp his hair firmly at the root.

He grins up at me, but his tongue doesn't leave my flesh. It only pushes me further into my oblivion.

My orgasm overtakes me like a freight train, the tingling sensation that crawls up my spine sending me into an all-consuming haze. My thighs quiver as he sucks my clit, not relenting as he stretches my ecstasy further than I think possible. I've had many orgasms in my lifetime—hell, I've had my fair share of partners—but the few orgasms I've received from Liam have been pulled from me so effortlessly and with such intensity that it has me in awe.

He manages to rule over my body with such finesse and confidence that it's starting to terrify me to think about what happens when this ends.

I refuse to linger on that right now, though.

Liam's lips press to my inner thigh as he ghosts a tender kiss against my flesh. His hand rests on the counter as he pulls himself up to stand. I watch as his tongue swipes over his bottom lip, wiping my arousal away, but the memory lingers.

My chest heaves as I attempt to catch my breath, my orgasm so intense that I think I forgot to breathe.

"So, pie?" He grins.

"Yes, pie."

TWENTY-EIGHT

LIAM

A blaring noise reverberates through the air. I jerk up in bed, blinded by the light streaming through the blinds and into my sleepy eyes. My phone wiggles on the nightstand, vibrating against a glass of water and making a telltale clink. A knot tightens in my stomach as I grab my phone and clumsily punch the answer button on the screen before pressing it to my ear.

"Hello?" My groggy voice is raspy and faint.

"Are you coming in?" At first I think it's my dad, but as I come to, I realize the voice on the other end of the phone is far too calm to be him.

"Huh?" I rub my eyes, both to dissolve the physical effects of sleep and to block out the sun.

"Are you coming into work? It's almost ten." The concern in their voice jerks me out of my daze, and the realization that it's Jackson causes my stomach to hit the floor.

It's Monday and, now that I think of it, I don't think I set my alarm last night—and clearly neither did Hannah.

"Shit!" I jump out of bed, stirring Hannah in the process. "I'll get there as quickly as possible."

"Hey man, don't sweat it. Hannah isn't here either, must be something in the air. Have you heard from her?"

"Why would I have heard from Hannah?" It comes out far too panicked and defensive for what the question warrants.

"Uh, because she might have texted you to let you know she's not coming in?" If he's suspicious, he doesn't let it show.

"Oh, uh, no, I haven't heard from her. I'll see you in a bit, man, I gotta get ready."

"Roger that. See you in a bit."

The clear click on the other end of the phone spurs me into action as I toss my phone onto the sheets. I desperately want to crawl back into bed; the beautiful blonde still fast asleep has me considering making up an emergency.

No, Liam. That's a terrible idea.

"Hannah." I attempt to whisper but it comes out more like a frantic gasp.

She, however, doesn't budge in the slightest.

"*Hannah.*" I try to be louder, to little avail.

She starts to stir, causing the white satin sheet draped across her naked body to fall down to her waist. I groan at the sight, tamping down any carnal thoughts I have in this moment. We don't have the time, but I wish we did.

I could go for round four.

"Princess," I whisper against her neck before pressing a featherlight kiss against her flesh. The small gesture is clearly a terrible mistake as the blood flow in my body shifts instantly.

She groans against her pillow, trying to ignore me.

"Hannah, we're late for work."

Everything up until this point hasn't ignited her urgency, but this seems to.

"What?" She's still half asleep and hazy, but I'm hopeful the question means she's getting up.

"It's 10:00 AM. We overslept for work. You need to get up," I say as I shift to sit on the edge of the bed, abandoning any sense of temptation to crawl back into the sheets with her.

Hannah lays there for a moment longer, but I can see the exact moment my words register on her face only seconds before she shoots up to a sitting position and yanks the sheets off of her bare body. "Shit! Why didn't you wake me up?!" She shuffles around the room in a frantic, discombobulated state.

"That's what I was literally doing..." I stand to start my shuffle around the space too, thankful that I had the forethought to bring clothes for today.

I finish getting ready in record time, pulling my socks on as I stumble from Hannah's room, my shoes hanging from one hand as I attempt to pull the cotton over my feet. Unfortunately, I don't realize until it's too late that Sage is home.

"Fancy seeing you here..." Sage grins up at me from behind her cup of coffee, the steam from the mug's contents billowing up around her chin.

"Don't start with me, Sage. I'm in no mood."

"Should be—at least from what I could hear, you should be in a great one."

Mortification doesn't even begin to explain the feeling crawling up from the pit of my stomach. I've been intentional in my quest to prevent people from knowing about me and Hannah. When people know, it encourages scrutiny; scrutiny I'm not ready to try to combat. However, there isn't much denying what happened last night.

"People hook up, don't read too much into it." I scoff as I pull on my left shoe. "I'd appreciate it if you didn't tell anyone about this. Doesn't have to be a big deal."

"Yeah, no big deal." Hannah's voice carries from behind

me and, if I didn't know any better, I'd say she sounds disappointed at my response.

She can't really be wanting people to know at this point, could she?

"I won't say a thing...besides, I'm not sure anyone would believe me if I did say it."

Mine and Hannah's tumultuous friendship, if you'd call it that, has never lent itself to the idea of us being together...or involved, as I'm not entirely sure what we are at this point.

As I shuffle around in my bag, the busted zipper rendering its contents on full display, I realize I don't have a tie with me. I could have sworn I'd brought a tie. While wearing a tie is encouraged, and I always wear one to work, people often forgo it for a more modern vibe, so I guess I can lean into that.

"Here." Hannah returns after disappearing back into her room, a blue- and white-striped tie in hand.

"Why do you have a tie?" I raise a brow, which pulls a laugh from Hannah.

"Okay, pervy..." She tosses the tie around my shoulders to sit across the back of my neck before she begins crisscrossing the fabric over itself, shifting her voice into an almost-whisper. "No, this tie isn't for that. Although, you're more than welcome to delve into that image another time. It was a gift for Jackson for the rehearsal, but I can get another."

As if I could forget that Sage is sitting mere feet away from us, she clears her throat, making it clear that Hannah's attempt at being quiet was not successful. Despite my irritation, I shrug Sage off.

She loves a good piece of gossip, but is fiercely loyal when it comes to things she's told in confidence or is asked to keep under wraps. Sage will be the first to tell you about her cousin's sister's brother-in-law's infidelity, but she would never divulge our secrets.

If anyone was to bear witness to this, I'm glad it was Sage and not Savannah.

"Ready to go?" Hannah taps on my shoulders after crafting my tie into a Windsor knot.

"Yeah," I say quietly, grinning down at her, still stuck on the fact that she managed to tie the knot so perfectly. It took me years of experience to make it not look like a five-year-old did it.

"Bye, you two," Sage yells as we head out the door, the amusement in her voice grinding my gears.

In the parking garage, I instantly start looking for my car.

"Oh, we can just take mine." Hannah speaks so matter-of-factly I almost say yes.

"No, I'll just take my car." I clear my throat as I reach for my keys. "We can't show up at the office together."

Hannah doesn't appear to like this answer as she huffs and walks away to her car without so much as a kiss goodbye.

Even if she might not like it, my refusal to flaunt whatever this is is with the intent to protect us both from the ridicule it would ignite. Not only would our families have a field day, but she works under me at not just my job, but my dad's company. It's so unprofessional it isn't even funny, but I can't shake the way the look on her face made my stomach plummet.

I find my car quickly and speed over to the office, thankful it's only about a fifteen-minute drive from Hannah's now that rush hour is over. Swerving in and out of lanes littered with parked cars and pedestrians, I find my parking spot in the garage with ease, thankful no one chose today to disregard the sign marked *Liam Park.*

My loafers clack against the tile floor as I step out of the elevator, the front desk of Baker & Park more of a warning than an invitation. I have no doubt in my mind that, despite Jackson's insistence that he'd keep it under wraps, my dad knows I was late today.

"Good morning, Mr. Park!" The receptionist grins from ear to ear.

I smile back. "Please, Pen. That's my dad—call me Liam. Being called Mr. Park makes my skin crawl."

"Of course. Good morning, Liam."

"Good morning, Penelope."

I walk past Hannah's desk as I barrel into my office, noting she's not sitting in front of her computer. She is typically the type to start her work the moment she walks in the door and doesn't typically say hello to me or Jackson until at least 11:00 AM.

As the leather of my briefcase hits the dark mahogany of my desk, Jackson clears his throat. I look at him, my movement only stuttering slightly at the sight of Hannah looking at me too.

"What's up?" I try to act nonchalant, but the way her green eyes bore into me has my stomach doing somersaults.

"Hannah just got in." At first I think Jackson is mentioning it because he clearly has caught on, but he just laughs. "She said she overslept too."

She couldn't come up with a more creative reason? Jesus, Hannah.

"Yeah, uh. I was up late. Raid night." This appears to quell his interest.

I haven't had as much time to game as I once did, which sucks. That being said, I also know it's a necessary evil to face when building a life and career in your twenties.

"Raid night? What, can't find friends in real life—have to

spend your nights playing video games with strangers online?" Hannah says.

The bite in her words doesn't meet her eyes, but I retort anyway. "At least I *have* friends. Online or not, at least people actually enjoy talking to me."

We've thrown these exact jabs at one another before; it's so common in my memory that I'm shocked Jackson doesn't realize just how fabricated our animosity is. To my delight, he doesn't say anything to imply he doesn't buy into the narrative.

"Damn, it's 10:45 AM. Talk about record time. Next time, at least let me finish my second cup of coffee before I have to be front row to the feud between the two of you."

"Whatever, man," I say as I make my way back to my desk. The stack of post-it notes from the morning I've missed causes me to sigh. Something tells me this is going to be far from a quick Monday.

TWENTY-NINE

HANNAH

The moment Jackson leaves, I find my way into his office and continue my workday from his desk. For the most part, I've been getting out of the office by 6:00 PM, but after showing up so late this morning, I opted to make up the time this evening.

Apparently, Liam had the same thought.

Silence sets in pretty quickly and I'm a bit surprised at our ability to focus on our work tasks so well after how things have been between us recently.

The ticking of the analog clock on the wall is a metronome of passing time, each minute seeming to stretch into oblivion. Liam hasn't looked up from the stack of papers in front of him in over an hour, the clock striking 7:00 PM a reminder of how long that's actually been.

"Everything okay?" I cut through the silence, earning a melancholy smile from Liam. My stomach ignites, swirling with anticipation but dying just as quickly when I see his exhausted eyes.

"Yeah, just trying to make sense of this transcript. I think I'm missing part of it." He leans back in his seat before bringing his hand to his eyes, wiping away the stale air that has settled over his skin.

Before I realize I'm moving, I'm standing at his side, peering over his arm to get a look at the paper in front of him. "Have you looked into the digital file? I know you prefer when you're given the printed-out version, but every document that comes into Baker & Park is catalogued digitally too. Maybe the missing snippet is just a matter of a lost piece of paper."

This lightens his expression, which makes me smile. "That's a fantastic idea, Hannah. Can you print that out for me?"

"Sure." I grin.

Liam's hand wraps around my wrist as I attempt to walk away from him, stopping me.

"Did you need something else?" My concerned voice seems to loosen Liam's grip and he drops his hand. I want to know what he was going to say, but I see his desire to say it leave just as quickly.

"Oh, uh. No, thank you, Hannah. Just get that printed for me."

I do as he asks, setting the exact same transcript he'd been inspecting in front of him, except it includes the missing block of text that he had been talking about.

"This is perfect, thank you." He is being weirdly kind today, but I'd like to attribute that to a night filled with multiple orgasms. However, the same great night has also led to us both being utterly exhausted today.

Stepping behind his chair, I place my hands on his shoulders, applying pressure against the back of his shoulders with my thumbs. He groans, leaning back from the desk, allowing my touch to consume his attention. As my fingers knead into his skin, I can almost see the tension melting off him. I want to take credit for that, want it to be because of my touch, but I'm sure his body would react just the same if any other person were to massage his shoulders.

I don't know why, but that thought stings... I like the idea of me being a factor in his comfort.

My fingers continue to push into his flesh, and the more pressure I apply, the louder his groans—both of pain and pleasure—seep into the air.

"Hannah." The way he says my name is like a symphony, so intoxicating that I think he could convince me of anything in this moment.

"Yes?"

"Come here." His hand lands against his leg, inviting me forward.

I do as he requests and sit on his lap, facing inward with my legs between his so I can look at him.

"Thank you."

"It's just a massage."

"That's not what I mean, Hannah." His eyes lock on mine as he speaks, but I shuffle through my thoughts at lightning speed, searching for why he would be expressing gratitude at all.

"For what, then?"

He sighs as he looks down at my exposed shoulder, my pale pink blouse pressed up to expose my flesh. "I don't think you realize how much you've helped me recently. I know you see this as just sex, but even if that's so, it's been what I've needed."

Liam's vulnerability nearly throws me off my axis. I've only seen him be this exposed one other time in our lives, so the weight of it sets in and doesn't relent. Something he says sticks in my mind.

You see this as just sex.

Is he implying that he doesn't?

I want to ask; I want to delve into it further. I want to crack open his head like a coconut and peer inside to get the answers to every question I've ever wanted to know.

I settle for honesty, my voice barely a whisper. "I don't see this as just sex."

Liam nods for a moment before pressing his lips to my shoulder. He doesn't reassure me that he feels the same, doesn't try to pry into what I mean. His lips linger against my skin, a tether between the two of us.

The knowledge that this isn't just sex for either of us should bring me solace, but I quickly remember that I thought that last time, too. This isn't the first time Liam and I have given into our desires and my heart got mangled in the process. I can't rely simply on implication this time around because my compass when it comes to Liam's psyche is, and has always been, skewed.

"Liam, how do you feel about me?"

At first, I think that he doesn't hear me, and I'm prepared to repeat myself, but then he quietly speaks. "I feel how you feel about me. We don't need to unpack that right now."

His lack of dedication to a solid answer makes my stomach plummet, but the hope that it ignites leaves me somewhere in the middle.

"Stay with me tonight," Liam mumbles against my skin as his arms wrap tighter around my middle. Us staying at each other's place has become increasingly commonplace, and while I want to merely exist in the feeling it gives me, I struggle to tamp down the fears that very same concept ignites inside my gut.

My trust in him has been misguided before, and while I

know with everything in me that I shouldn't allow him to invade my heart again, I worry that he already has.

Reaching up, I intertwine my fingers with his. My eyes linger on his lips resting against my skin, the sensation a direct arrow to my heart.

"Okay."

THIRTY

LIAM

I used to hate these bi-weekly meetings with my dad, but in the past few months, I've grown to miss their frequency. It used to be like clockwork: every other Thursday morning we would meet in his office to discuss what I've done, how I'm approaching certain things, and his plans for retirement and where I fall into that.

However, he's canceled our last two meetings, and one a couple months ago. I know he's insanely busy with Mr. Baker being less present, but I found a lot of comfort in touching base with him every so often.

I'll be the first to admit that I've spent the past few weeks... distracted. Hannah and I have fallen into a rhythm both in the office and at home. Most nights she's at my place, but sometimes we make our way over to hers. Although, I'll admit I've avoided her place like the plague since Sage caught me leaving in the morning a couple weeks ago.

Thanksgiving was weird. Hannah's parents didn't come up, so she defaulted to being with my parents here in Atlanta. While in the past I wouldn't even think twice about it, the change in our relationship has led to...less-than-opportune situations transpiring at the hand of our parents. I hate to admit it, but I'm glad her parents didn't come up from Live Oak and didn't require Jackson and Hannah to come visit them.

I don't like the way Hannah's mom treats her, and the further in I get with her, the more it pisses me off to watch and not say anything.

As I step out of the threshold to my dad's space, I notice a random brunette sitting at Hannah's desk down the hall. It's not uncommon for temps to fill in for our assistants when they're out of town, but I wasn't aware Hannah had a trip coming up.

Weird.

I walk past the temp without so much as a hello.

"Where's your sister?" I ask Jackson.

"She's in New York."

"What do you mean she's in New York?" I try to quell the panic in my response, but there's no hiding it—I'm freaking out.

Why would she go back to New York without so much as telling me? Does she really think the approach to whatever this is between us is to run back to New York without saying anything?

"I mean...she's in New York?" Jackson quirks a brow, a confused expression plaguing him.

In the past, I would take this as an opportunity to express how glad I am to have Hannah out of my hair, but as my stomach sours and I worry I may throw up, I realize that things have shifted far more than I'd originally thought.

How the hell did we get here?

"When does she come back?"

Jackson just shrugs at my question as he shifts his attention back to his computer. I feel like he should know when his sister is supposed to return from New York City. Does that mean she isn't coming back?

LIAM

when do you get back?

I stuff my phone back into my pants pocket as I attempt not to pace back and forth in our office. If Jackson sees through my attempts to hide why I'm frantic, he doesn't make it known. He just taps away at his keyboard, the sound of the clicks mixing with the ticking of the clock on the wall, my patience wearing with every passing sound.

Pulling my suit jacket off the back of my black desk chair, I push my arms through the sleeves, finding solace in the way the scratchy fabric grounds me.

"Where are you going?" Jackson looks up from his computer, a crease in his brow.

"Out." I throw my bag over my shoulder before fastening one button on my jacket, enough to secure it, but not so much that it looks weird.

"When are you coming back?"

"Dunno," I respond as I barrel out of the office, not so much as a goodbye leaving my lips. I turn to the unfamiliar female at Hannah's desk with a forced smile.

"Due to unforeseen circumstances, I'm going to be out of office. Do you have access to my calendar?"

"Yes, Mr. Park. Your assistant left me with all the logins."

"Great, please clear my schedule for today and tomorrow. Let them know that I'm sorry for the short notice, but that an emergency came up."

"Yes, sir," she awkwardly responds as she pulls up my

Google calendar, the same calendar that is filled to the brim with colorful meeting and engagement tiles.

"Thank you." I don't so much as ask her name as I step away, walking past my dad's office without even attempting to inform him of my pending absence. He'll figure it out...or he'll blow up my phone. Either way, it's done.

I step out into the chilly late November air with little concern for my decorum. Baker & Park employees mix with pedestrians on the street as I emerge from the building, hailing a cab, not caring where I'm going.

I'll figure it out when I get there.

THIRTY-ONE

HANNAH

The smell of roasted chestnuts and cinnamon wafts through the air as I wander down the sidewalk. The snow lightly dusts everything in sight, and the twinkling lights draped over every storefront create a merry ambiance. I watch as children run around with their parents, squealing with delight at the decorations and holiday window displays. To my surprise, even with Thanksgiving festivities being last week, this winter wonderland has wiped away the anxiety that New York City usually brings me.

Coming back to New York to audition was something I went back and forth on. While a lot of shows do hold auditions in Atlanta and Chicago, some only do a day or two in New York City. The city that never sleeps may be a necessary evil when it comes to the industry I chose, but coming back has only secured in my mind that I have no interest in living here unless it's specifically for a show.

"Hey, Blondie, would ya move?!" A white-haired man in a checkered brown suit, leaning heavily on a walking cane, pauses beside me on the sidewalk. He glances at me before thrusting his cane forward to jab me in the leg. His watery blue eyes twinkle with something like amusement as he limps away, resting most of his weight on the cane in his hand. I can hear him chuckling softly, even as I rub my bruised thigh and wonder why he chose to make a spectacle of me.

As I run my fingers over the tender area of my thigh that he just jabbed, my eyes linger on a group of women in black leotards and tights warming up only a few feet down the sidewalk. The studio isn't far from the theater district, so it's unsurprising that I would come across familiar faces. One figure stands out instantly. Luna is standing with the group of women, dressed in her rehearsal blacks. Her tanned olive skin and dark hair pulled up in a tight knot are easy to make out against the all-black ensemble. Our eyes meet, and I know she has seen me. She quickly excuses herself from the group and rushes over to me.

"Oh my God, Hannah! What are you doing here?" Her short arms wrap around my neck as she pulls me into a tight hug. The soft scent of lilacs flows from the top of her head, consuming my senses and lulling me into a calmed state. A friendly face in the chaos of New York City is a welcome reprieve to my anxiety after attempting to hail a cab during the busiest time of the evening.

"There are a few auditions in the city over the next few days, so I decided to come back for a bit." I smile at her, but the pleasant expression dies nearly instantly as another familiar face comes into my view. She's facing away as she talks to a petite brunette that I've never seen before. Our eyes lock, and I'm immediately transfixed by her piercing azure gaze. She pushes her fiery red hair over one shoulder, but her eyes don't leave mine. Her glance feels almost electrifying, and I am left wordless as my heart pounds in my chest. The mixture of intrigue and despair consumes me as she starts to walk toward us, abandoning her previous conversation with little regard.

Esme Eaton.

While I've embarrassingly kept up with her life via social media, I've found myself checking in less and less these days. There once was a time that she consumed my mind, whether it be because I was focused on our breakup—if you could even call it that—or, in moments of weakness, missing her. Esme and I spent a tumultuous four months together, and at no point did she ever want to label it. We discussed it at length, but she always said labels were restrictive and that I should know where her heart was at.

When she pretty much cheated on me, but then claimed we weren't in a committed relationship despite my thinking we were monogamous, I quickly learned why she was so set on not labeling it.

The heart-wrenching memory of the moment I found out about Sarah—the girl she'd been hooking up with—used to bring me to my knees. Now, as she approaches me on a crowded New York street, I don't feel the pain I once felt, but my stomach still twists as my eyes meet hers. Six months have passed since the awful night I found out about her betrayal. The sound of their laughter, the sight of them walking hand-in-hand; all these memories swim through my mind in an angry sea of emotion, but longing isn't one of them. Despite having no lingering affections, Esme's presence still causes me discomfort.

If anything, I feel like I haven't done enough. Esme just booked quite possibly a career-defining role. She's not just in the show, but one of the two leads, and I've yet to book a single production. I've been offered smaller projects over the years, but they were often unpaid and, given my situation with my parents, I needed something that would pay.

Esme's mile-wide smile is illuminated by the festive Christmas lights, and her eyes twinkle with glee. Just as she reaches us, I feel a hand run gently down my back. I jump in surprise; this is New York, after all, and sudden contact on a street corner could only mean one thing. Luna watches me intently as I shift away from the stranger's grip, only for me to feel their lips graze my temple.

"Shhh, princess. It's me." Liam's voice washes over me, the anxiety I'd been bathing in only moments ago instantly replaced with something new: safety.

"Oh, uh...hi." The surprise in my voice doesn't go unnoticed as Luna steps forward.

Esme stands to her side, arms crossed over her chest, but it's clear that it's not an expression of concern. "Who are you?" she asks, her arms not loosening even a millimeter from her body as she holds her ground.

"I apologize, that was rude of me," Liam says as he grins from ear to ear, his gleaming million-watt smile nearly knocking me over. He extends a hand to the redhead. "I'm Liam, Hannah's boyfriend. And you are?"

This causes her to shift on her feet and accept his pleasantry, taking his hand in hers. "Esme."

"Esme," he repeats, appearing to think through the Rolodex in his mind. I don't remember mentioning her to him, at least not by name. "I don't believe she's ever mentioned you, my apologies. It's great to meet you." The forced kindness in his voice crawls up my spine, and I wonder if he means it genuinely or wants to remind her of her place by telling her she's irrelevant.

This doesn't sit well with Esme.

"I find that hard to believe," she scoffs as she walks away, rejoining the group of castmates farther up the walk.

"What's the story there?" Luna's brows nearly reach her hairline as she stares at me.

My history with Esme is hardly a secret, but due to the nature of how she insisted on us keeping our relationship, it's unsurprising that people don't know.

"We, uh...used to date."

"Dude, that sucks," Luna says as she glances over her shoulder at Esme. "I can barely deal with her as a castmate, let alone being involved with her. You have the patience of a saint."

I nearly forget Liam is at my side until the hand he was resting on my lower back snakes around to squeeze my hip, pulling me flush to his side.

"It is what it is." I shrug before turning to Liam, whose eyes are already on me. "What are you doing here?"

He grins down at me, but I don't miss how it doesn't meet his eyes. "Just thought I'd surprise you."

"I gotta head back in to rehearsal, but let's try to get together before you head back to Atlanta, okay?"

"Sounds good!" I hug Luna quickly before she jogs back over to the group of women a few yards away.

Esme's eyes linger on me and Liam, but I realize for the first time that, whether it be Liam's presence or just some really impressive self-growth, I don't feel anything about it.

"Boyfriend, huh?" I chuckle at Liam, jabbing him in the side with my elbow. The warmth that blooms in my belly at the thought of that being true is unmistakable. I didn't realize until seeing Esme just how much the idea of being kept a secret hurts me. I've spent so much of my life being a second thought, never the most important thing to someone. The bonus child, the bonus friend, the runner-up, the understudy, but never the one they choose.

I deserve to be chosen.

"Is that what you want?" Liam's eyes meet mine, and I try with every fiber of my being to see what is hiding behind his eyes. He always does that—when I ask him how he feels, he turns it around on me.

I can't settle for a non-answer, not anymore.

"Is that what *you* want?"

He pauses for a moment before tightening his hold on my waist, pulling me against his front, my face nestled against his chest. "I want you," he says firmly as he pushes my chin up with his pointer finger to meet my gaze, holding me in place. His beautiful brown eyes glisten with intensity and seem darker than usual. His skin is flushed as he stares at me, seemingly searching for the answer in my eyes. "Hannah, I want you. Just you...just us. I don't share, and I sure as hell don't like the idea of entertaining other women when I'm with someone. So yeah, if that means being your boyfriend, absolutely."

As Liam speaks, my gut tightens and I feel an overwhelming sense of love. Heat spreads through my chest as his words crash over me like an ocean wave engulfing the shore. His gaze is intense and full of longing, and I finally realize that he wants me just as much as I want him.

The fear that consumes me in this moment is nothing compared to the realization that dawns on me. I'm irrefutably in love with Liam Park, and fuck if that's not the worst thing I've ever thought into existence.

Liam leans down, his lips pressed against mine, lingering there for a moment. The all-consuming feeling is mind-boggling and I'm admittedly knocked a bit off-kilter.

"Let's grab food," he says as he grins down at me, but all I do in return is nod.

We step down the sidewalk, and it hits me that Liam managed to find me in a city of almost nine million people.

"Wait, how did you know where to find me?"

Liam pauses, his shoulders tensing. "Well, uh...this is where your audition was!" he responds with a bit too much enthusiasm.

"And how did you know where my audition was?" The suspicion in my voice clearly reaches him as he avoids eye contact.

The silence lingers for a moment before he cracks. "I may or may not have lied to Sage and said there was an emergency at work and that I couldn't get ahold of you..."

The chuckle that crawls up my throat fights to get out, but I use all my effort to maintain composure. "Questionable ethics, Park."

He seems genuinely concerned until his eyes finally meet mine at the exact moment my laugh breaks free.

"Shut up," he chuckles, his voice low and husky. He yanks me closer to him until my cheek rests against his chest and his sturdy arms wrap around my shoulders.

As we make our way through New York City, I feel overwhelmed by this place. The bustling street traffic is a mass of voices and language, the roar of taxi horns mixing with sirens emanating from emergency vehicles, the sounds all compounding until they create one loud string of noise.

The scents as we make our way past multiple food venders has my mouth watering. From the savory aroma of hot dogs grilling on the street corners to hot cocoa from an old-fashioned pushcart, New York manages to have every possible cuisine one could want. The heavy traffic and bright lights illuminate the world to me. I take in my surroundings as we walk down bustling sidewalks, past men and women rushing from one place to another, each running their own race against time.

Nearby, the strains of a violin cut the air as a busker comes into view, fully encompassing in one action what the theater district of the city that never sleeps has to offer.

Music, art, culture—New York City has a never-ending supply.

"What do you want to eat?" Liam asks, squeezing my hand, the contact grounding me in the otherwise chaotic city that surrounds me.

"Anything is fine."

"*Hannah.*" He pins me with a glare as his words come out almost reprimanding. "I know you; you always have something specific in mind. So let's skip this song and dance and get to the point. What do you want?"

"I want to know why you came to New York." The words spill out before I can stop myself. He'd appeared by my side so quickly that I hadn't stopped to question why he's here and not in Atlanta. In all the years I lived in New York City, I don't recall a single time Liam came to the city, so it's a little convenient that he's here now.

"Can't eat that, Hannah."

"Liam!" I huff out as I stop in place, pulling his hand to bring him to a halt.

"It's not a big deal..." He nods toward the sidewalk in front of us, trying to encourage me to keep walking.

"Humor me."

Liam scans our surroundings as he seeks out something to pin his eyes on, anything to avoid looking me in the eye. The longer he diverts his gaze, the more my stomach starts to churn, the bubbling feeling at the pit of my gut leaving me in a constant shift between wanting to pass out or throw up. My palm grows wet in his hand, but he's squeezing it so tightly that I can't pull it from his grasp.

"I thought—" He sighs before looking down at me, an unfamiliar expression plaguing him. "I thought you were considering moving back."

The meaning in his words nearly floats past me before it hits me, causing a faint grin to overtake me.

"You were scared." My smile is on full display as he rolls his eyes, trying to yank his hand from what is now *my* death grip.

"I was not *scared*."

"Oh, you totally were!" I cackle as he yanks his hand from mine, giving me just enough reaction to know that I'm right.

"Whatever...what do you want to eat?"

The grin doesn't leave my lips as I slide my hand back into his, squeezing as he releases the tension he is holding. Whether he fights the revelation, a warmth grows in my belly at the realization that he's just as scared as I am.

"I could go for pizza."

"Finally, an answer," he says as he smiles down at me.

Troppe Pizze materializes, and the door of the family-owned restaurant swings open with a creak. A wave of hot air billows out, transporting a thick fog of steam along with it as it mixes with the crisp December air. The pungent scent of tomato sauce and oregano hangs heavy in the air, causing my mouth to water in anticipation. I inhale deeply, savoring the aroma.

Liam orders us a pie to share and it is delivered to us in record time. Despite my instinct to act reserved and not at all as ravenous as I am, I reach for it instantly.

The thin crust of the pepperoni pizza crackles as it breaks beneath my teeth, and the flavorful combination of tomato sauce and cheese explodes across my taste buds. I shovel another piece into my mouth with abandon, savoring every bite. I notice Liam's eyes locked on me as I do so.

"What?" I mumble, attempting to cover the unsightly contents of my full mouth.

"Nothing, it's just so sexy the way you shovel pizza into your mouth like you've been starving in the desert for the past two weeks." This earns him a kick under the table, which causes him to chuckle as he rubs the spot. "Okay, killer. No, I was just wondering where you're staying."

I swallow the last bite of my pizza before I speak this time. "My friend Anna's apartment in Midtown."

"False—you're staying with me at The Pierre."

"That's so interesting, because I don't recall agreeing to that." My brow raises, causing him to sigh.

"Hannah. Will you *please* stay with me at The Pierre?" While it comes off sarcastic, I take it as a win.

"Of course, all you had to do was ask."

He scoffs as he takes a sip of his beer, failing to bite back the grin that's clear as day.

THIRTY-TWO

HANNAH

Believe it or not, I came to New York City a lot as a kid. We often would travel up here as a family...before my mom decided she didn't enjoy my presence. My love for theater started at a young age, so when we attended a Broadway show as a family, it was the only time I ever felt connected to my parents, sharing something I loved.

We would all find ourselves engrossed in the stories and the musical numbers, a single focal point for each of us to let go of whatever consumed our daily lives.

When Jackson and I would come with our parents, we were always forced to share a double-queen bedroom while our parents got an adjoining room with a king bed. We would always stay at the same hotel near Times Square, and, while it was nice, it never even touched the level of opulence that is The Pierre.

Liam swipes his room key before he swings open the creaking mahogany door, and I am immediately hit with a wave of clean linens and aged leather. I step into a room that looks more like a museum than a hotel suite. Gold antiques, plush velvet curtains, and ornately patterned carpets fill the spacious area. The floor-to-ceiling windows look out onto Central Park, and an opulent chandelier looms over the four-poster bed. Ornate carvings cover every post, and gold garlands drape around each one. It's obvious this historic hotel is one of New York City's most luxurious accommodations.

Behind another mahogany door lies the bathroom; a room that feels like stepping into a palace. The gleaming gold clawfoot tub takes center stage, surrounded by white marble and illuminated by glimmering crystal sconces on the walls. An intricately carved wooden vanity stands to one side, complete with an ornately framed mirror.

The bathroom has an undeniable air of luxury about it. Soft, luxurious towels hang from the nearby towel rack, just waiting to embrace you after a warm soak in the tub. Tubes of aromatic bubble bath liquids line the shelves next to fragrant soaps made from honey and almond oil, while fine porcelain containers of lotion and shampoo sit atop a delicate antique walnut shelf.

"Liam, this is..." I trail off as I continue into the bathroom, my fingers ghosting over a fluffy white towel in the process. I'm completely in awe of this space.

Liam's arms wrap around my waist from behind as he squeezes my back flush to his front, the buttons of his shirt tickling my skin as my T-shirt rides up in the back.

"You like it?" He grins against my neck, which causes shivers to run down my spine.

"That's an understatement." My eyes are locked on the clawfoot tub as Liam's scruff tickles my cheek. I linger in his arms for a while, just basking in the calm that this space brings on.

He allows me to just exist as he holds me tightly. "Get

naked," he whispers against the shell of my ear, triggering me to arch into him further. Liam's fingers trace the hem of my T-shirt before pulling it over my head in one swift motion. As the cotton drifts to the ground, I turn around to face him, but Liam steps away from my embrace instantly.

"What are you doing?" A laugh escapes me.

He reaches down and turns the golden knob at the end of the bathtub, which springs to life as water starts to flow in a waterfall from the brass spout on the wall. The soft rippling sound of running water fills the room as Liam grabs a pale pink bottle off a shelf and pours it into the cascade of water. Bubbles disguise the water almost instantly as they replicate rapidly under the steaming stream.

"I said get naked." Liam peers up at me from below his brow, and a faint grin spreads to my lips instantaneously.

I strip off the rest of my clothes with urgency, the scraps of fabric a ball on the floor before the water even passes the halfway mark. Walking up behind Liam as he sits on the edge of the bath, I reach around and begin unbuttoning his shirt.

"What are you doing?"

"Getting you naked." I grin as my lips press against the side of his neck, not missing the way his breath hitches at the intimate touch.

The bubbles reach the top of the freestanding tub as Liam shuts off the spout. He moves to stand tall, his chest and arms rippling with taut muscles as he slowly undoes the button of his jeans. With a graceful motion, he peels off the rest of his clothing and tosses them in the corner to join my own before coming to stand over me. His stomach is pure, unadulterated perfection as his abs descend into an inviting V so intoxicating it would make Adonis jealous. His eyes sparkle with a mischievous grin, and I can almost feel my mouth watering with desire.

"Eyes up here, princess."

I roll my eyes at his remark, but it doesn't stop me from doing exactly as he demands.

His eyes meet mine and a mischievous grin stares back at me. "Get in the bathtub."

The moment my toes touch the scorching hot water, I wince. Liam jerks, clearly worried he'd run the bath too hot, but as my frigid toes grow accustomed to the new temperature, my muscles melt under the warmth. As I inch into the bathtub, I notice that Liam isn't joining me.

"What are you doing?" My brows pinch together as I glare up at him.

"Give me a second." Liam disappears into the bedroom before reemerging within seconds with two champagne flutes and a bottle of Dom Pérignon. I gasp as I notice the label, earning me a chuckle in return. "You weren't exactly raised poor, Hannah. Stop acting like the concept of a nice bottle of champagne is foreign."

"Yeah, but I've never had it."

"What? That's insane—your parents love buying expensive bottles."

"Yeah, but I was in New York for five years and tried to see them as little as possible. Don't get me wrong, I've been around people who frequently spend half my rent on a bottle, but seeing as my parents cut me off years ago, it's safe to say I've never been able to afford it."

A silence falls over the bathroom, the only audible sound the splashing of my slight movements in the bathtub.

"George and Linda cut you off?" He's still standing there with two champagne flutes in one hand and the bottle in the other. The concern etched in his brow would almost be cute if it wasn't accompanied by the stomach-dropping realization that he didn't know.

My parents have been pretty diligent in the information they divulge...even when it comes to Liam's parents.

"Yeah, uh...when I left for college. They didn't like that I didn't want to pursue a more stable career, so they pulled my college fund. After that, it was clear I was on my own."

"How'd you pay for school, then?"

"Loans mostly. I got a few that were federal, but most of them are private because my parents make too much money for me to qualify for much else."

"Damn."

"Yeah," I sigh as I lean my chin against the side of the bathtub. "Are you joining me or...?"

"Oh, yeah." He shakes his head as if to remove whatever emotion he was experiencing. He sets the bottle along with the glasses on the small bamboo table nestled against the side of the tub, then slides in behind me with little concern for the change in temperature.

He reaches for the bottle of champagne and expertly uncorks it, the pop echoing throughout the room. Bubbles race to the top of the bottle as he pours it into the two tall champagne flutes. I accept my glass, feeling its chill on my fingertips. We sit in silence for a while, the bubbles in the bath tickling my skin. Liam's strong arm wraps around my shoulders, and we silently lay together in the warm embrace of the swirling water. His face nestles into my neck, the rhythm of his breathing bringing me solace. Every muscle in my body releases its tension as my mind slowly starts to drift away.

"You made the right choice, Hannah."

"What?" My foggy state doesn't give me even the slightest inclination of what he's talking about.

"Going to school for theater. You made the right call," Liam mumbles as he presses his lips to my temple. "However misguided they were, I understand your parents wanting something stable for you. But they were still wrong. You're incredible as a performer. I know it hasn't panned out yet, but it's going to. I honestly think that they expected you to cower at the daunting future in front of you and run back to them, probably major in some bullshit like accounting. But you didn't...know what that makes you?"

"What does that make me?"

"A fucking badass who knew that her life was meant for far more than working at Baker & Park, then retiring with a 401K and a picket fence in the suburbs."

Despite the smile spread across my lips, a dampness begins to pool below my eyes.

I don't understand how Liam manages to know exactly what I need to hear despite spending years keeping me at arm's length.

His arms tighten around me, the water between us sloshing out with reckless abandon. As his lips linger at my temple, I melt into him further, allowing myself a moment of relaxation from the chaos of my life, resting in the arms of the man that I love.

My toes and fingers are pruned as I look around in the water and see that the bubbles are starting to dissipate.

"Do you want to get out?" I mumble in my sleepy, sated state.

"Yeah," Liam says through a yawn.

We step out of the steaming bath, and before Liam reaches for his towel, he tenderly swaddles me in a soft, plush one, his large hands gently rubbing my arms and back. I bask in the towel's warmth and the security of his embrace.

As we step into the bedroom, Liam drops his towel over the dark wood desk chair pushed up against the wall. He crawls onto the white-sheeted bed, holding out his arm for me to join him. I feel his warmth as I snuggle up beside him and he reaches over to switch off the antique brass lamp on the bedside table. The room falls into a soothing darkness.

My face rests against his chest, the peppering of hair tickling my jaw, but not so much that I want to pull away. We lay in silence for a moment before his voice cuts through the black.

"Can I ask you something?"

"Yeah, what's up?" I yawn out my words.

"Why did you hate me so much?" I don't miss the way he says it in past tense, a warmth blooming in my stomach before dropping at the memory his question evokes.

I pause for a moment, composing my thoughts. "Do you remember when we...the first time?" I wave my hand between our bodies, attempting to get the point across without going into too much detail in case he really doesn't remember.

"Of course..." His brows pull together, but he doesn't say much else.

"I was a virgin."

THIRTY-THREE

NINE YEARS AGO

HANNAH

I taste Bud Light on his tongue, and it should be gross, but it has the opposite effect—it's intoxicating. Maybe I could learn to like beer.

Liam presses me against the dryer, his body flush with my own.

The clean, fresh scent of the laundry room only eggs me on further as it successfully takes me out of my element. We're not at a party at the beach house; there aren't close to fifty people outside of that door right now throwing ping pong balls and shotgunning shitty beer. I'm completely consumed in a way that I've never felt.

A soft moan escapes me as he nips at my bottom lip, coaxing my mouth open for him to explore, which he does. His tongue tentatively dances over my own, inquiring at first, then quickly shifting to a frenzy. The scent of his cologne mixed with the smell of beer and laundry is weirdly comforting, and —dare I say—enticing.

He tightens his hands on my hips before lifting me without warning, pulling a yelp from me as he does so. My ass lands against the top of the dryer, but he doesn't waste even a second as he resumes his assault of my senses. His mouth collides with my own with far more urgency than before, and I dissolve into him.

A crash sounds outside the door, pulling us from the moment. Our gasps melt together as the realization hits us in unison. I'm ready to tell him we shouldn't, but he speaks first.

"Go to my room," he whispers. I want to bite back, tell him not to tell me what to do, but I just nod. "I need to check on what that was or my dad might kill me if something is broken. I'll be up there shortly. Go upstairs."

He hands me the oversized shirt from the hanger I'd been reaching for before. I pull the fabric over my head and it falls to hit a few inches above my knees. I escape the laundry room without drawing a look in my direction. I realize I was worried for nothing, because I'm sure no one here would even bat an eye at what we were just doing...so why am I freaking out?

Regardless, I'm not fazed enough to not meet him upstairs.

Liam has always been weirdly protective of his space. I've only ever been in his bedroom at the beach house a couple times, and even less at his house in Atlanta. He likes his space and, of all the things about him, I tend to respect this trait the most.

I meander, looking through the figurines huddled all over the top of his dresser.

"God, such a nerd." I chuckle to myself before turning on my heels to move over to the bed.

His bedding is insanely soft, the plush fabric like heaven against my sunburnt skin.

The door clicks, causing me to jerk before I realize it's Liam.

"Is everything okay?" I ask, a shortness in my breath that the situation doesn't call for.

"What?" He looks confused before he remembers. "Oh, uh...yeah, everything is fine. Some idiot knocked over the fruit bowl on the counter, but that thing is rock solid."

Liam steps toward me, crowding me again, this time with a much gentler touch. He's calculated, and I'm starting to think he may be sobering up.

"Hannah, how drunk are you?" he asks, a concerned expression riddling his features.

I was pretty drunk earlier, but I haven't had a sip of alcohol in close to two hours. This reminds me that I've officially sacrificed my full beverage sitting somewhere downstairs as I'm not dumb enough to pick up an abandoned drink at a party.

"I'm not drunk," I say matter-of-factly.

Liam stares at me for a moment as if trying to determine the truth. He seems to see something on my face that reassures his fear, so he nods.

"Okay, good."

He stands in front of me so that my face is level with his belly button before reaching down, snaking his hand around to cradle the back of my neck and tilting my head to look up at him. I expect him to say something, but he doesn't. He just looks at me for a bizarre amount of time.

"What are you thinking about, Park?"

This appears to shake him from whatever he was thinking as he leans down and places a gentle kiss on my lips. I want more, but he doesn't give it right away.

Liam pushes me back onto the bed and crawls between my legs. I instinctively wrap my legs around his hips, which causes him to grin.

I'm new to all of this, but nothing I've done has seemed to offend him, which gives me a new sense of confidence. His gentle kisses shift in intensity as I drag my tongue along his lower lip, spurring him into action. A groan escapes him and causes me to smile.

There is something invigorating about knowing that I cause the same reaction in him that he pulls from me.

Wrapping my hands around the back of his neck to pull him closer, I realize I want him more than I thought was even humanly possible. Don't get me wrong—I've liked people, I've been attracted to people, but I've never felt this. This all-consuming feeling of need is new and borderline terrifying. Despite my nerves, the feeling of his grin against my lips manages to ground me.

I squeeze my legs around him, pulling him closer, his hardness pressed flush against where I ache. He groans, which only coaxes me more. I want him, consequences be damned.

I want this; I want Liam.

"Liam," I say in a breathy moan. I don't know why I say it, but it seems to awaken something in him.

He doesn't respond, but simply presses into me further, pulling a matching sound from my mouth.

Liam's hands dance downward, leaving my hips and hooking under the hem of the shirt I'm wearing. He saw me in my underwear earlier, but something about the idea of him being able to touch me so intimately fogs my brain and stirs a newfound need in my core.

As he lifts the fabric achingly slowly, I try not to show my impatience. The moment it's bunched around my waist, he pulls my underwear down and tosses them onto the bed next to me. My stomach jumps in anticipation. I expect him to rush to get to the goal post. However, the moment his eyes meet mine, I feel a breath catch in my throat. He seems almost as nervous as I am, but probably not for the same reasons.

"Hannah—"

I don't know what he is about to say and I'm not sure I want to know, so I do the only thing I can think to do: I lean up and kiss him. Liam's lips are soft against my own, but I feel the moment he melts into me, his movements far more frantic than before.

He reaches down and, as his fingers wrap around my inner thigh, my breath hitches. Liam grips my flesh as he pulls me to the edge of the bed, but I don't miss the way his hands shake. His eyes lock on mine as he pulls down his swim trunks. When his erection springs free, a lump forms in my throat—I genuinely don't know how that is supposed to fit inside me.

Reaching into the drawer in the bedside table, Liam pulls out a little gold foil packet that I assume is a condom. He fumbles with the packaging as he rips it open, the trembling in his hand way more noticeable as he tries to get the condom free. When he finally gets it open, he surprisingly doesn't struggle with rolling it on.

I've known a lot of sides to Liam; he's been an asshole, but he's also been a friend. Growing up together, I've seen him through a variety of iterations of the boy and now man. However, the way he's looking at me right now is new. The deep brown eyes staring down at me—the unsure boy behind the man—has me melting, because despite the fumbling and nervous energy, I feel safe.

Liam lines himself up before pushing inside me. He eases in, but there is no level of attention or taking it slow that could ease the discomfort of being stretched so thoroughly for the first time. It takes a little while for him to be fully inside of me, but the moment he's buried to the hilt, he pauses. At first, I think it is to help me acclimate, but judging by the pained look on his face, I don't think that's the case.

His eyes meet mine as he takes a deep breath and starts to move, but he doesn't break eye contact as he does so. It feels weirdly intimate, but I can't seem to look away.

This continues for maybe another minute before he tenses, and I'm unsure why until, with a telltale grunt, I feel him twitch inside of me. He stays inside me for a minute, catching his breath, before he pulls out and walks to the trash can.

When you're told what losing your virginity will be like, you sometimes assume that it will be this insanely cosmic event. As girls, we're told our entire lives that our virginity is this huge gift, and once you've given it, your value depletes, so you have to choose who you give it to carefully. I've never bought into the idea that sex is for marriage exclusively; I'm not particularly religious. However, you only get one time to lose your virginity...even if it's not the earth-shattering, planets-aligning moment we're told it will be.

I'm glad it was with Liam.

Morning comes in a misty haze, flowing through the window in a serene cast over the room. The sun doesn't flow into my room like it does Liam's in the morning. Being on the other side of the house, my room is much more susceptible to afternoon sun and sunsets in the evening. I roll over to find a sleeping Liam, the scent of his cologne on the sheets that I didn't notice last night satiating me almost instantly. The faint smell of citrus and musk invades my senses in the most calming blanket I've ever experienced.

His alarm starts going off, jerking me from my sleepy haze.

I expect him to roll over and cuddle me, kiss me good morning, or at the very least acknowledge last night, but he doesn't do any of that.

"You should probably get out of here before Jackson sees you." He doesn't even look at me, just focuses on his phone in his hand, the alarm long since shut off.

I don't know how to respond. The thought of just running back to my room after what transpired has me on the verge of tears, but I try to keep it at bay.

"Can we talk about what happened last night?" I ask quietly, so quietly that I wonder if he even hears me.

A pregnant pause follows before Liam says anything, causing my calm to transform into a ball of anxiety. I'm on the brink of tears as he looks at me.

"Oh my God, Hannah. It's not a big deal. You don't have to be dramatic. People hook up—don't read into it."

Of all the things I expect to come out of his mouth, I never thought he would be so cold. We argue, sure, but it's never been *mean*. We bicker—I mean, we've known each other since we were babies—but this feels far crueler than anything he's ever said to me.

"Of course." My voice cracks as I stand up and pull my shirt from last night over my head. "Wouldn't want to be dramatic over something so...inconsequential."

He doesn't say anything; he's not even looking at me anymore. Liam just stares down at his phone, playing some mobile RPG game. How he can be so nonchalant, I'll never know.

I click the door behind me, thankful that it's hours before Jackson will be awake.

As the tears I've been holding back fall from my waterline,

I make the decision: I refuse to let that happen ever again. Not only will he never touch me like that again, but I also don't think I want to even be around him anymore. Any friendship we used to share is dead now.

Liam Stephen Park can rot in hell.

THIRTY-FOUR

PRESENT DAY

LIAM

My eyes widen and my jaw drops as I look down at her, the minimal light coming from outside just enough to make out the worry in her expression. It's a strange mix of fear and anticipation, like she's bracing for my reaction. However, nothing but guilt washes over me at the revelation of what happened all those years ago.

"You were a virgin?" I repeat it back to her as if it is going to change; as if I misheard her.

Hannah just nods in response.

I want to pry, I want to dig into why she didn't tell me, but as I open my mouth to speak, I clamp it shut again. We sit in silence for a while, the only sound in the room coming from the cabs down below.

"I don't understand why you hated me for that, though..."

The look she pins me with has my balls practically shrinking into me, anything to protect me from the wrath I'm about to endure.

"Are you serious right now?!" She shoots upright in bed before turning around to glare at me.

"Hannah, I'm sorry. I didn't mean it like that," I sigh as I reach to grab her hand. To my relief, she doesn't shove it away despite her clear irritation. "That was a really long time ago... can you refresh my memory on what I did?"

Hannah slowly pivots toward me, her eyes glistening with unshed tears. She nervously nibbles her lower lip as she looks down at me, wearing an expression of pain and confusion, and it's then I realize just how much my actions all those years ago hurt her. The thought that I am the cause of her distress makes my stomach sink.

"When we—" She pauses as she flails her arms around in my direction.

"Had sex?" My brows shoot up. I should be concerned, and I am, but something about the way she seems to be reverting to the level of comfort discussing sex she had at eighteen is adorable.

"Yes, that." Hannah clears her throat as her eyes meet mine. "The night we had sex at the beach house, I was a virgin. That night was fine, great, even. You were a perfect gentleman."

I don't know where she's going with this. My memory of that night is hazy, but I can remember how embarrassed I was. I lasted less than two minutes and I was humiliated. Now, as I look back, I think I remember her being aware of how quick it was, but with this new information, I'm wondering if I fabricated that in my nervous shame.

"Sounds like it went fine..."

"It did. It was great, everything I could have hoped for in losing my virginity. But..." She adjusts her position on the plush bed, crossing and uncrossing her legs, biting her lip to hold back a sob. A single tear drops from her long, dark lashes, quickly swiped away with the pad of her thumb. "The next morning wasn't like that."

I don't remember much beyond my embarrassment the night we were together, but I remember the next morning with startling clarity. When Hannah woke up wanting to talk, I went on the defense. The humiliation I felt from the night before had only compounded and the thought of talking about it gave me far more bite than the situation called for.

Hindsight is 20/20 and all that.

"When I asked you to talk about it, I wanted to tell you I was a virgin before we...had sex. Everything happened so fast, we didn't talk, and I knew we had to have that conversation. But you told me to stop being dramatic and that it didn't matter. So I made the decision that I wasn't going to allow you that close to me again." A pained chuckle escapes her, driving a knife through my gut. "Clearly did well on that front."

I pull myself up to sit against the wall, each breath a reminder of the icy chill brought on by the old hotel in December. My heart aches for her, urging me to reach out and pull her close. Yet something inside me holds back, knowing that this conversation has to be had without any physical contact. The sheets are rumpled around us, their softness a stark contrast to the hard wall behind me. It feels strange that we're having this talk in a bed, yet I find myself thinking it's somewhat poetic given how we got here.

"Hannah, I—"

"I'm not finished," she asserts, holding her finger up to shush me.

I wave in front of me, gesturing for her to continue.

"We had always been mean to each other. Kids and all that, picking on one another. Hell, for a while there I thought it was because you liked me."

Hannah's pained laugh pulls me forward from the wall. I lean in to be closer without touching her and invading her power. "Han—"

"Now, looking back, I realize it was just because I wanted that to be why. That year, I had the dumbest crush on you. I tried to fight it off, I tried to act like it didn't bother me when I saw you with other girls, but in retrospect it was obvious. I liked you."

Her words shouldn't be painful to reminisce on, but they're just another reminder of how royally I screwed up. The pained crack in her voice guts me as I knot my fingers together, anything to resist reaching out to touch her.

"Well..." She lets out a long exhale before continuing, "That day it went from playfully mean to just downright nasty...in both directions. I just figured that's how you always felt."

"No."

"What?"

"No, Hannah. That's not how I felt at all. I was terrified that night. I had had sex with one other person and it was like six months prior. In case you don't remember, I wasn't exactly fending off girls growing up. I didn't have sex until sophomore year of college. So, you were the only person I'd been with in a while."

Hannah's hurt expression morphs into confusion.

"When guys don't have sex for a while, it can have...less desirable effects. Like...not lasting very long."

"Okay?"

"I was embarrassed. Really embarrassed. I thought that you were disappointed in the experience and I really didn't want to relive it. So I made sure the conversation didn't happen. Looking back, I wish I could do it differently. But there are a lot of things I did and said at twenty that wouldn't even cross my mind at twenty-nine."

Our room grows silent as Hannah and I stare at one another, our eyes long-since adjusted to the darkness of the room. The diffused light from the street filters through the curtains enough that I can see Hannah's face.

Her adorable, broken expression.

I fucking hate myself right now.

Reaching forward, I grab her hand, sandwiching it between my own. I need her to hear this, even if it's just to give me peace of mind.

"I liked you, Hannah. I did for a long time, but you never saw me like that. Ever. Not until I came back from college sophomore year after learning what the campus rec center was, getting on Accutane, and getting contacts. It sounds douchy, but I went from nerdy as hell to moderately hot in the matter of a year. I thought I finally had my shot, so when I blew it, I was so sure that I'd squandered it. Now I know I did, but not for the reasons I thought...which sucks."

"You didn't squander it...at least not permanently." Hannah's mouth curves upward into a gentle smile, the first sign of relief since we started talking. She quickly uses her knuckles to wipe away the last trace of tears from her soft cheeks.

I reach out and brush my thumb across the spot where her tears trailed, and she leans into my touch. "Come here."

As she collapses into my arms, the panic from before and the memories that caused me so much shame finally expelled from the room, I know one thing with certainty.

I am in love with Hannah Thatcher-Miles, and that very well might kill me.

THIRTY-FIVE

HANNAH

Our cab skids and jolts its way through the bustling New York City streets, narrowly avoiding honking cars and weaving in and out of congested intersections. I have no idea where Liam is taking us, yet he exudes an air of confidence as he looks ahead, a small smile playing on his lips. As we pass through the dazzling lights of the theater district, I recall my audition earlier today, my last one on this trip.

I think it went well, and I genuinely mean that. Sometimes I convince myself it went better than it actually did just to avoid a nervous breakdown. This one, however, was exactly what I needed. It's for a national tour and, while it sounds like a dream come true, it's also a long shot.

"Where are we going?" I nudge Liam in the arm as he stares forward, but I don't miss the way he bites back a grin at my question.

"Like the seventeen other times you've asked me since we left dinner twenty minutes ago—we're almost there, I promise."

CHAPTER THIRTY-FIVE

The confidence he exudes should be irritating, yet I find it endearing.

Our yellow taxi speeds through the streets of Manhattan, dodging the other vehicles on the road with precision. The unmistakable sound of the brakes screeching across the concrete brings us to a halt in front of a grand theater with a brightly lit sign. The crowd of people gathering along the sidewalk buzzes with excitement, all vying for the chance to enter the illustrious playhouse and get to their seats as quickly as possible. I peer out my window, hoping for a better view of the marquee, but it is too far away.

Liam's grin only grows as he hops out of our cab and rounds to my side, opening the door for me in a far more gentlemanly manner than I would expect from him. I want to bite at him with a quippy response, but it dies on my tongue as he reaches for my hand, pulling me to a standing position among the bustling crowd. Our ride pulls away almost instantly, leaving me standing on the curb in what can only be described as an overly extravagant dress for such frigid cold. Liam seems to notice and reaches around, wrapping his arm around me before pulling me to his side.

The line begins to move, but Liam appears to be conspiring with the security guard at the front. Either he is highly persuasive, or the crisp Benjamin I watch him slip the tall, bald man does its job.

Liam's lips find my temple with a featherlight kiss. He's been far more open with his affection in New York. While I am actively reminding myself not to read into it, I still ruminate on the idea that he might be embarrassed to be seen with me back home.

We step into the Richard Rodgers Theatre and I am immediately breathless. The stage design of *Hamilton* is unmistakable, with its signature turntable center stage and a series of stairs and rafters weaving around the periphery to create an all-encompassing environment that brings the story alive. I've fixated on many productions over the years, but something about *Hamilton* makes it impossible to be anything but awed by.

Jackson and I caught a show a few years ago while I was living in the city, but we were seated in the rear mezzanine, nowhere near where Liam and I are being ushered now. The half-filled theater is beginning to condense as we find the seats from which we'll be enjoying the show.

"Liam, these tickets—"

"Don't start."

"They must have cost you a fortune!" I gasp.

"Sit down, Hannah."

Something about the look he's giving me causes me to sit down without further argument. My ass meets the upholstered seat, the velvet of my dress brushing along the grain of the synthetic pile.

The lights in the theater dim as a booming baritone fills the air, King George commanding everyone to power down electronic devices. Before the opening number even begins, I feel Liam's hand seek mine, his long fingers curling around my palm and his thumb making small circles against my skin. A warmth spreads throughout my body as the music swells, but the butterflies taking flight in my stomach are not for the Broadway show.

I feel the familiar thrill of anticipation as the orchestra begins to play. The lights shine brightly on the stage, illuminating a world of make-believe, and I am completely enchanted. No matter how many times I listen to the soundtrack or see this show, it is just as captivating each time.

The moment the show ends, we are ushered outside. The crisp December air bites my cheeks, making them rosier than normal. I shiver involuntarily before I feel Liam drape his suit jacket over my shoulders. This man—this version of him—is foreign to me, not that I've never known this version of him, but it's been a long time. He loops his fingers between mine, squeezing tightly before releasing the pressure.

Strings of twinkling lights decorate every building and lamppost we pass. The ambiance of the season fills me with delight, as it always does, and my joy is only exacerbated when we come upon a man selling hot dogs from a cart outfitted with a heater to keep himself warm. He tosses on gloves and a coat when he sees us approaching, but continues to cook the dogs.

"Two hot dogs, one with mustard and onion, the other with just ketchup," Liam instructs the man as he pulls out his wallet, the tattered and worn brown leather a stark contrast to the man who seems to always be put together. He hands the vender a twenty-dollar bill, tells him to keep the change, then grabs the foil-wrapped deliciousness before stepping down the sidewalk. He hands me the one with just ketchup and it's only then that I realize he ordered it with ease.

"How did you know that?"

"Know what?" He unwraps his hot dog and shoves one end in his mouth, yellow mustard coating the edge of his lip in the process.

"Know I only get ketchup on my hot dogs." I detest mustard; it's quite possibly the most disgusting condiment to exist...besides mayonnaise.

Liam swallows his bite before wiping the rogue mustard and sucking it off his thumb. His eyes meet mine as a chuckle falls from his lips. "Hannah, you're hardly a hard person to figure out. You get ketchup on your hot dogs, chicken penne at

Andre's, you hate mayonnaise, love chocolate cake. You hate strawberries, yet you still for some reason always get strawberry ice cream. Make that make sense." He starts to shove the hot dog back in his mouth, but my slack-jawed expression causes him to pause. "Oh c'mon, I've known you our entire lives. You pick up on things."

True, but not all of what he said ties back to us growing up together. We've only been going to Andre's for like a year, so for him to notice that is...

Well, it's interesting.

"Okay, stalker." I laugh as I smack his arm, nearly shoving the hot dog out of his hand.

"Yeah, yeah." Liam rolls his eyes before wrapping his free arm around my shoulders, tossing the wrapper in a trash can along with the last bite of food.

We finally return to the hotel, the warm lobby a welcome reprieve from the freezing temperature outside. The hotel is only a couple blocks from the theater, but with the December weather, you would think it's all the way in Brooklyn.

The second we get into our room, I'm tossing my heels into the corner and stripping my dress over my head. I don't really even think about what I'm doing until my eyes lock on Liam, his gaze fixed on my body with a hungry look. In an attempt to pretend I don't notice, I continue to strip down, leaving a trail of discarded clothing in my wake. Water starts to stream from the rain head above the clawfoot tub, but I don't step in right away. Pulling the curtain shut, I walk over to the bathroom door and close it only inches from Liam's face.

"That was rude." His unamused voice travels through the door, causing a grin to spread across my lips.

Stepping into the waterfall cascading from the ceiling, I

count to ten but only get to six as a now-naked Liam steps past the fabric barrier separating me from the rest of the bathroom.

"What took you so long?"

"Honest answer?"

"Always."

"Couldn't get my belt off."

A laugh bubbles up from my throat only to be silenced by his lips pressing hungrily against mine. His hands roam my body as the kiss deepens, and one of them finds its way to the back of my neck, entangling itself in the mass of wet strands there. He tugs firmly, making me open my mouth wider for him to explore. His tepid advances quickly shift to urgency as I'm pulled flush to him, his hard length pressed firmly against my navel, causing me to gasp.

We linger in the shower for a while, but I'll be honest—I've never been a fan of shower sex. You would think that the moisture would help, but in my experience it has the opposite effect. Water is an absolutely awful lubricant, so I personally feel that the shower is for starting, not finishing.

"Are you ready to get out?" I whisper faintly as Liam peppers kisses along my jaw. The tender, pruned skin on my fingertips ghosts along his arms as he leans away, taking the intoxicating feeling of his lips against my neck along with him.

"Sure." He turns the knob on the tub, stopping the water, and within moments I'm wrapped in one towel while I attempt to dry my hair with another. The chilly air has a bite to it, but any thought of it quickly subsides as Liam's lips ghost over mine. "Go lay down in bed...sans towel."

I glare at him for a moment, the instinct to argue when he tells me what to do dying on my tongue.

"Okay," I sigh, dropping my towel to the ground in front of him. A smirk paints my lips as I walk away, the warmth of

Liam's gaze as I sway my hips with more dramatics than normal causing my stomach to do flips.

I crawl under the silky duvet, allowing myself to sink into the plush pillow. Lingering there for a while, I find my eyelids growing heavier, with no Liam in sight. As I drift off to sleep, I'm bathed in far more warmth than the room provides.

THIRTY-SIX

HANNAH

Fluid silk ghosts over my wrist so delicately I almost don't realize it's happening. The fabric tightens around my left wrist, causing me to jerk in my hazy half-asleep state. I reach up to scratch my nose, only to realize one of my wrists is now bound to one of the posts at the head of the bed. This startles me, causing me to look frantically around the room. Wide-eyed, I find Liam leaning over me as he affixes my other wrist above my head in a similar fashion to the other.

"What are you doing?" I ask groggily, anticipation building in my stomach at what he might do next. As the silk tightens fully, it also restricts my movement. I can barely move against its restraint, but something tells me that is the point he's trying to make.

Liam doesn't respond to my question as he tugs on my wrists, ensuring that the knot of the tie is done properly.

"Are you comfortable?" His eyes twinkle in the moonlight cascading through the window as he looks me over top to bottom, hunger mixed with concern in his gaze.

"About as comfortable as one can be tied to a bed," I chuckle.

"Do you not want to, then?" He raises his brows. At first, I think he's taunting me, but then I notice a genuineness in his expression.

"I didn't say that."

"Okay, then shut up," he jokes with a smile before crawling onto the bed next to me. He rests his weight on his elbow as he gazes at me, an expression I can't quite place plaguing his face. "I'm serious, Hannah. If I do anything that makes you uncomfortable, I—"

"I'll tell you. If you do anything that makes me uncomfortable, I'll tell you."

Liam lets out a relieved exhale, causing me to smile. I watch as his demeanor shifts from doting boyfriend to stern, commanding lover, and I'd be lying if I said it didn't shoot straight to my core in the process.

He shifts again, this time to stand next to the bed. He stares down at me and the only thing I can hear is his breathing mixed with the radiator in the corner kicking on. With every breath he heaves out, my stomach jumps in anticipation. I'm aware of his every move, his every breath, his every being.

"Princess..."

"Hm?" I gaze up at him with hooded eyes, the mixture of darkness and energy consuming the room thrusting me into a dazed state.

"We've never...explored our interests together. Yeah, we've had sex, but we've never pushed each other. I want that to change." Something in the words he's saying has my pussy clenching in anticipation. "I'm going to push your body tonight, and I need you to feel empowered to ask me to stop if it's too much."

CHAPTER THIRTY-SIX

"Didn't think we should have this conversation before I was tied to the bed?"

"Hannah," he reprimands me, and I revel in it.

"*Fine.*" I glare up at him, but it's all fabricated. I'm completely engrossed in whatever this is, and the anticipation renders me lightheaded.

"What do you want your word to be?"

I linger on it for a moment. Don't get me wrong, I've needed one in the past. Liam is hardly my first partner. However, in this moment, my mind grows blank. I can't think of a single thing, and I don't want to say something boring like "banana."

"It's not the SATs, Hannah. Pick a fucking word."

"Seymour," I blurt out.

As soon as the name leaves my lips, Liam's brows pinch together.

"You want...your safe word...when having sex with your boyfriend..." He clears his throat as he bites back a grin, clearly amused. "Who, by the way—and I don't think I should have to say this—is named Liam...you want to use a man's name?"

"Yes." I could explain it, I could delve into the significance of the name, but I don't. It's more amusing to watch him try to unpack it on his own.

"Okay then, Seymour it is." He shakes his head as he moves from the edge of the bed and crawls toward me. He doesn't relax by my side this time, but simply hovers over me. His eyes are glassy in the minimal light, but it's unmistakable how he's looking at me right now.

With adoration.

As I think it, I watch his expression shift into something more sinister, more commanding, and I'll be damned if it's not the most intoxicating thing I've ever seen.

He places a chaste kiss on my lips before venturing downward, peppering kisses down my neck, down my collarbone, before enveloping his mouth over my semi-hard nipple. Liam swirls his tongue around the sensitive peak, pulling a gasp from me. The sensation is intoxicating as he releases it with a loud pop. Cold air whispers over the damp flesh, leaving my nipple rock-hard in its wake. He pulls away with a smile and devours the other nipple with the same attention, causing me to squirm.

"Liam," I whine.

He leans forward in response, wrapping his mouth around my nipple once more. This time, he bites. It stings just enough to cause me to yelp. The look he gives me is that of pure triumph; he must have been hoping for this reaction. He smirks at me before looking downward and continuing his descent.

As he traces his tongue over my navel, my stomach clenches instinctively. The lower he proceeds, the wetter I grow. He meanders further before pressing a gentle kiss against the patch of shaven skin just above my pussy. The anticipation overtakes me, but when he doesn't proceed, I glare down at him despite my restricted ability to hold myself up.

"Calm down, killer. Patience...it's a virtue, you know." He grins before dipping his head downward, languidly dragging his tongue from my entrance to my clit in one fluid motion. My entire body tingles at the contact, but it quickly dies as he pulls away again.

"Liam!" I groan, borderline yelling.

"Is this you telling me you want to stop?" He raises a brow, clearly taunting me.

I'm kinda pissed that it's working.

"No," I grit through my teeth before allowing my head to crash back against the pillow.

"I'm not stopping. It's a *pause*." Liam dips his tongue between my folds once more and I melt into the sensation. He pulls away again, causing me to tense. "I want you to keep count of when you come. Understand?"

"Wait, what?"

"You heard me."

He's not wrong—I did hear him—but seriously?

"No, I heard you. I just...let's be honest, it's not hard to count to one."

He pins me with a confused expression before standing up, abandoning what little hope I had to steer us away from talking as quickly as possible. Placing his hands on his hips, he just stares at me, a confused expression plaguing his face.

"What?"

"I can't tell if that was a dig."

"If what was a dig?"

"The orgasm thing."

"What? No. I just meant I've never had more than one orgasm in a sitting before. My body just can't do it. It's not a you thing, it's a me thing."

Something in my words spurs him into action, his perplexed expression shifting into something akin to defiance. Determination, maybe?

"We'll see about that."

I want to tell him not to bother, that it's not going to pan out the way he wants, but I kind of want to see him try and fail. He's gotten awfully cocky lately.

The moment his tongue darts back over my clit, a jolt of electricity shoots through me. Fuck, that feels good. He languidly drags his tongue up and down before flicking it with precision over my clit.

It's not that I question his ability to get me off—hell, he's managed to do it on numerous occasions—but multiple times? Those are some lofty goals.

Every thought I have leaves my mind the second he envelopes my clit between his lips, sucking just hard enough to cause a guttural moan to fall from my mouth. Yanking at the tie holding my hands above my head, the restraint makes the sensations all the more consuming. I can't escape it, although I can't say I would try if I could.

My orgasm starts to build far sooner than I would hope it to. We've barely done anything, so if I come now, it's over.

"Wait—" I try to halt him, but he only edges me further. The languid strokes of his tongue grow urgent, more frenzied. I gasp as I feel his tongue probe my entrance before being replaced with a finger. As he pushes a second inside me at the same moment he sucks my clit, I detonate like a bomb. The orgasm I've been fighting off envelopes me, and I'm consumed.

A tingling sensation overtakes me, the heady, euphoric state like being thrown off a cliff then staying suspended midair. My climax is so overwhelming I start to understand why they call them *Little Deaths*.

Liam presses featherlight kisses along my thigh, lingering there for a moment to allow me to catch my breath.

"Hannah." His commanding tone lets me know instantly what he's asking.

"One," I gasp out, earning a delicious grin in response.

"Good girl."

He hovers between my legs for a minute or two, allowing me a moment of reprieve to catch my breath. Then, he ghosts his thumb over my sensitized clit, causing me to jerk at the touch. I'm so sensitive right now, the slightest whisper of a touch against my bundle of nerves is too much.

Liam proceeds to press a finger inside of me. My post-orgasm tenderness makes the sensation overwhelming, but not painful. A soft moan escapes me as he continues to pump a single digit in and out of me, but he's strategic as he doesn't touch my clit. I begin to wonder if his goal is to get me to come again at all, but as soon as that thought sets in, a new sensation creeps back.

His thumb dances over my anus, which is somewhere I can honestly say no man or woman has ever touched me. Not for a lack of trying—some men are weirdly fixated on the idea of putting it in a woman's ass. I've never been interested in the idea. However, when Liam sucks his thumb between his lips before pressing it back against my puckered hole, I gasp as it presses past the tight ring of muscle.

At first, I think it is going to hurt, but he leaves it there without much movement as he continues to pump his middle finger inside my pussy and I realize that the sensation of being so full is...intoxicating.

"Fuck—" I moan loudly as he pushes a second finger inside, still maintaining the location of his thumb. The sensation of being this full is so foreign to me, but my God, it's indescribable.

A familiar tingling sensation begins to crawl up my back, leaving me with confusion as well as an unrelenting feeling of pleasure. I want to say something, anything. The foreign sensations have me discombobulated, so when Liam pulls his thumb out and replaces it with the tip of his tongue, I about jump out of my skin, the near-scream that leaves my mouth enough to have whoever shares our wall probably calling the front desk.

That's when it happens. The foreign feeling crests as he increases his speed, pumping his fingers harder inside my cunt, not relenting as he laps at my tight hole.

"Oh my God," I cry out as I unmistakably come. This orgasm is unlike any I've ever had, the total-body consumption leaving me in such a sated state that I'm essentially putty at his disposal.

Liam massages my thighs as the tension of my release slowly starts to fade. I continue to gasp, desperately trying to get air into my lungs. Blood whooshes in my ears, the intensity of the orgasm leaving me in a spent state.

"Hannah...?" He poses it as a question, a question I know the answer to. But do I give it to him without resistance?

"Hm?"

"*Hannah.*"

"Two."

THIRTY-SEVEN

LIAM

Fuck, if watching her come undone isn't the sexiest thing I've ever seen in my life. I'm twenty-nine, but I think I've lived a full life. Death by being so entranced by Hannah's orgasm? Hell of a way to go.

I press a kiss to her thigh before standing up from the edge of the bed. The tent in my pants is borderline painful, but I needed to make a point before doing anything except focusing 100% on her reaching orgasm, and nothing else.

As I pull my slacks off along with my boxer briefs, my cock springs free. Standing at attention, I stroke it, pulling the bead of pre-cum down against my shaft in the process.

Hannah's eyes are fixed on me as she peers through her lashes. I would honestly think her eyes were closed with how dark it is if not for how clearly I can feel her gaze on me. I climb between her parted legs and hover in place. Hannah's disheveled, sated state has me consumed; I want to bask in her for as long as humanly possible.

Knowing I'm the only person who's ever given her multiple orgasms isn't just ego-stroking; it also makes me feel weirdly possessive in a way I've never been before. I'm not a jealous guy, not usually. However, Hannah has completely flipped that on its head. Now, if a man so much as looked at her, I can't be sure what I would be capable of.

Leaning my weight on my elbows, I look down at her with a grin. "You like your ass played with." I mean to say it as a question, but it comes out more like a statement of fact.

She doesn't question me or even attempt to deny it. "I guess I do." She shrugs, but I don't miss the way her face flushes.

"My dirty girl," I say with a grin as I press my lips to hers. She melts into my touch and I'm consumed by it. I'm so in love with this woman it's honestly terrifying, and the more I want to run from it, the deeper I find myself being pulled under.

I'm starting to question if she did something to me—I wouldn't put it past her.

"You said you have an IUD?" I ask, the weight of my question not lost on Hannah as her eyes go wide.

I don't have unprotected sex; I've been adamant that I don't have sex without a condom. I'm not sure why I ask it, can't tell why I want to sink into her without a barrier so badly; I just know that I do. I've never had sex without a latex wall between me and the person I'm with, so it's not like I'm craving something I've had.

"Yeah, I have an IUD."

"Good." I press my lips against hers once more as I line my cock up with her entrance, the foreign feeling against the sensitive tip a startling reminder that I very well might be in over my head with this idea. I'm not going to last more than two minutes at this rate. Recreating her first time was hardly in the plan for tonight.

As I push into her, I groan with every passing inch.

Hannah is tight, vise tight, but without a condom it's almost too much to handle. Once fully seated inside her, I pause for a moment, trying with everything in me to maintain my composure.

"Are you okay?" she whispers. I almost think she's being kind, but when I notice the cocky grin on her face, I thrust forward to make a point.

"I'm great..." However, my actions provide a very inconvenient side effect as a not-very-manly moan escapes me and my words trail off.

I expect her to laugh about it, or at the very least make a snide remark. But as her glazed eyes meet mine, I see a sincerity in them.

"Can you untie me, please?"

My first instinct is to say no, to tell her to be compliant for one goddamned moment in her life, but I can't find it in me not to give her everything she asks of me.

My hands wrap around the silk of the tie, unknotting it from the wooden post with ease. It isn't a complex knot in the slightest, but it was tight enough to do the trick. She finishes pulling the scrap of fabric from her wrists before tossing it on the ground beside the bed.

Hannah wastes no time as she reaches up and cups my face in her hands, kissing me. It's not aggressive, it's not urgent, it's not frantic. It's...loving. Her kiss is tentative and languid and everything you'd expect in a kiss from someone you love. I know that should terrify me—I should be freaking out—but it doesn't have that effect, not even in the slightest.

I lean into her gentle touch as I push into her rhythmically, not fast enough to disturb the way our tongues intertwine with no regard for urgency.

The words are on the tip of my tongue, but the irrational

fear that she won't say them back keeps me from being completely truthful with her. I want this, I want her, but the idea of giving her that much control over me gives me pause.

Her eyes meet mine and something I can only liken to an electric current passes through us in that moment. As I sink into her deeper, Hannah lets out a sound that reminds me of heaven. The soft moans from before are dwarfed by the frantic moans and gasps rolling off her tongue.

I gingerly slide my hand down along her body and lightly tease my thumb over her clit. At first, she tenses, breathing through pursed lips and squirming slightly under my touch. I fear she'll ask me to stop, but then a shiver courses through her body as pleasure seems to take over. Her breaths shorten into shallow pants until all that remains is a faint whimper begging for more.

That I can work with.

Quickly, the stroke of my thumb begins to match the frequency and urgency of my thrusts. Every time I push inside of her, I'm transported into what can only be described as pure ecstasy. It's nothing like I've ever experienced, feeling her tighten around me with no barrier separating me from Eden.

"Fuck, Hannah," I grit through my teeth, trying to keep my orgasm at bay as long as possible. I'll be damned if I don't get her there a third time tonight, if for nothing else but to prove to her what I'm capable of.

"I'm so close," she whimpers.

This urges me to speed up my tempo, no longer focusing on my own release. Hannah's walls grip around my cock tighter with each stroke, and her breath comes out in pants as she nears her climax. Gripping me like a vise, her orgasm washes over her. I can't hold off any longer. The sensation of her muscles contracting around me pushes me over the edge and I let out a guttural roar of pleasure as I release inside her, my cum filling her in a way that consumes me with a possessiveness I've never known.

It's terrifying and exhilarating at the same time.

Our pants linger in the air, mixing together in a medley of exhaustion and pleasure all at once. I push her sweat-dampened strands from her forehead as I gaze down at her, completely enraptured by her. She manages to look even more intoxicating like this, her guard down and entirely spent.

"You know what they say, right?"

"Hm?" she mumbles in her sleepy state.

"That things come best in threes, and in this case...that would be you," I laugh.

"I love you," she says absentmindedly with a chuckle before her eyes go wide. The realization of what she just said hits her. "I, uh, I shouldn't have said that."

My brows pinch together as I stare down at her. At first, I can't think of the words, but realization dawns on me. "Shouldn't have said what?"

"That I love you."

"Why shouldn't you say that?"

"Because, I—"

"I love you too, Hannah." I smile down at her and watch intently as relief washes over her.

Tears glaze the edges of her eyes and my stomach instantly drops. There are a lot of ways a man expects a woman to respond after they say "I love you" for the first time, and that's not one of the preferred responses.

"Baby, what's wrong?"

"I don't know," she sobs as her eyes meet mine. "Overwhelmed, I guess. If I'm being honest, I didn't expect any of this to happen. For *us* to happen—certainly not me falling in love with you."

"I didn't expect it either..." I brush my finger over the rogue tear dripping down her cheek. "But we did...and I'm really happy we did."

"Me too."

I take this moment to pull out of her, the warm sensation of being inside her overtaken by the frigid chill in the air. Hannah hops up from the bed to run to the bathroom and it's then I notice my cum dripping down her thigh. It shouldn't make me feel any sort of way, but it does. It makes me feel a lot of things.

She's mine, just *mine*.

THIRTY-EIGHT

HANNAH

The week since returning from New York has been...hectic, and that's an understatement. When we got back, it was one of the first nights I'd spent away from Liam in a while, but Gen needed me since the wedding was coming up.

Fast-forward to today, the wedding rehearsal.

We got through the actual rehearsal rather quickly. It was surprisingly easy to pretend Liam and I aren't together, a charade we'll keep up until we have the chance to have a conversation about it. He kept jabbing me in the side and, while I think he meant it playfully, by the end of walking down the aisle it was getting on my nerves.

You can take the Liam out of the idiot, but you can't take the idiot out of the Liam, apparently.

We push open the door to Andre's Bistro, where a chaotic scene greets us. There is a line of people waiting for tables curling out the entrance, uniformed waitstaff scurrying around, and conversations floating through the air. The hostess is working frantically, her words lost beneath the cacophony of voices as she rushes to get everyone seated as quickly as possible.

Our group moves through the crowded restaurant, dodging waiters weaving between tables with steaming platters of food. We follow a set of stairs to an open door at the back, which reveals an invitingly quiet space surrounded by sweetly twinkling lights. The family-sized table sits dramatically under a majestic chandelier, adorned with delicate glassware, sparkling silverware, and perfectly arranged floral centerpieces.

Despite my desire to meet him at the end of the table next to Gabe, I know it would look weird if I sat next to Liam of my own free will. I hate that we haven't discussed what officially being together means for us now that we're home, and I haven't figured out exactly how to broach the subject.

He's mine and I'm his...but does that hold the same weight if the world doesn't know?

Plopping down next to my brother, I'm catty-corner from Liam. His infuriatingly adorable grin looking back at me causes my stomach to do somersaults, but he looks away just as quickly.

Everyone settles into their seats swiftly, pouring themselves a glass from the large water pitchers littering the table.

As everyone begins to settle in, Jackson clanks a butter knife against his water glass to pull everyone's attention in his direction. He stands from his seat and I notice the way Gen stares up at him adoringly. The idea that I ever wanted them apart fills me with guilt, but when her eyes meet mine, I know there is not a shred of animosity left between us.

"I wanted to thank everyone for being a part of mine and Gen's big day. Our family and friends that are basically family mean everything to us and we could not imagine embarking on this day without each of you with us..."

Tears begin to build as Jackson continues to talk, but my eyes still travel to Liam...whose eyes are already on me.

"Love is nothing without your loved ones to share it with. Gen and I would not be where we are without the love and support of everyone at this table."

Savannah hoots and hollers from the other end of the table, causing everyone to erupt in laughter. However, my eyes never leave Liam's even as he shifts to look at Gabe as he socializes with him and Kara, Gabe's longtime girlfriend.

Sage's shoulder brushes against mine as she leans into me. "How was New York?"

"It was good. The auditions went well."

"Oh, shut up, I don't care about that part yet. How was it when Liam showed up?"

I pin her with a glare, but she just stares at me with a grin. "How did you know about that?"

"Well, you went to New York and he disappeared the same day—it was hardly subtle. Does your brother know?"

"I don't think so, so if you could stop talking about it, that would be great."

"You haven't told him?" The confused expression Sage is sporting is anything but judgmental, only concerned. She's seen everything that's transpired between me and Liam, so it's logical that she'd be invested, but jeez, Sage, time and place.

"No, so shut the fuck up," I whisper aggressively.

Sage appears to get the hint as she settles back into her seat, Jackson's toast coming to an end.

"So, this is a toast to you guys, because Gen and I know this would not be happening if it weren't for your influence in our lives."

The preset meal makes it easy to wrangle the orders of everyone in our party. We submitted our desired dish out of three options last week and I naturally chose the chicken penne. As they set the dish down in front of me, I don't miss the way my mother's eyes linger on my plate.

She's always been intent on policing what I eat. Linda Thatcher-Miles is what the kids call an "almond mom." Despite never having had issues with my weight, she's convinced that I'll blow up like a balloon.

"Hannah." The fake cheery disposition doesn't meet her eyes as she grins across the table at me.

"Yes, Mom?" I look down at my food, pushing the chicken around so I have something to look at other than her.

"Are you sure that's the best route? I'm sure this kind gentleman could grab you a salad from the back."

I feel terrible for the poor server who is now standing next to my mother, a look of discomfort plaguing him.

"I'd be happy to grab you something from the back that you'd like better, miss."

"I think she'd enjoy that, Enrique." My mom makes a point of looking at the poor boy's name tag, no doubt not giving a single shit about what his name is.

"No, I'm good. Thank you, though. I'll have the pasta."

My mother's face drops when Enrique walks away, but she doesn't carry the conversation surrounding my choice of sustenance much further, thank God. She starts talking with Gen's dad at the other end of the table, giving me a much-needed reprieve from her scrutiny.

"So, Hannah! How did that audition in New York go?" Liam's mom, Caroline, peers across the table with genuine interest. Stephen must have told her about my taking PTO last

CHAPTER THIRTY-EIGHT

Friday, but I can't quell the hope that maybe it was Liam who told her.

"It went really well, actually. Fingers crossed!" I grin from ear to ear, my pride evident in my voice. I worked hard on preparing for the two auditions I attended while in New York and it shows.

However, I don't miss the way my mom scoffs. I'm prepared to ignore it and continue eating my pasta, but she doesn't allow that to happen.

"You really should be using your time more wisely, Hannah. With all the time you spend going on these silly little auditions, you could be putting in extra time to move past being an assistant at the firm. Isn't that right, Stephen?"

Stephen Park looks noticeably uncomfortable about being brought into the conversation. He's notoriously Switzerland when this happens, and he almost never has a quip to interject.

"I believe what Hannah does with her time outside of her scheduled hours at Baker & Park is her business."

At first I think it comes from Stephen, which is surprising on its own, but he's just as confused as I am.

It's Liam who interjected.

"Excuse me?" My mom scowls at Liam's clear insolence before continuing, "I don't believe your opinion was asked for. If I want my daughter to pursue something realistic rather than using that stupid theater degree she insisted on getting, then that's my right as a mother."

"It's also your right as a mother to treat your daughter like a human being."

"I beg your pardon?!" My mother nearly screams across Stephen and Caroline, who are sandwiched between her and Liam. I genuinely feel bad for them right now, but not enough to put a stop to whatever Liam is about to say.

"You heard me, Linda." He wipes his mouth with the cloth napkin in his lap before he continues, turning in his seat to look at my mother head-on. "Hannah is not a child. She is an adult with her own goals and ambitions. She wants to pursue theater, and she's damn good at it. So if you could stop making whatever your issue is with the way she lives her life everyone else's problem, that would be great."

My mouth drops open in pure shock. I want to say something, but I can't think of a single word. I expect Jackson to say something—he's notorious for defending our mother and the way she treats me; he says it's because she wants what is best for me—but as he looks at her now, he just seems sad. My dad is redder than a tomato, but it doesn't seem to be because of Liam. He's not a fan of dramatics or theatrics, so it's no surprise that we've never been particularly close. However, my mom's display of sparring with Liam is sure to get her an earful on their ride back to the hotel.

Liam, however, is so getting laid tonight.

"That's enough now, Liam. Let's salvage the rest of this evening and celebrate Gen and Jackson." Stephen finally breaks his silence as his eyes meet Liam's, an unspoken conversation happening between them right in front of my eyes.

Mom's eyes meet mine and it honestly seems like she expects me to defend her. However, as Enrique walks by to fill up the water pitchers, I grin up at him.

"Can you please send compliments to the chef? The chicken penne is delicious."

THIRTY-NINE

LIAM

The decision to have the entire bridal party stay at the hotel was initially a weird one as we all live in Atlanta. The wedding and hotel might be an hour outside the city, but it still feels like a bit much. However, if we're honest, as I tap my knuckles against Hannah's hotel room door, I feel like it was the most brilliant idea Jackson has ever had.

As her door swings open, Hannah reaches out and grabs me by the tie and yanks me into the room with little effort. We drove separately, but I was adamant that I wanted to see her the moment I got here.

I really am totally fucked, aren't I?

"Hey—" I start to say something, but before I can get the words out Hannah's lips are pressed against mine. The taste of Starburst candy is on her tongue and the smell of her hair fills my senses as she pushes me against the wall next to the door. I feel my heart beating faster as I laugh and tangle my hand in her hair, tilting her head back slightly.

"Calm down there, killer. What's this about?" Not that I'm

upset. Hell, I'd opt for this greeting every time I walk in the door, but it's just not how she normally is.

The room suddenly goes quiet, and her gaze shifts to meet mine. Her eyes widen with indignation as she asks, "Are you complaining?" Her lips are tight and her posture tense, shoulders rising slightly in anticipation.

"Of course not."

"Then shut up and kiss me, you idiot."

I do as she says because honestly, it doesn't take much convincing on my part.

My fingers tighten around the hair at the nape of Hannah's neck as I pull her to me. She tilts her head back and lets out a slight gasp. In one swift motion, I lift her up and feel her legs latch around my waist like a vise. The warmth radiating from her core against my hardened length sends a shiver through me, and I press her against the opposite wall of the entryway.

Hannah's chest heaves against mine with each breath, and I trail my lips down her throat. Her skin tastes of warm, sweet honey as I bite into the soft flesh at the curve of her neck. A pleasured moan escapes her lips as I pull her even closer, my hands roaming delicately along her curves.

Stepping away from the wall, I all but throw her onto the bed before pulling her dress over her head to find her completely naked underneath.

No panties, no bra.

"Wait, were you like this at dinner?" I laugh in shock.

"Of course not. However, I did get to the hotel twenty minutes before you and I was pretty set on jumping your bones the moment you walked in the door, so."

"That was a pretty solid plan."

"Thanks."

She exhales as I gently guide her down onto the bed. My lips dance lightly over the column of her throat and I nip at her delicious skin before my mouth travels lower to rest on the swell of her chest. I pause, hovering just above her body, and let my hand trace a tantalizing path between her breasts and down to her hips, where it comes to a teasing stop hovering over her heat.

"God, you're fucking perfect."

A soft moan pulls from Hannah's lips despite my barely touching her.

"I don't think you realize how long I've watched you. Dreamed about sinking into this perfect pussy of yours again." I ghost my fingertips over her glistening lips, but refrain from applying too much pressure yet.

"Liam," she whispers as she lifts her hips, but I don't change my pressure.

"Taste these perfect pink nipples," I say with a grin as I lean down and flick my tongue against one of the tantalizing peaks. Hannah gasps at the sensation. "Even when we were at each other's throats, I wanted nothing more than to fuck you so hard that you couldn't help being ruined by the man you hated most."

"Then do it."

"Do what?" I ask as I barely circle her clit, my touch so featherlight I doubt it brings her any sensation.

"Fuck me like I hate you—fuck me like you hate me," Hannah gasps, her words coming out as no more than a mumble. "Fuck me so hard that I'm irrefutably ruined for any other man, any other partner. Any other person who dares to touch me, knowing that you're on my mind."

Something in her words makes me snap; the simple

thought of anyone besides me touching her drums up something feral and animalistic inside me.

"Gladly."

My fingers tremble as I reach to loosen my belt buckle. My eyes never leave Hannah, who has settled back against the pillows on the bed, her face alive with anticipation and lust. With one swift movement, I pull my sweater and undershirt off and kick away my slacks. In a flurry of urgency, I yank off my boxer briefs and suddenly I am standing exposed in the room, illuminated by the soft light of a single lamp, with Hannah's hungry stare focused solely on me.

"Come here," I demand as I point to the edge of the bed.

Hannah quickly follows my instructions and sits on the edge, her glistening eyes staring up at me in anticipation.

"You listen so well." I grin down at her as she leans into my touch when I cup her face. "Do you remember your word?"

"Yes."

"What is it?"

"Seymour."

"Good," I say as I drag my thumb across her bottom lip, watching her go slack-jawed at the motion. "Now be my good girl and open that pretty mouth of yours."

Normally Hannah is resistant—even in the bedroom she could not be confused with someone compliant or docile. However, she concedes, and warmth invades my chest knowing she's willing to do that for me.

She opens her mouth wide and I rest my cock against her extended tongue. If I were a pictures kind of man, this would be the perfect moment: a memory I would love to imprint on my brain.

"Now suck."

Hannah's slender fingers encircle my shaft, her grip firm yet tender. She opens her mouth wider and carefully draws me inside. I feel the warmth of her breath on my skin as she works her tongue in long, pleasurable strokes. Her hands move up and down my length with each retreat of her lips, then she applies a gentle suction as she takes me deeper. My body shudders involuntarily at the sensation of my tip hitting the back of her throat, a wave of pleasure rolling through me like thunder.

"Fuck, princess. That feels incredible."

Hannah moans around my cock, the vibration only adding to my pleasure. I can feel the tension building and that just won't do—I have way more planned for tonight than shooting my load down her throat at this second. I reach around the back of her neck, grasping at the blonde strands, and use them to yank her backward. Her mouth hangs open as I pull my dick free.

"Tap my leg if it becomes too much. You won't be able to use your safe word." I make sure to make eye contact, needing to know she's comfortable.

"Yes, sir." A grin forms on Hannah's lips as she says it and I can't help the way my dick jerks at hearing her call me that. However, knowing Hannah, the slightest indication that I like it will cause her to use it against me.

"Open."

Hannah's mouth falls open again as I press past her lips and slide in in one swift motion. She gasps at the sudden sensation of my cock in her throat. I hold it there for a few seconds, allowing her to adjust before using my tight grip on her hair as leverage to push further down. Her eyes widen and tears form as I thrust in and out, slowly increasing speed until I finally pull all the way out, allowing her a moment to breathe.

I start again more forcefully, thrusting my cock down

Hannah's throat a little bit harder and deeper each time. She gags and I do it again and again until she's no longer fighting the gag reflex. Then I slowly slide it back in, a little deeper each time, until I'm in as far as I can go without choking her. I go slowly, holding my breath, forcing myself not to come.

Desperately, I want to come down her throat. I need it so bad despite my intentions not to. Her eyes are tearing and her hands are pulling at my ass, trying to force me to thrust deeper. I grab her hands before she can get them around my ass and hold them behind her back. I continue to fuck her mouth shallowly. She relaxes her throat and finally lets me slide all the way in. Then I hold myself there, my cock in the tight, warm crevice of her throat. My dick throbbing at the powerful sensation.

I pull free of her mouth once more as the suction releases with a loud pop.

"Are you going to let me come down that pretty little throat of yours?"

"Please," she says breathlessly.

Her response is unexpected, but I can't ignore how intoxicated it makes me feel.

"You want me to?"

"Yes."

"Be a good little slut then and ask me nicely." I grin down at her, but my stomach is in knots. Praise is one thing, but I haven't delved too far into degrading her. It's foreign territory but, God, if I don't want her to like it.

Lucky for me, she seems to.

Her eyes are glistening with tears, but they twinkle with mischief at my words just the same. "Please. Please come down my throat."

"You want my cum?" I drag my thumb over her bottom lip.

"Yes."

"Say it."

"I want your cum."

"God, if I knew you were such a little whore I would've fucked this pretty little mouth a long time ago."

Hannah squirms in place, rocking back and forth. I wait for her to bite back, but she doesn't, just stares up at me.

"Open."

She opens her mouth.

I thrust my hips forward, pushing my hardness deeper into Hannah's mouth. She gags as her lips press against the base of me. I withdraw slightly and push back in faster, eager to feel her throat around me again. She splutters and whimpers ever so quietly, but I continue, feeling the heat that is radiating from her. Each time, I drive into her hot mouth with an intensity that leaves us both trembling. Holding the back of her head, I thrust into her as deep as I can go, causing her to gag. I'm so proud of her when she doesn't tap my leg to bow out.

"Fuck. You are so good at taking my cock down your throat."

She hums in response, encouraging me further. I increase my pace as I watch my cock drive down her throat, her sigh enough to nearly make me lose it. Hannah's eyes pinch shut as I thrust into her.

I pause, seated so deep that her lips are wrapped around my base. "I want you to look at me while I cum in that pretty little mouth of yours."

Her eyes, glistening with tears, meet mine and something about the intimacy of her gaze causes my orgasm to crawl up my spine. I start frantically thrusting into her mouth as deep as I can go, causing her to swallow around my shaft. The tightening sensation pushes me past the point of no return.

I pump into her mouth once, then twice, but I pull out just enough so that I coat her tongue as I shoot ribbons of cum into her mouth. She doesn't jerk away, but revels in it as my cock jerks in her mouth.

When my orgasm finally dissipates, I pull out all the way, utterly fixated on the way Hannah sits there with her mouth open, my cum pooling on her tongue.

"Swallow."

And she does without hesitation. It's the single most intoxicating sight I've ever seen as I watch her swallow every last drop, her eyes never leaving mine.

Gasping for air, I stand there, cock in hand, staring down at her for about a minute. She doesn't go to move but stares up at me adoringly, awaiting instruction. As if this woman could get any more perfect, she manages to surprise me again and again.

I kneel in front of her, my eyes level with hers as she stares at me. The tears have long since dissipated, but moisture still lingers on her cheeks. I wipe them both dry with the pads of my thumbs.

"You have got to be the single most incredible woman I've ever known."

She rolls her eyes, and I realize as she tries to avoid my gaze that she doesn't even remotely believe me. I reach up, cupping her chin with far more aggression than I intend.

"Hannah, look at me."

She resists at first, but I squeeze her chin harder, forcing her gaze to mine.

"What?" The shitty attitude she normally has is back and while it's a relief to know she hasn't completely changed in the last half-hour, I don't like why she's biting back.

"Get up."

I'm surprised when she listens and allows me to cup her hands in mine so I can pull her to her feet. Guiding her over to the full-length, wood-framed mirror leaning against the wall, I stand behind her.

"What do you see?"

FORTY

HANNAH

"What do you see?" Liam's words reverberate off the shell of my ear as he forces me to stand in front of the full-length mirror, staring at myself in all my naked glory.

"Whatever you're trying here, Liam, it's not going to work. I have no issues with my body."

His arms wrap around my midsection from behind as he pulls me flush against him. "I didn't say you did. I asked what you see."

I roll my eyes at his ridiculous question as my eyes meet his in the mirror. "This is stupid," I say with a glare.

"Humor me."

A gulp rolls down my throat, the taste of his cum lingering, but his energy could not be further from what it was mere minutes ago. Despite my apprehension, I do as he asks, staring at myself in the mirror.

"I see me naked with your arms wrapped around my stomach."

"Okay, dumbass, dig a little deeper, please."

Resisting the urge to rear back and step on his foot, I look into the mirror once more.

"My lipstick is all over, thanks for that." I chuckle, causing him to laugh too.

"If you're expecting an apology for that, you've got the wrong guy."

"Yeah, yeah." I roll my eyes before turning my attention back to the task. "My mascara is everywhere too."

"Hannah," he says with that reprimanding tone that usually makes my knees buckle, but I honestly can't tell what he's asking for.

"I don't know, okay? I don't know what you're asking and you're starting to piss me off."

"Fine." He huffs before tightening his hold around me. "I'll go."

"Do I really need to be here while you compliment yourself? You've got an ego the size of the Empire State Building. Save me the preview, I've watched the movie."

"Hannah, please." His voice is soft and earnest.

I want to keep fighting him, but I don't. My eyes meet his in the mirror and he lets out a relieved sigh before continuing.

"When I see you, I see the most incredible woman I've ever known."

I scoff, earning me a pinch on the side.

"I'm serious. Even before all of this, I've always thought you were exceptional, and I hate that you don't think that too." He presses a kiss to the side of my head before continuing. "Who told you you weren't everything that I know you are?"

"You." I laugh, trying to cut through the tension in the air, but it has the opposite effect.

"Well, I'm an idiot. You really shouldn't listen to me 95% of the time."

Tears begin to build at my waterline as I struggle to hold them at bay. I don't like how vulnerable I feel right now, but as Liam's arms tighten around me, I know I'm not escaping it. The warmth of his embrace envelopes me in a cocoon of comfort, the chill in the air a whisper of a memory long since gone. The heating vent on the floor kicks on with a click before air begins whooshing out of the corner of the room. Our hotel room is spacious, but not big enough to give me an escape from Liam, though at this point I'm not sure I'd want one.

"I said a lot of things I'm not proud of. I worked for a long time to keep you at arm's length and I know in doing that I caused a lot of harm to us...to you. I still can't get over the fact that I could have had you this entire time if it wasn't for my stupid ego."

"It wasn't just you, Liam."

"I know that, but my dumbass decision to shrug you off the morning after we...after I took your virginity caused a nearly decade-long rift between us. I love you, and the thought of that now churns my stomach."

"I love you too."

Liam nods, a defeated expression plaguing his face as shame blankets him. "I know I was out of line with your mom earlier, and I'm sorry. I made a scene, but I can't stand the way she treats you. Half the time I want to punch Jackson in the face for not seeing it. More than anything, I hate the way her opinion has made you see yourself."

"My mom's opinion doesn't m—"

"Hannah."

A single tear streams down my cheek as my eyes meet his once more. All I can manage to do is shrug. My voice cracks as I speak. "She's my mom."

"And you deserve to be treated better."

"What? Is that gonna be you? Are you about to come and save me from the mean old Mother Gothel and fix everything?" Sarcasm drips off my words and I watch him mentally recoil.

Silence coats us, but we don't break apart as his gaze lingers on me in the mirror.

"Honestly, if I thought that were possible, there are few things I wouldn't do to make it happen. However, it's not about me. I want you to love you as much as I do because you believe you're exceptional, not because I willed you to."

Liam's arms tighten around me as he kisses the back of my head, and despite the weight of the conversation, I feel more loved than I've ever felt in my entire life.

"I'll get there...just give me time."

This seems to appease him as his tight grasp loosens, the loving embrace entrapping me no longer there for support.

"In the meantime..." His fingertips dance along my stomach, causing me to clench my abs at the contact. "...I'll just have to love you enough for the both of us."

My gaze is locked on his hand ghosting over my skin with a featherlight touch. Liam's pointer finger circles my navel as his lips press to my ear.

"Eyes on the mirror. You stop looking, I stop. Deal?"

I gulp as a heady feeling overtakes me. Locking my eyes with Liam's, I watch him intently as his fingers creep downward. His middle finger pushes between the folds of my pussy with a simple dip before pulling back. I swallow the lump in my throat as I fixate on his movements.

"Goddamn, princess. You're still so wet."

My stomach clenches again at the pet name, which used to bring me so much rage but now manages to reduce me to a puddle on the ground.

His finger slips down again, except this time he pushes past my entrance, causing me to gasp. As soon as he dips his finger inside, it's gone again. I groan at his taunts, but I don't risk breaking eye contact as my chest heaves in the mirror.

Liam lifts his finger and presses it to my lips. "Open."

I do as I'm told and he pushes the single digit into my mouth, the tangy taste of my own arousal coating my tongue. I don't miss the way his nostrils flare at the image in front of him, and that only makes me grow wetter.

"Please," I whine. I need him inside of me. I realize he's trying to do a thing right now, and I appreciate it and all the sentimentality of being loved and adored and all that shit. But right now? I need him desperately to fuck me like loving me is the last thing on his mind.

"Please what?" Liam's breath cascades over the side of my neck as he asks, clearly wanting me to verbalize it.

"I want you inside me. Please fuck me."

"How?"

The fuck does he mean *how*? I would venture to say it's a pretty self-explanatory process.

"What do you mean?"

"How would you like me to fuck you?" He chooses this moment to bite my neck, the sting melting into pleasure as a moan coats my lips. "Do you want me to make love to you and show you how much I love you? Or..." He dips two fingers inside of me, stretching me deliciously. "...do you want me to fuck you like I hate you? So hard that you have to rub your legs together just to find comfort as you walk down that aisle tomorrow?"

"The second one, definitely the second one," I blurt out, causing Liam to laugh.

"Eager little thing, aren't you."

My face flushes with heat, but I simply nod.

Liam reaches up, entangling his fingers in my hair. I expect a gentle tug like he's done many times before, but a yelp falls from my lips as he jerks my head back. The bite against my scalp only pushes me further into desire, drawing a whimper from my lips.

"Fuck, you're such a little whore. You love that, don't you? You love it when I manhandle you."

An even louder whimper escapes me, causing Liam to jerk me backwards.

"Fine. On the bed," he demands. At first, I think he sounds angry, but then I realize that it's all an act and I fold into it.

I sit down on the bed, only for him to pin me with a glare.

"On your hands and knees."

As my hands and knees meet the soft cotton of the duvet, I feel the sting of Liam's hand landing against my ass cheek, followed by a gentle rub in a circular motion. He dips his hand down only to find me not just wet, but soaked.

"Fuck..." He groans before his tone shifts again. "You love this, don't you? You love it when I treat you like a whore."

I moan loudly as he pushes two fingers inside my pussy. Liam gives me no time to adjust to the intrusion as he roughly fucks me with his hand. I back up an inch to chase his touch, but as soon as I move, he pulls his hand away, leaving me devastatingly empty, another whimper escaping me.

A loud crack lands against my ass, followed by the same kneading motion as before.

"If what I'm doing isn't good enough for you, then I'll just stop." He's taunting me, and I hate the way I grow wetter at his harsh response. "What do you want? Since you clearly aren't satisfied with what you're getting."

I don't respond, causing him to smack my ass again.

"Hannah, answer me."

"I want your cock," I whine.

The mattress dips as I feel him move onto the bed. Liam kneels behind me, his knees pushing my calves apart to slide between them.

"You want my cock?" he taunts as he slides the tip between my folds, the sensation tantalizing, yet still not enough.

"Yes."

"Say it—tell me again. Tell me you want my cock."

"I want your—"

My words are cut off as he slams into me, pushing deep inside with one swift thrust. I let out a sharp moan and quickly bury my face in the pillow to muffle my sounds of pleasure as he starts to move within me, each stroke more urgent than the last. His powerful thrusts send shockwaves of pleasure through my body that I can't contain any longer, and a loud moan escapes my lips despite my best efforts to keep quiet. He doesn't stop there, though, and drives into me even harder, his movements rhythmic and intense.

"You want me to fuck you like I hate you?" He increases his rhythm, nearly pushing me forward on the bed as I bite down on the cotton duvet in an attempt to quiet the scream building in my belly. "I'll gladly fuck you however you like. But just remember that you, along with this pussy—" He chooses this moment to slam into me, pulling a scream from my lungs. "—are mine and only mine. I don't take lightly to what's mine being mistreated."

Liam's grunts melt into the air with every harsh thrust, growing more and more ragged with every movement. "So remember that next time you let someone treat you like that. Now—" He pauses, giving me a welcome reprieve to breathe more fully. "Touch that delicious little clit of yours while I fuck you. I want to feel you come around my cock."

My middle finger finds the tender bundle of nerves and I begin to trace circles. The combination of feeling so full and fucked so roughly makes the contact almost too much.

Liam pulls one hand off my hip, but his thrusts don't relent. He's just as punishing, yet with the added stimulation it almost feels better. I nearly scream as his now-wet thumb circles the tight ring at my back entrance, teasing me as he presses the tip in. As he fucks my pussy with his dick, he keeps the same rhythm with his thumb in my ass and I reach the moment of no return faster than ever before.

I detonate, my orgasm taking me so violently, so intensely that I start to scream into the pillow.

Liam doesn't seem to like that; he yanks me backwards mid-orgasm, his free hand wrapping around my throat firmly, but not restricting my airway. He somehow manages to drag my orgasm out for what feels like forever and, just as I think I might pass out, I feel Liam's lips against my ear.

"Fuck, I love the way you come on my cock. I've never felt anything better." His words send shivers down my spine before he pushes me forward, causing my face to meet the duvet again.

His strong hands grip my hips tightly, and my body trembles with each thrust. He pounds into me relentlessly, dragging out each thrust until I can feel everything resonating through me. His voice is a low growl as he nears his climax. The last few strokes are but an echo of pleasure until his body finally stills. The heat of his cum radiates deep inside me, and I am overcome with pleasure as he slowly withdraws from me.

I feel so empty with him no longer inside me, but as his cum drips down my thigh, I feel entirely spent, and I can't think of a single other person in this world that I'd rather spend me.

The soft terrycloth of a damp washcloth drags across my sensitive core as Liam cleans me up. His tender touch is a far cry from how he was only moments ago. As much as I love when he's rough with me, that side of him pales in comparison to the doting man behind me. I roll over onto my back, allowing him easier access to drag the cloth against my flesh as he wipes my thigh with precision.

Liam tosses the washcloth into the hamper in the bathroom before returning to lay next to me in bed, grabbing me and pulling me into his arms without hesitation. His ragged breaths rattle me as I settle against his chest, the sound of his breathing a soundtrack to bring me calm.

He presses a kiss to the top of my head, causing me to smile. I open my mouth to talk, make a snide remark about his sudden affection, but he speaks before I have the chance to taunt him.

"Whatever you're about to say, don't. Just let me hold you for a while."

And I do.

FORTY-ONE

HANNAH

My knuckles rap against the bridal suite door twice before I hear footsteps briskly approach. Savannah opens it with a bright smile on her face, her attitude far more chipper than one would expect so early in the morning. Her copper waves are pulled tightly into a bun, and she wears a sage silk robe tied at the waist. On the back of the robe is written in fancy script: "Matron of Honor." We hug briefly before she steps aside to let me in. I take a moment to survey the room before us, the space filled with sunlight streaming in through the large floor-to-ceiling windowpanes. A queen-sized bed dressed in layers of white and blue sits against the far wall, vases of seasonal flowers scattered here and there, and a vanity mirror reflecting Gen's smiling face back at me.

"How's our bride this morning?" I smile as I set my overnight bag down on the floor and hang the garment bag housing my bridesmaid's dress on the clothing rack next to the vanity.

"Nervous," she laughs awkwardly before pulling what I assume to be a mimosa to her lips. Gen has never been great with massive amounts of attention on her, and you can't get much more center of attention than a bride on her wedding day.

"Why are you nervous?" I ask, but I'm sure I know before the words come out.

"Your mom insisted on us inviting close to 200 people on your family's side. We're going to have over 250 people there today and every time I think about walking down that aisle, I envision myself tripping and subsequently I get the strong urge to vomit."

And people say I'm dramatic.

"Viv—" I squeeze her shoulders as she breathes in, then exhales an elongated breath. Jackson and her dad are the only people I hear call her by her childhood nickname anymore, but if any day calls for sentimentalities, it's this one. "You are about to marry the love of your life, and if that's not enough motivation to push past the anxiety of today, you're also about to gain me as a sister. What gets better than that?"

Gen crinkles her nose at my joke, the years we spent apart a distant memory that I would prefer to pretend never happened. There once was a time that I willingly stood between her and Jackson and the idea of that makes me want to barf. Gen and Jackson are perfect for one another—I was an idiot not to see that.

"You've always been my sister, Hannah. Marrying Jackson doesn't make that any more true than it already is."

Tears threaten my waterline and I stare up at the ceiling, trying my best not to allow it to ruin the makeup I managed to put on before leaving my hotel room—much to Liam's dismay, mind you, as he made no less than three attempts to coax me back into bed. Despite my repeated reminders that we're both in the wedding, he kept reiterating that he isn't due to meet Jackson for another couple hours.

Gen reaches up, cupping her hand over mine resting on her shoulder. With a tight squeeze, my eyes are pulled back to hers in the mirror, the tears welling in my eyes reflected back at me in hers.

"I love you, you know that?" she says.

"What's not to love?" I laugh, causing her to squeeze my hand tighter. "Kidding, kidding. I love you too, Viv." I press my lips to the top of her unstyled hair. She's a stark contrast to me and Savannah, who already have our hair and makeup done, but Gen wanted us to be here while she's getting ready.

Now that I think of it, all three of us are supposed to be here. I look down at my iPhone to find no notifications from Sage before looking over at Savannah. She seems to get the message as she pulls her phone out to check for any missed texts or calls. Savannah shakes her head in disappointment at me. We still have a few hours, so it's not quite cause for concern.

"What was that?" Gen sounds frantic.

"What was what?"

"That look you two just gave each other?"

"We didn't give each other a look," I say with a laugh as Savannah comes to stand at my side.

"I'm going to go up to Sage's room. She just texted me letting me know that she needs help bringing down the extra champagne."

The blatant lie rolls off Savannah's tongue with ease and it appears to calm Gen from the impending spiral she was no doubt preparing to have.

Savannah disappears for longer than running up to a room in the same building to grab champagne requires, but when she appears in the doorway with a bare-faced Sage at her side and a bottle of champagne in hand, I breathe a sigh of relief.

By the time Gen is preparing to get into her wedding dress, Sage is ready. Her chocolate curls are pinned into a bun on top of her head, mirroring mine and Savannah's, and her makeup is elegant yet understated. Each of us steps into a sage-green, chiffon floor-length gown, but we each have a different neckline to accentuate each of our respective body types. Sage makes a menagerie of jokes about the color of our dresses being her name, but I don't miss the way Savannah hasn't stopped glaring at her sister-in-law.

What the hell is that about?

Whatever, we don't have time for that right now.

Savannah steps out of the walk-in closet attached to the bedroom with a large white garment bag, no doubt housing the gorgeous lace gown Gen found all those weeks ago.

The intricate beadwork mixed with the scalloped lace gives the gown almost an art deco style reminiscent of the twenties. Flutter sleeves melt into a deep V neckline, giving a peek of cleavage, but not so much that it looks distasteful.

Gen steps into the gown and, as she pulls it up over her hips, then all the way over her frame, it's clear that it was made specifically for her. It hugs her perfectly, and despite the bile that forms in the back of my throat at the thought of what my brother is inevitably going to think—and not all of it appropriate—I still admire how understated yet sexy it is. The fit-and-flare silhouette flatters Gen's ample curves in such a way that Aphrodite would be jealous.

Tears start to threaten, but I'm quickly pinned with a glare from Gen.

"Don't. Because if you start crying, I'll start—" Her voice cracks as she cuts herself off.

I stare up at the ceiling for the second time this morning in an attempt to keep my emotions in check as Savannah appears with a tissue for Gen, dabbing her waterline ever so delicately so as to not disturb her makeup.

"Are you ready?" Savannah asks Gen, and her question is met with a nod.

We line up for the processional and, as Liam steps to my side, I notice a tenseness in his demeanor that he didn't have when I left him this morning.

"What crawled up your ass?" I whisper, earning me a grin.

"Nothing," he says before clearing his throat. He leans in to my side as he brings his lips so close to my ear that I can feel the heat of his breath. "Just struggling with the fact that you look like that right now and I can't ravish you the way I want to."

A warmth spreads over me as he resumes his comfortable distance.

Biting back my grin, I look forward, but mumble in response, "Good answer."

A piano rendition of Barry Manilow's "Could It Be Magic" begins to play as each pairing walks down the aisle arm in arm. Our steps are carefully rehearsed as we approach the altar. I remove my arm from the crook of Liam's arm and step to stand behind Savannah as we await the bride.

Jackson's eyes meet mine as I feel the waterworks start to creep forward once again. This is everything he's ever wanted. Not a wife, but *this* wife. Genevieve Bennett, soon to be Genevieve Thatcher-Miles, my best friend since childhood, the first girl—nay—*only* girl he's ever loved.

Savannah subtly pushes a tissue into my palm as Édith Piaf's "La Vie En Rose" starts to play through the speakers discreetly placed throughout the chapel. The chill in the air is immediately dulled as the heavy wooden doors at the end of the aisle creak open once more, this time to reveal Gen.

The beautiful bride.

My gaze follows her as she floats down the aisle with her arm looped through her dad's, a man who has been through far too much in his lifetime but is consumed with so much pride as he gives his only daughter away.

"Who gives this bride?" the officiant asks.

"I do." Gen's dad's voice shakes as he responds, only exacerbated by the dam that breaks the moment he places Gen's hand in Jackson's. The tears that stream down his cheeks only make me more emotional. I quickly attempt to tap away the moisture from my face.

The moment they begin reciting their vows, my eyes ghost past them at the altar, only to linger on the tall drink of water already staring back at me. While his eyes aren't misty like mine, they're still steeped in emotion. I want to mouth "I love you," but based on the expression he's sporting, I'd venture to say he's having the very same thought.

"Do you, Genevieve Bennett, take Jackson to be your lawfully wedded husband?"

"I do."

"And do you, Jackson Thatcher-Miles, take Genevieve to be your lawfully wedded wife?"

"I do."

My attention keeps shifting back and forth between the happy couple and Liam, but his eyes never leave me. A few months ago I would have felt under scrutiny, like he's judging me, but when our eyes meet across the altar all I feel is this radiating warmth crawling up my stomach and pooling in my chest, where it has taken up residence for a while now.

"I now pronounce you husband and wife! You may kiss your bride!"

Jackson does just that as he cups Gen's face in his hands and draws her lips to his. The crowd hoots and hollers as "This Will Be" by Natalie Cole starts booming through the room, the familiar tone from mine and Gen's favorite movie when we were kids filling me with nostalgia.

As we pair off once more to make our way back down the aisle, I loop my arm through Liam's. Unlike before, he rests his hand over my hand in the crook of his elbow before squeezing it gently. No one in the room notices, but something about his touch causes my stomach to jump with anticipation—of what I'm not sure.

After an excruciating hour of being maneuvered by the photographer and Savannah yelling at everyone to stand just so, I'm relieved when we finally arrive in the reception hall.

I'm in awe the moment we walk into the room; twinkle lights mixed with sprigs of eucalyptus hang from the exposed beams on the ceiling. The rustic yet industrial feel of the space is softened by the feminine decor. Cream-colored tablecloths line every circular table, topped with a variety of trinkets and florals, all expertly tied in with the same eucalyptus that lines the ceiling.

Dinner passes quickly, yet the entire time I find myself searching for Liam across the space. It's a struggle to not be obvious. The bridal party is positioned at the head of the room at a long table, facing out over the guests. Over half of my extended family is here, most of which I haven't seen since high school. My mom is socializing with Aunt Sylvia, and I'm hopeful this means she'll be distracted from me tonight.

"Now it is time for the bride and groom to share their first dance," the DJ says into the microphone, his voice booming through the speakers.

Jackson and Gen are quickly on the dance floor, Gen's hand in one of Jackson's as his other rests on the exposed part of her back. An unfamiliar French tune fills the space as they sway to the music, the entire room engrossed in the love of the happy couple. As the song starts to fade, I expect them to move into father-daughter and mother-son dances, but the DJ's voice travels from the speakers once more.

"The bride and groom ask that the bridal party join them on the dance floor."

I want to groan—my feet are killing me in these insane heels Savannah picked for everyone to wear—but as Liam steps toward me with his hand extended, suddenly all my reservations are washed down the drain.

Taking his hand, I step out onto the dance floor. He pulls me close to him, my body flush with his front. This is the closest we've been in public since the start of all this and I find myself wishing he would kiss me; own this for what it is; claim our relationship for all to see. However, he does none of that. While he holds me close, it's not the same kind of adoring touch I'm used to. It's calculated and intentional, but a shiver crawls up my neck as his lips graze my ear.

"You look incredible," he whispers, causing a smile to paint my lips.

"Thank you," I respond, barely audible, but I know he hears me by the way he clutches me closer as we sway.

"Jeez, guys, just fuck already." Wes's voice carries from my left, causing Liam to freeze at his words. His clutch loosens as I feel him step backward, leaving so much space between us you would think we were at a seventh-grade dance.

"Yeah right, man," Liam chuckles, the sardonic nature of it leaving a slimy, uncomfortable feeling coating my skin. "You've got to be delusional if you think that's ever going to happen."

My every last joy of the moment is squashed as the denying, borderline hurtful words spill from Liam's lips. I release my hold on him, pushing him away from me in the process.

"Yeah." I laugh, but it doesn't meet my eyes. "I'd have to hate myself to get involved with an asshole like Liam Park."

Liam's hands drop from my sides as I step back from him entirely, the song thankfully coming to an end at the perfect moment.

And while the words roll off my tongue like a joke to the room, Liam's eyes lock on mine, a pained expression washing over him, all the shame he should have felt about denying me crashing into him at my harsh words, and I hate the way I feel vindicated by it.

FORTY-TWO

LIAM

Stepping into the Newmont building doesn't cause the same pep in my step as it normally does. The past few months I've found myself looking forward to going into work. Not because I'm doing something insanely rewarding—those aren't the words I would choose to describe helping yet another multimillionaire out of taking accountability for yet another white-collar crime—but because Hannah has slowly become the best part of my day.

At the end of the wedding Saturday night, I expected to go back to her room and stay there, so when the door was dead bolted and Hannah wasn't answering her phone, I assumed she just fell asleep. However, I tried to reach her all day Sunday and she's yet to return any of my calls, and I hate that I know why.

I was an idiot when Wes made that joke at the wedding. I don't know why I said it and the memory causes bile to crawl up my throat. Hannah and I haven't gone public with our relationship and I can't pinpoint why the idea causes me so much discomfort. I'm not embarrassed by being with Hannah

—hell, she's the hottest girl in pretty much every room we walk into—but the scrutiny I know we would face is enough to hold me back.

I like how things have been. The privacy of our relationship has been the only thing keeping me from losing my mind these days and I don't want to let it go just yet. There aren't these grandiose expectations of me when I'm alone with Hannah. Hell, if anything, she expects less of me, which means the bar is quite literally on the floor.

However, the look on her face when I brushed Wes off the other day has all but secured that she doesn't feel the same way about maintaining our privacy. What does she expect to happen, though? She doesn't just work for my dad's law firm, she works under me; Hannah reports to me directly. Well, and her brother, but let's be real, he never feels comfortable asking much of Hannah.

Which is precisely my point.

The moment people know that we're together, my entire job and all my business practices will be called into question regarding whether I did everything ethically or if I have been willingly letting her cut corners because we're sleeping together.

I refuse to have my professional career tarnished before it's barely begun.

So why is it that when Hannah walks right past me, latte in hand, without so much as a good morning or a hello, I instantly want to push her into the supply closet and force her to talk to me?

I can't do that, though, because this is a place of business and if she gets mad, I know everyone is going to hear us hashing it out.

"Hey," I say, reaching out and grabbing her arm as she

passes by me, nearly causing her Starbucks cup to spill in the process.

"Hey." Her voice is quiet and clipped, and given the fact that I nearly just caused vanilla, milk, and espresso to coat the side of her dress, I expect far more of a reaction. At the very least, I anticipate a snide remark. However, she gives me nothing more.

"Are you okay?"

"Why wouldn't I be?" Her eyes meet mine with zero warmth. She's pissed; I've seen it enough times to know the tells. I've also seen it enough times to know that she's going to pretend she's not mad until she quite possibly explodes, fragments of shrapnel flying at everyone in the wake.

"Hannah, I can tell you're mad."

"Well, I'm not. I'm working, so please let me do that." Something in her words causes me to release my hold on her arm. I've spent so much time thinking about the way our relationship being exposed could impact my career, the realization that Hannah is just as aware of prying eyes gives me pause instantly.

Hannah's phone starts to vibrate in her hand, pulling her eyes from my own. She's distracted and I hate that she won't talk to me about why. I thought we were past this dynamic of not telling each other what is going on—apparently, we're not.

"I have to take this." Her energy instantly shifts from that of anger to that of anticipation and I desperately want to know why. I try to get a peek at her phone, but it's out of sight within seconds. It must be something important...something important that she clearly doesn't want to tell me.

"Hannah, I—"

"Liam, I have to go." She backs up, stepping out of my space, and I have no time to argue further. She pulls the phone to her ear and offers her peppiest greeting, a stark contrast to her clipped tone only moments ago.

I'm prepared to go after her, ask her what's going on, but Jackson chooses the absolute worst moment to walk out of our office.

"Hey man, you got a sec? I need to brief you on my clients before Gen and I leave for Saint-Tropez tomorrow."

"Can this wait? I need to go do something."

Jackson pins me with a confused expression, no doubt wondering what I need to do...to which I'm not sure how to answer. I fidget with my hands as I attempt to think of something to say, but I draw a blank.

"Yeah, I have a sec," I say with an exhale, walking into our office, but my eyes don't divert from the blonde disappearing down the hallway, her phone pressed firmly to her ear.

I'm convinced Jackson needs to learn what constitutes an emergency and what can absolutely be pushed off by forty-five minutes to allow me to take care of my business. He hands me a manilla envelope full of documents, all of which are on the company server, leaving me unsure why he's handing them to me.

"I plan on setting up international service for my phone, so I'll be reachable, so you shouldn't have to do anything for anyone, but just in case, I wanted you to have the information." Jackson's phone starts to buzz and he lifts it up, the screen far more visible than his sister's with her privacy screen protector.

"Hey man, I gotta grab this. I think it might be the airline." Jackson disappears out the door without any explanation. However, unlike Hannah, any thoughts about what he's doing leave with him.

Settling into my desk chair, I rub my eyes, weirdly exhausted despite getting a moderately full night's sleep.

Hannah's distance since Saturday night has made it nearly impossible to focus, but there is no rest for the wicked and I need to have some level of focus at work.

Knuckles rap against the door before it creaks open. Veronica peeks into the office, a grin plastered across her lips.

"Hey, Liam!" She's far peppier than I feel in this moment, but I'll admit it makes me smile. She pulls her hair over one shoulder as she toys with the strands between her fingers, fidgety, though no more so than normal.

"Hey." I grin up at her. If she notices my demeanor, she doesn't let it show.

Veronica shifts to sit against the edge of the front of my desk, her proximity significantly closer than I'm used to—or, frankly, comfortable with.

"So I was thinking..." Her voice trails off as she leans in closer.

I attempt to back up to give her space, but my chair quickly hits my filing cabinet and I realize I have nowhere to go.

"...you had said we would hang out, but we haven't gotten to." She pouts as her voice shifts to something almost childlike. I don't like the way it makes my skin crawl.

"Sorry, V. I've been busy." Her office nickname slides off my tongue with ease, but it leaves my tongue coated in bile.

She shifts in closer as my entire body tenses. "Too busy for me?" She pouts.

Veronica continues to shift toward me and I realize too late that maybe I haven't been clear enough about my intentions—or lack thereof—with her.

FORTY-THREE

HANNAH

"Thank you!" Tears start to pool at the edges of my eyes, but they're fueled by nothing but unadulterated joy. The sour feeling I've been sporting since Saturday melts away with one simple phone call.

"We can't wait for you to join the cast of *Maybe, Definitely, No* for our inaugural national tour! You're going to be a perfect fit..." The man on the other end of the phone continues as he breaks down the details—when I need to report to New York to start rehearsals, when the first leg of the tour begins—but it's all information he said he'll be sending over via email, so I don't hear any of it.

"Thank you, seriously. Thank you." I don't know what to say or how to even use my words, apparently, because I can only muster the same two words that have been flying off my tongue since we started this conversation.

"We're happy to have you, Hannah. I'll get the details emailed over right away."

"Sounds great. Thank you."

"You're very welcome. Have a good rest of your day—and

"""

don't forget to pop open that bottle of champagne you've been saving for a special occasion. It sounds like you could use it right now." He chuckles on the other end and I smile in response, feeling my excitement surge with every word we exchange.

We continue chatting, and after a few more pleasantries, we eventually say our farewells. The joy from our conversation lingers, making me feel so energized, as if I could conquer the world.

I need to tell Liam.

We've hardly spoken since Saturday night, and while I'm still hurt, there isn't a single other person in this world that I want to tell first. This is the literal start to my career. Everything I've worked for since I was fourteen years old is finally coming to fruition. My stomach won't stop doing flips at the mere thought of it all. Despite the unfinished business between us, this is a moment I want to share with Liam.

My heart races as I barrel toward Liam and Jackson's office, picturing all the possibilities of what this next chapter of my life could bring.

I don't bother knocking, a formality I've long since abandoned over the past few weeks. Liam and Jackson have grown used to me just walking in, so I can't imagine today would be any different. My heart races in anticipation as I step inside, knowing that I am seconds away from sharing the biggest accomplishment of my life with the two most important men in it.

As I scan the room, my eyes instantly land on Liam. Where I expect him to be hunched over his computer, tapping away at the keys with laser focus and precision, the sight in front of me is much, much worse.

Veronica Tatum, the constant thorn in my side since I

started at the firm, is currently leaning over Liam's chair with her ass pressed against the edge of his desk and her lips pressed to his.

I want to scream, I want to yell, I want to throw the fucking stapler positioned at the corner of his desk at their freaking heads. But as I struggle to breathe amidst what I just walked into, I do none of that...I just turn around and walk away, delicately shutting the door so as not to be heard.

Jackson passes me in the hallway as tears stream down my face. I need to go to Stephen; I need to put in my notice so that I can start planning my move to start what was supposed to be one of the biggest, most exciting moments in my life. However, as Jackson's eyes meet mine, I just shake my head at him, managing, despite it all, to not want to throw Liam under the bus when it comes to us. It's not the first time Liam has made me cry, so when the words flow off my tongue, Jackson doesn't even question it.

"Liam is a fucking asshole."

His look of concern morphs into amusement, no doubt clearly thinking that Liam and I just got into one of our bickering matches. Little does he know that he's managed to rip my heart out twice in the span of seventy-two hours.

"Yeah, bug. I know." He wraps his arms around my shoulders and pulls me into a hug.

I hug him back, but all I want is to leave this building and never come back.

Fucking asshole.

FORTY-FOUR

LIAM

I freeze when I feel the warmth of Veronica's lips on mine. Everything around me stops as my brain frantically attempts to process this unfamiliar sensation. Instead of the tantalizing taste of Hannah's favorite Starburst candies, all I can taste is the sharpness of peppermint toothpaste. The shock of reality hits me like a ton of bricks, and I instinctively push her away, slack-jawed and wide-eyed as I stare at her.

"Veronica, what are you doing?"

Her flirtatious tone from before is nowhere to be found as she gazes at me, doe-eyed as shame washes over her. "I...I thought—"

"You thought what?"

"I thought you were...into me." Veronica diverts her gaze to the mahogany of my desk. A pink tinge washes over her cheeks, but it's not the kind that brings a smile to my lips. She's embarrassed and I don't have the bandwidth right now to try to reassure her and make her feel better.

"Veronica," I sigh, "I'm sorry that I made you think that. I should have been more clear."

Tears begin to well in her eyes as she looks at me. I anticipate a response, but she doesn't say anything as she stands. I expect her to leave without a second word, but she turns on her heels halfway to the door.

"Is there something wrong with me?" Her usually confident gaze is replaced with vulnerability as she asks me the question. Her full lips quiver as she waits for an answer, and I feel my stomach sink.

I don't know what to say. My hands curl into fists as I rub my brow in frustration, not at her, but at the situation we have found ourselves in.

"No, V," I finally manage to say. "It's not like that. If I were single, maybe, but—"

"You have a girlfriend?!" A look of utter disbelief replaces the pain on her face as she steps back and opens her mouth in shock.

"Is that surprising to you?" I quirk my brow, trying to keep any potential insult I might feel at her shock at bay.

"Yeah, kinda." Veronica rolls her ankle in a circular motion as she stares down at her foot, the simple motion giving her some level of calm in an otherwise uncomfortable situation. "In the entire time I've known you, you've never even mentioned a girl in your life. The only woman I hear you talk about besides your mom is Hannah, and we both know you're not dating Hannah. I realize my surprise may have come off a little crass, but Liam, you've never even mentioned her."

Her statement about Hannah stings and I realize for the first time that maybe my refusal to be outright about us has put our relationship in danger. In my fear of damaging my career, my fear of causing chaos in our families, I have been so adamant that we not be open about our relationship, so much so that, apparently, I managed to give a perfectly kind and attractive woman the wrong impression about my availability.

"Well, I do have a girlfriend. I'm a private guy, but that doesn't change that fact."

Veronica gnaws at the inside of her cheek as she nods. "You're right. I shouldn't have assumed."

I nod, but I don't find enjoyment in agreeing with her.

She offers an awkward bob of her head, shifting her weight between her feet. Her eyes flicker to the door, and she takes a small step toward it. With fingers that betray a slight tremble, she clasps the polished brass doorknob and slowly turns back to face me. "Whoever you're with is a really lucky girl. I'm sorry for not knowing that."

"It's not your fault."

She nods again, her brow creasing with a hint of satisfaction as she backs away and the tension in the air seems to evaporate. With a soft click, the door shuts behind her just as Jackson steps into my office, his determined strides carrying him forward.

"Hey, man." I rub my brow, the tension not dissipating despite my desire to move on with my day.

"What did you do?" He glares at me with an icy intensity, his clenched jaw visibly twitching.

I open my mouth to respond but realize I have no idea what he is talking about. "Great to see you too, buddy." I laugh, which is clearly not the response he wants as he slams his palm onto my desk, rattling its contents in the process.

"What did you say to Hannah?"

Seriously? This is about Hannah?

"Uh, nothing, actually. We haven't spoken all day."

"Well, you clearly said or did something, because she just went home in tears." He steps into my space, pressing his pointer finger firmly against my chest as he speaks, the words gritting through his teeth. "So whatever it is that you did, fix it."

He steps away, striding over to his side of the office without further elaboration.

Jackson's words hit me like a ton of bricks; I can't believe my ears. Hannah has been on edge since Saturday, but never has she seemed so upset that she'd cry so obviously at work. A wave of emotion floods my body, confusion quickly shifting to concern with each passing second. My heart rate quickens as the thought of her in distress fills me with burning rage and an undeniable urge to help.

"I gotta go," I say as I pull my suit jacket off the back of my chair. "I'm going to send my calls to voicemail, but if anything urgent comes up, call me on my cell."

Jackson pins me with a confused expression but surprisingly doesn't try to pry into what has me so frantic and ready to leave.

"Okay."

Without a word, I sprint down the hall and skid past my dad's office. The unmistakable sound of his voice calling after me reverberates through the air, echoing off the walls like thunder in a rainstorm. His words trail after me as I attempt to bolt out of sight, but he steps into the doorway, halting me in my tracks.

"Liam, come here, please."

"Dad, I really have to go."

"Liam," he says, his tone dropping lower like when he would reprimand me as a child.

"Okay." I instantly cower, knowing with certainty that there is nothing good that can come of me disregarding him. I step into his office, closing the door behind me, and sit in one of the two chairs on the opposite side of his desk. He settles into his chair.

"With Hannah quitting, I've decided to have HR post a job listing for a new assistant for you and Jackson. Both of your client loads have gone up significantly in recent months and I want to make sure it's as seamless as possible."

The panic from before is nothing compared to the racing of my thoughts now.

"Hannah quit?" I try to keep my panic out of my voice, but some of it seeps into my words, causing my dad to give me a confused expression.

"Yeah, she stopped by my office about twenty minutes ago. Her last day will be Friday. Seemed upset, but it's not my place to pry. Hannah aside, we need to start interviewing her replacement ASAP. I've already had HR post the job online. I'm hoping to start going through résumés next week."

His words start to fade into my periphery as my mind races, the weight of Hannah leaving causing me to nearly pass out. I don't know what I did—I can't help but think it's my fault. When she started at Baker & Park, getting her to quit was at the top of my to-do list, but now the idea nearly has me on my knees in anguish.

"Are you okay?" My dad leans in, placing his hand over mine. Where my hands are clammy and cold, his are warm and inviting.

The anxiety coursing through my veins does little to prevent me from spilling my thoughts, audience be damned.

"I need to go find Hannah." I jump up from my chair with little concern for the implication.

"Why would you need to go find Hannah?" His brows pull together, but I don't miss the amused smile that paints his lips.

He knows—to what extent I can't be sure, but he definitely knows more than I thought he did.

"Just...I need to go find her. We need to talk."

Silence falls as I step toward the door, the cold brass of the handle biting into my hand.

"Liam," he says, his voice drifting over my shoulder and up my neck.

"Yeah, Dad?"

"Go get her, son."

This stops me in my tracks. I turn to look over my shoulder and find him grinning from ear to ear. He's made comments over the years about me and Hannah, but nothing to allude to the fact that he actually thought we had something. Now, as he looks at me, I realize that he is far more observant than I've given him credit for.

"That's the plan."

I raise my knuckles to the cold painted wood of Hannah's apartment door, tentatively tapping out a rhythm. When there's no response, I find myself pounding on the door with increasing force until my fists are sore, yet still there is no sound from within. Five minutes have gone by and I'm growing more desperate for a sign that someone is home. The warmth of the takeout in my right hand is causing my palm to sweat, or it could be how wound up I am right now. Can't be totally sure at the moment.

"What?!" Sage's irritated voice carries through the wood before she swings the door open. Her face is flushed and her eyebrows are pinched together in a scowl. She wears a short silk robe, the belt cinched tightly at the waist. Her curly hair is unruly, as if she just woke up, but is snugly tied up with a silk scarf. Without any makeup, Sage looks younger than she usually does. Despite her unguarded, raw look, the rage in her eyes is palpable.

"Seriously, Sage? It's noon."

"Really? That's the attitude you want to take with me right now? I work at a bar, asshole. I didn't get home until 4:00 AM."

"Fair, I'm sorry," I say with a sigh, rubbing my eyes. "Is Hannah home?"

"Yes." As Sage doesn't move to allow me in, I pin her with a glare, crossing my arms over my chest.

"Can I *see* her?"

"Nope."

"Sage, please."

"Liam, *no*."

"Why?" I sigh, loosening my arms across my chest as I watch the tension in her shoulders relax.

She rolls her eyes before stepping into the hallway, allowing the door to click shut behind her. Her voice pitches low as she looks up at me, the anger from before melting into something like sympathy.

"Look, I don't know what happened. I don't know what happened between you two today, but you fucked up. She came home hysterical and, if I'm being honest, she hasn't stopped crying." As she continues to fill me in, my stomach drops with every word that leaves her lips. "That being said, I don't think this is the right time for you two to talk. Whatever happened has her in her head and I know nothing positive would come from you two talking right now."

While I know she's probably right, the idea of just allowing Hannah to stew in whatever she's feeling right now makes me nauseous. I've spent countless days being the cause of her anguish, and the thought of it actually has me ready to break down this door to get to her.

"Sage, I can't just not do anyth—"

"You can and you will. It'll only make things worse. So, put your ego aside and trust me."

I want to trust her. She is easily one of my best friends and I trust her judgment, but when it comes to me and Hannah, the idea of letting this linger for any longer sounds like a nightmare.

My worst nightmare.

The desire I feel to go into their apartment and force Hannah to talk to me is rooted in quelling this anxious feeling in the pit of my stomach and has nothing to do with whether it'll help Hannah.

With that, I let out a sigh, extending the brown takeout bag to Sage. "Give this to her, please. It's her favorite and she left before lunch."

Sage sighs as she wraps her fingers around the generic bag, nodding in recognition. "She'll talk to you when she's ready."

I nod in response before stepping away down the empty hallway. My pride is wounded, but my mind doesn't leave Hannah the entire drive home.

FORTY-FIVE

HANNAH

The front door to our apartment clicks shut quietly as Sage reappears in the living room, this time with a takeout bag. Despite my attempts to listen to their conversation, the walls in this building are surprisingly thick.

She drops the brown bag with "Andre's" scrawled across the side onto the coffee table, the smell of chicken penne wafting in the air. In any other situation, I would be yanking it open and inhaling it with little restraint, and, given how hungry I am, I *should* be doing that. However, the thought of eating anything makes me sick right now and all I want to do is hide away in my dark bedroom, but Sage is refusing to let that happen.

I am holding a plush throw blanket up around me, surrounding my face in a cocoon of warmth, but somehow I'm still shivering.

"He brought you lunch," she says as she plops down on the couch next to me with her legs crossed.

I stare at the paper bag on the table like it's going to sprout legs and a tail and walk away. Sage lets out a sigh as she turns in her seat before grasping the edge of my blanket. I tighten my grip on the soft fabric, desperate to keep its warmth around me, but Sage tugs relentlessly until I finally have to release my hold. With a defeated huff, I watch as the blanket slides off of me and onto the floor.

"Happy?" I pin her with a glare as I wave my hand over the discarded blanket.

"Um, no?" She lets out a sigh, far more dramatic than the last. "Seriously, Hannah. What happened?"

My eyes are red and puffy, my eyelids heavy with the tears that have been flowing since I stepped into Liam's office. Despite all of my efforts to keep it together, the floodgates open at even the slightest reminder of what I witnessed earlier. I wipe away the tears that fall freely down my cheeks, but nothing could stop the memories from coming back as if it were happening all over again.

"Hannah, please talk to me," Sage pleads, causing my eyes to drift to hers.

"What do you want to know?"

"Why don't you start at the beginning?"

And with that, I tell her everything. I tell her everything from start to finish. How Liam ended up here the morning she found him sneaking out of my bedroom. I tell her about Liam showing up in New York. We talk about what happened at the rehearsal dinner last week and how he stood up for me to my mom, and the entire time Sage sits silently and listens. She nods when it's called for and stays still when it doesn't.

When I get to this morning, Sage winces as the words tumble from my mouth.

"...and I found him kissing her in his office."

The conflict of interest I've been worried about is nowhere in Sage's expression. They're friends—sometimes I would even venture to say better friends than Sage and I—but you would never know that by the way she's looking at me right now.

"He's an asshole," she says matter-of-factly, standing from the couch before disappearing into the kitchen. The sound of glasses clanking and the fridge opening fills the room, then Sage reappears with two short glasses and a bottle of Johnnie Walker Black Label in hand. She sets the glasses down on the coffee table before pouring two healthy pours, what I would assume to be at least two shots each.

The moment she hands me mine, I down it in one gulp, earning a wide-eyed gaze of shock from Sage. The liquor burns on contact, causing me to wince.

"Jesus, Hannah. Pace yourself—it's noon, for fuck's sake."

Despite her words, Sage matches my actions as she throws back the glass in one gulp, her face contorting at the burn of the fiery liquid rolling down her throat.

I hold my glass out to her to request another, but she pauses before grabbing it from me.

"Fine, but pace yourself. I don't feel like cleaning up vomit today."

As she hands me the fresh glass of whisky, I do as she asks and don't down it quickly. She pours herself another before closing the bottle and pushing it back on the table in front of us. We sit in silence for a moment before she turns to me again.

"So you're clearly in love with him, right?"

I glare at her, but I don't have it in me to deny it. Then again, I'm unsure why I would want to.

"Yeah," I sigh, "I am."

"Don't sound so enthused." Sage rolls her eyes.

"Would you be enthusiastic about it in this situation, Sage?"

She raises the glass of liquor to her lips and tips it back.

The liquor appears to still have the same effect, causing her to grimace as she swallows before setting the empty glass down with a thud and saying, "Fair enough."

I take a sip of mine, the contents no longer giving me the warmth or calm as before.

"So, what are you going to do?"

It's then that I realize I'm not sure. The mere thought of forgiving Liam makes my stomach plummet, but the idea of not being with him anymore could quite possibly bring me to my knees.

"I don't know," I whisper as my head meets the back of the couch. I wish I had an answer—hell, if we're in the market of granting wishes, I'd ask that this never happened.

But it did.

Sooner or later I am going to have to deal with the fallout, but that won't be today.

"I booked a show. It's a national tour. I leave for New York next week." The words flow off my tongue, almost melancholy, causing Sage's eyes to go wide.

"Holy shit, Han! Way to bury the fucking lead. Oh my God, that's incredible!" She claps twice before falling back onto the couch. "Why don't you seem excited?"

"Because the one person I was excited to tell isn't here, and I can't even ask him to be."

"Well, you cou—"

"No."

"I'm not saying you *should*. I'm just saying you could. My personal opinion is that you should let him sweat it out. Go to New York, find a hot piece of ass."

"Aren't you and Liam, like, really good friends?" I ask, my eyebrows furrowing in confusion.

Her eyes meet mine before she rolls them in exasperation.

A moment of silence passes between us as her expression becomes more serious.

"Yeah, we're close. However, he's an idiot and I've never pretended that isn't true."

"Touché."

"You deserve better. Not that you deserve better than him, but you deserve better than him making you feel this way. No one deserves to be less-than. So yeah, ignore him right now. Ice him out, but when the time comes, I want you to do something for me."

"And what is that?"

"Give him hell."

FORTY-SIX

LIAM

Stepping into Andre's, I don't even begin to pretend like I'm not looking around hoping to find her. I know she isn't here—she's at home with Sage—but my eyes still linger on every blonde for a moment too long just the same.

"Hey, what was so urgent that I had to drop everything, including the fitness class I was in the middle of, to come meet you for dinner?"

Gabe is outwardly irritated, but he and I both know that he actually doesn't care...frankly, he doesn't even have a leg to stand on in this scenario. The number of times I've had to pick him up out of a gutter piss-drunk because Kara broke up with him again is actually concerning; I've earned at least one no-questions-asked, drop-everything kind of moment.

"How's Kara?"

He pins me with a glare before letting out an exhale. "Fair enough, but what was so urgent?"

I pull out the chair opposite him at the back of the restaurant and slide in. The menu in front of me is practically committed to memory at this point.

Unfortunately, they only serve their signature roast chicken on Tuesdays, so I'll have to settle for something else. Maybe I'll try the chicken penne Hannah doesn't shut up about.

"Hannah won't talk to me."

His eyes meet mine as he bites back a laugh. "Okay? Sounds like a dream come true for you."

Six months ago, I would have agreed with him. I used to wish for a time where Hannah would threaten not to talk to me and actually mean it. However, that hasn't been the case for a very long time.

"Well, seeing as I have feelings for her, it's less than opportune."

Gabe opens his mouth, bellowing as his shoulders shake with laughter so hard it makes his eyes water. His entire face turns a deep shade of red to match the fiery mop of hair atop his head.

"Gabe."

He continues to ride out his laughing fit with little concern for the fact that I'm glaring at him and only two inches from a steak knife.

"Gabe!" I shout, causing not only everyone around us to jerk their gaze in my direction, but also Gabe to shake out of his amusement.

His face is still beet-red from the lack of airflow, but he manages to bring his laughter down from a ten to about a two. "You're serious?"

"As death."

"Damn," he says with a sigh as he leans back in his chair, his eyes not leaving mine. "How did that happen?"

I shrug, not wanting to unpack all of that right now.

"Okay, well, what did you do?"

Once again, I shrug, at a complete loss as to what transpired to cause all of this shit to happen.

"And she won't talk to you?"

"Sage wouldn't even let me in the door."

"Do you want me to...?"

"No, involving you would no doubt just piss her off more."

He nods in agreement before leaning in to meet my gaze. "Are you okay?"

I think on it for a moment, my eyes locked on his in silence. Am I okay? I've spent the better part of my day trying to get information out of Jackson without divulging too much information. By the time he started prying about why I care, I left to meet Gabe for an early dinner.

"I'll be a hell of a lot better once my girlfriend gives me the time of day."

"Girlfriend?" His eyes go wide, the amusement from before on full display.

"Until she tells me otherwise, yeah."

"Well shit." He sinks back into his chair as he presses his water glass to his lips.

I've known Gabe most of my life. We weren't super close as kids, but started hanging out a lot in high school. He always knew about Hannah, so when everything hit the fan that summer, he was my sounding board through it all. He is privy to the intricacies of mine and Hannah's relationship far more than most people.

"It's Hannah," he sighs as the waiter approaches, filling our water glasses.

We place our orders and I opt to get the chicken penne. I might as well see what all the fuss is about. Our server walks out of earshot before I lean in toward the table.

"And?"

"What?"

"You said '*It's Hannah,*' then didn't say anything after that..."

"Oh yeah, sorry. I'm just saying, it's Hannah. She's never given you the silent treatment for more than a day. I don't know that she has it in her to not tell you what she thinks of you. Give her time—she'll come around."

I hope he's right, but there is a nagging voice in the back of my mind telling me that it might not happen this time. Whatever I did has her ready to toss me aside; I don't know that she has ever been this mad at me. Maybe the summer we hooked up, but even then, she talked to me.

"Fingers crossed, I guess."

Our meals arrive within minutes—a perk of eating dinner at four o'clock. An elderly couple two tables over turns to peer at me as I take my first bite of chicken penne, no doubt shocked by the two young men mixed in with the over-sixty-five crowd.

The creamy cheese sauce coats my tongue with warmth as I shovel my first bite of pasta into my mouth. It might not be Andre's signature roast chicken, but it'll do just fine.

"Does Jackson know?" Gabe asks as he takes his last bite of steak.

"No, and I'd appreciate it if you didn't tell him. I don't know if I'm ready for people to know, especially if we're in a bad place."

Gabe nods in recognition before leaning forward. "So what's your plan?"

"I'm gonna do what you said, wait her out. She's still got a few days at Baker & Park, so she'll have to talk to me in some capacity. Just have to see what happens."

Despite my words, I can't shake the feeling that maybe it won't be as simple as it sounds.

I step into the office, dreading the sight I fear I will find. Sure enough, Hannah's empty desk greets me with its eerie stillness. My mind races and my heart pounds in my chest. She isn't supposed to leave until Friday; what could be happening? I take a deep breath, pretending like it is any other day, and hang my suit jacket on the back of my chair, everything feeling heavier than usual.

Without even an attempt to dive into my work, I make my way out into the hallway to find Hannah, disheveled and exhausted, settling into her desk. Her hair is normally perfectly styled, but today it barely looks like she dragged a brush through it. Her typically sharp-as-nails eyeliner is nowhere to be found, and in its place is swelling around her beautiful green eyes from crying. Even though she is clearly trying to make it look like nothing is wrong, the pain she's radiating shoots straight to my gut.

"Hey." I speak softly, approaching uncertainly. I know that if I come on too strong, she'll cower away from me, and that's the last thing I want.

"Hello." Her voice is quick and clipped, a response I would expect if Jessica from Human Resources stopped by her desk, not the guy with whom she's been intimately involved for months.

My hand clenches then unclenches at my side as I attempt to calm my racing heart. We need to talk, and something tells me it is going to be a challenge. Though I originally planned to wait her out, as I look down at her now, I can't will myself not to try.

"Hannah."

She doesn't even look up from her computer screen. Her fingers fly across the keys with an intensity meant to rebuke me.

I shiver as the chill of her indifference fills the room, my stomach plummeting as realization dawns on me.

"Hannah, please."

Her gaze slowly drifts to mine, her icy impassiveness melting into something else—anger. "Leave me alone," she grits through her teeth.

"I'm still your boss, you know. Until Friday, you can't just ice me out. We need to be professional."

"Oh, do we? I wasn't aware we were still trying to maintain professionalism at this firm." Her words have bite, but I've argued enough times with her to not let it faze me.

"Hannah, can we please talk?"

While I try to keep my voice down, she doesn't seem to care about making a scene.

"Fine," she huffs as she storms past me into my office.

In the past, I've found a sick sense of amusement in her being angry at me, sometimes even a sense of attraction. However, in this moment I feel an invasive need to guard my dick.

I step into the room, the floor creaking beneath my feet. I shut the heavy door behind me and can feel its coolness against my back as I twist the lock into place.

Hannah sits down in Jackson's seat, clearly attempting to place distance between us for this conversation.

My feet begin to take me closer to her, but she raises a hand in warning. I pause immediately and my gaze burns into her as if hoping that my intensity will make her change her mind.

"Can we please talk like adults?"

"Fine, let's talk." Her previous distance is tucked away as

she approaches me with vengeance, but her arms are crossed over her chest as she keeps her distance. "How long have you been cheating on me?"

Of all the things I anticipate coming out of her mouth, that is low on the list.

"What?"

"Did I stutter?"

"Hannah," I sigh as I step closer. She backs up instinctively, and I stop. "I didn't cheat on you."

"I saw you." Her glare is toxic as her eyes meet mine. Where love once consumed her green gaze, hatred has taken over. Even when we were at our worst, she's never looked at me like that.

The hurt in her eyes makes me want to crumble to the ground. I linger on her words for a moment, trying to think of what she could be talking about. It takes me about a minute, but it hits me like a freight train.

Veronica.

"Princess, that wasn't what it looked like."

"Don't call me that. You don't get to call me that."

"I lo—"

"No."

"I didn't kiss her back. I promise you, I planned on telling you. I made it very clear I'm seeing someone."

"*Was* seeing someone." Her glare doesn't let up and her words send my stomach lurching.

"What?" I whisper, in utter disbelief of what is happening. "Hannah, I just told you that I didn't cheat on you. Why do you want to break up?"

Hannah rests against the edge of Jackson's desk as she lets out a sigh. The anger that previously radiated off of her melts into what looks like pain. She gnaws at her inner cheek as she stares at the short-piled carpet. I want to repeat myself, but I decide to give her time to sort out her thoughts. A couple minutes go by before she looks up at me.

"Why did she think it was okay to kiss you?"

This feels like a riddle, one which I don't know how to solve. It's not like I have insider knowledge of Veronica's psyche.

"I don't know."

"Yes, you do."

I don't have the slightest idea what she's referring to.

"You've spent our entire relationship refusing to tell people about us. I thought we were past that, but Saturday night you made it crystal clear we're not and that you're still embarrassed to be seen with me."

"Baby, I'm not—"

"You are."

Though she's wrong, I don't know how to convey that to her. It's never been about shame; it's always been about protecting what we have. Going public brings scrutiny. From our friends, from her mother, from the board at Baker & Park. Well, I guess the last one doesn't exactly apply anymore.

It's never been about shame.

Hannah continues as she steps toward me, but I know by the look in her eyes that it isn't to patch things up. She sighs as she continues, "You once told me that you don't take kindly to people treating me like I'm less-than. By my mom, by Jackson, but most importantly, by you..."

I know where this is going, yet I don't have the words to stop it.

"I've spent the better part of my life bending to the will of others. I may be stubborn, but I've realized recently just how much of a pathological people-pleaser I am. I've always been so focused on what others think of me and not rocking the boat that I forgot my value. I deserve better, even if I'm the only one willing to give it to me."

A hot lump gathers in my throat, and I swallow hard as tears threaten to spill down my cheeks. The weight of devastation and heartbreak crushes down upon me, but deep within, I still feel an ember of pride flicker. All I have ever wanted was for her to recognize her worth and put herself first. Maybe this was what she needed all along—someone to push her toward that...I just wish it wasn't me.

"You don't have to quit to do that."

"I didn't quit because of you."

FORTY-SEVEN

HANNAH

"Then why did you?"

My last twenty-four hours have been so consumed by grief about my relationship with Liam that I am just now realizing the only person I've told about New York is Sage. I didn't even tell Stephen when I quit, just that I had an opportunity, all while biting back tears. I couldn't get into it at the moment, and I still don't think I could have that conversation with him.

"I booked a show," I sigh. A faint smile creeps across my lips, but it doesn't reach my eyes. "It's a national tour. I'm going to swing for a few of the roles, so it's a really good opportunity for me. Actually..."

The memory from yesterday comes flooding back, context making it less painful but more enraging. I told him numerous times how Veronica clearly felt, but he wouldn't listen.

"...I was coming to tell you about it when I walked in on Veronica and you. You were the first person I wanted to know," I say as my voice cracks. Pain envelopes me as I remember what could have been between us. Maybe we'll find it again, but right now it's tainted.

CHAPTER FORTY-SEVEN

Our entire history is now overshadowed by something awful that could have been avoided if Liam had just been willing to tell people about us.

I deserve better.

Liam's face is streaked with tears, but his mouth widens in a watery smile of awe. His pain-ravaged eyes light up with joy. He smiles so wide despite the pain in his eyes—pure, unadulterated admiration.

"I'm so fucking proud of you." The pain in his voice doesn't hide the joy he's conveying. I genuinely know he's proud of me, I just wish I could celebrate with him. "I love you. Even if we're breaking up...know that."

"I know," I whisper, "but sometimes love isn't enough."

Even when you wish it was.

He nods, understanding washing over him, but it doesn't appear to bring him any comfort. "Can I hug you?" he asks awkwardly.

I just nod as I step into him, allowing the warmth of his body to radiate around me. The love I feel for him is far from gone, but the pain will fade with time. Liam's strong arms pull me in close, and a swell of emotion causes my breath to hitch. His scent is musky and familiar and it reminds me of happy memories. I feel the tension in his muscles as he squeezes me tighter in response to my sobs. Tears blur my vision, and I close my eyes tight, trying to will away the sadness as I bury my face deeper into his chest.

"Shhh," he coos into my ear, trying to calm me, but it only makes me sob harder.

I would give anything for this not to be necessary, but it is.

It's necessary for me, and that has to be enough.

FORTY-EIGHT

LIAM

For the rest of the week, Hannah and I don't talk much. While I want to, I know the result won't change, so what's the point? Every morning she settles into her desk and only communicates with me via email and Teams, and she leaves every day at 5:30 PM on the dot. It pains me not to reach out and touch her, but I know nothing I do is going to make a difference in how she's feeling.

Nor would it change the fact that she's leaving.

Jackson strides into the office on Monday morning, his skin glowing a golden brown from days in the Mediterranean sun. He and Gen returned home Saturday afternoon, so I have yet to hear about their adventures in Saint-Tropez. We haven't talked about what transpired with Hannah before he left.

I know I'm about to have to answer to Jackson today, but with the minimal sleep I've been getting and my constant state of anxiety, he had better not come for me about it.

"How was France?" I ask him with a nervous note of forced nonchalance.

Even though I keep my eyes on my computer screen, I can

feel the tension radiating in the air between us. His face is expressionless for a few moments before finally giving in to a slight upturn of his lips.

"It was good!"

"How's Gen?"

"She's good. I'm glad we decided to go back to Saint-Tropez."

With our pleasantries over, the room grows silent, unspoken words lingering in the air. I genuinely can't tell if he's going to bring it up or act like nothing happened—or worse, deck me. Then again, that's not really Jackson. But there are few things he wouldn't do for Hannah.

"Has Hannah's job been posted yet?"

"Yeah, Dad had HR post it last week when she told him. Should be interviewing this week."

Jackson's desk is a chaotic mix of papers, notes, and files strewn about. Sticky notes in neon hues adorn the sides of his computer monitor in a flamboyant display of color, seeping downward onto his desk. He grabs one off the mahogany surface with rough fingers, crumples it up into a ball, and tosses it into the trash can beside him.

The silence hangs heavy as we both sit there in contemplation. Then, with a polite cough, he breaks it and our gazes lock.

"Have you and Hannah talked?" he asks, straight to the point. Jackson has never been one to beat around the bush, something I'm thankful for right now.

"Yeah."

"Dude, what happened?" Concern lines his face as he leans forward in his chair, his fingers intertwined and his chin resting atop them.

"Got into a fight," I mumble.

"No shit. Elaborate, please."

I nervously tap my foot and run my hands through my hair while avoiding eye contact. I struggle to find the words, knowing that this conversation is long overdue but dreading it at the same time. My tongue feels heavy in my mouth as a lump forms in my throat. If I don't say something soon, the awkwardness will overwhelm us.

I wave my arms around the office as if that could help explain things. "You want to have this conversation here?" I ask, expecting an eye roll in response.

Sure enough, Jackson rolls his eyes at me before responding. "Well, seeing as our office is empty and locked, I see no reason why not."

Taking his answer as permission to proceed, I lean back into my chair and let my eyes wander to the ceiling tiles, still searching for the right words to say. Should I downplay what happened between me and Hannah? No, that's a terrible idea —Hannah already thinks I am too dishonest. Maybe it is time for some unabashed honesty so that maybe, just maybe, I have a chance of getting her back someday.

Taking an uneven breath, I meet Jackson's gaze and speak the truth. "Jackson, I'm in love with your sister."

He chokes on a sip of coffee and a coughing fit ensues before he can speak. "I'm sorry, what?"

My brows raise in amusement as his breathing levels. I speak with slow and exaggerated clarity. "I said that I'm in love with your sister."

Jackson's jaw tightens and his eyes glow like molten lava. He spits out the words, "I'm shocked, not hard of hearing, you asshole."

I act nonchalant and return to typing on my computer, but Jackson isn't done. Almost too quickly for me to register what is happening, one of my colorful stress balls flies across the room and collides with my forehead.

Jeez, I didn't know he even had that.

As I toss the ball back in his direction, I feel the weight in the room lift as he chuckles.

"You and Hannah, huh?"

"We were, yeah."

"Why *were?*"

Unpacking all of that sounds like my actual worst nightmare, but something in Jackson's expression tells me he's not going to let it go. His fingers tap against the hard surface of his desk, his eyes pinned on me.

"We broke up."

"Would you like me to throw something harder next time?"

"Fine," I sigh, exasperbated. "Hannah dumped me, okay? I fucked up and she dumped me."

Jackson nods in recognition, my words not seeming to even surprise him. He was initially shocked when I confessed my feelings, but now he seems to think this is normal.

"Why are you acting like that?"

"Like what?"

"Like you aren't surprised at all by this."

"Because I'm not," he says with an amused smirk. The pink tinge from the tropical sun is only made more prominent as he chuckles to himself. "It was only a matter of time before something happened. I'll admit, I didn't expect you guys to fall in love, but I definitely knew eventually you would at the very least hook up."

"And you're just cool with that?"

"Cool with it? Nah, but it would be a bit hypocritical of me to police who Hannah dates." Jackson leans back in his seat, his fingers locked behind his head. "Besides, I don't really have a say in that. It's not like you're my friend who she hooked up with. We've both known you forever."

I guess that makes sense. Every reason I was so dead set on keeping things private suddenly sounds trivial; I just wish I'd come to that realization before Hannah left.

"Did she tell you about the tour?"

His words sting on contact despite it being good news. She has worked her fingers to the bone for years, and now she is about to get what she has longed for: a spot on a national tour. I know I'll miss her while she's gone, but I also know that our bond is too strong to be broken by distance, even if she wants it to be. She's my parents' best friends' daughter. Hannah will always have a home with me, no matter how many miles apart we may be.

"Yeah, she told me."

"And what are your thoughts?" Jackson leans toward me, brows raised.

I can feel his piercing blue eyes boring into mine, and my stomach twists with nerves. I am sure he can see the truth in my gaze and know what I have been too afraid to admit out loud; that I'd willingly give her anything if it means she's happy.

"I'm really proud of her," I say finally, softly.

Jackson smiles knowingly, revealing a flash of white teeth, and his eyes sparkle with amusement. He chuckles lightly as he asks, "So you're really in love with her, huh? When did that happen?"

My heart sinks into my stomach as I try to answer his question. I pause for a moment, rewinding the last few months to pinpoint the exact moment I fell for her. We had been seeing each other for a couple months, but it feels like it was much longer. Since seeing her again over the summer, I've found myself hanging on every word or phrase she utters. I couldn't hold onto my animosity anymore, even though I desperately wanted to. Instead, I found myself chasing her every response, my entire body coming alive when she smiled or laughed, but more often than not, when I pissed her off.

It was like a high I couldn't obtain—it was as if I couldn't get enough of her.

"A while."

"Hm," Jackson hums with a grin.

"What?" I pin him with a glare.

"Nothing," he laughs, clearly thinking something he isn't telling me.

"Oh, fuck off, tell me."

"It's just..." He trails off as he leans forward. "I feel like it should have been more obvious to me that something was going on."

"Why?"

"Well, for starters, you snapped at my mom twice for being even remotely mean to Hannah."

Even now, even amidst everything that happened, he still refuses to acknowledge the weight his mom's scrutiny has on Hannah. It's not my place, and yet it spills from my lips without reserve.

"She's horrible to her, Jackson. Has been for years. It honestly bothers me a bit that you haven't stepped in. I shouldn't have had to, but I'd do it again if necessary."

He stares at me in a way that makes me think I've pissed him off, but then he nods in agreement. "You're right."

Of all the responses I expected, that's not one of them. Jackson has always had a rose-tinted-glasses approach to his parents, so much so that his mother's treatment of Hannah has managed to fly under the radar with him for *years*.

"She's lucky to have you, Liam." The sincerity in his voice causes my stomach to sour, the reminder of where Hannah and I stand washing over me.

"Well, she doesn't *have* me anymore."

"Oh, but she does."

"We broke up," I remind him, yet his fixed gaze is unwavering.

"You and I both know that doesn't mean shit when it comes to you being in her corner."

He's right, but I just nod in agreement. Any other approach might cause my shell to break, and I don't think either of us wants to be here when that happens.

"Thanks, man."

"For what?"

"For getting it."

Jackson shrugs. "If being with Gen has taught me anything, it's that sometimes love isn't easy...but it doesn't make it any less worth it."

Understatement of the year.

FORTY-NINE

LIAM

I cringe as I look at my slew of unanswered text messages to Hannah. If I'm going to make a fool of myself, I might as well commit and send another.

As I shove my phone back into my pocket, my mind ruminates on what Hannah might be doing right now. It's Christmas Eve and while I know it made little sense schedule-wise for her to come home, I still find myself disappointed that she didn't show up.

Linda has refused to look at me since they arrived a few days ago and, if I'm being frank, I don't care. If anything, it's a welcome reprieve from having to pretend that I don't want to rip her head off every time she makes a snide remark at Hannah's expense.

Despite everything, she has still said some things that I've had to bite my tongue about.

Hannah is touring the country, doing exactly what she's worked her ass off for years for, and yet her mom still finds a way to drag her down.

Christmas passes with little fanfare. In years past, it's been an extravagant event, but between the wedding and Hannah being gone, it doesn't seem to make a ton of sense to pull out all the stops.

Honestly, I don't really feel like celebrating anyway.

Jackson mentioned a few days ago that Hannah was trying to come home for my parents' annual New Year's party, so I find myself anxious as I step into the hotel. My eyes rove around the ballroom, taking in the vibrant holiday decorations. Scarlet and gold garlands hang from every surface and mini evergreen trees sit in the center of each table, their branches covered with twinkling fairy lights. Gleaming golden chargers are perched on top of each place setting, catching glints of light from the fixtures above. Nostalgia washes over me as I admire my mom's attention to detail when it comes to holiday celebrations.

"Hey there."

My body tenses as the sweet sound of a feminine voice calls out to me. I spin quickly around, my heart racing with anticipation, only to be met with defeat when I see Gen standing in front of me instead of Hannah like I had hoped. My shoulders slump and my heart sinks as the reality of the situation settles in.

Is this how it's going to be from now on? Hannah slowly fading out of my life with little closure on the matter? I refuse to believe that.

"Hey, Gen," I say as I try to plaster on a grin, but judging by the expression she's sporting, it feels crystal clear that she sees right through my facade.

"Are you okay?" she asks quietly.

"Why wouldn't I be?" I look away as I respond, pulling my champagne flute to my lips.

"Liam." Gen sighs as her body turns toward me. "I know we're not super close, but I know Hannah and—"

"Jackson told you?"

Gen nods before continuing, "I don't think her not showing up tonight is any indicator of where you two stand right now. She was trying to come, really. But her rehearsal schedule is insane right now, the tour starts the second week in January."

I know this should bring me comfort, but it stings as it secures the truth that Hannah for sure isn't coming.

"Have you talked to her?" I ask.

Gen nods softly, but isn't forthcoming.

"How is she?"

Something in my eyes causes her shoulders to relax as she lets out another sigh. "She's okay. Misses you."

"She said that?" My brows shoot up, hopeful.

"No, but it's pretty obvious."

Nodding to myself, I wash down the rest of my champagne in one big gulp. The sparkling liquid tickles my throat as it goes down, but the alcohol doesn't have the desired effect of mellowing me out. I'm half tempted to hop on a flight to New York, but I know that would only push Hannah away more.

There is nothing I have to say that is going to change her mind. She's decided.

"Can I give you a bit of advice?"

"Why do I feel like you're going to whether or not I say yes?"

"Because you're smart," Gen says with a grin before clearing her throat. "As you know, Hannah can be difficult to figure out. She might exude confidence most of the time, but it's an act."

I hate how well-acquainted I am with that fact. How, even now, Hannah doesn't see how incredible she is is a mystery to me.

Gen continues, "If there is one thing that is a non-negotiable for Hannah, it's being chosen. Like, truly chosen above all else. Her family isn't perfect."

My brows shoot up again as my eyes meet hers. I would have expected her to coast through life with the same rose-tinted glasses that Jackson sports, but as she nods, I know that's not the case.

"She's spent most of her life feeling like she plays second fiddle to her brother. It's a big reason we didn't talk for a long time." I knew Hannah and Gen had a rocky past—I mean, they didn't talk for a long time after Gen and Jackson initially broke up—but the reason never crossed my mind. "And don't even get me started on Linda. If Hannah had even an inkling, justified or not, that you were ashamed to be with her, I could see her reacting emotionally to that."

CHAPTER FORTY-NINE

With everything that went down, I never thought about it that way. While in my mind it seemed clear why I wanted us to be private, it suddenly makes sense why Hannah was so upset about it.

At no point have I ever wanted to make her feel like she doesn't matter or like I'm embarrassed to be with her. Suddenly, though, I'm seeing that's exactly how I made her feel, and my stomach churns at the realization.

"Gen?"

"Hm?" she responds as she pulls her glass from her lips.

"Can you help me with something?"

FIFTY

LIAM

I clench my fists, my knuckles whitening against my slack-clad legs. With shaking hands, I rap lightly at my dad's office door. My heart thuds in my chest and sweat trickles down my spine as I wait for a response. While I've been wanting to talk to him for a while, it's never been the right time. With everything with Hannah recently consuming my mind, it's fallen to the wayside, but with the new year starting, I know I have to prioritize this conversation.

No matter how uncomfortable it may be.

"Come in." His voice radiates from behind the door as he ushers me in.

Stephen Park's office is one of two extremely large offices, and I'll bet you can think of who the other one belongs to. Baker & Park tries to maintain a modern approach to layout and interaction among employees, but this is one of the areas where they stick to a traditional setup.

"Hey, Dad." I grimace as I step into the space, standing in front of his desk.

He looks up at me. "Liam," he says with a smile, waving his arm to instruct me to sit.

I sit in the chair, taking in the large mahogany desk that is almost three times larger than my own. There isn't a single scribble of paper marring its polished surface or a dusty file folder tucked away in a corner. Every pen and pencil is placed meticulously in its place, a habit of my father's for as long as I can remember.

Large, gleaming brass frames hang on the far wall of his office. They display various diplomas and certificates of accomplishment, his extensive knowledge no doubt being a major factor in where he is today. On his desk, however, is a single framed photograph of me, him, and my mom standing on a beach. The photo is from when I was fifteen or sixteen on our annual summer trip. He has one arm draped over each of our shoulders, joy radiating from his face as he grins from ear to ear.

"Can we talk?" My voice comes out far more timid than normal, but given the nature of the conversation, I cower.

"Of course. What's up?"

"I, um—" I twist my fingers, my hands intertwined in my lap, my clear anxiety causing my palms to sweat. "I don't want to do corporate law."

His expression of pride and admiration falls, replaced by a frown, one which I can't quite read.

"What?"

I can't tell if he didn't hear me or if he is looking for clarification, so I go for a mixture of both. "I don't know if Baker & Park is for me, at least not in the capacity that you want it to be."

My dad nods silently, processing my words. He's not a typically angry guy, but I could see this being the moment I discover a different side of my father. I tense as I wait for his response.

"Okay..." He stands before walking over to a bar cart in the corner of the room, which I've seldom seen him use. "What do you want to do, then?"

That's unexpected. I anticipated him at the very least reacting negatively even if short lived, but he seems eerily supportive.

"Oh, I, uh—I am wanting to do more pro-bono work. I want to feel like I'm making a difference." I freeze as the words start to tumble out, feeling they're potentially far too stark. "That's not to say that what Baker & Park does isn't important, but I don't want to spend my life going over contracts and, when I do step foot into a courtroom, defending our corporate clients from accusations of white-collar crimes."

He nods again, but his brows are pinched and I can't tell if it's in thought or irritation.

"And you don't feel like you can do that at Baker & Park?"

"Not really. We aren't exactly a firm that specializes in pro-bono and family law."

He carefully unstoppers an intricately cut crystal decanter and pours a generous measure of the dark, amber-hued liquid into two heavy tumblers. He holds one out in offer as I nod my agreement. His long fingers curl around the second glass and his gaze lingers on me for a moment before he speaks. "We do pro-bono work...not near as much as we used to, but we still do our part where we can."

"I know, but when we downsized, I know that fell to the wayside. I don't want you to think I'm—"

"I've been wanting to change that."

"You've been wanting to change what?"

"I've been wanting the firm to start taking on more pro-bono work again. It's important to give back to the community. I can relate to where you're coming from about our clientele. We'll figure out a way to have you focus more on that and less on our corporate clients."

"Wait, really?"

"Don't look so shocked, son." He laughs as he presses his glass to his lips, taking a large swig of what I now know to be bourbon. I do the same, taking a sip of mine, and it seems to help quell the unrest crawling up my spine at the mere thought of this conversation.

"There is something else..." I sigh as I lean forward in my chair, setting the crystal glass on the hard surface.

"Is someone pregnant?" He laughs awkwardly before the amusement leaves him at my expression. "Liam Stephen Park, did you get someone pregnant?"

"Hannah isn't pregnant."

"Hannah?!" His eyes nearly bug out as the tight grip on his glass grows stronger.

"Dad, not the time. I need to talk to you about something."

"Is that why she quit?"

"No."

This appears to appease whatever worry he was holding onto. He waves his hand, signaling for me to keep going. His gold wedding band gleams in the overhead lighting as he again pulls his tumbler to his lips.

"I don't want to be groomed to take over Baker & Park."

He nearly chokes on his bourbon, taking almost a minute to level out his breathing.

This is more the reaction I was expecting.

Once his coughing fit subsides, it's as if a blanket has washed over his expression. He's entirely void of emotion.

"Dad?"

"I need a minute."

So I give it to him. We sit in silence for five minutes before he clears his throat, pulling my eyes to his.

"Why?"

"Huh?"

"Why don't you want to take over Baker & Park? It's all you've worked for your entire life. The plan has always been for you to make partner and take over my shares in the firm. What changed?"

While he's right about that, it was never about wanting the firm. I went into law because I loved it, that is still true, but it was never about being anyone's boss. I want to make a difference in this world, even if it includes not making corporate law kind of money. That, and I don't want to be tied down to Atlanta, at least not entirely. I like the idea of not being locked in to Baker & Park until I retire.

"I don't feel that I'm the right fit."

"And who is the right fit? You're an only child, and Richard doesn't have children. It's always been you."

The pressure to carry on my dad's legacy has never been outwardly discussed between us, but it's always in the air. He's not getting any younger, so it's been expected for a while that it would come up soon. There isn't any putting it off anymore; we need to talk, even if it sucks.

"Jackson."

"Jackson isn't a Park." He says it so matter-of-factly, like it's something I haven't considered.

"He might as well be," I say before gulping down the remaining liquid in my glass. "Name or not, you and I both know Jackson has what it takes to carry on your legacy, and probably better than I would have, anyway."

"There is no undoing this decision, Liam. You know that,

right? I bring this to Richard and you're committing to this—are you sure this is what you want?"

"I'm sure."

"And is Jackson even interested in that path?"

I shrug. We haven't actually discussed it at all, but I know Jackson. His desire to go into law has never had anything to do with practicing law, at least not in the way I want to. I want to help people, not oversee them. I don't want to be someone's boss, especially not if it takes me away from being able to make an actual difference. "I'm pretty sure he'd be open to discussing it."

"Then we'll discuss it."

"Just like that, then?" My brows raise, earning me a chuckle.

"Would you prefer I yell?"

"No," I laugh.

"Good. I'm not a fan of yelling." He swallows the rest of his drink before leaning back in his chair, far more relaxed than I've ever seen him at the firm.

"So, tell me about you and Hannah."

And I do, unabashedly.

FIFTY-ONE

LIAM

As I step off the plane, the frigid air of Chicago slams into me with all its might. The bitter wind stings my cheeks and numbs my nose. This is a far cry from the warm and welcoming climate of Georgia, but we had to come here for Hannah's big performance.

When she told Jackson that she would be playing the lead this weekend in Illinois, we knew we had to make it happen, no matter how challenging the weather would be. Bundled up in layers of clothing, we brace ourselves against the harsh gusts and trudge toward the theater district. Our breath billows out in front of us with every exhale as we walk through streets lined with towering skyscrapers as far as the eye can see.

Despite the biting cold, I feel a thrill of excitement coursing through my veins as we head to watch Hannah perform under bright lights onstage.

Sage skips ahead as we approach the theater. I still don't understand how the cold isn't bothering her, but I'm quickly reminded that she is a different breed of human entirely.

A force of nature.

I don't miss the way Gabe walks at her side, their dynamic having vastly changed in the past few weeks. When Hannah moved out last month, Sage was left without a roommate. Simultaneously, Gabe and Kara broke up again, but this time it was bad enough for him to move out. I just hope this break-up sticks. He deserves better.

I take a step into the theater and immediately flash back to when Hannah and I saw *Hamilton* in New York. But as my eyes adjust to the dimly lit room, I notice that this theater is much smaller, with worn-down seats and faded curtains decorating the stage. Instead of massive props and intricate costumes, this production has modest designs, but is still elegant in its own way.

The theater goes dark and my heart rate spikes. My eyes lock on the stage, the cast's presence as palpable as electricity in the air. A stirring from behind the curtain reveals an ensemble of bright-eyed actors spilling onto the stage. My gaze darts among them, searching for a single familiar face amidst the crowd.

Then suddenly, there she is. Her signature blonde strands are pulled back beneath a brunette wig to reveal her striking green eyes sparkling under the spotlight. I draw in a deep breath, butterflies fluttering in my stomach.

Her voice fills the small theater like a gentle caress. Each word that comes from her mouth seems to be suspended in the air as I lean forward in my chair, captivated by her performance. My heart flutters with anticipation and I feel completely entranced.

I'd be content doing this forever, watching her perform.

A hand lands on my forearm, causing me to jerk. Only then do I realize it's Sage squeezing my skin with a grin across her lips.

There haven't been many conversations between the two of us that didn't revolve around Hannah in the past few weeks. Ever since I made the decision to try to mend things with her, I've spent an abhorrent amount of time talking Sage's ear off. Asking for advice, mostly, but sometimes just to vent.

Intermission comes and goes but I don't leave my seat, even when everyone else goes to the bathroom and grabs drinks. It's like I'm fused to my seat.

The second half is more entrancing than the first, and I find my eyes locked intently on Hannah with little desire or ability to let go.

We step out of the theater and as my skin chills in the winter air, I feel a new sense of contentment I haven't experienced in months. Whether she's willing to talk to me or is even happy I'm here, it gives me a sense of calm knowing that I've seen her again and she's okay.

Jackson steps onto the sidewalk, eyes focused on Gen as they walk. His left hand is firmly tucked inside hers, and his right arm is around her shoulders, warming her from the cold breeze that blows through the city street amidst the frigid night. He removes his jacket with his free hand and carefully drapes it over her slender frame.

"Hannah said for us to meet her at some restaurant named Stage Left—I guess the cast is going there after the show."

"Did she say anything?" I ask, my voice more timid than normal.

"About?"

"About me being here?"

"Oh, she doesn't know."

"You didn't tell her?" I say, my voice climbing in volume.

"Not my place. She'll see you in like twenty minutes, so chill."

I resist the urge to smack him upside the head as we make our way down the sidewalk to find a hole-in-the-wall restaurant.

The tables are covered with red- and white-checkered cloths, and the smell of garlic and melted cheese fills the air. Steam drifts upward from the bubbling cheese of deep-dish pizzas, their doughy crusts glistening with olive oil. Several of the makeshift tables have two or three pizzas placed in the center as groups huddle around, scooping pieces onto their respective plates.

Dimly lit, the room is humming with chatter and laughter, but as soon as an employee wheels a microphone stand onto the empty stage at the back of the room, all eyes shift toward it. Every wall is filled with memorabilia; however, my gaze is drawn to the large poster next to the stage that announces tonight as open mic night. The barstools along the small bar are now full, and some people have even taken to standing around the edges of the room, waiting for the show to begin.

Makes sense why the cast wants to come here, no doubt to continue the performance and keep their skills sharp.

"Liam," Sage calls, and I realize I'm still standing near the door, taking in the expanse of the room. My friends are now crowded around a table far too small for five people. I'm suddenly glad Wes couldn't get off work—as a result, he and Savannah were not able to come. This setup would be a disaster with seven—actually, including Hannah, eight people.

I hesitantly make my way along the edge of the crowded room until I spot the DJ booth and a selection of instruments behind it. Swallowing hard, I walk up to the counter where the open mic night sign-up sheet lays. I grab a pen from beside it and write my name down with shaking hands, my fingers tingling with anticipation.

If I'm going to make a complete idiot of myself, I might as well do it in stride and go out in a fiery blaze of glory.

My heart skips a beat as the door to the restaurant slams open, gusts of cold air rushing in with her. My breath catches in my throat as my eyes find Hannah darting toward the table to embrace Sage in a hug. She is oblivious to me, so I take the moment and allow her presence to consume me.

Hannah Thatcher-Miles, the love of my life.

FIFTY-TWO

HANNAH

"I can't believe you guys are here!" I squeal as I go down the line, hugging Sage, then hugging Gen and Jackson, then giving Gabe a fist bump because Kara very well might send a hitman after me if I get too close to her boyfriend. I awkwardly step back to Jackson's side, where he wraps me in another embrace.

"We wouldn't miss it for the world, bug," Jackson says as he presses his lips to the side of my head. We talked briefly when he came to say hello after the show, mostly about mom. He apologized for not saying anything sooner. While I appreciate him finally noticing it's a problem with her, I'm too excited to see him to care about that right now. He's here and that is more than enough.

Leaving again has been lonely, but nothing like it was in New York.

There's something comforting about knowing I have a home to go to, friends to go home to, a family. A few months ago I never would have said Atlanta was home, but it feels a lot more like home than Live Oak or New York ever did.

However, the singular person who has made Atlanta feel

that way for me is nowhere in sight and my stomach drops with the realization that he's not here.

I guess I should have expected that, eventually, he would get tired of waiting for me to respond or give him the time to talk, but a small, delusional part of me still hopes that he wants this...even if I can't figure out a way to let it happen yet.

I don't think he tried to hurt me.

For a little while there, it felt intentional—like a form of payback for years of disagreement—but in the two months since I've seen him, I've gotten a lot more clarity on the issue.

He didn't mean to hurt me, but that doesn't mean he didn't.

The microphone squeals as the MC steps up onto the stage to announce the beginning of open mic night. The cast of *Maybe, Definitely, No* tries to catch as many open mic and karaoke nights as possible. While I realize we do plenty of singing while on stage, there's something comforting about letting loose but also being able to have that creative outlet.

I'm not sure what I plan to sing, but I definitely plan on getting over to that sign-up sheet soon and getting some stage time.

"Thank you to everyone for coming to our weekly open mic night here at Stage Left," the MC says with his lips almost flush against the microphone, "for the first song, I'll admit it's definitely a first. I've never heard this one at all, let alone performed at one of these. That being said, here is Liam Park." He steps back from the microphone as a figure emerges from the wing.

My eyes go from the stage to my brother, who simply shrugs. My heart is pounding in my chest so loud it consumes me. The cold winter air does nothing to comfort the burn as blood rushes to my face, my skin no doubt a startling shade of crimson as I shift my attention back to the stage where Liam is now standing. He's staring down at me with an acoustic guitar in hand. It's not his guitar—this one looks to be light wood, whereas his has a dark, rich hue.

He looks at home with it slung over his shoulder just the same.

Liam's fingers tremble ever so slightly as he adjusts the mic stand and clears his throat before speaking. "Hi, everyone...I'll admit, I'm not typically one to do this. In fact, I don't think I've ever performed in an open mic night."

He takes this moment to drag a guitar pick across the strings, causing an angelic sound to emanate through the air. "But the girl I'm in love with said to me recently that I'm not forthcoming enough with our relationship. I'll be honest, at first I didn't get it...but now I do. She deserves someone who would shout it from the rooftops that they're hers, making it crystal clear to the world...so with that, I'm going to make an absolute fool of myself. Hannah, I love you."

My eyes brim with tears, my face a mix of pain and joy as I attempt to contain my growing smile. All eyes in the restaurant are glued to us—me taking in every moment and him strumming the guitar on stage. The guests watch, entranced and captivated by his music, and I'm right there along with them.

The sound shifts from random notes to a song I know well with a distinct backing track playing through the speakers. It's a song that he has told me on no less than two occasions is the cheesiest song he's ever heard from the most poorly written show he's ever seen. He starts to sing "Your Biggest Fan" from *Jonas L.A.*, and while I'm completely enamored, I'm also consumed by secondhand embarrassment.

Something tells me that is by design.

The song is written for Nick Jonas's tenor voice, so Liam has to pitch the song down to work as he's a natural baritone. At first, I register the decision as a cheesy choice on his part, but then I remember the context the song had in the show.

Nick's character had been dodgy about sharing his adoration for his counterpart, Macy. The song is used in a scene where he makes the conscious decision to outwardly and vocally own his feelings for her, allowing her the opportunity to be wholly honest with those around her.

My cheeks burn as I sink into my chair, using the collar of my shirt to shield my face. His commitment to the rap portion of the song feels like a physical punch in my gut, but he raps with no sign of embarrassment or shame. I want to scream, but instead stay silent and motionless as I allow him to show his commitment.

If it wasn't so sweet, I'd punch him for embarrassing me. As the song comes to a close, I find my feet moving of their own volition. The crowd claps as Gabe and Sage hoot and holler with little restraint, causing the pink tinging Liam's face to grow to a full crimson. He strums the guitar one last time before setting it on the stand. He steps off the stage, meeting me on the floor, a timid expression painting his brow.

"Hey, princess." He exhales with a grin.

"Hey." I smile back at him, my eyes misty from the emotion of seeing him again for the first time in months.

"Can we talk?"

I give a barely perceptible nod in response before he turns and guides me through a doorway at the back of the restaurant. The tables here are arranged with extra space between them, all covered by red checkered cloths that rustle against the background noise of hushed conversations. A few couples sitting nearby can't take their eyes off the stage as they cling to each other's hands, ready for what lies ahead.

"How are you?" He asks the question far more tentatively than I've ever heard him speak.

"I'm good," I laugh lightly. "You seem nervous—maybe don't do that? It's making me nervous."

"Oh, I'm sorry that my nervousness causes you discomfort." Sarcasm drips off his words as the tension leaves his shoulders. "I miss you, Hannah."

My mouth twists in a slight smile before I go to speak, but as soon as his familiar brown eyes look into mine, the words get stuck in my throat. His gaze is heavy and intense, and suddenly, my stomach feels like it is filled with fluttering wings.

"I love you," he whispers as he steps toward me.

My instincts tell me to melt into him, but as his lips ghost close to mine, I feel myself back up.

"Liam."

"You're right, I'm sorry." He winces as he backs up, his defeated expression shooting straight through my heart.

"It's not that." I gulp before allowing my eyes to meet his again. "I love you too, but that was never the problem."

He stares into my eyes for a while, but doesn't fight me on what I'm saying. If we do this again, it needs to be on my terms. I've spent far too much time allowing my choices to be wielded by the whims of other people; I need to know that, in jumping back into this, it's for the right reasons, not just because I miss him, and not without diving into any of the reasons we broke up in the first place.

"I'm not saying no," I say, watching his shoulders relax at my words. "But I need time. We can talk again when I get back to Atlanta in May, but right now I need to focus on what's best for me."

"I've never wanted anything else for you, Hannah."

"I know, but right now I need to be the one to make that happen."

He nods again, but no words leave his lips. I take the opportunity to step into his space, wrapping my arms around his waist. Liam's arms tighten around my shoulders as his lips press firmly to my temple.

And for the first time in two months, I feel at peace.

FIFTY-THREE

LIAM

im going on as martha tonight!! annabeth
has the stomach flu

thats awesome! im gonna assume that is a
big role

seeing as there are only three main female
roles, yeah id say so

so mean

youll kill it

Mon Mar 11 at 12:42 PM

Andres took your penne off the menu

youre not funny

im a little funny

Fri Mar 15 at 9:14 AM

you really need an iphone

why would I do that?

because you love me

why do I feel like one day you'll make me
regret that decision?

because youre smarter than everyone says
you are

wait, who says im not smart?!

Thur Mar 21 at 10:53 PM

whatre you up to?

laying in bed

same

wish you were here

oh?

dont make me regret texting you

down tiger

why do you wish i was there? ;)

goodnight park

Fri Mar 29 at 12:34 AM

have you ever wondered why camels
evolutionarily formed their humps?

were in denver this weekend

i cant sleep

same

but thats because my phone has been
vibrating because someone is high

im not high!

ok, maybe a little

ft?

youre going to make me regret getting an
iphone arent you?

probably

Fri Mar 29 at 10:23 AM

i am running on fumes today, so if I get fired thats on you

something tells me your DAD isnt about to fire you

he could, you dont know

maybe ill fall asleep in a client meeting, because SOMEONE kept me on facetime until after 4 am

you werent complaining last night when you saw my boobs

you make an excellent point

Mon Apr 8 at 8:43 PM

I thought of you today

and here i thought you thought about me every day

omg i was kidding

nvm

oh fuck off, tell me

[Picture Message]

is that...

a venus fly trap? yep, i finally watched that musical you mentioned, and now these things haunt my dreams audrey 2 isn't a venus fly trap

keep that energy when I stick your finger in it when youre sleeping

your brain scares me sometimes

Wed Apr 17 at 1:23 PM

hey

oh, she is alive

time flies when you want to stick your head in an oven

that bad?

not really, just an asshole in the cast. are you avail to ft?

for you? always

Fri Apr 26 at 3:37 PM

next week

whats your plan?

what do you mean?

...well seeing as gabe is now living in your apartment

oh, im staying with jackson and gen

or...

oh darn, gotta get to makeup, tudaloo!

Sat May 4 at 5:37 AM

kinda freaking out

your flight isn't going to disappear for five years hannah

you dont know that

you really shouldnt be watching manifest the night before you board a flight

you may be onto something

taxying, g2g

FIFTY-FOUR

HANNAH

I take slow steps up the stone walkway and survey the window boxes filled with bright yellow daisies. Letting out a deep breath as my hand touches the worn brass doorknob, the smell of freshly brewed coffee hits me first as I step inside, and I feel my chest swell with warmth.

Jackson had been intent on picking me up at the airport, but when I reminded him how early my flight was slated to get in, the idea of me getting a rideshare from the airport got progressively more attractive. The sun is settled just over the horizon as I step fully over the threshold, the balmy May air thankfully being left at the door as I become enveloped in their central air conditioning.

"Hey," I call out into the quiet house.

Gen and Jackson aren't particularly known for their early morning activities, so I fully anticipate them both being in bed. If I couldn't smell the nutty aroma of the coffee being brewed, I would head up to crawl into bed and talk to them in a few hours.

"I'm in the kitchen," Gen responds just as I step into the expansive space.

The kitchen is a stunning blend of old and new. The tall, light wood cabinets dwarf the space but provide a cohesive look with the lower half painted in the same natural hue. The light granite countertop glistens under the early morning sun that streams through the window above the sink, illuminating an otherwise modern yet traditional atmosphere.

As soon as her eyes meet mine, Gen is handing me a mug of steaming hot coffee, the scent invading my senses as I take a deep breath.

"Thank you."

"Of course. How was the flight?"

"It was a flight," I laugh before pulling the cup to my lips and taking a sip. "I was sat next to a family going to Disney and I guess they had a connecting flight in Atlanta. I don't have an issue with kids, but damn, this kid wouldn't shut the fuck up."

"Yeah, that's no fun."

We continue recapping my travels, both from today and from touring with *Maybe, Definitely, No*. I ask where Jackson is, and she lets me know that he's still sleeping and well— neither of us are particularly surprised by that.

"Have you and Liam talked?"

I nod in response.

She grins. "Does he know you're home?"

I nod again.

"I see."

She stares at me for a moment before I roll my eyes. "Spit it out, Viv."

"What is going on with you guys?"

I start to respond, but then I realize that I don't actually know.

Liam and I have spoken frequently over the past few months while I was gone, and we've pushed the line between friends and more—a lot—but as for specifics, I have no idea.

"Not really sure."

"Why?"

"I don't know," I sigh as I set my mug down on the countertop. "He really hurt me. I told him I needed time to focus on me and he gave me that, but now I worry that maybe I held off too long."

"Why would you think that?"

"What kind of man just waits months for a woman to decide if she wants to be with him?"

"The kind that knows what he wants and is clearly in love with her," a male voice rings from behind me, and I find myself hoping it's Liam, though I know it's not.

I don't mean to appear so disappointed when Jackson comes into view, but it's glaringly obvious.

"Happy to see you too, bug," he laughs as he steps into my space, wrapping me in a hug.

I hope that his walking in is the end of the discussion, but he latches onto the topic like a vise.

"Have you called Liam?" Jackson doesn't even pretend to entertain pleasantries as he steps toward the coffee machine and pours a cup of black coffee from the pot.

"How do you drink it like that?"

"Don't deflect, answer the question."

I sigh as his eyes meet mine before settling against the counter. "I texted him before the plane left New York and he had my flight details. He knows I'm home."

"You didn't call or text him when you landed?"

The moment I shake my head, Jackson laughs.

"You're going to give that man a complex."

I shrug as I say, "Meh, builds character."

"Hannah," Jackson chuckles.

"Fine, I'll call him." I push away from the counter to walk down the hallway to the foyer, allowing myself the slightest bit of privacy. Although, I'd bet they can hear everything from the kitchen anyway.

The line starts to ring and my stomach forms into knots. Liam and I have talked on the phone and on FaceTime at length, but something about being back in Atlanta, knowing I'll see him soon, causes butterflies to take flight in my stomach.

"Hello?" Liam's groggy voice carries through my phone speaker, causing a grin to pull at the corners of my mouth.

"Hey."

"What's up?" I hear him yawn.

"Are you not up yet? It's almost 9:00 AM."

"Well, I was up texting someone at like 5:00 AM, so excuse me for getting a couple more hours of shut-eye."

I huff in mock exasperation. "I'd suppose you're right. I just thought you might want to come to Jackson's, but I'll just ca—"

Loud shuffling carries through the receiver and Liam sounds breathless when he says, "I'll be there in twenty minutes."

The moment the line goes dead, I burst out laughing as it's the only response I can muster to quell the anxiety building in my belly. The sound of it reverberates through the room, echoing off the walls until it fades into an awkward silence.

"Are you okay?" Jackson yells from the kitchen.

"Yeah, Liam is heading over."

"Good."

Twenty minutes my ass.

Liam steps through the front door with minutes to spare,

frantic as a bat out of hell. His hair is disheveled and chaotic and his typically perfectly groomed scruff is borderline unkept. His eyes meet mine as he steps into the kitchen, where I sit next to Gen at the table, but words don't pass between us initially. He lets out a slow exhale, peering around the room, all three of us with our eyes locked on him.

Jackson clears his throat as he steps up behind Gen's chair and latches his hand onto her shoulder. He whispers quietly, but loud enough that I hear, "Let's give them some privacy to talk."

They dart out of the room and up the stairs to their bedroom, Gen's laughter echoing as Jackson disgustingly swats at her ass.

My grossed-out expression causes Liam to laugh before he sits down in the chair next to me, our knees brushing beneath the table.

"Hey," he says quietly, almost tentatively.

"Hey."

We linger, staring at each other in silence for what feels like minutes. My mind is racing with all the things I planned to say when I saw him again. We've talked, but there are a multitude of things I've convinced myself needed to wait until I was home.

I love you.

I miss you.

Let's get back together.

Yet, when my mouth falls open, all I can muster is the same greeting I already gave: "Hey."

"You said that," he says with a grin. "Never thought I'd see the day that Hannah Thatcher-Miles was at a loss for words."

"Sometimes Batman has to take off his cape."

His brows shoot up as I laugh.

"Don't get too excited. It's an *Office* reference, not a DC Comics reference."

"God, you just saying the words *DC Comics* is so sexy."

"You have really low standards, Park."

"Fell in love with you, didn't I?"

I smack his arm and this seems to lessen the tension in the air. "Yeah...you did."

"Still do, you know."

Our eyes lock for what feels like an eternity until suddenly the weight of all my emotions becomes too much to bear and I break down in a fit of uncontrollable sobs. My vision blurs with tears as I am overcome by all the feelings I have been trying to keep hidden over the past six months.

"Hey," he says quietly as he reaches over and pulls me into his lap. His arms wrap firmly around me as his face buries into my neck, the rhythm of his breaths like a metronome to count my own. "Nothing has changed, princess. Six months apart doesn't mean anything in the grand scheme of things. I'm just as consumed by you as I was the day you left...maybe even more so."

He pulls away slightly so our eyes can meet and, without restraint, I lean in and press my lips to his. Every rogue emotion, every tough night, every celebration over the past six months does nothing but pale in comparison to the joy I feel right now.

"I love you," I sob against his mouth, causing a grin to spread across his lips.

"I love you too."

FIFTY-FIVE

HANNAH

The moment I step into Andre's, my stomach lurches as if I'm in freefall. My palms begin to sweat and my heart races at the thought of seeing my mother again. It has been six months since Jackson and Gen's wedding, and I can feel an impending panic attack coming on.

The lunchtime hustle and bustle has quieted as the restaurant is now almost empty save for a few couples scattered across the dining room. Most of them are well over fifty-five, speaking in low murmurs, their faces wrinkled with age but radiating contentment as they enjoy Andre's early bird special.

In recent months, the signature roast chicken has gone from being a Monday delicacy to a fixture on the permanent menu, much to Liam's delight. The smell of the dish causes my mouth to water as we're ushered to our seats—a table at the back of the restaurant where both Liam and my parents sit. Initially, Jackson and Gen were slated to join us, but the more we thought about it, the more we thought that it would be better to do this alone.

Over the past six months, I've thought at length about what I might say to my mom when I saw her again. We didn't talk for the expanse of the entire tour, so I can't imagine her attitude toward me has changed for the better.

"Hannah." Caroline grins from ear to ear as she stands and envelopes me in a tight hug. The warmth of her welcoming embrace gives me the comfort I need as I sit down to what is sure to be the most tense meal I've had since Jackson and Gen's rehearsal dinner.

"Hey, sweetie," my dad says with a smile.

"Hi, Dad."

We all exchange pleasantries as I settle into my seat opposite my mother, this time with Liam by my side. His fingers are looped through my own, a far cry from the dynamic we had at the last meal we shared with our parents together.

"You have no idea how happy this makes me," Caroline says as she beams with delight, her grin a stark catalyst to my mother's scowl.

To my understanding, things have only gotten more estranged between my mom and Liam. I know I should be concerned; I know I should hope that the man I love would have a good relationship with my parents, but I can't will myself to care about it.

Why would I hope for him to have a relationship with them when I barely want a relationship with them?

Liam's lips land against my temple as he squeezes my hand tightly at his mother's words.

While I haven't spoken to my parents since leaving for the tour, I've spoken to Caroline and Stephen on more than one occasion. They've not only been supportive of mine and Liam's relationship, but they've been so enthusiastic it's almost terrifying.

"How was the rest of the tour?" Stephen asks as he takes a bite of the side salad in front of him.

"It was amazing! We go back on the road in August for another leg of the tour, but this time it'll be a year. The initial reception was more than they were expecting, so they're confident in adding more shows."

"That's incredible, Hannah. We are so proud of you."

"Thank you, Stephen."

My mom scoffs and I fight everything in me not to cower at her response. I knew she would have an opinion. Despite me successfully earning my union card and booking a major tour, it's still not good enough. At this point, I can't say for sure if anything I do will ever be good enough for her.

"Did you say something, Mom?" I turn to find her looking at me with a disgusted expression, but rather than allowing it to pull me down, I simply return the energy.

"When do you return to Baker & Park?" she asks.

"I'm not?" I pose it almost as a question, but the idea is so preposterous that I am thrown off.

"Why not?!" she nearly yells, and in the almost-empty restaurant, various sets of eyes travel in our direction.

"Because I have a job?"

She scoffs again, this time not bothering to hide her disdain. "You need a real job, Hannah."

"I have a real job," I grit through my teeth, trying not to lose my cool entirely. Sage was able to get me a part-time bartending job at Harry's with her for the next couple months until I leave, but my mother doesn't need to know that.

"Hannah, you're being ridiculous."

"No, Mom, I'm really not," I say as the last bit of restraint I've been holding onto falls apart. Liam squeezes my leg below the table, his silent support giving me the confidence to do what I've never had the will to do. "I am not a child."

"You're acting like—"

"Don't interrupt me," I shoot back before clearing my throat. "I'm twenty-seven years old, almost twenty-eight. I've worked my ass off for well over half my life to do what I do. What you think of it quite literally could not matter less to me."

"Hannah, you're being—"

"I'm not finished." To my surprise she clamps her mouth shut in response. "You're my mother, and for only God knows what reason, I love you. However, Mom, I love me more. So going forward, if you can't figure out a way to unpack whatever your issue is, you will simply cease to be a part of my life. Do we understand each other?"

The intensity of her gaze is almost searing as she stares me down, her lips pursed tightly and her cheeks flushed bright red. I can feel the anger radiating off of her in waves, yet I refuse to look away. Time seems to stand still as we lock eyes, and I can almost swear that I see a vein throbbing in her forehead.

"You ungrateful lit—"

"Linda, enough!" my dad yells, his fist landing against the hard surface of the table, causing the silverware to rattle.

My mother's angry gaze shifts from me to my dad in an instant, but the rage dies as her eyes meet his. I expect her to bite at him—she's hardly ever been afraid to tell him what she thinks—but something in the way he's looking at her now leaves me wondering what he's said before this moment.

"I think it's time we go," my dad says as he stands, his cloth napkin landing firmly against the table.

My mother instantly gets up without so much as a goodbye

to any of us, but my dad pauses to press a kiss to the top of my head as he leaves.

Something tells me that is about to be an excruciating ride back to their hotel.

FIFTY-SIX

HANNAH

"Are you planning on helping?" Jackson huffs, dropping the box marked *Bedroom* onto the hardwood floor. He pushes his dark brown hair back, the combination of the sweltering Atlanta heat and the five trips he's already made up to Liam's high-rise apartment today clearly leaving him exhausted.

"But you do it so well..." I pout, but a grin pokes through.

"It wasn't cute when you said it before, and it's not cute now. Come help."

I sigh as I jump off the barstool I've been seated at as I unpacked a random box containing a slew of random items. When I packed everything and put it in storage to move out of mine and Sage's apartment last year, I wasn't particularly concerned with it making a lick of sense, just ensuring it made it into my storage unit.

Today, as I move into Liam's apartment, I'm reminded of what a terrible decision that was.

The month and a half I spent living with Gen and Jackson again wasn't bad, but I felt like I was constantly in their way. I can't imagine I'd want Jackson in mine and Liam's space, so I can't say I necessarily blame them.

Liam appears in the doorway of his—uh, our apartment with a massive cardboard box in his arms. His dark eyes are filled with irritation as he glares at me. The scowl plastered on his face gives me a feeling that he and Jackson share the same sentiment as I move toward the door.

"No time to relax, gotta go grab a box," I say far too enthusiastically as he blocks the doorway, his irritated expression from before morphing into amusement.

"What have you been doing?"

"Organizing."

"What have you been organizing?"

I point to the box on the counter, earning a far-too-dramatic eye roll from Liam. "That box is just as full as it was three trips ago."

"I'm very thorough."

Liam chuckles and sets the cardboard box he was holding down on the floor. As he steps toward me, I can see his once-crisp shirt now stuck to his skin with sweat. His musky scent mixed with the muggy air is almost too much. He encases me in a hug and I feel every inch of his soaked body pressed against mine.

"You stink!" I joke, pushing him away from me with my palms on his heaving chest. He tightens his grip but doesn't move an inch as I pretend to gag.

"Shhhhhh," he says, holding me tighter. "Just let it happen."

My gagging gets louder and more dramatic the longer he holds me in a vise grip. His tight hold shifts to his fingers digging into my side, eliciting a yelp from me. My laughter consumes the room as I try to yank myself from his grasp.

"Fine, fine!" I laugh so hard my breath is choppy. "I'll help!"

"Too late, this is your fate now. Accept it, relish in it."

Jackson appears in the doorway and I instantly reach for him. "Jackson. Tell him to let go of me," I whine.

"Not my circus, bug."

"Asshole."

Liam finally loosens his hold before looking down at me. My cheek is moist with sweat and it only looks like a trophy to him.

"You're a dick."

"You love it."

I don't even fight him on it, because I do.

As the last echo of departing footsteps vanishes, we both release a deep sigh of relief. We slowly collapse onto the soft gray couch in the living room, sinking into it, its plush embrace like a warm hug. I close my eyes and let out an exhale as exhaustion takes over, grateful that this day is coming to an end. The soft light of sunset filters through thin curtains, casting long shadows across the room. A gust from outside carries in fresh air, and I'm thankful for the breeze against my skin. It is just what I need after moving around all day long.

"Hannah..." Liam's tone is ominous as he stands from the couch to walk to the other side of the room.

My stomach erupts into knots as he pulls a familiar figurine from the box open on the countertop.

"Yes?" I nervously grin up at him, knowing that the cogs in his brain are moving at full speed.

"When did you take this?"

"A couple years ago."

"So you just watched me tear apart my apartment looking

for it last week for fun? Hannah, this thing wasn't cheap. I thought it was lost in my apartment."

"You're so cute when you're frustrated," I say with a mocking pout.

He steps closer to me, his strong jawline and angular features softening slightly, a glimmer of hope shining through the scowl that was threatening to consume him moments before. I feel my stomach fill with thousands of tiny butterflies, wings fluttering in anticipation.

"You're gonna get it."

And I hope I do.

READ MORE JUST PEACHY

Second Chance Vacation (Just Peachy Book 1)

Gen & Jackson's story

Available now!

ABOUT THE AUTHOR

Nicole fell in love with writing at a young age. She started out with short story competitions in middle school and went on to take various creative writing courses through high school and on into college. She participated in short-form writing communities online for years, but over time lost her muse for storytelling.

In 2020 when the world turned on its head, Nicole found a lot more extra time on her hands and started typing away. Many a WIP have come and gone since then, but nothing captured her heart until the Just Peachy series enough to share it with the world. She lives in Ohio with her amazing husband, two cats, and their two dogs.

facebook.com/nicoleryanbooks

instagram.com/nicoleryanbooks

tiktok.com/@nicoleryanbooks

ACKNOWLEDGMENTS

As always, I owe an endless amount of gratitude to my incredible husband Danny, without whom I not only wouldn't have finished this book, but I also would not have gotten through this past year. This year has been equal parts exhilarating with the release of Second Chance Vacation, and difficult due to the loss of my grandmother.

My Nana was—nay, still is—the most inspiring and incredible woman I have ever known. She was the person who introduced me to storytelling at a young age and while it has been immeasurably painful since losing her, I find comfort in knowing that she was able to see me release my first book and was incredibly proud. Thank you for being my lighthouse.

To my incredible editor, Erin, thank you. You were instrumental in this book coming to fruition. Our shared hatred of color names will live rent free in my mind.

Thank you to my amazing beta readers: Anna, Arianna, Bekki, Liz, Megan, Nicola, Ruthi, Sammey, Stephanie, Tori, and Ycel. This story would quite literally not be what it is without each of you. Also, your live reactions are seared into my brain, take with that what you will.

A massive thank you and shout out to Miss. Joné from Theatre Kidz Inc (R.I.P. TKI), for fueling my love of theatre at such a young age and subsequently giving me the stories of which I drew inspiration for Hannah's time in Little Shop of Horrors.

Lastly, I'd like to give a massive thank you to the incredible community of female authors I've met over the past year. It's baffling to me that this time last year I was only writing the first draft of Second Chance Vacation, and now Mostly Loathing You is out in the world. The phrase 'community over competition' has never held as much weight as it does to me now, and it is all because of you guys. Here is to a kick ass 2024 for all of us.